Praise for Book One

Dawn of Fire: Avenging Son

by Guy Haley

'The beginning of an essential new epic: heroic, cataclysmic and vast in scope. Guy has delivered exactly what 40K readers crave, and lit the fuse on the Dark Millennium. This far future's about to detonate...'

Dan Abnett, author of Horus Rising

'With all the thunderous scope of The Horus Heresy, a magnificent new saga begins.'

Peter McLean, author of Priest of Bones

'A perfect blending of themes – characters that are raw, real and wonderfully human, set against a backdrop of battle and mythology'.

Danie Ware, author of Ecko Rising

HAND OF ABADDON

A DAWN OF FIRE NOVEL

More Warhammer 40,000 from Black Library

• DAWN OF FIRE •
BOOK 1: Avenging Son
Guy Haley
BOOK 2: The Gate of Bones
Andy Clark
BOOK 3: The Wolftime
Gav Thorpe
BOOK 4: Throne of Light
Guy Haley
BOOK 5: The Iron Kingdom
Nick Kyme
BOOK 6: The Martyr's Tomb
Marc Collins
BOOK 7: Sea of Souls
Chris Wraight
BOOK 8: Hand of Abaddon
Nick Kyme

LEVIATHAN
Darius Hinks

• DARK IMPERIUM •
Guy Haley
BOOK 1: Dark Imperium
BOOK 2: Plague War
BOOK 3: Godblight

HURON BLACKHEART: MASTER OF THE MAELSTROM
Mike Brooks

VOID KING
Marc Collins

GENEFATHER
Guy Haley

BLACKSTONE FORTRESS
Darius Hinks

THE LION: SON OF THE FOREST
Mike Brooks

HAND OF ABADDON

A DAWN OF FIRE NOVEL

NICK KYME

A BLACK LIBRARY PUBLICATION

First published in 2024.
This edition published in Great Britain in 2024 by
Black Library, Games Workshop Ltd., Willow Road,
Nottingham, NG7 2WS, UK.

Represented by: Games Workshop Limited – Irish branch,
Unit 3, Lower Liffey Street, Dublin 1,
D01 K199, Ireland.

10 9 8 7 6 5 4 3 2 1

Produced by Games Workshop in Nottingham.
Cover illustration by Johan Grenier.

A CIP record for this book is available from the British Library.

ISBN 13: 978-1-80026-281-2

Printed and bound in the UK.

To Stef, for always being there and for getting me over the finishing line.

For more than a hundred centuries the Emperor has sat immobile on the Golden Throne of Earth. He is the Master of Mankind. By the might of his inexhaustible armies a million worlds stand against the dark.

Yet, he is a rotting carcass, the Carrion Lord of the Imperium held in life by marvels from the Dark Age of Technology and the thousand souls sacrificed each day so his may continue to burn.

To be a man in such times is to be one amongst untold billions. It is to live in the cruelest and most bloody regime imaginable. It is to suffer an eternity of carnage and slaughter. It is to have cries of anguish and sorrow drowned by the thirsting laughter of dark gods.

This is a dark and terrible era where you will find little comfort or hope. Forget the power of technology and science. Forget the promise of progress and advancement. Forget any notion of common humanity or compassion.

There is no peace amongst the stars, for in the grim darkness of the far future, there is only war.

DRAMATIS PERSONAE

AGENTS OF THE EMPEROR

Leonid Rostov	Inquisitor
Syreniel	Oblivion Knight of the Palatine Vigilators, Silent Sisterhood
Katla Helvintr	Rogue trader
Benidei Antoniato	Interrogator
Hayden Lacrante	Investigatus
Cheelche	Xenos gunslinger
Yamir	Rogue trader
Nirdrangar	Inquisitorial storm trooper

ASTRA MILITARUM

Isiah Falden	Colonel, 84th Mordian
Magda Kesh	Sergeant, 84th Mordian
Abel Munser	Lieutenant, 84th Mordian
Lodrin	Trooper, 84th Mordian
Mavin	Trooper, 84th Mordian
Vosko	Corporal, 84th Mordian
Nakaturo	Colonel, 116th Catachan
Hagan	Captain, Catachan

SERVANTS OF CHAOS

Tharador Yheng	Sorceress, acolyte of Tenebrus
Tenebrus	Sorcerer, the Hand of Abaddon
The Iron Magus	Dark Mechanicum magos
Augury	Entity, the Hand of Abaddon

RENEGADE ASTARTES

Graeyl Herek	Red Corsair, pirate lord and captain of the *Ruin*
Vassago Kurgos	Red Corsair, chirurgeon

Rathek	Red Corsair, called 'the Culler'
Clortho	Red Corsair

ADEPTUS ASTARTES

Maximus Epathus	Sixth Company Ultramarines, captain
Ferren Areios	Sixth Company Ultramarines, lieutenant
Maendaius	Sixth Company Ultramarines, Librarian
Cicero	Sixth Company Ultramarines
Drussus	Sixth Company Ultramarines
Helicio	Sixth Company Ultramarines
Valentius	Sixth Company Ultramarines, Apothecary
Vitrian Messinius	Lord lieutenant, White Consuls

THE KIN

Vutred	Kâhl of Omrigar Kindred
Othed	Grimnyr
Utri	Einhyr Champion

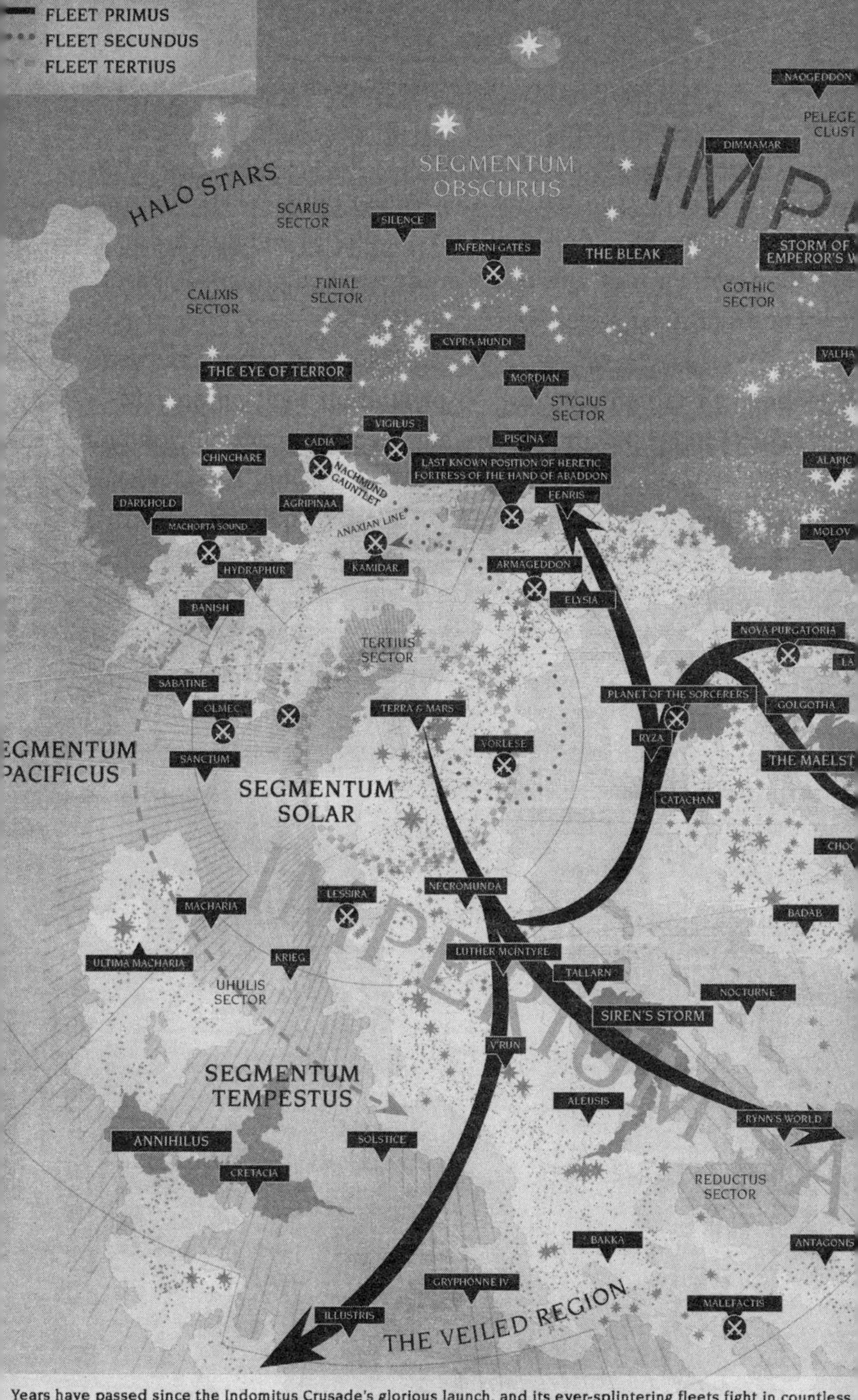

Years have passed since the Indomitus Crusade's glorious launch, and its ever-splintering fleets fight in countless warzones across the galaxy. No cartograph, even this one, should be considered all-encompassing due to the immeasurable scale and fluidity of the crusade as it battles to save the Imperium of Man from total annihilation.

Prologue

Fathomless black surrounded Yheng.

Absolute and suffocating.

It was a palpable *otherness* emanating from the walls of the vast ritual chamber, in the very stones beneath her feet. The stone shone like glass as she walked, her soft-soled feet padding on dark mirrors. Only it wasn't glass, though her pale skin was reflected back at her. And the mirror wasn't a mirror, not in the mundane sense.

It was all an illusion, perpetuated by the alien nature of this place and the primordial darkness the Hand had summoned into being. She knew this to be the black heart of their hidden fortress, where they had gathered in secret the pieces of a weapon so ancient its existence in the here and now defied belief. The prospect of that weapon and what it could do, in pieces though it still was, excited her.

Close enough to power to be able to step forth and touch it, close enough to something that had laid low the demigods of an elder age... The hairs arose on the backs of her arms as its name coalesced in her mind.

Anathame.

Its reacquisition was the Hand's great purpose, overriding any personal agendas or enmities. And there were many between the members of the Hand.

Now the culmination of that goal drew near as they brought forth the supplicant into the ritual chamber and Yheng, like the rest of the gathering, took her place to bear witness. The supplicant was stripped of all trappings and naked, his skin a canvas upon which eight sigils would be written. She had paid rapt attention to her master as the 'bestowing' ritual was described to her, eager for knowledge, keener still to use that knowledge and everything else she had gleaned to step out of his shadow.

Soon... Much like the supplicant, her time was approaching.

He was led by a hooded acolyte to a large stone dais in the centre of the room. Eight thrones stood around it, carved with ancient sigils and the markings of the gods. The supplicant's head was low, as if in abeyance, his muscular body together with the stark metal ports punched into his flesh revealing that he was one of the Traitor Astartes. Yheng smirked cruelly. She doubted a lesser being would survive the rite. As he knelt down, he bowed his head further, ready to receive the blessings of the Eight – otherwise known as the Hand of Abaddon.

Yheng's master went first. Tenebrus had been standing just in front of her, a subtle reinforcement of his position and hers. She despised him for it. He was known in this dark covenant as the Sorcerer, a tall, hairless creature with corpse-like flesh and a cruel mouth that put Yheng in mind of the doktor-surgeons she had met when she was still in the bone-whittler's gang on Gathalamor. How far away that seemed now... How small she had once been. No more.

Tenebrus stooped, his dark robes pooling around his feet like spilled ink, a narrow arm extending like a pallid proboscis, his outstretched finger as the quill. He inked a hex, and sombre chanting stirred from the room's periphery where the hooded acolytes in attendance sang praises to the gods. Their voices echoed from the vaulted ceiling and soaring walls.

Eight shards would be bestowed upon the supplicant, the formerly disparate pieces of the Anathame reunited within this mortal flesh, one for each sigil made by the Hand. The first slid through skin and meat with ease as if the piece of scarred metal were eager for this union, as if it had sentience of its own.

Yheng knew little about the mythic blade that, legend said, had pierced Horus' side – he who had forsworn his father, the Emperor of Mankind, and incited a war that brought a nascent Imperium to the brink of destruction. If the power she tasted in the air was a mere fraction of the whole then she understood in that moment why the Hand had risked so much, and sacrificed so wantonly for its acquisition.

As Tenebrus retreated from the dais, he took care not to disturb the bloody runes painted onto the floor around it. Yheng could smell the bloodless bodies who had given up their vital fluids for the rite, could feel them staring sightlessly from the deeper shadows.

And so the weak are punished for their weakness...

'Thus is the first anointing made and there will be eight and from the eight a great doom shall be made anew...' Tenebrus uttered as he returned to her side. The air felt thicker all of a sudden, warm like an oven. As Yheng went to steady herself she made the mistake of touching one of the columns that stood between each of the thrones. Every nerve lit like a burning ember, white hot and searing. Yheng gasped but quickly mastered her pain. She would show no weakness here, not to the Hand.

Not to anyone.

Tenebrus turned, and laid a thin claw on her shoulder. Little, she admitted grudgingly, passed his notice.

'What do you feel, Yheng of Gathalamor?'

Yheng spoke through gritted teeth, surprised at how thin and rasping her voice had suddenly become. 'Pain...' she hissed. 'I feel its pain. How is that possible?'

She wasn't talking about the supplicant. And Tenebrus somehow knew this.

He smiled, too wide, too deeply, his mouth like a crescent moon. 'It is more than a place, more than a mechanism or a mere fortress. It has concealed us from prying eyes and allowed the shards to be gathered in secret.' He gestured to the chamber and all the corridors and halls beyond. 'It is ancient, Tharador Yheng. It can *feel*. It writhes in sympathetic agony for its twin that fell upon the Gate World of Cadia,' he whispered. 'Think of it as an animal, once wild and rampant. It has been shackled, bent to the will of the Hand. Chains will chafe if you pull against them.' His eager gaze drifted to the supplicant, Yheng following with her eyes. 'For in the end we are all slaves to the darkness, whether we want to admit it or not.'

The ceremony continued. Two of the Hand had returned to stand by their thrones: the Butcher King and the Host of Masks, their marks made. The Butcher King did not linger, his ragged crimson cloak trailing behind him as he stalked away to marshal his warriors, leaving the scent of hot copper in his wake. An impatient beast was the Butcher, a brutish instrument who craved battle. Yheng had heard his murderous rampages across the fortress echoing through the walls and had wisely steered away.

In contrast, the Host of Masks retreated with slithering poise after it had impaled another one of the shards into flesh, the face it was currently wearing etched with studious rapture. What lay behind that false face Yheng did not know, but she imagined scars or hideous mutation. Perhaps it was unsettlingly blank, a shapeless canvas upon which the Host could impress its moods. It wore a bodyglove of dark leather that did nothing to reveal who or even what it was. Like so many of the Hand, it was an enigma.

Less so, the maker of the fourth mark.

This was inscribed by the Iron Magus, a hulking shape whose black robes hid a plethora of cybernetics, a devotee of the Dark Mechanicum. As they ascended the dais, the Iron Magus turned their hollow and hooded regard upon Yheng. At the same moment, the light in the chamber darkened and she saw a bleak aura exuding from the kneeling supplicant. It suffused him in an unlight that ate the pale glow of lumens and the crackling blue fire of electro-flambeaux overhead. Yheng watched as their glow was devoured, and by the time her attention returned to the Iron Magus they had performed their part of the ritual and resumed their place in the covenant.

The fifth and the sixth marks were given by the Wretched Prince, a twisted, mutated creature whose withered form drew sneers of hatred from the assembly, and the Sin of Six Knives, a warp-born thing whose ethereal body flickered in and out of reality with only its sextet-blades and hooked grin persistently visible. A wind howled through the throne room at these two inscriptions, carrying the voices of the damned and the promises of the malign yet unborn essences of the warp. Reality shuddered, and for a fleeting half-second Yheng felt a hundred thousand eyes regard her with eager hunger. It was almost overwhelming, the insignificance of her existence never more achingly apparent. She took an involuntary step back, inwardly cursing herself for her weakness and doubly so when Tenebrus held her fast with a grip of iron.

'You must witness!' he snapped. 'The eye of the gods is upon us.'

Six shards down, only two remained.

At the seventh shard, a bell began tolling, as if from far away, as if from a place beyond the throne room, beyond reality. The Scion of Plagues stepped back, his gauntleted hands resting on the pommel of a massive axe. He leaned backwards, a chuckle slipping through the grille of his bucket helm. A late ascension, this one, his appointment unexpected but needed. A putrescent reek wafted from this grim headsman, who was a warrior of the old war.

Upon the dais, the supplicant was barely a juddering silhouette in the unlight, feathered at the edges like a paint smear on a damp canvas. His back arched in apparent agony, limbs rigid by his sides as the culmination of the bestowing neared.

The eighth figure wore a formless cloak, white skin peeking from within the folds of a voluminous hood.

Augury.

As they placed their mark, long fingers caressing like a tongue tasting their prey and fed the last piece of jagged metal into flesh, they turned towards Yheng. At first, she thought it was her imagination, but the gaze of Augury was unmistakable. They had literally stopped to stare at her. Not a glance or a challenge like the Iron Magus – that had been blatant, obvious – though if any others of the Hand noticed Augury's sudden interest in Yheng, they did not stir. Not even Tenebrus, who appeared almost entranced, locked out of time and place.

This moment was only for Yheng.

Augury's lipless mouth curved into a sickle grin as the eighth pulled back its hood to reveal...

The demagogue who had recruited her on Gathalamor. Yheng had killed him herself, a sacrifice to the gods to ensure her rise to cult leader of the Blade Unsheathed. A shadow passed over the man's face and, in its wake, his features thickened, his head broadened, old Colchisian runes marked his skin, and he became Kar-Gatharr. She had once called the Word Bearer master until–

The face changed again, thinning as if all its vital Astartesian vigour was draining away, to leave...

Tenebrus. The sorcerer eerily looked back, both simultaneously by her side and standing across the dais. She did not flinch, nor breathe, her heart thudding against her chest.

If the true Tenebrus thought anything amiss, he gave no outward sign.

Though it disgusted her, Yheng felt the urge to run. *Flee or die,* her body screamed. She should not be here in this place. This was beyond her, the wagers of gods and monsters. The ambitions she had harboured were nothing but the foolish dreams of a child grasping for the sun. Her overreach would destroy her.

No. She didn't believe that.

Her expression hardened, the revulsion she felt for her former masters galvanising her, spurring her on.

I am Tharador Yheng, she asserted to herself. *None will master me.*

At this the simulacrum faded, sloughing away like dead skin, a mask of dust and nothing more, Yheng's brief sense of disquiet fading with it. Augury's pale visage remained, eyes hidden by the low hood, that lipless mouth still smiling. White and gelid, like a creature of deep places, of fathomless ocean trenches that had never felt the touch of sunlight.

And though the mouth did not move, Yheng heard its voice nonetheless, like a lover's promise into her ear.

Behold...

Unlight filled the chamber and as it touched her, Yheng heard screaming – a long-held cry of agony, out of phase, echoing through displaced time.

Behold...

Through the pain and the tumult, Yheng felt it. The malign regard of the gods of Ruin. The rapture of it, the sense of being *chosen.* The sheer magnificence of it all...

Until it consumed her, and she fell screaming.

Chapter One

DAUGHTER OF MORDIAN

TARTARUS

WHISPERERS

Kesh awoke to screaming, and in the quiet dark of the underground it took her a few moments to realise it was only a dream.

She was alone in her bunk and even upon waking could not be sure if she had been the one screaming or if it was someone else. She stood and moved to the basin beside her cot, first dashing water onto her face, then trying to rub the stiffness from her neck and shoulders with her other hand.

She felt a scar there, one of many old wounds earned from past battles. It wasn't the scars she could touch that bothered her, but rather the ones she could not. The scars that were memories. Of Gathalamor in the catacombs, buried alive under the bones of the dead. Of Kamidar in the palace, and the dreams of fire and blood, of black sackcloth wings.

When does a memory become a dream and a dream a memory? When is reality and fiction so intertwined that the one is no longer readily distinguishable from the other?

Kesh shuddered at the thought. She found Dvorgin's old flask amongst her belongings and took a swig to settle her nerves. The *rupka* stung like a bastard but it was warming and had enough of a kick to make her feel almost alive. When her hands stopped shaking, she dressed fully. She had been wearing her fatigue trousers and under-vest already, so the rest didn't take long to throw on, and then she was out.

She found Lodrin and a few of the others sitting around a table in a part of the tunnel designated as barracks. It was one of many such chambers that had been cored out of the rock and earth, a few tables and chairs thrown in, a stove for recaff with bunks adjoining. Sodium lamps flickered over the scene, lending it more atmosphere than it deserved, the soft lighting kind to the shithouse condition of everyone and everything inside.

Of the group, only Lodrin evinced any kind of cheer. Ruddy-cheeked, dark brown hair cut short but not shaved, he always managed to look simultaneously neat and out of breath. Gently spoken was Lod, though his build was that of a brawler, thick-necked and wide-shouldered. He carried the squad's flamer, some of the shadows beneath his eyes soot rather than lack of sleep. His cap sat on the table next to a steaming mug of recaff, and he looked up from staring at the fan of cards he held in front of him as Kesh approached.

The game was Sickles, a firm favourite amongst the ranks, easy to learn and fraught with gambler's peril.

'I can deal you in, sergeant,' he offered genially.

Kesh wondered briefly if he and the others had heard her screaming, or if it had just been the dream.

Mavin, their vox-operator, glanced at his own hand, but like the other trooper he kept his feelings as well guarded as his cards, giving nothing away. Mavin hailed from Tarnus, one of the hives on Mordian, the world where the entirety of the 84th came from. Tarnus had a cut-throat reputation, its clans miserly and distrustful. His narrow, angular features and thin chin seemed to exacerbate this trait in him, and like most of the hivers, he had stark white hair from where the rains had bleached it. Kesh had always found him fair and shrewd, if a little tight.

The mood was tense, the pile of Munitorum chits high.

Garris had the highest pile. He leaned back in his chair, his face pensive. 'Not until this round is concluded,' he said, flat as ice.

A soldier through and through, Garris had a gift. He knew knives like a Catachan knows the jungle, although Kesh had seen him turn most any sharp object into a deadly weapon. On Brevin, he had killed a cultist with a fork, stabbing every artery and point of critical injury in a matter of seconds. He also doubled as the squad's battlefield surgeon when the need arose. There was no one more capable than Harkus Garris with a needle, and he always kept his stitches small.

'Wouldn't want to break your streak, trooper,' Kesh replied, earning a sharp glance from the veteran. She gave a nod of thanks to Lodrin, who offered a half-hearted smile in return. Perhaps he had hoped she would change his luck, or perhaps he didn't know what else to say.

There had been a lot of that going around since Kamidar. Hundreds dead, many of those slain in cold blood, massacred by the Queen of Iron, who also now lay in her grave. Kesh's rank permitted her to know very little of the particulars, but the world had been pacified in the wake of internecine war and made a redoubt of the Anaxian Line. She had come back to a regiment much changed since the early years of the crusade. Fellows had died during that time, replacements had come in to maintain the ranks and then those replacements had died, and so it went. Kesh endured. Some amongst the 84th thought she was lucky.

She didn't feel lucky.

Hence she left the game of Sickles well alone.

'If there's any of that recaff going, I'll take a cup,' she said, briefly choosing wakefulness over sleep, glancing around for the pot.

Garris took a handful of bone dice and threw them into a tray in the middle of the table. His grin widened as the octagonal dice came to rest and he laid down three cards, taking up two in return. Kesh glanced over the spread that remained, her interest casual.

'Only dregs left,' said Lodrin apologetically, and he shaped as if he was about to rise. 'I can brew up some more if you–'

Kesh stopped him. 'No need.' She cast her eye out to the softly lit darkness beyond. 'I'm sure I can scrounge up something from one of the other squads.

'Enjoy your game,' she added, leaning in to Lodrin before she went. 'I'd take the Preceptor and the Veteran if I were you...' She winked at Garris, who growled under his breath, something filthy, an expletive from his old hive.

And then she was out into the tunnels, hunting sleep, grasping for a mote of peace.

According to the chrono, another item bequeathed by her dying commanding officer, it was late. Or early, depending on your perspective, she supposed. The sentries were active; Kesh nodded as she passed by their patrols. Their pale, mud-grimed faces were swathed in the shadows of phosphor lamps hanging from the low ceiling on looping strings of wire.

She saw troops from the Vardish and Catachan regiments. Good fighters, disciplined but ill-suited to the dark and narrow places under the world. She and the Mordian 84th shared lodgings with one other regiment besides these two. Whilst the Vardish and Catachans had been brought in for manpower and fighting grit, the Gunbad 204th were loners when they weren't mustered or in combat but deadly with their trench axes. Tunnellers by military trade, they excelled in the 'Hellway', the name the troops had given to the miles-long network of passages and chambers painstakingly excavated by the teams of Mechanicus sappers that Kesh could hear by the distant echoes of drilling engines deeper in the subterranean complex.

Above her, sixty feet of hard earth and bedrock, was Barren. A fitting name for a bleak and unimpressive world. What little she had seen of it, anyway. They had landed by night, over three months ago, and it was less than two days after that when the Martians had forged an underground beachhead with the Termites, and the Militarum short-strawed as underminers had been sent below to make a garrison.

A grim fate for some, though Kesh didn't mind the dark. As a native of Mordian she was used to it.

'Having trouble sleeping, sergeant?'

She met Captain Rellion coming the other way. Tall, straight-backed and dark-haired like some Mordians, Rellion looked almost pristine for someone who had been living underground for the better part of the last few months. Though he had taken to wearing his combat helmet instead of his officer's cap ever since Colonel Arber had been struck by a loose piece of rock and stretchered off the line. Geologians from the Martian cohort had performed a rapid structural analysis of the tunnels in the aftermath of the incident and replaced steel wall braces with synthwood. Then they had sprayed any weaknesses with a bonding polymer, declaring Tartarus – the name the Militarum had given this tunnel network – safe, but Rellion didn't trust it. He was keeping his helmet on. Kesh wondered if he slept with it on and stifled a grin at the thought of the man wearing little but his helm, deciding it was not so bad an image.

'Is it that obvious, sir?' said Kesh, and made a crisp salute.

She knew she must look ragged, and felt the dark circles

around her eyes, her gaunt features. The roughly cropped hair like a thick tuft of snow-grass on her head. Never mind the scars.

Rellion reciprocated the salute, putting Kesh at ease. 'Looking for something to take the edge off?' he asked.

'Would that be inappropriate, sir?'

'Not at all. I think there's a medicae somewhere around this section that has been handing out low-dose morphia like it's standard issue.' He pointed vaguely to one of the tunnel branches behind him. 'You're not the only one who's ill at ease down here.' He gave a furtive glance at the ceiling as if at any second it might give way or that piece of rock that took out Colonel Arber would somehow find him too.

'Oh, I don't mind the dark and the deeps, sir.'

Rellion quirked an eyebrow as he looked back at Kesh. 'Night terrors then? I thought I heard screaming.'

Kesh cursed inwardly at this confirmation. It also meant the others had been hiding their knowledge of it. *What else have they been hiding?*

Rellion went on. 'I think there's a regimental priest hereabouts too.' He looked around. 'But Throne of Terra, I couldn't say exactly where. This place grows by the hour. I swear the only reason I walk these halls is so that I don't wake up one day and realise I'm lost in them. Wandering forever, never finding my way back to the line.' He smiled.

'Don't tempt me,' Kesh joked but took care to note if any of the Commissariat were in earshot first. 'I suppose we'll be prepping for the assault soon?' she asked.

Rellion nodded, his gaze faraway for a moment. 'This place'll be choked with troopers by then. A lot of men and materiel underground.' Another look at the ceiling. 'I hope these cogheads know what they're doing.'

Kesh doubted the Martians had much regard for the flesh-and-blood troopers of the Militarum, but she trusted their craft. The tunnels would hold, even with two thousand boots rumbling through them. At least, she hoped they would.

'Are you alright, sergeant?' he said, noting something in Kesh's manner.

'Just a little insomnia, sir.'

'You seem a little off.'

Kesh shrugged; she couldn't disagree.

'I'm surprised,' Rellion continued, and gestured to her rank pins, 'that you're still at squad level. After Kamidar and what you did... I could scarcely credit Munser's report, but here you are.'

She felt her chest tighten, a vice pincering her ribs and pushing out her breath. Lieutenant Munser and some of his men had found her in the halls of the Kamidarian palatial capital not long after the shield wall had come down and the Black Templars had made their surgical strike. It had ended the war, or cut it off at the knees before it could properly start at least. Kesh had been hailed a hero, even if the exact circumstances of how she had survived couldn't be fully established.

Munser had brought her on as his sergeant and part of his command squad, and she found she liked the change. The lieutenant was a decent man, and the others in her squad had their quirks, like Garris, but she trusted them.

Rellion was still talking, Kesh having drifted out and only now picking up the threads of their conversation again. 'I heard they tried to give you a platoon. And pinned a medal on your chest.'

Kesh nodded, trying to gather her composure.

'Remarkable valour, Kesh. And to have lived through all that...' He shook his head and Kesh prayed he wouldn't say it. *Please don't say it...* 'Miraculous.'

She couldn't decide if Rellion was probing, looking for something hidden, some truth Kesh wasn't willing to reveal, that she *couldn't* reveal because she understood as little about what had transpired in Gallanhold as anyone else. Except she had been there. Her and Syreniel. Though the Silent Sister had stayed true to the name of her Order, she had still managed to communicate something of what she saw in Kesh. To think of it made Kesh's skin crawl and her hand slipped to the gold coin the Oblivion Knight had given her upon her departure. It still felt warm to the touch despite the chill of the under-dark.

'I'm just a soldier, sir,' said Kesh, 'one who wants to do her duty. I see better with my boots on the ground.' She tugged at the forester's cap tucked under her epaulette, but it was stuck tight enough. 'I have no desire to lead. I find the way so that others may lead, that's the pathfinder's creed.'

She nodded briskly, about to move on, when Rellion held up a hand to stop her.

'Here,' said the captain, proffering a smoke stick from his jacket pocket. 'Won't help you sleep, but...'

Kesh took it with a wan smile. 'Much obliged, sir. Though I should be on my way if I'm going to find that medicae.'

She made a swift exit after that, and headed in the rough direction Rellion had indicated. She could not fault his assertion that getting lost down here was a distinct possibility. All the tunnels looked much the same, and was it her imagination or did the ceiling seem to be getting lower? Kesh suppressed a shudder at the sudden thought of several tons of earth and rock pressing down on her and silently cursed the captain for putting the thought in her head.

A couple of troopers passed her, wearing flak armour. They had low-lumen torches on their uniforms but the shadows couldn't hide the fact they looked on edge. After weeks of dogged preparation, the assault was coming. Alarms had been set up throughout the complex, poised to signal everyone to arms.

Kesh nodded to them, turning her face from the light as it

shone her way. She saw just fine without a lumen, her world of origin having prepared her for it. Every daughter and son of Mordian was born to the dark, half the global hemisphere perpetually benighted whilst the other burned eternally in the light of Mordian's vengeful star. It had left her pale but with exceptional night vision.

The troopers barely acknowledged her, lost in their own thoughts.

On she went, and after a while she started to think she might have taken a wrong turn or somehow double-backed without realisation. It was only when she saw the sentry up ahead that Kesh breathed a small sigh of relief.

He sat on a metal footlocker at the entrance to a larger section of the tunnel complex, sharpening a bayonet. He was of the Gunbad, the tunnel fighters. She noticed a savage-looking trench axe tucked in his belt. Bright eyes like burnt umber regarded Kesh as she approached him.

'Thought this was the medicae?' she asked.

'It is,' came a slightly gruff reply. He looked young, just a trooper, his stubbled chin pockmarked with thicker patches of hair, and she guessed he used the trench axe for more than just hacking at earth. 'Medicae's dead, I'm afraid,' he said.

Kesh caught a glimpse into a chamber beyond. No body to see, but a cut rope swayed gently in an underground breeze, hanging from a synthwood support beam. All the excavated caverns were shored up in this way. Wood was better than steel. It bent with pressure. Kesh tried not to imagine the creak and then the crack of timber surrendering to the mass above. The earth crashing down to bury her alive.

Bloody Rellion!

Dying. *Again.* This was the dream, she realised. Her death. It felt real. It always felt real, every time.

'Yet here I am...' she murmured. Just as the captain had said.

'Beg pardon?' said the sentry, as Kesh realised she had spoken a little too loudly.

'What happened?' she bluffed instead.

'Self-execution.' He raised his eyebrows as if suspicious, then spoke into the side of his hand, in a mock stage whisper. 'The commissars won't let us say suicide. Bad for morale. Ironic, eh?'

Kesh thought he had a lot of candour for a sentry.

'What's your name, trooper?'

'Ghates.' He tapped his ident with a dirty fingernail. As if really noticing her for the first time, Ghates stopped sharpening. 'What do you need, Nighter?'

It was the name some of the troopers in the other regiments gave the Mordians in reference to the fact that Mordian was a world of eternal darkness. As cognomens went, it wasn't bad.

'Something for sleep. Anything in there still? Maybe a sedative, something to take the edge off. And you can call me Kesh.'

'Whole kit and caboodle's still in there, Kesh. The black hats never touched a thing.'

Kesh looked but hesitated, almost afraid to enter. As if it was sacrilege or something.

She really needed to sleep. Or wake properly. One or the other.

'Why he'd do it?' she asked.

Ghates shrugged and went back to sharpening the bayonet. 'Maybe he felt the world pressing in. Or maybe dealing with the pain of others day and night drove him mad. Maybe the whisperers got him...' He made the sign of the aquila.

Kesh frowned. 'What do you mean?'

'Nothing. Something. I just think maybe we've been down here a little too long. Folks hearing things. Seeing things, too.'

'Such as?'

He shook his head, suddenly concerned. 'Oh, not me. I'm buttoned up nice and tight. Nothing ailing me, Nighter. But there's a reason that frayed rope is hanging from the rafters...'

'Can I get in there, see what I can find? I just need a sedative,' Kesh repeated. 'Something mild.'

'Next medicae is north.' Ghates pointed with his bayonet. 'That way.'

Her heart sank at the thought of the trudge back through the tunnels. 'But that's about two miles under all of this shit...'

He gave a wry smile, and jerked his head sideways towards the room.

'The Emperor protects...' she said, about to enter when she paused again. 'Thank you, Ghates,' she said and offered the smoke Rellion had given her. She wasn't going to use it.

Ghates took it with a nod of gratitude. 'I'd be quick if I were you.'

Kesh stepped inside, about to begin her search when the alarms started ringing. She shared a weary glance with the tunnel fighter and about-faced.

Sleep would have to wait.

Chapter Two

KITH AND KIN

HERALDS OF THE HAND

A PRISONER

Yamir had not the fortitude of his stocky hosts, and greatly desired to sleep. Fatigue dragged against every sinew and bone in his body. He was not built for such rigour, Yamir decided to himself, as a particularly savage battle played out in the background. His fine trappings, his frock coat and trousers would need a thorough cleanse. As soon as he was able to return to the *Buccaneer* he would take a bath too. Even the mere thought of it was a balm. He doubted the Kin, in which he had made company, were as fastidious. They looked at home in the dust and the blood. Not that he would voice it; he was far too experienced a diplomat for that. A rogue trader in service of a distant master, he had come here to this barren moon to gain favour with and potentially form an alliance between the doughty warriors of the Omrigar Kindred, many of whom were still fighting amongst themselves.

Automatic weapon discharge and the shrieking refrain of more exotic firearms laced the air. The low, bellowed oaths of the Kin contrasted with the death-rattle defiance of the cultists, who fought like zealots but without any hope of victory. They were outgunned, outmatched. Undone.

A largely barren expanse characterised the battlefield, where the Kin had arranged their vehicles and mass extraction engines in efficient camps around their find. The moon was dead, perhaps inhabited once, but its seams of titanium and metathane still ran deep. It was this that the Kin coveted, their kâhl most of all.

Her name was Vutred and she stood just ahead of Yamir, a small cohort of her finest and most heavily armoured warriors around her. She had taken a prisoner, a wretched thing in the ragged garb of a Navy captain, his Imperial sigils besmirched or removed and those of the gods of Ruin daubed in their place.

Vutred gave a curt signal, the chopping motion of her armoured hand like a blade.

'Don't let it fall unconscious, Utri,' she growled.

The Kin leader was a stout figure, broad-shouldered as an auroch and skin cracked with scars like fissures through rock. She was clad in a suit of heavy powered plate, the edges worn to sharp silver in places and begrimed with dust, her weapons disengaged, her trappings flecked with enemy blood. Some of it had dried in an interrupted scythe-blade curve across her cheek. A deep scar above one eye stopped at her crest of flaxen hair.

One of her Einhyr stepped forward at her gruff command with a grind of servo-driven exo-armour, like an anvil had been miraculously animated and turned into flesh and blood, and slapped the prisoner across the cheek.

Already dazed, the prisoner hissed in pain but became instantly focused as Utri's crackling gauntlet drew close. Faint lightning arced over the knuckles, picking out the cultist's face in the glow. His countenance had been noble once but now it was disfigured, like so many of those who worshipped the Dark Gods, with crude sigils seared into his dark skin as if by a torturer's brand. An eight-pointed star, a three-tined fork, a sickle moon and a fiery eye, amongst other less identifiable runes. The wounds looked angry, almost raw.

The Einhyr pulled back his arm for another blow, his red-bearded face framed in a snarl.

'Enough, Utri.'

He paused, before withdrawing silently to join the other warriors. They stayed close, a cordon around their kâhl, though in truth she needed no such protection.

The battle surrounding them continued.

Given how badly the cultists were faring, Yamir felt confident they regretted their decision to attack the seemingly vulnerable Kin.

Not long after landing, drawn by the esoteric readings of their augurs, the Kin had set to work establishing a mine-head. Rigs had been fixed in place, harvesters primed. Then drilling and extraction had begun. The mineral-rich heart of the moon was where the real treasure lay, but the Kin wrenched every iota of material from the site, always gauging their efforts against the potential rewards to the extent that the expenditure of resources in having to fight the cultists appeared to have offended them.

The cultists had come upon the Kin as they were closing up their operations. Seeing only a modest band of prospectors, their stout voidship at low anchor above the moon, they must have appeared easy pickings to the cultists, who had launched landing craft in abundance.

What the attackers hadn't known was that Vutred and her other warriors had been deep inside the primary borehole they had made in the moon's core, surveying extraction and carefully tabulating yields. Every grain and particle accounted for.

Waste feeds the void, or so the Kin would say.

As the cultists were being blunted on the bolt cannons of the Hearthkyn left to watch the entrance, Vutred and her Einhyr had appeared from the heart of the moon. A band of heavily armed fighters in even heavier armour had followed – Yamir had learned the name for these fighters was 'Thunderkyn', an apt moniker considering their impressive and explosive armaments – and for the cultists, the fight went precipitously downhill from there. The Oathband were merciless in their destruction of the enemy, herding them into kill-zones, harrying them relentlessly and otherwise ending any real threat.

Little more than dregs of the enemy remained now, mainly half-armoured militia and bestial acolytes, their ship a listless ruin drifting in the upper void. Pieces of space-borne detritus followed it in a shattered wake like the leavings of a half-picked carcass. Bodies littered the ground underfoot with only a handful of Kin slain in reply. Yet, even for that there would be an accounting, as it was in all things for the Kin.

All of this Yamir had come to learn during his time with the stocky pioneers. The rogue trader had seen few braver and none shrewder. Every price paid would be measured from this conflict to the last, every expenditure, every acquisition – as the scion of the Lotha-Venz Dynasty, and with a Warrant of Trade to his family's name, he could understand that. Though Vutred, who cast a glance over her shoulder at her warriors rounding up the last of the enemy, looked less than pleased with the cost.

'Speak now, filth,' she demanded of the cultist, her creased features as tanned and worn as boiled leather. 'I give you this one chance. What did you hope to gain by attacking the Omrigar Kindred?'

The prisoner grinned, the insane look in his eye rekindled for a moment. Old scars marked his face – from his former life, Yamir assumed. His moustache, not an uncommon sight amongst the Navy elite, was lank and greasy with corruption.

The defaced rank pin of the Imperial Navy shone amid his battered wargear. A golden shoulder guard shaped like an eagle had been defaced and blackened by fire. Defections were not unheard of in Imperial forces, but to see one of their shipmasters fallen to Chaos was unsettling.

'Answer me!' snarled Vutred, and Yamir saw the prisoner's grin widen.

'We are the heralds,' he spat, 'the splinters of dissolution, when the pantheon will reign and Ruin is ascendant. We are the disciples, those who follow the Apostle, his servants and the servants of the true gods whose eye is upon us!' Neck bulging, he lurched forward against his bonds until Vutred kicked him in the chest, smashing all the air from his lungs and sending him sprawling back in fits of gasping agony.

'Wretched creature,' she said and turned to another of her company, a grey-bearded sage, his void armour draped in a charcoal-coloured hooded cloak. Still as stone this one, unmoving as a statue. 'Othed...'

At his name, the Grimnyr's eyes glowed as he raised an ancestral staff carved with strange angular markings. The atmosphere chilled, faint flakes of snow crystallising out of air. They had something of the warp about them, these battle-sages, but Othed was unlike any psyker Yamir had ever encountered.

A machine of some kind followed in the Grimnyr's wake, like a robotic torso impelled by anti-gravitic technologies. It hummed as Othed approached the prisoner, his gloved hand raised in a claw.

It took a few moments, the chill of his presence seeping into bone, cooling blood to ice, before the gentle storm ebbed and the Grimnyr's eyes faded back to grey.

'I detect no falsehood, my kâhl,' he uttered, in a voice like creaking oak. 'He believes his ravings. They came here to pillage, to kill and capture. Whatever greater purpose he speaks of, this warband are no longer any part of it. They are wild dogs left to roam. And a wild dog will always piss where it is not wanted.'

'As true as wrought,' agreed Utri, the Einhyr eager to finish this.

Vutred rubbed her chin with a well-worn gauntlet.

'What of you, Imperial?' she asked, none too kindly. He had found her fair but fierce. The kâhl had problems of her own, he knew. Detail was sparse, but he had deduced her Kindred were facing something like fiscal ruin. For the Kin, this was disastrous. Vutred sought what she referred to as the *mother-lode*, some lucrative discovery, a prospect that would change her fortunes. As such, she had little patience for becoming embroiled in petty skirmishes. 'Is any of this known to you?'

Yamir nodded, weathering her stern regard. 'An old friend of mine was particularly adept at wrenching the truth out of scum like this,' said the rogue trader. He risked a glance at the Grimnyr. 'I mean no offence to your sage's abilities.'

The Grimnyr inclined his head slightly, showing there was none taken.

Vutred barely noticed as she raised an eyebrow. 'Is he nearby?'

'Alas, no. Well, I don't think so. I haven't seen him in some time. I could reach him, but you'd be in for a wait.'

She sniffed desultorily. 'I am not without patience, Imperial, but I need to know if this one has more allies in this region. I can ill afford further losses.' She bit her tongue at that remark, the consternation plain as a map on her face. 'This friend of yours, did he pass on any of his craft to you?'

Yamir tilted his head regretfully. 'Also, no.'

'Then I don't suppose you're much use to me here, are you?' She muttered something else under her breath, but he had not learned enough of their language to decipher the phrase.

In any case, he struggled to disagree.

A tearing sound suddenly came from the prisoner, followed

by a snap as he cut himself free of his bindings, a concealed knife brandished in his hand. Screaming, he lunged for Vutred.

'Let the Dark Gods bear witness!'

Eyes shimmering with uncanny hoar-frost, Othed raised a gloved hand, fingers crackling with power...

Vutred was faster.

She seized the cultist by the neck, stopping him short, her other gauntleted hand around his wrist. With a twist she broke the bone, eliciting a cry from her would-be assassin, the knife clattering to the ground, where Othed claimed it, spiriting the blade into a force shield emanated by his robotic familiar. The Grimnyr hawked and spat, muttering the Kin word for 'cursed'.

It happened so quickly, Utri and the other Einhyr had barely had a chance to move, much less comprehend what was happening.

'Look to my own protection, shall I?' snapped the kâhl, her gaze withering as it fell upon the chastened Einhyr.

Her attention returned to the cultist who was squirming in her grip. She threw the wretch down, looming like a storm. 'I don't know why you came here, but I'll waste no further resource on you.' Vutred's plasma blade unsheathed from her gauntlet, the dormant weapon suddenly igniting forge-red.

'Wait!' The urgent cry came from Yamir before he realised he'd spoken.

A host of angry Kin faces fell upon him.

'Look...' He pointed.

There was another mark on the prisoner's chest. Partially revealed when he had lunged for the kâhl and his already torn Navy jacket and shirt had parted. It was red raw, despite the scar tissue framing it, carved into skin, a wound that refused to heal.

Yamir thought he recognised it as something described to him years ago, not long after the outset of the crusade. He leaned in for a closer look, the Einhyr about to intervene until Vutred warned them off.

'Let him be, but hold the wretch down,' she said, gesturing to the prisoner.

Two of the Einhyr grabbed an arm each to prevent the cultist wriggling. He submitted readily, a flash of tapetum in his eye as the light caught it. Feral, predatory despite his obvious disadvantage.

It made the rogue trader hesitate for a moment before gingerly baring the cultist's chest, wincing at the stench. And there it was. Unmistakable.

A hand print, its long fingers ending in talons.

The cultist started muttering feverishly.

Dour, Vutred looked on. 'What's he saying?'

Feeling the cultist's rank breath on his cheek, Yamir drew closer. He half expected the wretch to try to bite him, but the prisoner appeared almost catatonic, entranced by his own rasping mantra. Discerning a single word, the rogue trader paled. A name. Yamir withdrew as if stung, turning to the kâhl, whose brows had knitted together in a thunderhead of consternation.

'Hand of Abaddon. He's saying "Hand of Abaddon".'

Vutred frowned.

'What, by the ancestors, is the Hand of Abaddon?'

Chapter Three

A RETURN TO TERRA

THE ARCHIVE

A DARK DISCOVERY

This place had been grand once, during the days of Rostov's distant ancestors. In these benighted times, it was a hollow and gilded shell, a decaying edifice, its grandeur long faded.

And yet he loved it anyway, for it was where He resided, His Throne and His crown.

Terra.

He had come to a scholars' district, one of the oldest and less well travelled, though the Via Gnosis still groaned against the mass of servitors, priests, bent-backed scribes and notaries, the passing sutlers bound for the void docks, the zealots and orators cramming its miles-long expanse. Few ever went by anything other than foot in this particular district, unless they could travel via lighter or transport ship, and here such a luxury was impossible, the many arches and bridges, the spires, the statues and lofty balconies making a labyrinth of the skyways. Not to mention the flocks of cyber-cherubim fluttering on dead wings, and held aloft by anti-gravitic motors.

The roads were equally congested, clustered also with carts and rickshaws, palanquins and auto-pulpits. The ink-fingered inhabitants dragged stacks of vellum or bore string-bound clusters of manuscripts lashed onto their backs or else cradles of scrolls.

Rostov moved steadily through the throng, his leg still stiff on account of his injuries. They had removed the metal callipers and he no longer needed the cane, but he would never fully heal. So he patiently made his journey and resisted the urge to brandish his rosette as he edged through the crowds.

Let them think me one of them, he decided. Secrecy was one of the chief weapons of the Inquisition after all. As he walked, taking in the smells of sweat and toil that were only half hidden by the cloying fragrance of incense, he rubbed idly at his hand. It had been paining him of late, worse than before and growing more problematic by the day. It was no longer just the hand, either. He felt it in his arm and shoulder too, a profound itching across his back reminiscent of scar tissue. Rostov had scars aplenty. In the Ordo Xenos of the Holy Inquisition, it came with the territory. But this was different, and not like his other injury. At times, the pain was stabbing, burning. An indelible wound.

This represented a consequence.

Or perhaps even a warning.

He put it to the back of his mind, and focused instead on the structure looming ahead. It was curved and formidable, made from sandstone and ouslite, and chromed with silver – more a fortress than a repository of knowledge. They had just turned onto a wide processional, a paved avenue lined with artificial trees and the statues of prelates, theologians and saints.

'At the risk of sounding trite,' a voice behind Rostov began, raising its volume to be heard above the general hubbub of the mob, 'are we almost at our destination, my lord?'

Rostov smiled. 'Are your feet hurting, Antoniato? I thought a veteran like you would be used to campaigning...'

The former Guardsman turned Inquisitorial agent grunted something unflattering, and shucked his plasma rifle into a more comfortable position against his shoulder. Benidei Antoniato was well-muscled, with dark brown hair, his weathered face suggesting his age. He wore a patched uniform, heavy flak armour over the top with a grenade belt around his body, and a short blade strapped to his leg. Rostov heard him clank and clack as he adjusted his pistol belt, too.

'I told you the arsenal would not be necessary,' the inquisitor lightly chided.

'I prefer to be prepared, and this is Terra, and the largest hive city in the Imperium. More places to get lost and forgotten here than on some death worlds I could mention. You trust these bloody priests and scribes? I know I don't.'

A coterie of scholars coming the opposite way dared a scowl in Rostov's rough vicinity which he assumed was meant for the ex-Guardsman.

'Let's not goad them, shall we, Antoniato. Writers can be savage if spurred.'

Another grumble, the muttering fading into a long, drawn-out sigh.

'How we must suffer in the Emperor's service,' said Rostov with a rueful smile.

They passed under the shadow of statues, half listening to hymns piped through numerous vox-casters stationed throughout the via. Not all functioned, and several of the statues were merely feet and ankles attached to marble plinths. Gilded but very much tarnished, Terra still bore some evidence of the incursion nigh on a decade ago when the Throneworld was besieged for the third time in its storied history. At least, the third time that Rostov knew about. Much had been lost through war and indolence.

God-Emperor, he had been through similar trials to reach this crucial point in his hunt for the Hand. All that he had seen and experienced – the Dark Apostle captured at Machorta Sound, the sorcerer he had encountered on Srinagar. Each claiming knowledge of this prey and its machinations that had so haunted Rostov's waking nights and weary days. Every evidential shred, every scrap of information, all of it had led him back to Terra and its Grand Librarium. He had exhausted every other avenue of enquiry first, for no visit to the Throneworld came without price. Every underworld contact, every low-level heretic and recidivist, every cult and arcanist. Any with knowledge of the esoteric, the ancient. It had yielded little and taxed him a lot, so he had made the journey, although it interrupted his other plans. But he must know. He *had* to know.

He scratched at his shoulder, certain it was becoming a compulsive tic, and wondered at what other cost, what hidden price, he was paying for his diligence. Another price he could ill afford, but pay it he would nonetheless.

At last, they came to the threshold of the Grand Librarium. Rostov passed under the shadow cast by soaring stone above, a smaller postern gate opening within the colossal doors granting him admittance.

Hulking guardians stood either side of the doorway, wearing ancient war plate and wielding immense halberds. Auto-turrets cunningly worked into the embrasures tracked him through fluted mouth-barrels, their arsenals hidden behind cherubic masks.

Through the postern gate and into the librarium interior, he noticed monitor servitors cast soft detection beams over them both. Even here, at this outer marker, the very edge point of the much deeper labyrinth, piles of books and scrolls were in abundance. Tapestries lined the walls, banners hung from columns, feathered-edged manuscripts were stuffed into high stacks, diligently archived. The smell of it, all that parchment and vellum... The dust of ages fell thick on the recycled air.

Passing through a second arch between two columns, less grandiose and more functional in its aesthetic, Rostov detected an energy field powering down. As he crossed its deactivated aegis, he tasted the remnants of its bitter flavour on his tongue and realised it was a killing field.

No chances taken here. Knowledge was power and that power was well guarded.

Gratefully, he crossed this hidden gauntlet and entered the librarium proper. Dinginess reigned within, marginally lessened by electro-sconces and flambeaux hanging down from the vaulted ceiling.

'Now what, my lord?' groaned Antoniato. At the outer marker, he had been divested of his weapons, his arsenal secured in a sealed casket for retrieval upon his exit from the librarium. He sounded less than pleased.

Rostov had brought no weapons of his own. At least, none that were overt or easily detectable. His status as an inquisitor lent some anonymity too.

'The archive, Antoniato. That is where we are bound.'

Farther they descended, through several more checkpoints, each more severely defended than the last. This shadowed place harboured many secrets, some of which were not meant for the eyes of man. As he reached the lowest of the deeps, a grave chill in the air despite the apparent lack of atmospheric devices, Rostov was stopped by a final gatekeeper.

This one he knew was the Archivist itself, a strange, quasi-mechanical individual with retractable lenses for eyes and long, stilt-like legs. Swathed in heavy black robes, with a long, curved stave clutched in a skeletal hand, it reminded Rostov of a spectral ferryman, here to shepherd lost souls into the stygian underworld.

Further guardians resided here, stock still in alcoves, their halberds firmly planted, a barricade of tower shields facing outwards. Tracked servitor units lingered nearby, armed with deflagrating weapons, their eyes dead but for their targeting lasers, fire-red and searching...

Rostov stood at the edge of the dimly lit gallery, before a broad set of steps leading into further darkness.

He suppressed a shudder of unease, despite the power of his office. Even to inquisitors, the lowest levels were restricted. He presented a seal to the Archivist. It was not his own, but rather his inquisitor lord's, a seal of sanction granted to only a few and not easily. Rostov thought she must have called in several favours for this. Another price he would be expected to pay back.

After a few tense seconds of verification, the Archivist stepped aside. The latent energy hum from the alcoves powered down and the servitors' targeting lasers blinked out. Despite himself, he let out a breath and, after being handed a lumen-lantern by some scuttling homunculus, proceeded down into the last darkness.

Antoniato, uneasy despite his mental conditioning, stayed behind. He gave nary a grumble nor voiced any complaint, wise to keep his peace. Though when Rostov glanced back, his companion looked none too pleased at being left alone with the Archivist and its cohorts.

The lowest level was even more labyrinthine than the others. A vast expanse unfolded from the base of the stairway, yawning away into a half-dark haunted by the shadows of slow-moving servitors. Rostov briefly wondered who else might be down here and what they might be like.

Navigation proved taxing, the librarium stuffed to the eaves with esoterica, exotica and mirabilia. It was a hoarder's paradise. Incomplete, bewildering. Rostov applied his intellect to the task and narrowed the search to a single wing. Anti-gravitic platforms provided access to the higher stacks, so Rostov hooked his lumen-lantern to the guide rail, mounted one of the platforms, and went in search of the clandestine and the forgotten. He pulled every scrap of data he could find, the authors of these works ten thousand years dead in the main.

Hours riffled by like pages as Rostov scoured countless tomes and scrolls. He took up station by one of the many tables, the wood groaning under the sheer weight of material. Teetering stacks of manuscripts threatened to collapse at every turn, the research painstaking and arduous, but his solitude remained unmolested at least. As far as he could tell, he was the only one present, a solitary voyager in a place apart from the rest of the world. It was a unique and unsettling feeling.

As he searched, deploying paperweights to hold down scrolls, maps, and old star charts and other esoterica, he tried to recall everything about the artefact, committing to memory precisely how the thing had worked, its colour, its smell, the way it caught the light, the psychic resonance it left in its wake on Srinagar.

He also brought to mind the shard that had been found and then lost by his comrades in the Inquisition aboard the battle cruiser *Judgement of the Void*. The report had been brief but stark and would all but confirm his suspicions if he could ally it with knowledge gleaned in this benighted catacomb.

The artefact he had seen on Srinagar appeared to be a reality-severing knife, like a piece of obsidian glass or stone. He found many references to such blades, all variations on the same theme: some were recorded as destroyed or housed within the strictly controlled archives beneath the Imperial Palace itself. He would not be granted access there, no matter whose seal he carried. Only Captain-General Trajann Valoris himself and the black-clad keepers sworn to ensure its inviolability had the authority to breach this vault. Rostov must do without.

After what felt like it could be days, a dry hunger wrenching his stomach, Rostov pulled forth an old parchment from a cluster of unmarked volumes. He had nearly missed them, the codification down in the lowest deeps leaving much to be desired. Idly, as he tugged on the ribbon, he wondered if that was intentional. There was writing on the scroll, descriptions of provenance and form.

The name of the author caught in his throat, but he needed to speak it aloud to prove it was real.

'The solemn account of Roboute Guilliman, Thirteenth Primarch of the Imperium and Master of Ultramar...'

A jagged shard, a piece of a greater whole... two sighted now by the Order in recent months.

He wished he could deny it, but the evidence was compelling.

Sweat prickled his back and forehead despite the grave chill in the air. He read on, taking in the exactness of the primarch's description, the comprehensive detail. Turning the page, he found a second scroll beneath, concomitant to the first. An illustration in dark red ink took up half of one page. Beneath it more writing. Rostov read a name. Then he read it again to be sure, a sick feeling rising up in his gut.

'God-Emperor...' he breathed.

Chapter Four

A GATHERING

ARE WE TO FALL TO RANCOUR

THE PATH OF THE HAND

The dominion of the God-Emperor and mankind would fall, so swore the Hand.

And all present believed the recovery of the Anathame a significant step on the road to the Imperium's destruction, though they had made their own individual pacts with the Warmaster for their part in it. In truth, Yheng reflected as she took her place behind Tenebrus once more, it was all that had held this fragile alliance together. Without it, she feared what would happen next. This was precisely why the covenant had gathered again, albeit in part and mere hours after the ritual, in another cyclopean chamber. It was one of only several chambers deemed safe by the Iron Magus, who both maintained the fortress as well as slaving it to their will. A dark metal ziggurat dominated the space, its summit the meeting place for the Hand. No thrones here, just a stark black expanse, huge cables dangling from above like the entrails of some great beast. Just another part of the fortress wreathed in mystery.

Yheng found her eye drawn to these shadowy vaults and wondered what purpose this room might have once had. Before feeling the alien sentience of the place, she had assumed it was a machine or perhaps several, once interlinked but now severed. The ache of that separation impressed itself upon her somehow. Perhaps when she had touched the column in the black chamber, she had connected with it, the machine, its *mind*. The thought both chilled and excited her. She had recovered from her experience there, but the sheer unfathomable regard of the Dark Gods remained. Indelible, like a scar on her psyche. No one else, not even the warp-born thing with the blades, had appeared to notice what had happened and, as such, Yheng had begun to question whether it had happened at all. She had begun to question many things. Only Augury seemed to have any insight, but they were as inscrutable as the fortress and currently beyond Yheng's reach to understand.

She was one of the few acolytes present, though she noticed the Iron Magus had left a proxy in their place, a robed creature of metal and tendrils, massive and hunchbacked, its retinal lenses burning from the shadows of its hood like balefires.

The Wretched Prince had brought a coven of psykers, the pitiful human degenerates half hiding their mutations under rags and threadbare cloaks, and clutching staves and icons of Ruin. Yheng knew not to underestimate the creature or his witchlings. Twisted in body, almost perpetually warped by the magic that coursed through him, thin-limbed and shambling, the Prince made up for his physical limitations with his sorcerous mastery.

Even Tenebrus, Yheng knew with no small amount of petty satisfaction, was wary of him. It was part of the Prince's curse to be reviled, a fact which none of the Hand bothered to conceal. As such, he had no allies amongst the covenant, but she doubted any would openly challenge him either.

The seventh, the Traitor Astartes known as the Scion of Plagues, had a pair of risen corpses standing in his wake. Between them, they carried an immense bell-shaped mace, a chain that was attached to the mace trailing behind. Their pearl-white eyes were downcast, their bent limbs and bodies rotting and foul.

The rest had come alone, the Sin of Six Knives carrying with it the sulphurous stench of the warp, its sinuous movements flickering and indistinct. It hurt Yheng's head to try to follow them, so she quickly gave up.

That left the Host of Masks, who wore what could only be described as a bored expression on its eerily porcelain face. An assassin of some repute, rumours persisted that it had once served the Imperium but had defected or been corrupted. Another story suggested it was a daemon inhabiting mortal flesh. A further account claimed it was xenos in origin, the last of its otherwise extinct species. The only thing Yheng knew for sure was that according to Tenebrus it could not be trusted, but then many amongst the covenant had false faces, even those who did not wear a mask, Yheng reflected.

Absent was the Butcher King, the Iron Magus themself and, curiously, Augury.

That gave Yheng pause, and her mind could not help but wonder what the latter was up to. Secrets, she had long ago learned, were practically currency amongst the Hand. It was a minor dark miracle the alliance had persisted long enough to achieve what it had.

That, however, appeared about to change.

'A pity that all of the Eight are not present for this communion,' remarked Tenebrus, the first to speak. Yheng knew it was to assert his will.

The proxy replied, the voice of the Iron Magus issuing through the vox-emitter built into the mechanised creature's chest.

'Not all of us are so enamoured with the sound of their own voice, Sorcerer. Unlike many amongst this council, I had much

to attend to. Unless you wish this fortress to cease functioning, of course.'

'At least you have sent a representative in your place, Magus,' Tenebrus remarked, urbane. 'It is incumbent upon all of us, I feel, to determine what must now transpire in the wake of our success.'

'And what success,' uttered the Scion in a guttural, choking gurgle that put Yheng in mind of seeping virulent diseases, 'do you believe we have accomplished?'

The question was asked honestly without agenda. Of all the chosen of the Hand, the Scion of Plagues seemed the least affected by infighting. Perhaps it was a symptom of the fact he was a recent addition – or, as Yheng suspected was the case, his place in one of the old Legions put him above such concerns. She believed this was true of the Butcher King also, both Traitor Astartes wishing only to return to their Long War.

'The shards are gathered, the blade can be reforged,' answered Tenebrus as if these things should be obvious and did not necessitate an explanation. 'A weapon, I might add, that has felled primarchs nigh unto death. I know you probably have little interest in such matters,' he went on, addressing the Scion in particular. 'That you, no doubt, have greater schemes to enact.'

'Ever is the toil of the Grandfather unfinished,' the Scion chuckled, 'and my own father bids me to my tasks. I serve here as a favour to the Warmaster. What transpires after this is of no concern to me.'

'Then it bears the question...' rasped the Wretched Prince, his tone simultaneously odious and obsequious. Yheng saw several of the Hand clench their fists. 'Of whether this alliance has reached its terminus.'

The Host of Masks, possessing not one but several overlapping voices of varying gender and timbre, spoke up. 'You speak of alliance, yet I see only disparate warlords who had common purpose but are now free to do as they wish.'

'And what might you mean by that, Host?' asked the Iron Magus through their proxy abomination. *'That you mean to break whatever amnesty exists between us?'*

Tenebrus said smoothly, 'None here are advocating violence, I am sure. Though it intrigues me that you would broach that unenviable possibility whilst you are far from unfriendly staff or blade.'

'I am not the one who is the lurker in shadows,' the Magus rejoined, the enmity between the two of them obvious.

Again, the Scion chuckled as if entertained by the petty squabbling. Even the Host's false face had shifted to one of wry amusement.

'Regardless of our differences,' Tenebrus began, eyeing the Magus' proxy acidly, 'it is difficult to deny the potency of our union. As Hand of Abaddon, we can still–'

'I cannot speak for the will of the Warmaster,' said the Host. 'Can you?' it asked Tenebrus before turning its frowning visage on the Scion. 'What of you, of the Traitor Legions, have you insight that we do not?'

The hulking warrior merely shook his head as a maggot slid idly from a gap in his gorget.

'Perhaps the warp spawn has some forbidden knowledge to impart,' said the Host of Masks, swinging its hollow gaze onto the Sin of Six Knives, but the thing merely grinned wider as it slowly drew its blades one against the other in a scraping cacophony.

Yheng felt the animosity in the room thicken to a palpable thing. She detected the faintest hint of warp sorcery around Tenebrus as he dug deep into his power. He feared a conflict. That was why she was here, she realised – as reinforcement. He might come to regret that blind trust.

Even the Wretched Prince, who was accustomed to being reviled, appeared defensive, having retreated amongst his coven, though his gaze flitted back and forth amongst each one of the Hand without a specific enemy to focus on.

Like predators who suddenly found themselves caged together and without an obvious alpha, the Hand prepared for violence. All except the Scion, who looked relaxed and unconcerned, though Yheng did not doubt he could destroy them all swiftly if provoked.

In half a second, the Mechanicum abomination powered up, weapons emerging from its robes, crackling and humming dangerously. Quicker still, the Host of Masks whipped forth a blade from behind its back. Yheng hadn't even realised it was armed as it cut the creature apart in a blur of swift strikes. Oil, offal and butchered machine parts lay in a heap. The vox-emitter, dulcetly hissing, was still live.

'The Magus, it appears,' said the Host, 'sought a pre-emptive solution.'

The vox hiss went dead a second later. The Magus would be holing up in some part of the fortress, Yheng suspected.

With a gurgling sigh, the Scion of Plagues unslung the massive axe from his shoulder. Dark magics crackled around the Wretched Prince and his witchlings.

'Are we to fall to rancour then?' declared Tenebrus, as the shadows began to coalesce around him. +Be ready, Yheng!+ his voice hissed urgently in her mind.

The Sin of Six Knives stopped sharpening its blades.

'Shall we kill each other and leave what remains to the Butcher King or perhaps the Magus, who only risks provocation when they are safely out of harm's way?' Tenebrus pressed.

He didn't want this, Yheng realised. It would interfere with his plans. He still *needed* the Hand for some reason, or else needed to be here. A chilling moment of clarity made Yheng wonder if *she* was the reason, if he had by some eldritch means become aware of what had happened in the black chamber. Of the regard of the gods that had fallen upon her.

That would be of profound interest.

'And what of Augury?' Tenebrus continued as a confrontation between the Hand drew closer. They had all sought the Warmaster's favour for their allegiance to him, and this alliance was part of their compact, but the disciples of the Dark Gods were ever prone to animus. 'Where is the architect in all of this? They who supposedly have the gift of foresight, absent as violence erupts in our ranks.'

'*They* are here...' Augury uttered from the darkness, appearing on the summit of the ziggurat as if from the ether itself. Drifting sylph-like into the midst of the brewing conflict, Augury appeared untroubled, a formless figure in a hooded cloak, their pale mouth the only visible part of their body. 'Our path, the path of the Hand, is plain enough.'

Weapons were lowered, the crackle of warp sorcery abated. Even the daemon-thing retreated into flickering ephemerality.

'Then speak it,' said Tenebrus, trying to conceal the relief in his tone, but Yheng knew the sorcerer too well to be fooled.

'Aye,' gurgled the Scion, 'let it be known.'

The Host of Masks sheathed its blade as it attended Augury. The Wretched Prince kept his head low and his eyes up like a beaten dog, listening intently.

Augury smiled deeply, their regard falling obviously upon Yheng, who felt the eyes of the covenant of the Hand fall upon her in turn.

'There will be killing to come but not yet, not between us. All that remains for the Hand to do is wait.'

Chapter Five

MUSTER

SIGNAL TO ADVANCE

THE LIGHTS GO OUT

The waiting was over. The Mordians mustered with haste, the call to arms ringing throughout Tartarus like a deathsong.

Kesh stood alongside her regiment, the Mordian 84th, having gathered her kit swiftly. She was no stranger to rapid deployments. Her rifle sat against her chest, hanging by a leather strap around her shoulder. Its power pack charged, spare packs in a belt around her waist. Her Militarum-issue combat knife in a boot sheath. Her laspistol was holstered at her hip, the left side on account of Kesh being right-handed. She wore a helmet in place of her usual forager's cap, the underground environs making adequate head protection a necessity. Dvorgin's flask and chrono – she still couldn't think of it as her own property – and the precious coin gifted to her by Syreniel were ferreted away in her uniform jacket. Her regulation stimm-vials, provided to every trooper on extended front-line duty, were tucked in an inside pocket protected in a small metal case. She was armed and armoured, with flak vest and bracers.

Readied for war, just like all the rest of the faceless horde.

Men and women in full battle-gear crammed the large underground space, the section they were mustered in excavated by the Mechanicus for the purpose of mass assembly. Every trooper amongst them awaited the order to move out. Hundreds of Mordians were crisply arrayed, grim-faced. They were hard folk from an even harder world. One regiment in the grand assault force. Four thousand souls near-as, or so Rellion had reckoned, all preparing to do their duty.

All of a sudden three months of waiting felt like seconds, time and reality rushing up to meet them. Kesh touched the coin tucked away in her pocket, its curious warmth reassuring.

As the regimental priests in their dirty robes and flak armour passed, spitting catechisms and flicking holy water before strapping on their chainswords and joining the troops, Kesh felt the ceiling shake. Garris swore under his breath but his face was set, the lasgun held close to his body, bayonet as sharp as a razor, its edge glinting like a promise. Standing next to him in the line, Lodrin pulled his helmet straps a little tighter, while Mavin made sure the vox-unit strapped to his back still had its blast shield.

Only Lieutenant Munser looked untroubled. His dark stubble had the appearance of a mask in the shadows, but it was his discipline that he wore so convincingly. Straight-backed, chin like a cliff edge with a sheathed sword at his waist, a silver-chased bolt pistol in his gloved hand, he looked like he could carve through the earth and rock with his glare alone, never mind the Mechanicus' drilling machines.

And still the dust motes cascaded like dying moths and earth trickled downwards like minute breaches in a dam. Kesh's theory about the braces was about to be tested. Half a mile above, the god-machines were walking. Combined with the timing of the muster it meant the ground assault against the walls had begun. She noted the Imperial strategos and their magos counterparts going over attack plans one final time. This huge chamber was one of three, each snaking to a nexus where Martian sappers prepared to undermine the enemy fortress above. No battle tanks – the tight confines of the tunnels did not allow for that – but unlimbered heavy guns were wheeled up alongside her, their sweating crews stripped at the arms and thick with muscle. Crew-served weapons, spotters and loaders and gunners besides.

The Gunbad tunnel fighters were ranked up next to the Mordians, clutching hatchets and trench-clubs. Kesh was surprised to briefly spot Ghates amongst them before he was lost to the throng. The smoke she had given him poked from his top pocket. She hoped to catch his eye, but he didn't see her amongst all the shifting, shuffling troopers.

An undercurrent of unease pervaded, a heavier version of what she had felt in the tunnels less than an hour earlier, just before the alarms had started up. Soldiers on edge, wound tight enough to snap. And something else that gnawed deeper than the usual pent-up tension before battle. Kesh couldn't quite define it but saw it in the gritted-teeth grins, the hard-set jawlines and clenched fists.

A captain she didn't know started barking orders, softening the piano-wire tension for a moment with the imminence of action. Several followed the officer's example, including Rellion, calling for ranks and readiness, for faith and fury. They were shouting now, the need for quiet entirely moot what with the Titans abroad above them. Orders were dispensed, squad by squad, each one named for their ranking officer and then by platoon, identified by numeric. She was in Platoon Seven, Squad Munser. Seventh in the line, seventh to hit the Martian breach after the Termites broke through. With five platoons at a time, they would be in the second wave. She eyed the sea of troopers ahead of her, all destined for the grinder. Commissars overlooked the throng from vantage points of banked earth, searching for evidence of desertion, their hands resting easily on holstered pistols. Somewhere there was a gunshot. The closed acoustics of the tunnels made the echo of the shot hard to pinpoint, but it sounded close. Kesh exchanged a glance with Mavin, the vox-operator turning deathly pale.

'Eyes forward,' Munser said, having caught the scared look, raising his voice to be heard.

Then she heard Lodrin quietly asking for a blessing from the Emperor. The squad's flamer sat ready in his grasp, a volatile piece of kit but a deadly one. Kesh tried not to think about what would happen if the fuel tank got breached during the assault. The thought had come unbidden, heralded by nothing more than the man's presence. She gripped her rifle tighter, whispering, 'I am a daughter of Mordian, born in darkness, I fear no shadow, not even death.' Others in her vicinity echoed the mantra under their breath, sons and daughters of the night-world both.

The lights would be doused, the captains were saying, every word a shout, and then a whistle would sound...

'This is the signal to advance,' Rellion hollered as thunder shook the great cavern and clods of earth dropped from the ceiling. A particularly large piece hit a trooper and she collapsed, felled. Orderlies from the medicae in Militarum fatigues dragged her clear of the line, her helmet cracked and bloody, the trooper unmoving.

Someone bolted. Kesh didn't see who or from where exactly, but there was movement from within the ranks of the Vardish, a sudden rippling of bodies, shoving and parting. They didn't get far. As soon as they breached the edge of the massing troopers and broke for the open tunnels a commissar stepped forward from her vantage point, extended her arm and shot the deserter through the back of the head with her bolt pistol. The head exploded. Nearby Vardish got hit with the spatter of blood, bone and brain. To their credit, they barely flinched, but the mood was becoming dangerous, like a magazine about to cook off.

Another trooper fled, then another, and for a few moments it looked as if the commissars might lose control, but the executions were swift and the officers and regimental priests restored order soon after. They called for calm, they called for strength.

Kesh felt Mavin glance her way again, but she didn't look back this time. Garris had become almost a statue, his thousand-yard stare fixed like his bayonet.

'Hold to your duty, the Emperor is watching,' she reminded them. 'Hold to your faith in Him and He will see us delivered.'

Munser nodded to her, approving of the words.

From somewhere came a pent-up wail, a scream that reverberated, barely drowned out by the god-machines such was its pitch. It rose and died away, a necessary release of nerves. It quietened after that, a resentful, anxious hush stealing upon the crowd. Every commissar had drawn now, pistols at the ready. One even pulled his chainsword and Kesh dared not imagine the carnage that would wreak amidst the packed ranks of troopers. Something was wrong, she could sense it, a prickling at the back of her neck. She thought again of the medicae who had hung himself. Despair thickened the air, almost tangible like fog.

Even Munser pulled at his collar as a tiny bead of sweat trickled down the back of his neck.

'At the sound of the whistle, advance,' Rellion repeated as soon as a fragile sort of stability had been established. The other officers spoke in train, their words an out-of-synch echo of his own. 'Follow the strips daubed in lumen paint on the ground, they will lead you along your attack route. It *will* be dark. Follow your lines, listen to your sergeants – sergeants, listen to your officers. Once underway there is no route back, only through. Back is death. Death and dishonour.' He paused to moisten his lips, his breathing hurried despite his efforts to hide it. 'We march ahead for glory, for the Emperor, for the Reborn Primarch.'

At this every priest roared, 'Ave Imperator!' Others took up the chant and a chorus of Throne-sworn affirmations resounded in the tunnel space. Despair eased, albeit fractionally, but Kesh was suddenly beset by other thoughts.

Of Gathalamor.

Of Kamidar.

Of miracles.

Her hands were shaking. She quelled the tremors by touching Syreniel's coin. The Silent Sister had disappeared as mysteriously as she had appeared, a living embodiment of the God-Emperor's will. Kesh wondered at its meaning, at all of it. She was still caught up in her thoughts as the lights went out. Darkness fell heavy like a lead cloak. A few seconds later, the first of the whistles began to shrill.

Chapter Six

HOOKS

LUNA

CONCLAVE

The engines shrilled through the hull, setting Rostov's teeth on edge. In the shadows of the transport's hold, his thoughts were turbulent. Foot drumming on the deck floor, hands wringing, he knew he must look on edge.

He had left Antoniato behind on Terra, and the rest of his retinue aboard ship in Solar dock. Lacrante would be overseeing the crew and there was no way by the Nine Devils that Cheelche would have been permitted on the Throneworld or where he was headed now. The district watchmen would have trussed her up and skinned her in the streets... assuming they could catch her.

No, it was better this way, better that he went alone. Besides, Rostov didn't want the others to see him like this.

Agitated.

Afraid.

He caught a watery reflection of himself in the dull chrome plating the walls. Haggard was the best definition he could find.

His blond hair lank, his beard unkempt. He had a handsome face, but even that was drawn and ashen from lack of sleep, the dark eyes haunted. As an inquisitor, he had seen the true horrors of the galaxy and knew its darkest secrets. It was his sacred charge to bear such truths and remain loyal, remain sane in order to prosecute his holy duties, but this... *this* was of a magnitude he almost dared not consider.

It had been several hours since his departure from the Grand Librarium. Doubtless seeing his ghastly pallor, Antoniato had asked exactly what the inquisitor had unearthed but Rostov had fended off the ex-Guardsman's concern, given him standing orders to wait, and hurried off to find a ship.

He was grateful for the darkness of the hold, for it smothered his thoughts to a degree, the inner voices dulled to an ache, but despite all that he could not stop staring at the casket he had brought with him from Terra. A lockbox of sorts, of baroque grey metal with a silver skull clasp, it secured the scrolls he had retrieved from the librarium. Ancient and containing proscribed knowledge as it was, he had to take the appropriate precautions during their transit.

The casket sat across the hold from Rostov, unmoving, for why would it move? Innocuous, in and of itself. But the knowledge and the potential consequences that came with that knowledge... that was deadlier than a virus bomb.

And so he watched and waited, and failed to silence his creeping terror.

He focused on the other news he had discovered at the Erudine Outpost, before departing Terra. The outpost doubled as a filtering station for any vermilion-encoded messaging meant for ordos ears only. It carried Rostov's personal sigil-ident, which only a few people knew and fewer still had the temerity to deploy. Rostov thought of them as his 'hooks'. Each one was tethered to a line that was in turn tethered to an investigation or several investigations, each ongoing and long term. A tremor on the line meant potential evidence, a sighting or a contact, a suspicious transaction that might lead to more. In this case, it came from an old ally from his younger days as an inquisitor, before the Great Rift, before the necessary obsession with the Hand. An agent of the Ruinous Powers, the Hand of Abaddon remained a mystery, but one Rostov was convinced he needed to solve. A plot was afoot, something he could not yet see but felt in his bones represented dire peril to the crusade and even the Imperium itself. Any lead, therefore, must be followed. In this particular instance, the ally might be an old one but the investigation was far from it.

Rostov took out the voxcorder, a simple Munitorum-standard unit, shaped like a large iron key, and replayed the encrypted message.

'Leonid...' it began, the audio broken, with a static hiss, passed down painstakingly from listening station to listening station, refabricated and facsimiled until it reached its intended destination. *'Leonid... it has been...'* the audio paused here, as if the speaker were struggling to find the right chronological denomination but then settled for being vague, *'...a very long time, old friend. I know you have not had cause to call on me for many years. Throne, so much has changed in the intervening time... But I still check in on the networks when I am able – a 'hook' in your great net, that's what you called us, isn't it? I assume you left me active to be eyes and ears, I have a broad scope after all. My warrant speaks to that, and I'm grateful to you for what you did to help me keep it. I am, eternally, your servant.*

'I have come upon information which I believe is relevant to an endeavour of yours. It might yet be nothing, but I think we both know it's the nothings that end up leading to the revelatory. I think there's a proverb or adage in there somewhere, I can never tell the difference honestly.

'Coordinates are embedded in the vox-code of this message. I trust you will be able to extract and discern them without difficulty. I include also the case cipher, double encrypted of course.

'I think you will find it of interest.'

There, the voice ended, and Rostov found himself surprised at the nostalgia it provoked. Simpler times, he supposed, although such things only ever felt that way through hindsight. Decoding the case cipher was straightforward enough and Rostov did so with ease. It glared at him from the voxcorder's vis-slate, decompressed and reconstituted in lexical output.

Diabolus.

A cipher for a specific one of his investigations. He had named it thusly. Rostov did not consider it providence that this had come to him now, at this time. It was too much of a coincidence. It meant the night was more advanced than he had first believed and lent even greater significance to the meeting ahead.

The cipher translated to 'Hand of Abaddon'.

The vox crackled as the pilot's voice came through from the cockpit, a welcome distraction. They were making their descent. As the landing thrusters kicked in, shaking the hold entire, the lumens flared. With a squint and a clench of teeth, Rostov recoiled like a neanderthal emerging from its cave into searing sunlight. He clutched his arm, the pain refreshed, shoulder and back a field of needles biting into flesh.

'Lights doused,' he snarled into the vox, and after a few seconds he saw white retreat to grey again.

Taking a nip of drink from a flask, he cuffed spilled alcohol from his mouth and approached a viewslit cut into the side of the hull. A soft, watery glow emanated from the narrow slice in the metal, and through shielded glass, he saw her. Silver, beauteous, her cratered lands and valleys swathed in abalone grey, a dust desert in all but name. That stilled white pearl who had suffered in recent days.

Luna.

Beneath the surface, the citizens of Terra's moon toiled in vast subterranean hive cities. Above, the evidence of their industry was visible in the form of massive factorums, military compounds, great walled citadels and other defensive structures. Luna was a bastion, armed and armoured for perpetual war, but it had once been so much more.

A landing pad came into view, still relatively far off across the Mare Vaporum, the jagged walls of the Stevinus crater rising up around it to form a natural barrier to approaches from the lunar surface.

Rostov prepared himself. He cinched the clasps on his armour, secured his weapons belt. After a few moments of gentle shuddering, the ship touched down on the landing pad and Rostov stood and approached the casket. A second's hesitation and he took it, and carried it one-handed out of the hold as the ramp lowered, admitting him to Luna.

Two guards met him at the edge of the gang ramp clad in dull carapace the colour of charcoal. They held heavy-gauge lasguns across their chests, muzzles aimed downwards, and exercised military trigger discipline. Visored helmets obscured their faces and they spoke through rebreather masks. Despite the fact that this region of Luna benefited from artificial gravity and atmosphere, the regolith was still an irritant, making filtration necessary.

'Welcome to Sylem, Inquisitor Rostov,' the first guard said in a cold monotone. 'The lord inquisitor is expecting you.'

Rostov strode past them brusquely, refusing the meek offer of refreshment from a helot cowed behind the hulking guards in black, and made for a fortified and well-defended bridge. Manned weapon emplacements watched the approach and a garrison tower squatted at the far end, two guards patrolling its battlement.

A stone keep stood on the other side, its high walls sloped and decked with gun slits. Three hexagonal turrets held fixed heavy bolter emplacements, and a Deathstrike missile array stood dormant but ready. More of an outpost than a proper Inquisitorial fortress, it served the needs of the Imperium in keeping watch over its lunar domains and happened to be the current habitation of his conclave master.

Through a gate overlooked by two more guards, he walked briskly on through a narrow and high-walled gallery. Murder slits in the canted ceiling betrayed its true purpose, a kill-box for any hostile enemy seeking to force ingress through the main entrance. Beyond the gallery, the interior opened out into a circular lobby, its cardinal points punctuated by statues of dour saints and soldiers. He recognised the well-noted puritan Sebastian Thor amongst the masoned luminaries: founder and promulgator of the Thorian creed, the belief in the concept of a Divine Avatar and the eventual rebirth of the Emperor into an unbroken and living host.

Passing beneath the severe regard of these stone effigies of order, Rostov climbed a long stairway to an upper gallery and through there to a sparsely decorated solarium, where a figure swathed in shadows waited.

'Does it not terrify you,' said the figure, her voice a little cracked with age but no less formidable, 'the vastness of it all?' She had her back to him, stargazing through a massive circular aperture. Bulk trawlers and mass-transit craft plied the unfathomable black, bound for Terran shipping lanes. 'Such an expansive galaxy and yet our eye needed on every crack, every forgotten hollow and dark alley on every Throne-forsaken world...'

Rostov stepped forward, the casket clutched in a gloved hand. Low lamplight gave the room an undeniably sepulchral mood.

'I see only darkness.'

'Precisely my point.'

He followed his master's eye as it averted from the stars to travel downwards towards the lunar plain. A hundred miles or so distant, he discerned the outline of the forbidding citadel that had been on Luna since the earliest days of the empire, once forgotten but renewed in this bleak era that presaged humankind's extinction. It stood out, stark and sharp like a lance. A grim place whose ominous denizens he had no desire to meet.

Somnus.

It meant 'sleep', or perhaps to some, 'silence'.

The fact his master regarded it through the great aperture boded ill.

'So, you have news then, I take it.' She took her attention from the endless void outside but did not face him. It was as if she regarded her own reflection instead. Rostov noticed her hat set aside on a low table, one of the few pieces of furniture in the room. Her crossbow hung off a nearby chair arm, and she was wearing her armour.

'Expecting trouble?' he ventured.

Inquisitor Greyfax turned then, bestowing a cunning smile on Rostov that he at once found unsettling and reassuring. He expected she deliberately crafted it that way. There was little that Katarinya Greyfax did that was not carefully considered and crafted.

Although they were from different ordos, the Inquisition went wherever it was needed, and as an inquisitor of the Ordo Hereticus, Greyfax had a particular interest in the Hand, given the likelihood of psychic or sorcerous involvement.

'I have learned many things in my years,' she said, stepping more clearly into the chamber's wan light, her gilded armour shining. 'Those that came before I was incarcerated in that monster's vault and those after, that I now live out. One fact remains true, Leonid, that as an inquisitor one should always expect trouble.'

Rostov gave a shallow bow of the head, her words sage as ever.

'Indeed, my lord.'

Greyfax had an intriguing history, one whose vicissitudes saw her the prisoner of an ancient creature, an enemy of the Imperium. Though a matter of some quiet conjecture, it was believed that there she had stayed, stasis frozen for many years until fate, and perhaps the Emperor's grace, saw her freed – an anachronism, believed centuries dead and returned to the galaxy in perhaps its direst hour.

A faint glint entered her eyes, piercing as a rapier, and Rostov detected the slightest hint of amusement. *Am I so easy to read?* he wondered.

He held out the casket in one hand, both purity-sealed and bio-locked. The skull's rictus grinned almost mockingly.

'With your sanction once more...' he invited.

Greyfax raised an eyebrow, regarding the object as if it were an enemy she was assessing. Descending a set of steps from the raised dais in front of the great aperture, a black cloak sweeping behind her, she muttered, 'Out.'

Guards, hidden from Rostov's sight until that moment, quietly departed. Armed with sabres and entirely clad in midnight-black war plate, these were a cut above the highly trained operatives outside the chamber and upon the walls.

'Alone at last...' Greyfax said with a smile, and for a moment Rostov struggled to parse her meaning. He suspected this was deliberate too. 'Hand it over then,' she said, as she came to within a pace of the inquisitor. 'You won't get back into that thing without this first.' She brandished an obscenely sharp knife, the hilt embossed with an Inquisitorial sigil.

Rostov did as he was told, and Greyfax pricked her finger with the knife tip. At the merest touch of her blood, the skull that sealed the casket shut unclenched its jaw. A hiss of escaping pressure briefly filled the room and through a dispersing stasis cloud, the pair of scrolls he had borrowed from the librarium were revealed.

Gingerly it seemed to Rostov, Greyfax took both pieces of parchment and rolled them out on a table, pushing aside the galactic maps and missives currently occupying it. She read, and in the silence that followed, Rostov held his breath.

'And you're sure about this?' Her eyes narrowed. Something like concern flickered in them, the mildest tremor of a nerve in her neck. A dab of the tongue moistened her lips.

Rostov cleared his throat.

'Certain. A reality-cutting knife, primordial in design. It was one of the shards.'

Greyfax looked on, but Rostov knew she had already assimilated everything on the scroll. She let out a long exhalation.

'Holy Throne... You think this is what they're looking for?'

'I am certain of that too. The Hand, whoever it is, wants this artefact. They are actively seeking it. A piece of it was seen on Kamidar, we have the reports of the Black Templars to thank for that. Alas, I have been unable to track them down – or the fragment of the artefact. I know of at least one more piece in the Archenemy's possession on Srinagar. The discovery of a third, via coded astropathic message sent by Interrogator Il Moro, was received by Domus Tower. It and his whereabouts are unknown.' He paused, letting the magnitude of his words sink in. 'I do not believe these events to be unrelated.'

'Nor do I,' said Greyfax. 'It is what we feared then.' She looked ashen, a breath caught in her throat.

Rostov felt it too, the fear that they had been trained to suppress, reaching up from the pit of his stomach. The old, mortal frailty they were supposed to be inured to when they had been told the secrets of the universe, and then stared into the abyss without blinking. Inquisitors were not meant to balk at anything.

But *this*... This was the physical representation of the primordial enemy; this was old corruption, a piece of the Heresy War. If the myths were true, a weapon like that... Throne, it could have repercussions for the entire Imperium.

'Yes...' Rostov's voice was almost a rasp, 'They are attempting to remake the Anathame. The mythic blade that pierced Horus' side.'

Greyfax rolled up the scrolls, lingering for a few seconds on the artistic rendering of the knife, a cruel and ugly thing from an elder age, and returned them to the casket. A second prick with her own knife and her blood resealed it.

'You know its provenance?'

'Only what I have read,' said Rostov, regaining his composure, 'and even that comes across more like myth than fact.'

'There are only myths about such things, Leonid.'

That was true enough but it didn't make them any less unsettling, and he saw his concern echoed in Greyfax's eyes.

'That it has the power to slay a god, if you believe in such things.'

She quirked an eyebrow at him. '*If* you believe...?'

'I have heard the returned primarch be referred to thusly,' he replied, letting the implication hang in the air like a noose. 'Regardless, if this is the Hand's plan then this agent must be found and stopped. At any cost. I fear for the outcome and its impact on the Imperium if we do not. I fought a sorcerer on Srinagar that claimed it was the Hand, and I believe I have seen visions of a second individual also claiming this title. I cannot yet parse the truth of it, but I was recently contacted by one of my agents, a rogue trader, who has a traitor in his custody believed to be a servant of the Hand. Or perhaps even something more.'

'You do not need my permission to investigate.'

'I already plan to, the synchronicity of these events is too compelling. But that's not what I need.'

'Then what do you need, Leonid?'

'An army. To hunt the Hand and bring it down. End this threat before it becomes too great to stop.'

She laughed, and it was an altogether unpleasant sound.

'I can't give you that, Leonid.' She stepped away from the table and returned to the dais. At her unspoken request, Rostov joined her.

'Much is being asked of the crusade,' she said, once he was standing by her side. 'It is stretched in every conceivable direction, and even this is only to hold on to the gains we have made, let alone any attempt to push out further. Half the galaxy is enshrouded by darkness, lost to us through the hell of the Rift, the other teeters on the brink.'

'Even now?' Rostov hated the ignorance in his voice, but he hadn't realised it was that bad.

'Even now,' Greyfax confirmed. 'Nachmund remains heavily contested, our only sure route through to Imperium Nihilus, and whilst the primarch's generals push for the Gauntlet, it is far from certain that we will break through. And yet our efforts cannot lessen, for to do so invites the enemy to attack from a second front.' She shook her head ruefully. 'With Cadia and the Cadian Gate gone, we are sorely pressed. A bulwark like that is not easily replaced.'

'What of the Anaxian Line?'

A coterie of redoubt worlds stood in chain corewards of the collapsed Cadian Gate. They had been raised as a secondary defensive border against aggression from enemy forces amassing out of Cadia's ashes, providing vital resupply and reinforcement to the fleets trying to staunch the advance of the Warmaster's armies there, and dubbed the 'Anaxian Line'.

'It holds,' said Greyfax. 'For now. Barren is under attack, and without its materiel reserves for the other worlds in the chain...' She sucked the air through her teeth. 'Well, our stalwart rear supply lines would become much less reliable, shall we say. Kamidar still reels in the aftermath of civil war. And Garrovire is being fought over as we speak. The Militarum strategos regard Garrovire as a lynchpin – without it the entire enterprise could be in jeopardy. Only Helsvorn, Aggrandis and Phykus hold with any surety. A thin strand of wire holds our combined armies together by a most tenuous thread and shivers under this current tension.'

'I need but a few regiments. If my ally has a true lead, it could prove significant and with the apprehension of the Hand, its further plans revealed under excoriation, is it not worth the effort for such a prize? Surely something could be spared? There must be reserves within the fleets...'

'There are none,' Greyfax stated emphatically. 'Another muster is being raised with any and all reserve forces joining it. A second passage through the Great Rift has been discovered at the Attilan Gate. Reports claim it is sizeable, though as to its stability I cannot attest. I will send you the relevant information to fill any gaps.'

Rostov nodded his thanks.

She gave him a side glance. 'So, you see, there are no regiments to send. Nothing remaining. Not for a mission without clear objective.'

'The Hand *is* the objective.'

'And where does it reside? You do not even know who it is, let alone where.'

'A matter I plan to resolve. And then with a few ships, troops at my disposal, I could–'

'It cannot be done. I am sorry, Leonid.'

'Then I am alone in this.'

'Oh, I know you have friends, Leonid.'

'They are unfortunately few. I had hoped for the help of the ordos and your authority with it.'

The slight curl at the edge of Greyfax's lips suggested a smile. Rostov decided he didn't like it in the least.

'I did not say I couldn't help.'

Rostov frowned, confused.

'I can lend you a few men from the fortress here, but I can't give you an army,' she said, and he followed her gaze until it alighted on the Somnus Citadel. 'I can, however, also give you an ally.'

Chapter Seven

OLD WEAPONS

SILENCED

A WAY TO SERVE

In truth, the Silent Sisterhood had been blessed with few allies. In the aftermath of the Great Heresy War, the Order fell into severe decline as its followers became pariahs in both name, function and regard. As with many longstanding institutions that could be deemed a 'necessary evil', the Silent Sisterhood were marginalised when they became less politic to deploy, and their ranks were culled.

During those days Somnus became a near-empty ruin, haunted by a handful of caretakers, and gratefully forgotten by the Imperium, a sword left to rust in its scabbard. That had changed in the aftermath of the Great Rift and the calamity that followed. Somnus was rebuilt on the orders of the primarch himself, its garrison and prior function as a military outpost restored.

Much of its millennia-long neglect remained, however. The old fortress walls bore unsealed cracks, several of its towers still partially ruined. Only the orbital docking spikes for the Black Ships remained in a state of good repair, for the stewardship of these crucial vessels was the remaining duty required of the Silent Sisterhood after their disbanding and before the Guilliman reformation.

Old weapons, it seemed, were back in fashion again.

A blunted sword hastily sharpened will as likely cut its bearer as its enemy, thought Syreniel as she trod the dilapidated halls of the citadel, her great blade sheathed upon her back, her armour clinking dully with her booted footsteps.

Despite its recent resurgence, it was a haunted place of lonely corridors and stilled chambers lit by brazier flame. A mausoleum to a dead culture, ineffectively resurrected. For Syreniel, the return to Somnus held an especial dread that had nothing in common with the Imperium's fickle favour.

She saw one of her Order, the first since entering the citadel, a Knight-Centura of the Argent Lynx cadre, but found no warmth in her Sister's iron gaze. If anything, her eyes hardened to the edge of hostility as she regarded the silver-armoured Vigilator and put herself in Syreniel's path.

Clad in Vratine armour herself and wielding a power axe, a crimson half-cloak hanging over her left shoulder, she looked every inch the formidable sentry.

The corridor was narrow, the dark stone seeming to press in; there would be no moving around her.

I seek the Knight Abyssal, Syreniel signed, her thoughtmark rusty on account of how little she had used it in recent months, and resisting the urge to meet this challenge with hostility of her own.

The other Sister hesitated before replying, as if gauging whether or not Syreniel was worthy of response. For a few seconds, crackling flame was the only sound. Her hand movements were swift, complicated, as if trying to outwit her comrade. It took Syreniel a few moments to discern their meaning.

You carry a penitent's mark, the other Sister signed, *your plume shorn and eyes tarred to black.*

Nothing in this held a question. Purely accusation, a judge preparing to give sentence.

I seek the Knight Abyssal, Syreniel repeated, unwilling to be baited. *Either tell me where she is or stand aside. My coming is known to her.*

The gorget the other Sister wore over her mouth shifted up like a portcullis with her imperious scowl. *It is known...* A snarl in the eyes with this, the movements clipped and sharp. Her gauntlets rasped as they scraped against one another like a sword angrily leaving its sheath.

If I am delayed... Syreniel began, choosing a different approach.

The other Sister appeared to consider this. At length, she relented and gave a curt gesture towards the end of the corridor. East.

Syreniel nodded, despite this aggression directed her way. The other Sister did not acknowledge it but appeared to glare through her as the Vigilator moved on.

She found Sister Etruvia in an anteroom, amongst a slew of astropathic messages translated and transcribed onto parchment. The room, one of several, she would later learn, was almost overburdened. Tables and desks stood piled high as missives from across the various sectors of the galaxy funnelled into this nexus.

Amongst the minutiae, Syreniel saw reports from the Black Ships, the witch-tallies and unconfirmed sightings yet to be investigated by the Order, as well as military operations and requests for aid.

Loitering at the threshold, Syreniel had the air of an unwelcome guest as her cadre mistress turned to regard her.

Pariah, she signed, adding disdainful inflection through her movements. If the Sister in the corridor had been hostile, then Etruvia held only unyielding ice. At her bidding, Syreniel entered and hoped her findings would spur a thaw.

She spoke without utterance of her posting to Battle Group Praxis, where she had served as enforcer and assassin to Admiral Tiberion Ardemus. The fact Ardemus had perished, his flagship with its entire complement along with him, presented little consternation to her audience, who listened stony-faced throughout. Only when Syreniel reached the part about the entity and their apparent immunity to her pariah nature did the other occupant of the room, who stood to Etruvia's right, sign an interrogative.

Both had been conversing in the way of the Order when Syreniel arrived, ruminating on the endless ill tidings. Both were armed and armoured in the manner typical of the Sisterhood, only Etruvia had a red cloak and bronzed Vratine, whilst the other, the Knight Abyssal, wore silver-azure artificer armour and a black cloak to denote her station.

And she had the touch about her? His grace?

Syreniel gave a solemn nod to the Knight Abyssal. *I saw her survive enemy fire, breach a plexi-shield with only the strength of her arm.*

A quirk of fate could explain the enemy fire, a hitherto unseen weakness in the plexi-shield the breach, Etruvia countered. *What convinces you she is a conduit?*

Instinct. A feeling.

The cadre mistress sneered, and Syreniel saw the glint of bared teeth through the narrow slits in her gorget. *And what has instinct brought you, pariah? You are not fashioned to listen to your feelings.*

Nonetheless, signed Syreniel, *it is the only answer I have.*

Etruvia was unwilling to let the matter pass. *Perhaps had you denied your feelings, you would not have broken the oath of tranquillity on Hyrelion and we here now would be having a different conversation. Perhaps had your discipline been more robust, your Sisters would not have died there.*

Syreniel gritted her teeth at the unwelcome memory, of

Angared and Villenia slain in the temple at Merita. A witch hunt gone awry. Her feelings having got the better of her. Composure came with difficulty, but it did come.

I cannot attest to what is not, only what is, my cadre mistress.

Etruvia's eyes burned with well-stoked anger. *And insolence into the bargain–*

She would have gone on had the Knight Abyssal not raised her hand to stop her.

Tell us of this entity. It did not recoil at your presence?

Syreniel shook her head. *I perceived no visible effect.*

Then it could not be Neverborn, Etruvia stated with a definitive hand gesture.

The Knight Abyssal appeared unconvinced, her mood pensive. *And yet the pariah gift impresses itself upon any being. Only we of the soulless are unaffected.* Her studious eye appraised Syreniel. *Did she have a name, this individual?*

Syreniel gave it but it yielded nothing by way of recognition. *She appeared a servant, albeit one of rank...*

Yet there is more, isn't there, the Knight Abyssal coaxed.

Syreniel found her stare penetrating but braved it regardless. Her sins had been laid bare long ago, after all. *I think the face she wore was a mask, her entire persona in fact. It brushed up against my mind, searching for weakness.*

A witch?

It had the psychic spoor, I am certain of it.

And you were alongside the other, when you encountered this creature, the one you believe touched by His grace?

Another nod.

And what of her reaction?

Fear, undoubtedbly, but also resolve. As I felt her touch, the presence of the other receded and we parted ways with it.

You let one of the Neverborn escape? Etruvia cut in, spite exuding from her every pore.

The Knight Abyssal came to Syreniel's defence. *Not a moment ago you claimed it could not be Neverborn. You cannot have it both ways, Sister.*

Subtly chastened, Etruvia bowed her head in contrition but her glower remained on Syreniel. The other's regard was more inquisitive though.

Much is obfuscated, but none of this inspires confidence. She paused to think, the many missives around her a tangible reminder of the ongoing peril the Imperium endured. *I am aware of your transgressions, Syreniel, a misdeed that can never be forgiven or forgotten, but you have done well bringing this to the Order. Much may be revealed in coming days and only He knows how this latest intelligence may benefit Lord Guilliman's cause. Alas, we cannot ask Him. But I see a way for you to serve, Sister...* she signed, reaching for a curled scroll sitting atop a nearby stack.

Syreniel noticed it bore an Inquisitorial stamp.

Chapter Eight

ONE HELL FOR ANOTHER

THE ONES WHO LIVE

LET ME BE THY INSTRUMENT...

The stamp of booted feet resounded in the tunnels as troopers ran to the blaring of whistles. Following the scuffed tracts of lumen paint, a frantic stampede that would brook no stopping had broken loose. Like an auroch herd fleeing a wildfire, it would not even slow until it was free. And that freedom was the light, a killing light where the enemy awaited.

Kesh saw a man trip, fall. He became lost at once, swallowed in the frenzy, a choked-off scream his last contribution to the war. And he was not the only one. Others who stumbled did not rise, for the throng did not wait, could not wait. The dark closed and the light ahead promised. Madness held them, impelled them, and amongst the huffing, heaving masses she felt that creeping dread again, that unease like an unsettling visitor who refused to leave.

Her squad held each other together, hands on shoulders, gripping collars and coattails, the staunch discipline of Mordian tested to its limit. It helped that they could see better than most, being born of a night world having its advantages. Sight brought calm, at least a measure of it, and the more practical benefit of clearer navigation.

Munser shouted throughout the advance, urging courage, promising retribution if that courage failed, and then convincing in his affirmation that it would not.

Ahead of her, Kesh made out the next section in the line, the bellows of the commissars in her ears as they roared the soldier-horde on. Into the dark, into the light, into death... She shook her head, the seep of despair near tangible. A stumble, her feet tangling with a boot left in the tunnel, lost by some poor soul lying dead somewhere, and she nearly took a tumble herself but for Garris yanking her up. Still running, she flashed a grateful glance his way. A curt nod was the only acknowledgement and then they were in the flow again. It felt like miles, hearts hammering, breath heaving, but it was merely feet. At the barked orders of their captain, they took the second left fork.

Munser repeated the order, every order. Firm and clear, that was his way. It served them now as they sped on.

Out of Tartarus, and trading one hell for another.

Light expanded, bled deeper as they closed on its source, and Kesh could practically feel the relief. No war shouts yet. They were too far away for that, and the heavy thunder rumbling above as the god-engines walked was drowning out almost everything except her inner voice.

God-Emperor, let it hold, let it hold... Don't bury us here, in the forgotten dark.

Spills of earth teemed regularly now, gathering on shoulders, around packs and bandoliers. Banks of it built up in the corners and recesses. With every step, they were filling their own graves a handful of dirt at a time.

Still several feet out, they heard the Termites, their drilling engines giving out a shrill whine that cut through air like a blunt knife. Nails scratching glass, teeth on edge.

More light, brighter, wider, a dull clamour coming from above now. The scent of foetid air, musty on the breeze. The tang of cordite and fyceline. A muffled explosion and the rattle of automatic gunfire, the whip-crack fizzing of las-beams. Now the shouts, now the screaming. Voices bellowing in foreign tongues through laud hailers, reacting to the attackers in their midst.

'On, on!' roared the commissars. 'He is watching! He bids you bring them death!'

Death! the soldier-horde roared back. *DEATH!* One mass, a single organism bent to the same purpose. A beast giving over its fear to hate. The Imperial way.

As Kesh's platoon reached the last few yards and the threshold of a wide ramp of earth flattened by the Termite's tracks, the din of battle reached them in earnest and the yellow light of the upper world, a world they had known for months, flooded over the troopers. Rising then, the booted heels of their comrades ahead of them in the line, grinding upwards towards a wide lip of earth, they dug in to the climb. She reckoned on another fifty feet to the summit, loose dirt and grit slipping underfoot.

'Up, up!' roared the commissars again, a shot ringing out as someone faltered.

A feverish rush towards that light above, eyes blinking, pulses racing until–

The earth split and the walls caved against the relentless pressure, a mucky avalanche slewing down the shelved ramp and into their midst. A man cried out, a fear scream presaging their imminent deaths. In seconds dirt rode up around Kesh's ankles, then her knees. She strove, they all did, desperately climbing, but they were wading through mud and the milky wash above was closing like an eyelid shutting out the world. And the light.

Darkness fell then and choking terror, the muffled shouts and scared fighting. Their fear, the dark, each other.

Kesh heard a gurgled death, someone stabbed in the neck most likely. A commissar dared raise his voice, tried shooting a few but got mobbed, dragged down even as the earth continued to bury them. Despair washed over the troopers, thicker and more pervasive than the dirt clogging their throats. A lumen torch flared but quickly failed, its bulb smashed in the scrum. Men and women digging, clawing with trench shovels, with knives and bare hands. Backs bent, elbows pushing, spitting, huffing fevered breaths.

Ghates, grossly displaced from his unit, fixed Kesh with a look as the chaos dragged him down and the earth rose above his mouth. She reached but was too far to grab him, fingers snatching air. She couldn't say his name because the air was too thick with dirt and she was choking anyway. He blinked once before the black deluge took him, buried alive in an improvised grave.

Out of panic the section was tearing itself apart as every fear became manifest in that dark, claustrophobic space...

And then, the trembling of the earth slowed, stopped. The cave-in abated. It had swallowed some – poor Ghates' gloved hand frozen in a claw, grasping for the light – but not all. It didn't have to. They were killing each other anyway, giving in to that undefinable pall of dread. She saw Lodrin swing a trench-club, wild-eyed and near raving. Kesh blocked his arm, held his wrist fast.

'Stop! Stop this... Breathe. Just breathe and be still.'

Lodrin paused, fear turning his eyes large.

Others had stopped to listen, the fighting beginning to ebb. She saw Garris turn to look, releasing the gun strap he had been using to strangle a fellow trooper.

There was light here, Kesh realised, issuing through some crack perhaps, or maybe it was–

'Be still,' she said again, terrified but seeing the attention of the survivors was upon her. Her hand closed around a lumen torch and she lit it, the flare refulgent in the darkness. 'We are the Guard. We are His soldiers, His hammer. And we do not give in to despair.'

Rellion was dead. The captain had a bayonet lodged in his chest, his hands wrapped around another trooper's throat. Kesh averted her eyes to focus on the ones who lived.

'The earth has stopped. We are still alive,' she told them. 'But we have to fight to *stay* alive.' She turned then, the torch snagged in her belt, and moved the first clod of dirt. Then a stone. Then another. 'Dig,' she said. 'Find the light.'

'You heard her,' bellowed Munser, a gash on his forehead like a crack in stone. 'Dig, damn you!'

Lodrin, who she had just let go of, joined her. He went to work with trench-axe and shovel. Others followed. Garris and then two more. Soon an entire labour gang toiled at the collapsed earth-face, pulling and digging, hacking and hefting, chains of troopers funnelling rock and dirt. They did it wearing scarves wrapped around their faces to keep out the dust, or rebreather masks if they had them. The trenchmen did the bulk of the digging, remembering their old skills, but Kesh stayed at the forefront, unable to stop. Their fear ebbed with the salve of honest work until a tiny shaft of light pierced the gloom and cool air filtered through.

Faint grey light turned to yellow and got brighter, wider, until an aperture the size of Kesh's fist was made. She thrust her hand through it, pulled more earth aside, dirt seemingly falling away at her merest touch, until it fell away entirely. Light and sound rushed in.

Blood pulsing, she cried out in defiance, shaking loose the dirt around her legs and ankles, hauling herself out and up.

'With me! With me!'

They followed, many hundreds strong, not in platoons but as a mass of warriors, and swarmed into city streets.

It had been Varta once, but that was before the war, and the occupation. The enemy named it Slaugheln, but the Guard had simply taken to calling it the Last Stronghold. For were it to fall, there would be no others. Here, this place, would be where the fight for Barren and a vital part of the Anaxian supply chain would be won or lost.

As Kesh ran, the heady fuel of freedom feeding tired muscles, the battlefront imposed itself in all its glorious and bewildering fury. The Last Stronghold was an immense, fortified city. It had once housed hundreds of thousands, but many of those citizens were dead or enslaved, or else turned to dark masters. Beyond its towering outer walls lay manufactoria and hab-blocks, refineries and depots. At their backs was the great Citadel Wall, garrisoned by enemy guns and foot soldiers garbed in black iron. They paid little heed to the interlopers below, intent instead on the attack from without, the tremor of the city's abused void shields turning the sky purple with every bruising impact.

In a vast courtyard before the sealed gates, bands of Imperial soldiers stood and fought. These were the forces who had made it through the tunnels and out the other side. Skirmishes had broken out in all directions, the Imperial troops stretched thin and waning against the enemy defenders. Swathes of robed cultists and the more heavily armed Guard defectors had reacted to the loyalists in their midst. The surprise attack, meant as a swift hammer blow, had failed to materialise and the Imperial assaulters were struggling to capitalise.

A large band, several platoons strong, had erected makeshift defences and fired from behind weapons crates and collapsed statuary. They made their stand around one of the Termites, its armoured skin threaded with bullet impacts, point defence guns blazing. A handful of red-robed Mechanicus troops fought alongside them, their deflagrating beams adding to the fusillade of lasguns and autocarbines. A gallant stand, but enemy fighters mobbed their position.

Only one of the breaches had been wholly successful and only part of another, the one to which Kesh belonged. Those from the first platoons had all but been destroyed, scrap companies forming in an attempt to stave off total annihilation. A third attempt at undermining had entirely collapsed, perhaps due to some malfunction or some unknown agency of the enemy, trapping and burying hundreds of soldiers within. Those who had emerged from the other two tunnels were therefore outnumbered and losing ground.

In short, in those few seconds of stark revelation, the situation looked bleak.

Kesh felt a surge of pride and anger. She hadn't endured the horrors of Gathalamor, survived a massacre in the royal palace on Kamidar, lived through a burning hell-storm and been almost buried alive to capitulate without a fight. She lifted her arm, a clenched fist raised to the heavens, and roared.

'If we die, we die in His name! Ave Imperator!'

'Ave Imperator!'

'Ave Imperator!'

'Ave Imperator!' they chorused, turning to righteous hatred for their courage.

Her massive warrior band swept out with abandon, almost immediately overwhelming several skirmishes taking place throughout the streets, purging enemy positions and consolidating allied ones. They rose, her host, like a crushing tide and the cult army was driven back, hemmed in, slowly destroyed. Gained ground stayed Imperial.

In short order they had taken the courtyard and the major arteries feeding into it, though thick tranches of agitators remained beyond this fragile cordon. Cries of victory rose up, premature, driven by relief. It wasn't over. More would be needed.

Above Kesh, the great walls of the city loomed large and forbidding. They cast a shadow across half a district, rumbling to the steady percussion of macrocannons, static weapon emplacements and rocket batteries.

'Those guns,' she said, a cluster of troopers having gathered around her even as the bulk dispersed. One amongst their number was a captain of the Vardish. 'We have to silence them.'

After the maddened rush to wreak carnage, order had begun to assert itself. The soldier-horde broke up as officers took charge, coordinated, rallied and redeployed. Tactics, if not strategy, became part of Imperial thinking again. They took fire from the raised battlements, but it was a light rain. The enemy's storm was turned outwards.

She paused for but a second or two, looking to Munser for confirmation.

He shook his head at Kesh. 'I follow you,' he told her.

The others nodded in concert. A gathering of a few had turned into several squads. Then two platoons. Priests began to sing their throaty catechisms, zeal in their eyes. More officers arrived, Mordian and others besides. All waited on Kesh's next order.

Swallowing down her momentary unease, Kesh swiftly organised three assault groups who divided up and hit stairways and ladders. She felt powerful, inspired. They rose quickly, almost unopposed, the bulk of the enemy fighters occupied with what came for them outside the walls. By the time they had realised saboteurs were in their midst many of their positions were overrun.

Hurrying across a lower battlement Kesh shot a cultist point-blank, his body falling noiselessly off the wall and onto the courtyard below. Another she gutted with her bayonet, but the blade became trapped and she had to release her rifle, which plummeted away with the dead. Pulling her sidearm, she shot another. Leading the charge now, she quickly scooped up a slain comrade's sabre and let the killing mood take her. Cultists and defectors fell to her sword, her wrath.

Wings as black as sackcloth, fire unending...

Old waking dreams assailed her as she fought, a lick of flame in every flash of gunfire, every shine of metal as the light struck it.

Kesh pushed it down, forced herself to see what was there. The solidity of the hilt in her hand, the acrid bite of smoke in her throat. Every lung-bursting stride. Higher, higher.

Near breathless, she gained the summit of the Citadel Wall, and took a few seconds to gaze between the massive crenellations at the mighty war engines braced and blistering in the scorched fields beyond. Imperial Knights, their pennants fluttering in the hot wind. Livery as bespoke as each war engine, sigils of rampant beasts of myth and ancient weapons rendered in dark silhouette. Only two machines, the muzzle flares of their weapons like a dying star unleashed, a baleful aura coruscating around the capacitors as they built to fire.

A rippling halo of heavy blasts ringed the Knights, their activated ion shields crackling with ozone and energy displacement. They held their ground but did not advance, stymied by the relentless barrage of the guns.

A flare of light against her face made Kesh turn. In the distance, promethium fires burned as the wells and silos rose up in great jets of black and red. Smoke ran thick like an aurora, an oil slick across the veil of night, the sky transformed to funerary black.

The first of the guns on the wall fell to the northernmost assault group, a loud explosion followed by a thick grey plume further polluting the war front. Kesh led two squads to the second, spiking it with a pair of fused krak grenades and letting the stowed magazines do the rest. It caused carnage amongst the enemy ranks, their positions utterly undone and overtaken. The attackers moved swiftly, disengaging as soon as their ruthless work was complete. Horns had begun to sound, a wall garrison raised.

Kesh signalled to Lodrin and a spurt of flame cleansed the steps beneath them.

Mavin pointed through the thinning smoke. In the city below, a surge of traitor forces had joined those contesting the outer streets. An armour-clad giant in pitted brown and fever yellow, vibrant with oxidisation, led the horde. A barbute helm bulged around his lumpen forehead, his armour straining to contain his girth.

'Emperor's mercy...' hissed Munser, and for the first time fear edged his voice.

The dread warrior's spike-hammer took a heavy tally, turning the mood of the fight in several places, bludgeoning through men as though they were nothing more than rotten bone. Emboldened, the traitors rallied. Kesh felt the swell of the battle shift, the inevitable push as the tide turned, and knew they had to return to the courtyard.

Seconds before they were about to embark on the difficult climb back down to the courtyard, a huge blast shuddered through the wall. One trooper tripped, lost her footing and fell to her death. Others stumbled, on both sides, enemy combatants swift to seize on any advantage.

The great gates pinwheeled inwards, splitting and fragmenting as they turned, buoyed on a dust-filled pressure wave. Half of one of the gates cleaved the Termite where the Imperials had made their last stand, severing it into two pieces. The resulting explosion killed over fifty men. The other flattened a horde of cultists, crushing them bodily beneath its incredible mass. The heathens did not even have time to scream.

Through the morass of dust and smoke, flames reaching thirty feet or more into the city, strode another hulking warrior. This one wore a red crest upon his helm, white armour dirtied but still gleaming. He raised an axe to the heavens, a ragged black cloak snapping in his wake. Kesh made out the lightning-and-axe sigil on his armour, her blood chilling as the warrior declaimed, '*Jagun hak sang tal!*'

At the Storm Reaper's arrival, his counterpart clad in corroded metal seemed to quicken, as if recognising a fellow apex predator in his hunting ground. The Traitor Marine swung the haft of his spike-hammer across his body into a guard stance and stood his ground. A challenge in any language. Rabid cultists and other followers of the Dark Gods flowed around him, a foetid boulder amidst a sea of carnage.

Before Kesh realised what she was doing, she had descended the stairs, Munser, Lodrin and the others in tow, a host of Guardsmen following on after. Fifty men against the horde. Fifty to join the fighters emerging through the shattered gate being led by the Storm Reaper. It had been several months since she'd even seen, let alone fought alongside, a Space Marine. The crusade had stretched everyone, even the mighty Angels of Death. Many amongst the Guard warned against battling hand in glove with the Astartes.

No fight ever ended well with or against the Angels, Dvorgin had always said. Thoughts of the old man dying on the cold Gallanhold floor turned to grief before hardening into determination and finally vengeance.

'Into them!' Kesh roared.

The growing melee seethed like a turbulent ocean as the Mordians chased the wake of the Storm Reaper's forces. A few stragglers had joined them, a lieutenant of the Gunbad amongst them. The woman's face was awash with crimson, her teeth starkly white, her trench-axe darkened with dirt and blood.

They clashed, the Space Marines, the lightning against the immoveable cliff. Kesh couldn't see much; she was fighting through the masses, clashing in close combat before the melee broke apart or shifted and became a firefight again. Lodrin's flamer tanked out and he slipped the heavy rig off his shoulders, pulling a laspistol. Mavin kept up the pace, features cold as alabaster, teeth gritted against the madness. He fired on endless repeat, steady despite his fear. Garris took to the killing work like he was born to it, his bayonet slick and red. Munser did his best to marshal the rest, calling out orders, trying to keep everyone up.

Garris overextended in his eagerness to vent his fear and anger. Arterial spray got in his eyes, and he was wiping it away when the axe blade caught him in the neck. He died quick, swallowed in the mass like so many others. Kesh watched him go, feeling detached from reality. They just had to keep going. To survive.

A large armoured cultist, her bulky frame lined with steel plates, stymied the advance. Kesh skidded to an abrupt halt as the traitor swung a chainblade. She ducked, barely avoiding the growling teeth, clods of chewed-up skin and gristle spattering her like a grisly rain. A stab of Kesh's sabre raked metal but failed to penetrate, and she was bowled over by the cultist's sheer girth. Others of her kind had rallied to her, clutching hatchets, clubs and dirty pistols.

Several fighters went down on both sides: brief, close-ranged fire exchanged, then it was blades and bayonets. The old way.

Kesh scrambled back, rolled aside as the chainblade hacked down at her, taking a chunk out of the paving beneath. She was chanting, the cult demagogue, offering up Kesh as sacrifice.

An Imperial priest, spitting litanies like they were daggers, hurled himself at the cultist, but she cut him down, splitting him from shoulder to hip. The awful, noisy churn of tearing flesh and muscle was all that Kesh could hear, but it gave her a moment to clamber to her feet. Still shaky, her improvised parry scarcely turned the chainblade meant for her chest. The sabre cracked and shattered, ripped apart by adamantine teeth, but the shards got stuck in the mechanism. A few strangled sputters and the engine died. Grunting, the cultist threw down her weapon and came at Kesh with bare hands. Kesh shot her once through the throat and again through the eye, scorching a third hole through a dirty sacking hood.

As the cultist fell back, a gap emerged in her wake and Kesh quickly exploited it.

'Forward, forward!'

Revealed through the narrow window in the melee, the Storm Reaper was on his knees. Deep rents scored his armour, leaking eagerly with blood, his axe fallen beside him still crackling with energy but no use to nerveless fingers that could barely grip, let alone heft.

Time seemed to slow for Kesh as he raised his gaze to his killer, a retinal lens in his helm broken and showing the flesh-and-blood man beneath. His eye narrowed with hatred as the traitor stove in his head.

She wanted to turn away, to cry out in anguish and fear, but instead Kesh ran. She ran *towards* the duel, towards the body of the Storm Reaper tipping sideways, his face a red ruin.

Lodrin and Mavin called after her, so did Munser, his deep voice unmistakable. They were calling her back from her death. But Kesh knew, she *knew* without any uncertainty, that in this moment the battle would be decided. Allow the dark champion to prevail and the Imperial assault would falter. Already the guns were being retaken, the cultist horde finding courage in their warlord's victory.

God-Emperor, thought Kesh, and knew not from where the next words came. *Let me be thy instrument.*

She had holstered her pistol – it would be no use in this fight – and instead reached down for the axe, caged lightning running across its blade. Into her. She felt it sear her skin, send spikes of pain through her arm. Felt its sheer weight, the immense thickness of the grip. She used two hands, shoulders buckling, blade dragging as it spat sparks along the ground...

He laughed as he turned his eyes on her, his baleful mirth like poison in Kesh's veins. Being close to him, she felt her resolve ebb and knew this creature or some part of its essence had been used to taint the tunnels. They had known, the traitors, and had taken precautions. None of that mattered now.

Kesh scraped the axe, like a child wielding an anchor, and saw her opponent stride towards her. He swung the spike-hammer from hand to hand, like a pendulum counting down to her doom.

Throne... the axe felt as heavy as a battle tank, how could she even raise it?

Around her, the sea of fighters had parted as if they understood on some primal level that they needed to bear witness. Kesh barely saw them. Her eyes were scrunched in pain, her fingertips blackening.

The stench of him was the worst thing, of offal and septic pits. His presence brushed against her as a miasma and Kesh felt that hopelessness again, the despair that had nearly killed them all in the tunnels.

Close now, so close... and Kesh still dragging the axe.

He spoke, the Traitor Marine, said something in his crude language. Words to put teeth on edge. Briefly, she wondered if it was admiration, but she was less than a worm to this warrior. It was amusement, she realised.

The spike-hammer lifted, about to strike its death-knell.

Shoulders and arms seething with agony, Kesh felt her burden lighten. For a fleeting second, she thought she might be dead and this feeling a symptom of the afterlife, but the axe was still in her hands, rising, lightning arcing... She struck, a bolt of such fury that it cut through the Traitor Marine's war plate and burned through the corruption of his innards.

He died, painfully, horribly, consumed by conflagration and crashing backwards to the ground, still aflame.

A shockwave rippled through the cultist horde, who moaned in dismay, a cry of triumph rising in counterpoint from the Imperials.

Kesh felt light, a pure and pearlescent light. She couldn't figure out where it was coming from, but it bathed her entirely... And all her doubts fled before its touch.

Chapter Nine

HUNTED

AT LEAST OUR END WILL BE BLOODY

SUSURRATION

Though it stabbed at his pride, Graeyl Herek, lord of the Red Corsairs, fled.

As a Renegade Astartes, he was unaccustomed to running from his foes, but then again he had not been expecting this *foe* and certainly not in such force. Someone wanted them dead, and so the hunters had become hunted. A fringe world, a nothing city: he and his brothers had come here seeking slaves. It should have been easy, a minor inconvenience as part of a much longer journey. Then came the ambush and the cold realisation the Red Corsairs were not alone.

They had fought at first, Astartes arrogance coming to the fore, but the first attack had been costly. Bitter-tasting though it was, Herek had ordered his warriors to retreat.

Fall back, regroup, regain the upper hand.

It had bought them a small respite, lost in the warren of unknown city streets.

But the stalkers were coming and they had overwhelmed

the Red Corsairs vanguard already. The red and the black of his warriors' armour had turned mainly to red. Hargul and Unrith were dead, and he doubted Baruss would rise to see the next dawn of this world's star. Kurgos, the ship's chirurgeon, carried the gasping warrior on his back without complaint or apparent hardship. Slow and ponderous was Vassago Kurgos, but indomitable.

A rueful smile curled Herek's mouth at the thought before he patted Rathek on the shoulder as the shadow passed over them from above. The buildings either side were tight and close, but the stalkers weren't using the streets. They had taken to the rooftops. The swordsman stopped at once, his plated form drenched in gloom as he crouched beneath the ragged awnings that stretched across the narrow market alleyways and looked upwards...

Rathek made the sign for *enemy close.*

Aren't they always, Herek thought ruefully.

The Red Corsairs needed fresh crew for the *Ruin*. They had already been forced to scuttle their other vessel, the *Fell Lord*, stripping its bones for everything of worth, the cult priests sacrificing the weakest of the slaves in a bid to earn the favour of the gods. And though Herek placed less faith in the deities of Chaos than some of his more zealous followers, he could not deny divine providence would be useful right now.

He had eight in his company, another sixteen spread across the rest of the marketplace in three smaller groups, moving from alcove to alcove, human and Astartes alike. A raiding party, confident in their pre-eminence until the stalkers fell upon them, drawn by only the hells knew what. Now they ran, like dogs. Hurt and bleeding. Trying to remain hidden.

The shadows moved on, the distant hiss of their binharic war-argot fading as they went. The Red Corsairs waited a few moments longer, staying down, never rising much above a crouch.

Gothar had made the error of climbing for the rooftops. The iconoclast had gained the lip but only for a second or two, his headless corpse falling back, neck cauterised with nothing above it but a red mist. Stay down, quiet, goad the attackers to them. Not for the first time since landfall, Herek cursed ever coming to Felsrath and Rancor City.

It had been several weeks since they had left port, buoyed on the success of wrenching his old sword – though in truth something far more significant than that – from the mailed fist of the Black Templars. A hard fight, and ultimately, for Herek, unsatisfying on account of the fact that Morrigan still lived and their feud remained unresolved. Still, a victory was a victory, and taking the sword back from him had felt like a coup.

He had another purpose now, a path he must follow.

At first, Herek had felt destined. *Chosen.* His previous feats now rang hollow, the *Fell Lord* a gutted ruin left adrift in the void after a warp storm tore through it, altering a great many of the crew and driving the rest to madness. Some malignancy had befallen them, so said Clortho, and had clung on like barnacles accreting to a ship's hull.

Herek had begun to suspect he had angered the gods.

And that was before the voices had started.

Gods, he hoped they were his guide and not malicious sirens sent to scuttle him and his warband against the rocks of his ambitions.

Ahead of them the narrow street, flanked by flaking walls, came to an end. The alley mouth widened into a large communal square. They had been here before and in their retreat had somehow doubled back, the vendors' carts and hawkers stalls upturned or collapsed. The dead remained where the Red Corsairs and their cultists had struck them down. A cohort of local watchmen amongst the bodies, woefully outclassed. Herek felt the bite of irony as he regarded their harrowed faces.

First to the alley mouth, Rathek turned, keeping low with his back pressed as close to the wall as he was able. *This was not the path we took,* he signed.

He was right. Herek had been driving them towards the heart of the city's labyrinth, not to this kill-zone. Not for the first time, he shut his eyes and tried to focus. At the edge of his mind, in the liminal borderlands between sleeping and waking, he heard them. The old words from a place unknown, the *susurration* he had come to call it.

Are you a tether I must follow? Where are you leading me?

Or had they given him that name? The things he knew now, the dark truths purloined from a forbidden realm intruding on his imperilled present, they haunted him.

'Silence...' he hissed through a barricade of teeth.

A hard grip on his forearm brought him around. It was Kurgos, the groaning body of Baruss still strapped to his back. The chirurgeon was too malformed to crouch, but his back had shaped him into a permanent stoop, a hunched and tumour-ridden monstrosity. Like the others, he was dressed in red and black, the mark of the Tyrant's claw emblazoned on his armour. Besides Rathek, he was Herek's most trusted ally. A brother, for brotherhood still existed for the damned.

'A little farther, Graeyl,' he said, his voice a cancerous rasp, the uncle encouraging his ward. 'And then I can administer the serum.'

Letting out a gasped exhalation, Herek nodded.

The serum would take the edge off, give him some peace. Quiet the voices, though he knew he needed them if he was to follow the path before him. First, though, they needed to survive.

How quickly one retrenches their immediate goals in the face of annihilation.

He gestured to Rathek, a quick flurry of battle sign. *No more hiding.*

Rathek drew both his blades with a scrape of metal against scabbard. A keen-edged spatha and a hand-and-a-half sword.

They will come as soon as you show yourself, signed Herek.

Rathek nodded, understanding his role.

I can send one of the serfs... Herek added, having no desire to put his brother in harm's way without good reason or gain. It was the pirate's calculus, the careful balancing of effort versus reward, and it had served them well over the decades.

Rathek made a snorting gesture and ventured out into the square.

He ran headlong on an oblique route, the stalkers descending at once on bent-back, mechanised legs, believing their trap sprung. Volkites and fusion weapons flashed, deflagrating metal carts or the corpses left to rot on the street. Steel turned to rust, skin to bone... both to ash.

No beam struck Rathek as he jinked and turned and leapt, sword flashing...

One of the stalkers fell, oil and fluid spewing as gorily as blood. It twitched in its end-state, bladed limbs whipping then falling still, its cyclopean eye flaring brightly, as red as a dying sun, until fading into black.

They were spindly, but strong. *Very* strong, not nearly as brittle as their narrow frames and long, multi-jointed limbs suggested. Hargul and Unrith had learned that to their cost, along with a score of cultists.

Like black arachnids they scuttled after Rathek now, transonic blades humming. Six he had teased out of ambuscade, targeting reticules painting the gloomy market in skeins of red. Kurgos killed a second, emerging with Herek and the others. He put a bolt-round straight through its main vertebrae, shattering it with the explosion impact. A third turned to Herek, blurting out a warning code for its cohort. Herek swung Harrower and beheaded it. Grimy matter fountained from the ragged neck wound.

Three against three, at least in that split second. Herek had reinforcements coming, the rest of his eight-strong company – only three of whom were Astartes, and one of those languished in his death throes on Kurgos' back.

Gethir burst into the square, chainaxe swinging, a curse on his lips. It died when Gethir did, cored through the chest by a conflagrating beam as the second group of stalkers entered the fray. They had been waiting for the enemy's true strength to reveal itself, and now that Herek realised the real trap he swore under his breath.

'Should we withdraw?' asked Kurgos between bursts of fire, calmly shredding up what was left of the market stalls and clipping one of the stalkers, blasting off a trailing leg.

Herek checked a signal emitter mag-locked to his thigh. It blinked dully, repeating every three seconds. 'We hold here or we die here,' he said to Kurgos, and rallied his warriors.

The last of the Astartes, Clortho, joined them, his plate and mail armour chipped and scorched from numerous glancing impacts. A deep rent in his right shoulder guard was evidence of a more tangible blow and he held his right arm to his chest, taking shots with the plasma pistol in his left.

All the Red Corsairs regrouped to their captain. Despite Harrower's impatient hunger, Herek stowed his massive war axe and pulled his bolt pistol.

Better to keep the cyborgs at arm's length.

Back to back, the renegades blazed at every silhouette as the stalkers came for them in a tide, scurrying over rooftops and spilling from alleyways like metal marionettes. Black as an oil slick, with a shimmering, beetle-like carapace, they drooled acid and carried vibrating blades and fusion cannons. The latter flashed like hellfire, immolating what little cover the renegades had found. The last of the cultists died in seconds to the stalkers, several fleeing in abject terror from the cybernetic monstrosities only to be scythed down or disintegrated. Those that stood their ground did so isolated and without the iron discipline of the Astartes, and were slaughtered all the same.

In the market square, amongst the corpses of the massacred citizens, a pall of darkness had fallen. It blanketed the sky, the smoke from numerous fires causing the blackout.

Turning his helm plate to heatsight, Herek's visual world turned sharp and visceral, the stalkers rendered as edged outlines, teeming into the square like ants attacking a rival nest. As they closed, surrounding the tiny knot of renegades on all sides, the stalkers paused, then fell back into a perimeter. With a raised hand, Herek signalled the ceasefire.

'Conserve your rounds,' he growled over the vox.

His ammo counter blinked amber.

Clortho had a spare powercell and slammed it home. His last. The sidearm looked close to an overheat anyway. Rathek had not even touched his pistol, his two blades slick with greasy oil and ichor. Kurgos had stowed his bolter and instead had drawn a chainbladed knife. A surgeon's brutal tool, it was used for cutting through an injured warrior's armour.

'At least our end will be bloody,' remarked the chirurgeon, unconcerned as he set his blade's teeth churning.

'I for one have no intention of dying here, but then all dead men would say the same,' uttered Herek.

A veritable army of ocular lenses and sensors analysed them from the shadows, blades and cannons humming. An eerie silence drifted over the scene, broken only by the crackle of flames. An awning collapsed, crashing noisily to the ground in a scorched heap. No one moved.

What are they waiting for? signed Rathek, ever eager for the killing. He was known as 'the Culler' for good reason, though his humours had levelled out of late, ever since Herek's old sword had been destroyed. Herek would have wanted that frenzied berserker by his side right now. Instead, he held up a hand to his brother.

Hold, it said.

'They are waiting to see if this is a trap...' muttered Clortho, earning a slow nod from Herek as the captain eyed their foes.

'Wouldn't you, Clortho, if your prey willingly stepped into a killing field?'

Kurgos shifted his bulk ever so slightly, the mildest cant of his head, the gentle turn of his shoulder.

You let us be herded, he signed, using an argot known only to his kin amongst the Red Corsairs.

'Stand ready,' Herek replied, shooting a glance at the signal emitter: still blinking. 'This will get bad before it's over.'

Amongst the cybernetic host – almost forty in number now as their other clades returned from their kill-missions, amassing for the decapitation strike – a hooded princeps straightened and blurted a binharic attack command.

'Here they come!' shouted Clortho.

He fired, one last shot before the pistol burned out and he threw it down, a second later unhooking a flanged mace from his belt.

The stalkers ran the gauntlet, fifty feet or more between them and the renegades, opting for sabres over any volkites or fusion arms. They scurried at first, coming in low and fast, before breaking into long and loping strides. Herek sprayed one of the stalkers against the side of a metal cart before his pistol clunked empty. Harrower swept from his back to replace it, her blade singing.

Kurgos shrugged Baruss off his shoulder, the helmless renegade white as ash, dead eyes staring. He gave his fallen brother a last look of regret before pulling a second knife, its edge savagely serrated.

A soundless roar came from Rathek, who kicked over a cart to stand atop its ruin and point his longer sword at the princeps.

Clortho arched his head to the stygian heavens, bellowing, 'Gods... bear witness!'

And then the stalkers were amongst them.

The air turned thick with actinic heat as a blur of transonic blades whipped at Herek. Harrower proved equal to the task, parrying but more often lashing out, hacking at metal limbs and necks. Machine parts flew in silver rain, oil splashing like blood. Herek's face was lathered with it, a greasy, snarling mask.

From the corner of his eye, he saw Kurgos raise one of the stalkers on his surgeon's blades. A sword pierced his side, right through his armour, but beyond a muffled grunt the chirurgeon gave no sign he had been stabbed.

Rathek beheaded his aggressor before impaling another. He moved on to a third, shearing a sword hand off at the wrist, a thrust through the stalker's ocular socket finishing it. Designating the blade-master a priority target, four of the cyborgs ganged up on him and Rathek fell back into a defensive posture before Herek lost sight of him altogether. He swung Harrower in a wide arc, more scythe than axe, reaping a heavy tally of claws, antennae and other components. She kept the stalkers at bay, but the tactic would only stall the inevitable...

They took Clortho first, burying the warlord under a pile of cybernetic bodies. He roared as he fell, mace swinging wildly even as they cut his ancient armour to ribbons. Then Kurgos shuddered, a blade transfixing him through the stomach. Blood welled up from under his helm, spewing out of his mouth grille. He snapped the sword with his gauntleted hand, losing a couple of fingers in the process, and managed to turn to Herek, who fought his own last stand.

'I regret nothing...' rasped the chirurgeon through foaming blood.

He would have fallen, half a transonic blade sticking from his gut, but from the rooftops came thunder as twenty or more boltguns opened up in unison. Weapons fire swept through the cybernetic horde, tearing them apart as their sensors failed to notice the blanking field coming from Herek's signal emitter, a little piece of scrapcode buried in the three-second pulse. And that wasn't all. It had been transmitting their loc-ref and distress code.

From aboard the *Ruin* at low anchor over Felsrath, the Red Corsairs reinforcements had come. These men were loyal to Herek, despite their many depravities. He had brought them glory and fortune in the eyes of the gods. At least until of late. Their loyalty held, driven by their greed and for some, their fraternal beliefs. They would follow him wherever the path led.

Realising their tactical error in having been drawn into their own killing field, the stalkers attempted to adjust, but the renegades were meticulous in the cyborgs' destruction and it was over quickly.

Kurgos staggered, spitting up more blood, and Herek helped steady him.

'Can you walk?'

Painfully, the chirurgeon nodded as Herek took in his wounds, the ragged shaft of metal protruding from his body.

'I hope you can still stitch with fewer fingers...'

A strangled cough came from the chirurgeon, a failed attempt at mirth. He wrapped his good hand around the broken blade and wrenched it out. Little blood came with it, the fluid that ran through Kurgos being thicker than most. He also endured pain like no other man Herek knew. Spitting up a gobbet of black gore, he gave a gargled rasp and began hobbling over to Clortho. The warlord lay on his back, breathing but badly skewered, his old armour in pieces. He had lost his helmet in the scrum and a face riddled with scars stared wild-eyed at the chirurgeon.

'I'll return him to the ship,' Kurgos said to Herek, visually assessing Clortho's wounds.

'See that he lives. I can ill afford any more losses, especially so far from our goal.'

'Aye, he'll live,' Kurgos rasped, 'and when your business here is concluded, I will treat you as well.'

'Any ailment of mine can wait,' said Herek, already walking away.

Through dissipating smoke, he found the princeps alive but dismembered. The other renegades had descended into the square and together with Rathek were dispatching any stalkers showing signs of anima. Their scraped blade thrusts provided a grim chorus as Herek knelt to regard his mutilated enemy. Its ocular lenses pulsed fever yellow, the rhythm not unlike a heartbeat.

'Many good fighters died to your abominations,' he told it. His hand, a bionic replacement for the flesh and blood one he had lost to an old enemy, clenched around its jaw. Herek tightened his grip a fraction, just enough so the metal squealed. 'I hope you can still feel something, creature...'

The pulse increased in tempo.

Herek released the princeps' chin, and stood up. As the adrenaline faded, the voices had begun to gnaw at his mind again. He took off his helm, its confines stifling. A well-defined, chiselled face appeared from underneath with little to suggest the inner corruption to his soul, barring two small horns that protruded from either side of his forehead, one of which had been shorn almost to the root. More harrowed than he had been, though, because of the *susurration.*

It had put him in a bad mood. He decided he would take it out on the princeps. Make it suffer, as much as one of its kind could experience suffering.

'Bring this one with us. Let's find out what it knows.'

They had dissected the princeps, its remains now lying on a table in one of the *Ruin*'s chambers. Kurgos had brought it with him on a grav-sled at Herek's request, the captain needing to work as he received treatment. Despite his own extensive injuries, the chirurgeon betrayed no sign of discomfort apart from his usual belaboured gait.

A grimace creased Herek's face as the serum filled his veins but his mind stilled, if only for a short while.

'Better...' he said, voice breathy with pain.

'It will serve for now,' Kurgos replied, packing away his instruments, 'but a more potent solution will be needed soon.'

'Increase the dosage.'

'It's not a matter of how much, it will simply cease to function. When I made the serum for Rathek, I never envisaged it would be used to treat something this... *esoteric*. It shouldn't work at all.'

'I have the utmost confidence, Vassago.'

The chirurgeon gave an irritated grunt. 'Where is he, anyway? I need to review his biologicals.'

'Last I saw, he was headed for the oubliettes. I think he sleeps down there still. We are all indoctrinated in our ways.'

Another grunt, agreement this time. 'Perhaps for the best...'

Herek had stripped down to half-armour, the upper sections lying in a corner of the room. The scars on his shoulders, arms and back were extensive, and a few fresh wounds would soon join them. Not all had been received in war. There were ritualistic marks too. He gave Kurgos a sharp look.

'I speak no lies here, Graeyl. Be wise to the fact that Rathek is a beast still, albeit tamed or perhaps sleeping. I have yet to decide which.' He turned to appraise the dissected remains.

Herek came to stand alongside him. 'And what truths are revealed here, brother?'

The creature had been pulled apart, and there was evidence of biological matter amid the machine: blood, sinew, even entire organs. Herek suspected it would have screamed had it still possessed vocal cords when Kurgos had conducted his work. They had found other things too – mutation, marks of the diabolic. There was something festering and unnatural beneath all of that metal.

Reaching into his belt pouch, Kurgos produced a vial of fluid. He shook it, activating the chemicals within, then, applying a few drops to the exposed flesh, he sniffed at the reaction and scowled.

'Sulphur and something else I can't identify. Potent though.' Gruesome as he was, Kurgos possessed attuned olfactory senses. 'It was tainted by a magister's touch. Something Neverborn clung to its flesh, twisted it.' He gestured to the black lesions, the corrosion around the metal where it conjoined to mutated flesh. 'A lesser entity, I have to assume, or it would have revealed itself when threatened.'

'For what purpose?'

'To see and hear for its master, so it could follow us, would be my guess.'

'That's... troubling.'

'Agreed. It puts a cloud over our current endeavour.' He turned a mildewed eye to the star chart laid out on the table near to where they were standing. The leather had curled at the edges and there were rough patches here and there, gnarled and callused, the odd wiry hair jutting out. The map had been inked in blood, the cartographer's marks old, almost feverish – as if this path had only been seen in a dream or some other pseudo-somnambulant state.

'I recognise none of these destinations,' Kurgos admitted. 'Nor the language in which they are written. Together with whatever remnants or marks of warp spawn remain on this creature, it suggests a certain kind of adversary.'

'It's daemon speak,' said Herek, not knowing how he knew – no, that wasn't entirely true; he knew, he just didn't want to acknowledge it. He gritted his teeth, his fists suddenly clenched as if considering the map and their journey across its uncanny contours had triggered something.

'I have more serum,' offered Kurgos, seeing his distress.

Herek shook his head. 'Three doses is enough. It'll have to suffice.' *Besides,* he thought, as he regarded the lunatic's map, *I might need the voices.*

Between the voices and the soul mariner, the *Ruin* had maintained the right course.

'As ship's surgeon, I have to caution you, captain,' said Kurgos. 'Your condition is worsening.'

'You already have. And it makes no difference. I feel it, Vassago... the pieces of it crawling beneath my skin. Embedded. Every scratch is a word or a phrase that finds its echo in my subconscious mind. The closer we get, the louder it becomes.'

'To what, though?'

Behethramog.

Herek felt certain it was a place, their final destination and goal. He had heard the name in the cuneiform runes, scratched by a madman's hand onto the map. Kurgos still awaited his answer.

'To an ending, to what has been promised.'

To be chosen.

To become one of the Hand, perhaps, or something greater? Either way, it was a form of apotheosis that he sought. Herek knew he must have faith, and that the whims of the Dark Gods were never transparent. His patron had promised him glory, and had he not fulfilled his part of the bargain thus far?

The chirurgeon frowned, his hideous features made even more distorted. 'You still trust it, *the other*? I know it only speaks to you, Graeyl, but unlike Clortho I have never placed my faith in the word of daemons.'

'*They*, Vassago, not it. And I trust them because there is no other choice.'

'The captain of the *Ruin* and Lord of Corsairs *always* has a choice, Graeyl.'

Herek's expression darkened but he gave nothing of his true thoughts away. 'Our patron remains absent,' he confirmed instead. 'I have made the ritual six times and every time there is nothing.'

'A symptom of your burden perhaps?'

'I don't think it's the susurration. And they gave it to me, why would it place the patron beyond my reach? This is something else, some ploy I'm not seeing. Perhaps we are meant to triumph alone. It doesn't matter. We have our map, our heading...' He turned his attention to a silent figure in the room. 'And our compass.'

The Navigator was naked but for the spiked and eyeless helm encasing its head and bent over on its knees as if in penitence. Bloody wounds raked its back, lit by a shaft of twilight from above.

'Are you ready for another foray, soul mariner?'

Its eerie voice resonated from behind its helm as it arched its head towards the light.

'I serve your will, lord. Let me ply the Devil's Road and cross the Straits of Lunacy. At the Burned Spire to the Threefold Wytch and the Abyssal Nadir... It is beauty and horror, and yet there is yearning in me for more. For the further truths hidden by the Great Ocean...' It bowed then, as low to the floor as possible, practically folded over, its skeletal limbs contorting, and whispered, 'It will be dangeroussss...'

Herek replied with disdain. 'When is it not?'

He shared another look with Kurgos, who had begun to re-examine the princeps' corpse. A scalpel pulled back a flap of skin, exposing a rune. Not one made by mortal hands.

'I have the distinct impression,' he said, 'that we are being hunted by more than just men.'

Chapter Ten

LED INTO DARKNESS

GHOULS

I AM BUT AN ACOLYTE

Yheng could not shake the sense of being hunted. Even though she knew this part of the fortress and had been here on one of her several excursions, she could not help her growing paranoia. Perhaps it was the prospect of war between the Hand, despite Augury's intervention. Their timely proclamation had cooled heads but left Tenebrus sullen. He had dismissed Yheng immediately afterwards, to see to his own machinations, no doubt.

And so she had ventured out, but the creeping disquiet had followed, it seemed. Several times she had stopped and turned at half-glimpsed movement or a sound but found nothing on her heels.

She chastised herself for her weakness. If something did trail her, and gods knew she had heard creatures in the deep nooks of the fortress, it would regret doing so.

Her long robes flared in her wake as Yheng strode deliberately, head raised to let her disdain be known. Her staff's ferrule thudded as it struck the floor, the small blue flame at its forked tip wavering and flickering as her pace increased. Colder here in this lower deep, a bone-gnawing chill that her powers could not soften. She had taken to wearing a thick cloak, the same night-black as her acolyte's attire. The silver piercings in her eyebrows and the chains embedded in her scalp chimed sharply with each step. The jewels cut into her flesh flashed as they caught the ambient light. They gave her a fiercer aspect, made her more predatory.

She sought the sentience she had felt in the black chamber, though had been unsuccessful thus far. The exhilaration of a little fear was worth it. Cleared the mind. Annoyingly, her head still ached, the regard of the gods heavy in her thoughts and just as unfathomable. The awe of it was yet to fade, and Yheng wondered briefly if she were still sane. No, she was master of her own mind and perceptions. This felt different though, like a shift, potentially seismic. It thrilled her. Ever since her recruitment to the ranks of the Cult of the Blade Unsheathed, the gods and their gifts had been an abstract concept. She had seen things in her apprenticeship to Tenebrus, and had considerable warp sorcery of her own, but what had happened to her in the black chamber was the first time she had personally experienced the sense of something greater. And her part in it.

Of being chosen.

She liked it. And craved more of it.

She wandered on, growing accustomed to the strangeness of the benighted corridors, accounting for it like one would accept sunlight or gravity. The halls looked old, the metal worn and corroded with rust. Deck plating thrummed beneath her feet and she wondered what engine was at work, and where. Surely, it must be powerful? Mist lay heavy over everything. It had depths, this hollow place, untold fathoms like an ocean trench, half-forgotten and seldom travelled.

Passing through a doorway, a vaulted arch of angular metal,

she stopped. The pathway extended another few feet and then came to an abrupt halt, the way plunging down into darkness like a well at the edge of the universe. Had the mists not thinned, she felt sure she would have plummeted to her death. She snorted at the thought, convinced enough of her destiny that she would not meet such an ignominious end.

The shaft before her was wide, hexagonal, and the tiny veins of light that ran through it showed little of what lay below. Yheng had never been to this part of the fortress before, though she trod the same steps, took the same paths as she had previously. She must have got turned around somewhere or taken a wrong path. She glanced back over her shoulder but found only the same nondescript passageway, the mist thickening again. Had it changed too? A slight alteration to its direction. She couldn't recall *two* branching corridors from its junction.

Irritated, she glanced ahead, half hoping it had changed too, but saw only the well before her, a faint breeze emanating up the shaft. The lightest sound came with the breeze, a murmur. Yheng stepped towards it, straining to hear.

Then another step, as the murmur grew louder.

Another, she almost had it now...

'No further, Tharador Yheng,' rasped the voice of Tenebrus.

Yheng opened her eyes, belatedly realising they were closed.

And snarled at the immense, gaping drop a few inches from where she had placed her feet. Another step and...

She calmly stepped back, and found the sorcerer a few paces behind her. He smiled, at once knowing and sinister.

'I told you it was alive.'

Gods of the abyss, she would have liked to flay him in that moment, but she bowed as an acolyte would to a master. 'You said it could feel, master.'

Tenebrus' cobalt eyes narrowed in what might have been annoyance. She smiled inwardly at his irritation.

'That I did. You have a good memory, Yheng, but little common sense.'

Her expression hardened as her hand tightened around her staff. 'I appear to have been turned around,' she confessed, the bile rising in her throat at needing his help.

'You have. It brought you here, do you understand? It sought to take you, Yheng.'

Yheng scowled, briefly confused, and Tenebrus swept before her, a shadow given form. A bony arm snaked around her shoulder, sharp fingers biting through her clothes and into flesh. His touch... repellent and unwanted. His death, when the moment came, would be an unpleasant one, Yheng decided in that moment.

'Observe...' uttered Tenebrus.

Unfurling the fingers of his other hand, the sorcerer gestured to the changed corridor.

At first Yheng saw nothing, only a path she did not know, but then it began to move. Ever so subtly, near imperceptible. The second branch closed, sealing shut with silent finality. As she watched, fascinated, Yheng felt a cold dampness in her side. She touched it and brought back reddish fingers. She looked at Tenebrus.

'Master, you appear to be bleeding.'

Perhaps that death she had envisaged for him wasn't so far off after all.

'Ah yes,' Tenebrus sighed, 'I had forgotten about that... I had an encounter before I found you.'

He gestured to the shadows.

Several pallid creatures appeared in the darkness then; blind, judging by the hollow perforations they had instead of eyes, nasal pits sucking at stale air.

'What are they?' she hissed, aware of the lethal drop behind them.

'The true denizens of this place.'

They loped, knuckling across the ground, their skeletal frames rangy but tough. Hunched over, thick claws curling from long fingers, they found the sorcerer's scent, lifted their heads and snarled. Needle teeth glinted wetly in the light, pinkish from where they had already tasted blood. A pack of six emerged entirely from the mist, the leader rising to its full extension and throwing back its head to bellow. A ululating cry, altogether too deep, too resonant.

'It cries for flesh,' said Tenebrus.

'Then slay them, my lord,' said Yheng, reaching for her own power.

'I cannot.'

She too found her power absent. Something in this place was blunting it.

No... wait. She felt something new, a well of strength that was both alien and enticing at the same time. For a moment, Yheng almost tapped into it, but something prevented her going any further. The murmur... Trusting it, she hesitated.

Yheng risked a glance over her shoulder, the precipice nearing...

The creatures stalked towards them now, hissing back and forth as if coordinating their attack.

Again, Yheng suppressed the urge to defend herself. *I could kill them all myself,* she realised, but an instinct stayed her hand.

'Stay still, Yheng,' rasped Tenebrus as the shadows embraced her like an immense dark cloak. Uttering a cry, the creatures lunged, clambering off the walls and ceiling, and through the blackness that swirled around her Yheng saw different monsters, and realised they had ascended from the pit.

Mechanical aberrations, the sorcerer's creatures now.

Clothed in ragged shadows, they were all blades and scythes. They fell upon the ghoulish predators with their own weapons, churning and rending, the arrow-sharp screeches of the wretches echoing strangely off the walls.

In a few moments it was done and the dismembered bodies of the ghouls lay scattered about. Several pieces had been flung into the pit.

Tenebrus breathed hard, his narrow frame heaving with the effort.

'The wound is not severe,' he said, referring to the blood leaking from his side. At a click of his tongue, the monstrous machines retreated back into the pit, slowly slinking down into shadow. 'It is merely taxing in this place to call upon the ether. The stone, this blackstone. *Noctilith.* It can... disrupt the essence of the warp, nullify its potency. It's why this place remains undiscovered by our enemies. For now. But it has certain hostile proclivities.'

And yet she had felt reserves of strength. Yheng glanced down at the butchered ghouls, their remains steaming in the cool air.

'The sentience you spoke of, master.'

'Yes... and no.'

She looked back at Tenebrus. The sorcerer had paled, his flesh even whiter than before, and waxen, as if feverish. She knew she had changed too, the darkening around her eyes, the pallor of her skin. She reached out to offer a steadying hand but was rebuffed with an impatient hiss. That stung, the barb of anger she already felt sharpening further.

'I believe the Hand has all but served its purpose. The gathering has confirmed that. We came here to unite the shards. That mission has been successful. Each of us has followers, forces at our disposal. Internecine conflict was inevitable. It has caught up to us sooner than I anticipated. And you, Yheng, *you* have a part to play.'

A trill of alarm rippled through her as she realised Tenebrus had some awareness of what she had felt in the black chamber.

'I am but an acolyte, your servant,' she said, trying to deflect.

Tenebrus' eyes narrowed, as if he peered into her soul. The

touch of it sent ice down her spine and she shivered despite herself.

'You are more than that, I think. And you have power. But we must be sure.'

Yheng wasn't sure what Tenebrus meant by his last comment, but she did realise one thing.

'Those creatures, they were sent for me? To harm or kill?'

'It is possible. Maybe they were meant to capture and I was in their way, or perhaps it is something else. Much is obscured. I know only that there is a plan beyond what we, here, have achieved. To see it through, we have to survive what comes next. I take little reassurance from Augury's words. They are not to be trusted. Few are. An ally may be found in the Wretched Prince, and I do not believe either of the Traitor Astartes are interested in any war they could fight here. The rest, though... I wonder,' said Tenebrus, briefly wistful, 'if this is what the Warmaster intended, that the covenant would devour itself.' Then he turned his gaze back onto Yheng. 'Tell me, Yheng, have you ever felt the regard of the gods? Their eye upon you?'

Yheng froze at this sudden confirmation. Until then she had still clung to the hope that no one, barring Augury, had been aware of her experience in the black chamber. The sudden memory spurred unease. Once again, she struggled to fully bring the encounter to mind. It was dreamlike, fading like ice against the sun. The sorcerer had a way about him, though. A *knowing*. It was uncanny.

But Tenebrus was not infallible, and here Yheng had a strength seemingly denied to him.

'I saw what you saw, my master,' she lied, silken and with confidence, 'the glory of the Dark Gods.'

'You felt nothing?' The furrowing of his brow suggested his frustration at not being able to see through Yheng's lie. A warm sense of satisfaction grew in her.

'Only awe, who would not?' She frowned, her feigned ignorance flawless, the fortress she had raised around her mind without weakness. 'The ritual... the sheer momentousness of it all. Humbling, my lord.'

'And the screaming,' hissed Tenebrus, shaking now. He coughed, blood flecking his pale skin, and a thin red rivulet trickled from one corner of his mouth. 'Why were you screaming, Yheng?'

'I was... overwhelmed,' said Yheng, scrambling a little at the revelation that the scream had been real and not imagined. Her words to him were true, but obfuscated and reshaped to her purpose.

Tenebrus gave a sharp intake of breath, as if he had been about to press for more, but instead his hand went to his side. It came back drenched in crimson, and he gasped, 'I may have been wrong... about the severity of my injuries...' and sagged into a ragged heap.

As she looked down upon the sorcerer in his weakened state, Yheng experienced a moment's indecision. She still had her ritual knives and knew enough of the rites to make an offering. Her hand even closed around a hilt... until she released it. Not here, not yet. Besides, he was still conscious and might have been trying to trick her.

She helped him instead. He was obscenely light; she lifted him easily so his arm was draped over her shoulder, supporting his weight, and faced off against the corridor as it changed again, blackstone moving to reveal the path she needed.

'This place was not meant for the eyes of men...' uttered Tenebrus as he leaned on Yheng and took them through another unexplored part of the fortress. Despite his injuries, he remained awake, but his breathing was laboured as they went together into the deeper darkness.

Through a corridor and across an expansive platform that

eerily possessed no echo, the sound of their footfalls deadened, their breaths becoming still and flat, Tenebrus led them to a tall and lightless shaft that soared up into the vaults of this bizarre place. Creatures flocked in the vaults, flesh and mechanical, though Yheng could discern little more than that.

'Do not trouble yourself,' rasped Tenebrus, his voice faint. 'They will not venture down here.'

A fissure in the facing wall became a crack then widened into a door, which the sorcerer bid her to take. They passed through the door and into another chamber, this one as foreign to Yheng as the last. Though she could not be sure, these looked like quarters the sorcerer had taken for himself. A few books and artefacts sat in niches or were simply piled in corners. A sigil daubed in ash and blood covered the entire floor, and when she stepped across its threshold Yheng felt her skin prickle.

'A warding circle,' said Tenebrus, as if reading her mind. 'To keep out unwanted guests and unwanted minds...'

Detaching himself from her arm, he shuffled over to a black wooden box banded with dark iron and pulled forth a foul-smelling salve. He applied it to the elliptical wound in his side, which was darkly red and ringed with small puncture marks, and shuddered with relief. A vial of yellowish liquid was downed next, and Tenebrus' pain visibly eased at its imbibing.

'Better,' he rasped.

Yheng had been sleeping wherever she might, praying to the Dark Gods that she would not wake to some horror bearing down on her. She had never been to these chambers before.

'Why I am here, master?' she asked, her eyes straying to a strange mural daubed on the wall in chalk and what might also be paint. She frowned, trying to make sense of the scratched images, but saw only slashes of darkness against grey.

'Do you remember what we took from Gathalamor, Yheng?'

asked Tenebrus, taking a seat upon a crude-looking cot where he made his bed, perhaps more injured than he was letting on.

'Of course, my lord. The ring. Of the old heretic, the demagogue cardinal.'

'Bucharis, yes.'

'I thought that plan was ultimately unfulfilled.'

'It succeeded in part.'

Yheng's silence bade Tenebrus to talk further, as she knew it would.

'Much remains veiled by the gods, Yheng. The ring is a tool, a means for us to achieve a lasting victory. Kar-Gatharr sought to use it to empower a weapon. Crude and unambitious, he tried to yoke the essence of the warp to his will, to *direct* it. To lay waste to ships, perhaps even to fleets. He overreached his ability and was found wanting in the eyes of the gods. His rotting corpse is testament to this. His small-minded ambition blinded him to the ring's true purpose. Properly harnessed, it can pierce any aegis, whatever or whoever the source.'

Any aegis... That was interesting. Yheng felt certain Tenebrus had chosen the word deliberately. She wondered what he meant. So many secrets... If only she could crack open his skull and spill them out along with his blood and brains.

'I believe we are on the cusp of great change,' he continued, 'a shifting of hierarchy and an end to old empires that should have died out long ago. There is a being that is destined to become a vessel for a power not seen in ten thousand years. I have seen it, Yheng, on Srinagar I was afforded but a glimpse. It heralds a new galactic order and whosoever controls it will be beyond reckoning, beyond any challenge. For its ascension to be assured, the current pretenders must be removed. But do not let that trouble you now.' Tenebrus smiled then, his grin reminiscent of a shark's mouth.

Her own smile hid a snarl. She hated how he assumed her weak. *It will be the death of him,* she thought.

'And this...' Tenebrus added, gesturing to the mural. 'Each mark represents one of the shards of Erebus. What do you know of them, Yheng?'

Yheng shook her head. 'Almost nothing, master. Only that rejoined, they will forge the Anathame.'

Tenebrus nodded. 'Yes,' he said, 'the Anathame. The blade that almost killed the arch-traitor Horus himself.'

She had witnessed the fell power of the shards before, but her master did so delight in the self-aggrandisement of sharing his knowledge.

Tenebrus went on. 'They are truly ancient, Yheng, almost as old as the decaying empire itself. And they have power... Enough perhaps to kill even a god. Or something very like one.'

At this, Yheng turned to face him, her expression suddenly receptive.

Tenebrus merely smiled again. 'It was our purpose to gather the shards and reunite their dark glory. A supplicant was chosen for this purpose, to be their bearer.'

Her face soured as Tenebrus recounted what she already knew, but the sorcerer wasn't finished.

'They had other bearers once,' he said, 'and have since... Kor Phaeron, Morpal Cxir, Foedrall Fwel, Hol Beloth, Quor Vondar, Phael Rabor and Kolos Undil were the first.' He winced, slightly shifting his posture, and all at once the sorcerer's regard changed. Gone the lecturer, in its place the cold-eyed interrogator. 'Think now, Yheng, does *none* of this resonate?'

Tenebrus outstretched a bony finger and suddenly Yheng felt her body seized and pulled upwards as if by invisible, psychic strings. She tried to resist but he had caught her unprepared. In his own chambers, within the runic circle he had made, he was far the greater power. Her neck strained, her limbs grew painfully stretched. She struggled to breathe, her reaching toes scraping the floor.

'I swear, I have no further insight, master.' Gods, she wanted to kill him.

'Search your mind, acolyte. *See* the shards and their history, their legacy...'

'There is nothing...' She snarled, her rage a buffer against the pain. 'I do not know what you want me to–'

And then she saw it, a war across the heavens, of gods astride the galaxy, of armies beyond counting, rebellion, of Terra benighted and the predations of the Ruinous Powers from beyond the veil. And across the gulf of millennia, they turned their regard on her, watching ten thousand years in the past. Yheng felt again the touch of destiny on her shoulder and the promise of something greater...

I am *chosen...*

Immense, overwhelming, her mind reeled.

The spell broke in a sudden explosion of force, casting Tenebrus across the chamber until he hit the wall. Smoke drooled off his body as he clambered to his feet.

Had that been her, or something else?

As Tenebrus wiped a bead of blood from his mouth and smiled, she realised it was the latter.

'Good... very good.'

Trembling with unleashed power, awed by everything she had seen and experienced, Yheng ran.

He did not try to stop her, though she suspected the sorcery he had employed in his quarters had overtaxed him anyway. She had no destination in mind, only to escape, to find some quiet place to think. *It* led her, or so it appeared, the fortress reshaping, moulding itself into pathways that closed behind Yheng as soon as she had taken them. She quickly lost all sense of her bearings, content to plunge further, deeper, ripples of sympathetic pain dancing through her fingertips whenever she brushed against a column or archway.

Mist engulfed her, and she was scurrying blindly, hoping no chasm would open up beneath her; that she would not impale herself on some spike of black glass. She heard voices in the mist, old and young, known and unknown, a kaleidoscope of identities that merged into a single siren song, calling her onwards...

Until she reached the edge of a mirrored pool. In it she saw herself reflected, haggard and dishevelled. This place was taking a toll on her, she realised, mentally and physically. But she sensed no malice in it, merely a desire to impart revelation.

Tenebrus had said a war was coming between those of the Hand, now that their task was done and the shards had been gathered. She thought of the ghouls again, cannibal denizens of the fortress. They had only appeared when Tenebrus had revealed his presence.

Her hand had been stayed for a reason. That moment of instinct when she had hesitated.

I could have destroyed them, she realised.

And then as the mists lifted, revealing the one who had brought her here, Yheng wondered whether the creatures had been sent after her at all.

Chapter Eleven

GARROVIRE

SONS OF ULTRAMAR

ORACLES

Through parting mist, Brother-Lieutenant Ferren Areios saw them.

His cobalt armour stood out amid the filth of the mire in which he stood, the white Ultima still resplendent on his shoulder. A giant clad head to foot in powered war plate, a warrior born and then forged. But the creatures he had fought ever since this campaign had begun were not bearing down on the Ultramarine. They had other prey in mind.

The creatures ran in packs, huffing and spitting like beasts. Long, loping strides through grimy marshland. Hungry and driven. A thin line of soldiers faced them, tired-looking men and women who had already seen battle and would soon see it again...

The soldiers had dubbed their enemies the 'Turned'. The one in front was amongst the biggest and lumbered feverishly, hacking at roots and vines with a sharpened piece of shrapnel. A lumpen creature, swollen with muscle, a diminutive additional arm protruding from its back. Scraps of clothing clung to its scrambling, top-heavy form, its skin the colour of over-boiled meat.

It had been a man once.

It led the others of its kind, those with horned appendages or fingers melded into claws, the tumour-ridden and the scaled, a great herd of the malformed and the changed, milling and splashing through foetid water.

Thick air, turbid with marsh gas and swarms of mosquitos, clung to the troopers like a second skin. Forest-green fatigues, khaki vests beneath, wearing ranger caps, combat helms and red bandanas, they were well-muscled and clung to carbines and shotcannons. They waded through the sludge and the foetor with gruff indifference, lasguns cracking and fizzing at the first sightings of the mutants through the fog, sharp stabs of cerulean blue against cesspool brown. Across the Deromir Swamps of Arrandius, the soldiers of the Catachan 116th and the ragged hosts of the Divine Eye met and fought.

And Areios watched. Half a mile from the battle line, he watched as the enemy attacked in overwhelming force and felt his jaw tighten.

It had been one hundred and thirteen days since the first of the Turned had emerged in one of the civitas majoris. Other cities of the Arrandius region had followed swiftly, some seemingly responding to a silent siren call, whilst others erupted with spontaneous and sudden change, a biological transformation on an unprecedented scale. Entire populations became Turned almost overnight. Order collapsed. This was Garrovire, a redoubt, a world of the Anaxian Line and Arrandius its greatest continent, but even stalwart loyalty and unwavering courage was no proof against the vicissitudes of the enemy.

At first the Imperial government had tried burning the contagion out, anything to slow or stop the rot. Preachers had performed rites, watered the earth with holy philtres, spread incense to cleanse the air. Culled the weak. Pyres fifty feet high had been seen in cities the world over. Eventually the spread abated, but that had been only the beginning. The masters rose up from within the ranks of the Turned, arcanists and diabolists. From where, none could truly say. A pandemic became a revolt, revolution of the darkest stripe seemed inevitable. Holed up in their bunkers, the last remaining vestiges of the Administratum, the Imperial law on this world, had sent out a desperate plea.

And in the churning heavens of a turbulent galaxy, that plea had been answered.

'It is here, brother,' the calm and certain voice of Cicero assured Areios over the vox.

'I see only Turned,' Areios answered, a half growl. He had nothing but ire for this wretched place, its bogs and marshland. The mud and filth lapped at his armour, his bolt rifle a useless anchor in his hands. His fingers tensed, eager to be put to use.

The Catachans had dug in and created a defensive picket across the breadth of the marsh. It had stretched them; to Areios, the weakness of this strategy was plain. But the Guard were trying to tackle the sweeping horde on every front, whittle them down with their crew-served guns and rocket tubes. As if possessed of no more sentience than one of the buzzing insects that thronged the marsh, the Turned ran headlong into fire. Bodies were ripped apart. A scarlet haze hung in the air. Yet they persisted, the first ranks bullet shields for the second. Shouts were coming from the Guard as the Turned got closer, the inevitability of the Catachans' doomed plan becoming evident.

Areios was not here for them. He could kill Turned easily enough. He already had done. He and his brothers had different prey.

'Then we must look harder, Areios,' Cicero told him, *'for mark me, the Oracles are here. This many Turned, where else could they be?'*

The name 'Oracle' had been coined by the campaign commanders and given to the masters of the Turned.

'You are mistaken, brother,' Areios replied, not liking what he was seeing on the line. The Catachans had been breached in several places. Order had begun to fragment.

'We should relocate north to Landhope,' suggested Helicio over the vox. *'Sightings have been reported in that region.'*

'And miss the opportunity to purge this filth?' said Drussus, his pugnacity as loud as a shell-blast. The bombastic Calthian moved up on Areios' flank.

Together with Gravus, Helicio and Cicero, they were one half of Victus Squad, the other being stationed half a mile east. 'Dispersed tactical deployment', Brother-Captain Epathus had called it. Useful for hunting. Inquisitorial intelligence suggested the Oracles were puppet masters and propagators of the Turned. As such, they had been marked as priority targets. The proverbial head of the serpent.

And we the axe, thought Areios, rueful at their lack of viable enemies, though his attention had not wavered from the Catachans as their platoons were slowly being overwhelmed.

'Helicio,' said Areios, 'hail the brother-captain. I request intercession.' His gauntleted fist tightened around his bolt rifle.

'Our orders are to hold until an Oracle is sighted,' the officious battle-brother replied. Sometimes, Areios thought Helicio had been placed in the squad to keep an eye on him by Messinius.

That would be just like you, my old mentor...

'Raise and send the request regardless...'

His eyes narrowed, focusing on a Catachan officer as she was gored on a Turned's horn. She killed the creature, a point-blank shot to the head with her pistol, but others were bearing down on her. One of her men got in their way, heavy stubber blazing. It was a brief respite before he was dragged down into the mire and killed. Time enough for her command section to grab her underarm and haul her back, the officer raging but powerless to prevent the retreat. Troopers died up and down the line as their positions were overtaken. An ammo crate left behind cooked off. An explosion tore into the air, casting up limp bodies from both sides in a dirty plume of smoke and water.

'Cicero,' Areios said, 'what are their odds?' He knew the answer but wanted his brothers to hear it.

'At the current rate of attrition, the Militarum forces will sustain eighty-five per cent casualties before they are able to successfully withdraw.'

'A high rate.'

'A high rate,' Cicero echoed.

'And yet our orders are clear,' Helicio countered.

'Every weapon taken from the hand of an ally is one put in the hands of an enemy,' said Areios. 'Have you heard that phrase, brother?'

For Areios, its meaning was simple – save as many as you can to fight another day.

Helicio remained dogged as ever. *'Protocol states our objectives are–'*

'I am familiar with our objectives, Helicio.'

The Catachans were dying, pulled down into the dirt, cut apart where they stood.

'The hells with this,' Areios murmured as he broke into a run, then louder said, 'Kill Team Exemplar, on my lead. We engage the Turned.'

None would gainsay him, and the four battle-brothers in blue war plate bounded after their leader, shouts of 'Courage and honour!' on their lips.

Never had the mark of the Ultima felt heavier.

Areios set a fearsome pace, his long and powerful strides eating up the distance between him and the breaking Catachan line. Tactical data overlaid his vision, delivered through his retinal lens array. It described distance and temperature, as well as biometrics, the relative positions of his kill team. As he charged through the mire, an icon lit on the left-hand read-out. Private vox interrogative.

Areios engaged it.

Cicero's voice issued into his ear. *'Queries inbound from Paragon,'* he said, naming the other kill team, led by Sergeant Trajus.

'Have them stand, maintain coherency and position,' Areios replied, not missing a beat nor a stride.

A pause, the link not yet closed.

'Speak, Cicero,' Areios invited.

'I am disinclined to agree with Helicio, but the brother-captain will see this as a breach of discipline. Probable outcome will be interrogation by the Chaplaincy.'

'Theoretical – I will face censure for my actions. Practical – if I do not act then good and loyal servants of the Imperium will die and our position on this world will weaken. Extenuation of crisis is justification enough.'

'I will it so, Areios.'

'Do not trouble yourself, Cicero. And when we are in combat, refer to me by my rank. As per operational procedure. Let us not add to the infractions.' He smiled, and heard it reciprocated in Cicero's reply.

'Right you are, brother-lieutenant.'

The feed cut and Areios, who was two hundred feet away from his brother, reached the edge of the conflict zone.

Running and gunning, he strafed a mob of Turned, chewing them to pieces with controlled bursts from his bolt rifle. The mass-reactives shattered bone and cratered flesh. Nothing but chunks of meat and gristle remained.

Switching to a one-handed grip, he unclipped a grenade from his belt and tossed it into a group of Turned where dozens of the creatures had converged into a horde. An explosion tore up the swamp in his wake. Still running, he homed in on the Catachan officer being dragged from the fray. She still fought her saviours, but blood loss appeared to be taking its toll and her protests had weakened. The Turned had her scent, and closed in.

A Turned tried to get in Areios' path, the mutants only just now reacting to the Space Marines' presence. He barged it aside, shattering its ribcage and tearing off one of its arms with his sheer momentum, and never broke stride. Others split off from the growing mob pursuing the Catachan officer. Areios counted over fifty. Kill Team Exemplar destroyed them. Drussus' roar sounded above all else.

Areios smiled grimly, glad to have his brothers by his side.

The latter half of the mob had almost reached their prey, barely a handful of fighters left protecting the Catachan officer. Areios boosted into a sprint, the servos in his power armour building to a high-pitched whine. He hit a ramp of banked earth, one of the abandoned fortifications, and raced up the incline, locking his bolt rifle to his power plant behind him as he went and drawing his sword. The weapon hummed with power, the crackle of a disruption field rippling down the blade.

'Avenging Son!' he cried, loud enough to shatter eardrums, and as he reached the end of the ramp, he leapt...

...and launched into the midst of the Turned. Areios killed two before he had even hit the ground, a lateral cut severing heads. He landed in a crouch, a low sweep of his blade cutting knees and waists. The Turned squealed and shrieked in pain. Rising, he stabbed a hulking mutant bloated with excess fat and flesh through its rubbery gut, cooking it from the inside out. Pivoting, he struck down two more with rapid diagonal cuts that formed a cross of aerosolised blood in the air.

All this in under three seconds.

Heedless of death, the Turned attempted to swarm, but Areios reaped through their ranks with surgical precision. Unsatisfied with the rate of destruction, he pulled his bolt rifle and started shooting.

After a few more seconds, it was over and the Turned lay dead and dismembered about his feet. The Catachans gaped in awe as Areios looked back, his armour splattered with gore. With the immediate danger passed, the officer shrugged off her protectors and began to make her way over to the Space Marine. In the background, the sounds of more distant fighting renewed, the sudden intervention of the Astartes kill team enough to embolden hearts. Dismayed, the enemy's rampage was stymied.

Areios spared a glance for his brothers and saw they were moving methodically through the Turned, before settling into a loose perimeter around their lieutenant. Multiple vox-interrogatives scrolled down his retinal feed. Areios cancelled every one of them with a blink.

'I can still fight,' wheezed the gruff Catachan to her overly cautious men, one of whom was still trying to prop her up. Age marked her face, her olive skin like old leather, but her eyes were bright, her muscles still firm and threaded with ropey veins. She wore a ranger's cap, turned backwards, and camo paint swathed her features in green, brown and black. White teeth shone like an ivory barricade. A shotcannon hung from a strap on her back and an oversized pistol sat snug in a krokodil-hide holster. On the other hip sat a sheathed combat knife. Her pack had a canteen, map case, her gear, and a chainsword wrapped up in tightly bound tarp. Short and squat, she put Areios in mind of a stubborn spur of granite resistant to the elements.

Someone must have bound or cauterised her wound and put a stimm-shot in her. She looked wired.

'Then stand and fight,' Areios told her, bringing the full weight of his regard to bear.

Fear, pain and awe warred in her expression. To her credit, she marshalled each emotion to stand unaided before him.

'I owe you a debt, lord. That my men are not all dead is because of you.' She dipped her head a fraction, then paused to light a cigar. Her bloodstained fingers only shook a little as she lit it, puffing out violet smoke that hazed the marshland air around her. 'Colonel Nakaturo,' she introduced herself.

He pulled off his helm, uncaring of the minor infraction, to reveal a stone-like countenance that had more in common with a tor than a skull, a face framed by short black hair that was shaved at the temples. His skin was the rich hue of walnut and his amber eyes held warmth but also warning.

'Areios,' he said, his voice deep and sonorous.

'Lieutenant,' ventured Nakaturo, noting his rank badges. 'In terms of martial command, I outrank you,' she joked.

The smile didn't reach his eyes. 'You are bold, colonel.'

'That has been confused with rash.'

'I can believe that.' He gestured to the troopers who had begun to establish a position around their officer. 'These are your men?'

'That they are... The Hundred-Sixteenth Death Eagles,' she said proudly.

Areios saw little to be proud of in that moment. The soldiers looked ragged, at the edge of their endurance and viability as a regiment.

'We have seen better days, lord,' Nakaturo admitted, noticing the Space Marine lieutenant's appraisal.

'You have nothing to prove to me, colonel. Though tell me, how did you run afoul of the Turned?'

Nakaturo described their mission, how they had been tasked with reinforcing the army at Harrow Bight. They had been marching through the marshlands when the Turned had been sighted. An initial skirmish four miles east of their current position had become a retreat after the enemy's masses had spiked far beyond the projections of Militarum intelligence for the region. At western Deromir, near an old command post, Nakaturo had declared a last stand.

'A stand that would have killed us all,' she concluded, her shame evident.

'Death in battle is never ignoble,' said Areios.

'Tell that to those drowning in this shitting marsh.' Realising what she'd said, she looked abashed. 'Apologies, lord.'

Beyond a minor nerve tremor in his neck vein, Areios gave no reaction. Instead he asked, 'How many did you encounter when you initially went east?'

'At least a thousand, maybe more.'

His eyes widened by the slightest fraction, before he sent out a series of sub-vocal interrogatives through his armour systems to his brothers in the vicinity and farther afield.

'Is that significant?' asked Nakaturo, sensing his interest.

'Sightings of the Oracles coincide with the proliferation of the Turned,' Areios replied. 'It could be.'

Cicero reached his side first. He had a purity seal on his left pauldron, bestowed by the Master of Sanctity for his service at the Nachmund Line. An old, long war, and like so many others, still raging. He took off his own helm so he could speak to his lieutenant on equal terms. Cicero had narrow features for a Space Marine, with fair hair and grey eyes. A scar ran down the left side of his face, a gift from the renegades he had fought at Nachmund.

'It appears you may well have been right, brother,' said Areios.

Cicero glanced briefly at the Militarum officer before returning his attention to Areios. His eyes held an unspoken question.

'We have updated intelligence on the primary objective,' Areios told him.

'An Oracle.'

'Within the vicinity.'

Helicio arrived at that moment, bolt rifle held across his body in perfect firing discipline. He kept his helm on and stood stiffly alongside the others. Areios looked his way, stony-faced, and told him to inform the brother-captain about the change of status.

After a brief pause, Helicio turned and went to his duties.

In the meantime, a Militarum adjutant had brought up a data-slate at his colonel's request. Nakaturo took it from the man, who kept staring at the Astartes and was unable to stop shaking. She dismissed him with a curt, gruff command.

'The horde we fought was overspill from the larger mass,' she began as Areios bent down to one knee to listen at her head height.

On the data-slate was a series of operational maps. As she talked, Nakaturo cycled through each one, Areios absorbing every detail and contour, every landmark. When she was finished, he stood. He had already subvocalised coordinates to Sergeant Trajus, and ordered him to converge on their current position.

'Gather up the squad,' he said to Cicero, who nodded and set about it.

That left Nakaturo and her men.

'So then...' she said, taking a long pull on her cigar and blowing out smoke as she spoke, 'Are we fighting or what?'

The skirmish at Deromir was all but over. The Turned were running and dying, the Catachans shouting and punching the air in triumph. A banner snapped in the wind, depicting an eagle in flight, its claws extended.

Areios looked down at Nakaturo, and donned his helmet.

Chapter Twelve

MINISTORUM RIGOURS

WE ARE GUARD

A PROMOTION

They had removed her helmet. It sat beside the rest of her armour on the only table in the room. The roof was low and strung with cables feeding sodium lamps that fizzed and hissed like unquiet spirits. Tremors rattled the bunker walls, sent little twists of dust from the ceiling. The Ministorum notary sitting at the table looked untroubled, the *scritching* of his autoquill uninterrupted. The spills from above put Kesh back in mind of the Tartarus tunnels and the partial collapse, the fighting in the darkness, fighting each other, the mindless killing as the taint inside the earth took hold. Good men and women. Her comrades. Some she had counted as friends. Rellion was amongst the dead, and his face floated to the surface of her mind like a corpse in a river, buoyed by putrefaction. And then Ghates, desperately drowning in mud. She shook them off, feeling the residue of the thing that had claimed the troopers of her regiment and the others sent to live in the darkness for months on end. A shiver ran down her back at the recent memory, a bead of sweat chasing it despite the chill.

Another tremor, more lazy spills of dust.

Kesh gritted her teeth, eyes front like she'd been taught by the drill-sergeants, by her officers. By Dvorgin, his chrono still heavy in her pocket. It was one of the few items she had been permitted to keep. Her rifle she had handed over last, unloading it and laying it reverently alongside her other trappings. At the final moment she noticed a piece was missing, the regimental badge that had been attached to the grip. A good-luck charm. She couldn't remember the last time she had seen it. Was it as far back as Kamidar? Too late now to find it or to worry. It seemed to have brought her little favour anyway.

Her mind turned to the ongoing conflict. The outer city had been claimed and much of the inner was currently being pacified and made safe. This she had learned from a corporal, talking too loudly to Colonel Falden, who was in overall Militarum command and was being debriefed in one of the bunker's many antechambers. After the fall, when the enemy's opposition had wilted against Imperial aggression and stubbornness, much of the command cadre had moved their staff and their persons into the established bunker complex at the edge of the combat zone. Several still feared hidden enemy insurgents or further arcane traps like that which had so decimated the Guard underminers.

Skulls, partly decomposed and etched with strange runic symbols, had been found buried in the upper soil beneath the city. Upon their discovery, the Commissariat had swept in with the utmost urgency. Priests had been summoned, hammers and flamers brandished. The dust that remained had been conveyed with paranoid care to null chests and hex-marked caskets. A sorcerous minefield, Kesh supposed. Unnatural and inexplicable, even to the sanctioned psykana cohorts.

It was why she stood here now, the notary making his marks, taking account.

They had told her she awaited the Ecclesiarch but knew not of whom they spoke, only that he would come and assess her. The Guard platoons had several priests amongst their number during the assault, their faith alas proving little use against the enemy's malign deterrents. Not only had Kesh been more effective, her rhetoric reportedly steeling and safeguarding the military body, she had also, according to the sworn testimony of more than a dozen witnesses, taken up an Astartes weapon and killed the enemy general, a Traitor Space Marine.

She had learned this from the notary himself, who had listed her deeds like a judge recounting the accused's crimes. If the stripping of her trappings, her weapons and gear was any barometer, she felt distinctly like she was under some form of arrest. All petitions to speak to her commanding officer had been denied and a pair of Adeptus Sororitas in scripture-etched armour and full-faced helms stood by the only exit to the chamber, their silver masks impassive.

Dead on her feet, her mind abuzz with what she had seen and felt in the courtyard when she had taken up that war axe, Kesh fought not to sway where she stood. So it was with a mixture of dread and relief that she met the Ecclesiarch when he finally arrived.

Tall and broad as an ox, he wore red leather armour and cream vestments. He had the frame of a pugilist, his flat nose betraying the sign of numerous badly healed breaks, and his knuckles well-callused from frequent scabbing. A scar down one side of his face looked like an old knife wound, something jagged, the cut deep. He wore it like the rest of his attire, with grim severity. A confessor: she knew the kind. They were the Ministorum's torturers and, if needed, executioners. Years of brutality lurked in this man's eyes, which were hard like pieces of sharp flint. He appraised her with those eyes, his scrutiny unsettling.

What could he see that Kesh could not? Or rather did not *want* to see?

Her heart began racing and she fought to still it.

From his belt, he produced a pair of callipers with which he proceeded to measure the distance between fingers, from elbow joint to wrist, between her eyes, forehead to nose, diameter of the skull. He did this without speech or request, breathing slowly as he conducted his work. Up close, he had the aroma of milk and rancid sweat. She doubted she smelled any better. Next came a vial, as one instrument was swapped for another. The liquid felt cold against Kesh's exposed skin. A drop for each eyelid, the backs of her hands, her forehead. At a curt, silent instruction, she stuck out her tongue and here he placed three drops. The fluid tasted vile and brackish, though she tried not to grimace. A hot iron he placed against her thumb and then her fingers, each in turn as he forced her hands into the shape of the aquila. She bore every searing touch stoically, her arms already bandaged from where the medicae had patched her up. Through each and every trial, she kept her eyes front and did not flinch, not even when he applied thumb and forefinger, pushing up her eyelid and examining her cornea with a candle flame. Lastly, he examined her burns. The skin underneath the bandage was still raw and painful, despite the low-grade morphia she had been administered. She bit her lip to stop herself crying out, her eyes watering with every agonised unbinding of her wrappings. The caged lightning of the war axe had ravaged her flesh, turning it black in places, where all feeling had numbed, the nerves seared into oblivion.

After he was finished, he wrote every finding, every measurement in a small leather notebook, his handwriting thick and ugly and daubed with a wax pencil. Throughout the examination, the notary had remained still and pensive, his autoquill poised in readiness. As the confessor turned, he straightened and raised his chin.

'Clean,' the confessor growled, but then paused when he caught sight of something amongst Kesh's belongings on the table. It glinted faintly in the low light, tucked half in her jacket pocket from where it had spilled loose.

Syreniel's coin.

Kesh stiffened, suddenly concerned. She hadn't realised how attached to it she had become, and despite carefully secreting it away, it was here in plain sight.

The confessor teased it out of the pocket with a thin metal rod, another of his tools, careful not to touch it. Kesh knew if he did, he would find it to be warm. Like a stone caressed by fire, like blood in a body.

He raised an eyebrow and uttered the only other words he would speak throughout their encounter.

'What is this?'

'Nothing,' Kesh lied, 'just a trinket, a token from an old ally.'

The gold coin bore the mark of the Talons, as clear as lightning in a cloudless sky, the Emperor's own warriors.

The confessor lingered, as if reluctant to take his eye away from the coin, as if searching for the truth of its provenance. In the end, he left without looking back and tromped off into the shadows, his forbidding warriors behind him.

If he took stock of any of this, the notary did not show it, but merely bowed his head to the departing confessor, reverent, uttering, 'Your eminence.' The autoquill scratched a fresh mark before he stamped the parchment, then rolled it into a scroll and sealed it with wax. Then he rose to his feet, briefly made the sign of the aquila and left.

Bewildered, hurting, Kesh looked around as if a stranger in a foreign land. She would have fallen then, had Munser not caught her elbow and had she not leaned on his strength. He wasn't alone but brought friends rather than guards.

'I think we should get those wounds re-dressed, soldier,' he said, his concern evident in his voice. He smiled kindly at Kesh, but his gaze hardened when it wandered in the direction of the recently departed notary.

Kesh nodded. Her fear had kept fatigue at bay, but now it rushed back like a rip tide, threatening to pull her from her feet. Again, Munser steadied her.

'Lodrin, get her gear. Mavin, the rifle...'

She made to protest, but the words failed to form on her lips and she relented as Lodrin bundled up her armour, though she kept a close eye on Mavin as the vox-operator gingerly handled her rifle.

The next few moments passed in a watery haze, sights and sounds rising and falling as Munser helped her from the room, a few glances coming her way as they passed through the expansive tunnels of the bunker complex until they reached the infirmary, where one of the Vardish medicae awaited.

The medicae applied analgesic balm to Kesh's skin, and after fresh gauze and bandage had been layered over it, the pain ebbed and Kesh felt her senses returning. Another morphia shot, laced with a stimm compound for alertness, didn't hurt either. The medicae worked swiftly and efficiently, though Kesh noticed the nervous glances, the slight tremble in her hands, the lump she quickly swallowed in her throat.

Is she afraid?

Munser looked on, his face unreadable, though seemingly rumpled into a perpetual frown.

'Here,' he said after the medicae had stepped back from her work before making a muttered excuse to leave, drifting deeper into the infirmary to treat another patient.

Kesh took the proffered flask from the lieutenant and had

a sharp pull. Instinctively, she patted her jacket for her flask, relieved to find it still there. The rupka burned her throat and warmed her belly. She could understand how Dvorgin had acquired a taste, and the thought of him never enjoying a nip again gave her a tiny pang of grief.

'I should be dead, shouldn't I?' she said, her eyes moving from Munser to Lodrin and then Mavin. The other two lowered their eyes, only Munser meeting her gaze.

He was a stout man with trimmed, neat dark hair and grey eyes. She knew little of his background beyond soldiering but had heard the limp he carried was on account of getting shot in the leg by a cultist's stub gun when he had gone back into a fire-zone to drag out one of his fallen men. In her eyes, that and the fact he had saved her from being burned alive at Gallanhold meant he could be trusted.

'Lieutenant...' she pressed.

Munser moistened his lips, looking like he was about to answer, but then said something else. 'Colonel wants a word. He sent me to fetch you.' He gestured to the two troopers standing quietly by. 'I thought you might appreciate some familiar faces.'

But Kesh looked at *his* face, at everything it was telling her. Something had happened, something she could not remember beyond the searing pain of the war axe and the light... the heat of that light like a furnace ablaze. Her skin raw and blackened but healing. She could feel it already.

I should be dead.

Just like the catacombs under Gathalamor.

And just like Kamidar. First the weapon jam and then the fire. Every time surviving when she should have not.

She thought about pushing the matter, pressing Munser to say more, but instead she settled on, 'Then you had best take me to him, lieutenant.'

They walked largely in silence, with only the odd comment

from Lodrin about the regiment or how he missed Garris despite him being a miserable bastard, in a failed effort to spur conversation. He looked at her as he spoke, but in snatches, as if wary to hold her in his eye for too long. For his part Mavin kept his eyes front, Mordian through and through. His knuckles were white, though, where they gripped his lasgun strap, and he was breathing a little fast.

Munser made some remark about rations, but the words, his low exasperations, and Lodrin's chatter, washed over her like odourless smoke, leaving no impression. Eventually, they both gave up and the last few yards went by in a tense quiet until they reached the warm glow of Falden's quarters.

Colonel Isiah Falden had thickened over the years. Still a line commander, he nonetheless saw fewer and fewer combat actions up close, having to send his captains and lieutenants to die in his stead, should the Imperium call for it.

Dying is a young man's game, he had been quoted as saying on occasion. He and Dvorgin had never got on, in all their many years of knowing each other, or so the rumour went. Kesh could understand why.

'Abel,' he began, addressing Munser by his first name, as he did all of the officers in his immediate command, 'I think I can take it from here.'

Munser sketched a firm salute, turned, and took the two troopers with him, leaving Kesh on her own.

Falden observed her through a pall of smoke from a cigarillo he had pinched between the fingers of his left hand. He was a fearsome-looking man, scarred like many officers of his long tenure. The right sleeve of his uniform jacket and shirt had been rolled up to accommodate a chrome bionic that appeared to begin at the colonel's elbow. Part of his chin had a metal plate, a matching one on the left side of his forehead. She couldn't see it, hidden as it was by the large wooden desk that looked stout enough to withstand a mortar shell, but both of his legs were also augmetic. The servos ground as he shifted in his leather-backed chair, a grimace creasing the contours of his craggy face.

'Questions, Sergeant Kesh...' Falden said, his voice grating as he leaned back, the chair creaking with the weight. 'That's all I hear.'

'Pertaining to what, sir?' asked Kesh. She would need to be careful here. After the confessor and now this, she felt wrong-footed.

'You, sergeant,' he answered flatly, pausing to blow out a large plume of smoke. 'Pertaining to you.'

'I understand I was cleared by the Ministorum, sir.' She remembered that much at least.

'Indeed you were.' He leaned over to shuffle a piece of parchment in her direction, grunting in pain as he did so.

Kesh recognised the notary's report, the wax seal now broken. 'Am I to read this, sir?'

'No,' Falden said, 'you already know what it says, or at least enough of what it says. I just wanted you to see it.' He tapped the ash tip off his cigarillo, and his gaze fixed on Kesh.

'I'm not sure I follow, sir.'

'It's to remind you of who you are, *what* you are. You're Militarum, Kesh. One of us. A soldier.'

'I see, sir.'

'Do you?' Falden sucked at his teeth, picking a small piece of cigarillo that had snagged between them. 'Do you know how many battles I've fought, Kesh? How many campaigns?'

Here, he looked to the portrait hanging on the wall, its gilt frame catching the light of the yellow overhead lumens. It depicted Arcadian Leontus rearing up on his horse, sword in hand, rendered in oil on canvas. A fine painting, as much as she could tell anyway, and by far the most opulent furnishing in an otherwise austere room.

Falden was a staunch Leonite, his devotion to the Lord Solar bordering on idolisation.

'I could not even guess, sir.'

'Nor I. But I have seen a great deal during my days of service. I have seen a lone Guardsman hold off a battalion and a half-dead cavalryman rise up despite his wounds to defend a fallen horse. I've witnessed a band of conscripts take down a war party of hardened veterans. I've seen it all, Kesh, and on each occasion there were questions. How? Why?

'It is a comfort to believe we are watched over, that He protects...' Falden made the sign of the aquila, and signalled to some imaginary place above him. 'There are those among our ranks who claim you are blessed, Magda Kesh. Are you aware of that?'

'I am now, sir,' she said, inwardly writhing, wanting to be away, out of the spotlight and back amongst the anonymous many.

'They believe the Emperor Himself moved through you when you struck down that bastard renegade. Perhaps He did, perhaps you are... I believe in what I see, not what I am told. I hope He sees you, Kesh. I really do hope He does. We are in need of His blessing. But I do not care for talk, nor the sort of reckless behaviour that comes from blind zealotry. We all have faith, Kesh. We must.' He seized the lasgun propped up against his chair and for a moment she flinched, fearing what he might do. He merely brandished it, the weapon almost totemic. 'I have faith in this,' said Falden, and then tapped a finger to his temple, the cigarillo still cinched in the same hand, 'and in this' – he tapped his chest – 'and most of all in this.

'We are Guard, Kesh. We are not Angels, nor those who command god-engines, just men and women devoted to the cause of the Imperium. I believe that a soldier with stout heart, faith in the Emperor and a good lasgun in their hands is the equal of any enemy. You proved that. Such courage, Magda...' He sucked in a stirring breath. 'To take that wall, to take the courtyard, lead those men. God-Emperor, that's strength I can use. *That* I believe in.'

'I beg your pardon, sir. I don't think I follow.'

Falden rose up from his chair, bionics whirring, the desk creaking from where he pushed himself to his feet. He proffered something for her to take: a set of gold rank pins.

'Congratulations, I am making you captain to replace Isak Rellion.'

She frowned, fear riding high within her. This was the opposite of what Kesh wanted. 'Sir?' To be under the spotlight, an officer no less... Throne, how could she avert this? 'I am honoured,' she lied, 'but is not Lieutenant Munser a more appropriate candidate?'

'Let me judge who is appropriate or not. I have made my decision. Abel is a good officer, solid, dependable. He will serve you well, and I have spoken to him already of your promotion. He can lead. You, Kesh... you *inspire*. As an Imperial commander, I use every advantage at my disposal.' He scowled then, patience waning. 'Do not make me give you an order, *captain*. You will not like where that road takes you. Service to the Throne, to the Imperium, takes whatever shape it must.'

Kesh bowed her head, contrite. Straightening again, she took the rank pins and made a firm salute.

'For the Throne, colonel.'

Falden gave a wry smile, but there was a fire in his eyes. 'Aye, for the Throne.'

As she left, Kesh tried to marshal her thoughts. Try as she might, though, she could not keep denying the truth. She should be dead, several times over, and yet she had been spared. Not luck, not fate. Providence.

As she headed back to the barracks, to meet with Munser

and look a man in the eye she had once saluted who would now have to salute her, the clerks and priests bowed their heads. One woman even genuflected, whilst another, an adjutant, made the sign of the aquila at her passing. Kesh tried not to notice, but her heart hammered and a nervous sweat crept over her skin like a clammy veil. She fought to stop from running, to quell the unease coiling in her gut.

She knew the signs; she had seen them before in Ministorum priests, in the devout: a rising of the faith. A cult.

Chapter Thirteen

THE FORLORN TEMPLE

EPATHUS, MASTER OF THE RITES

COVEN

It had once been a temple, though the name of the Imperial cult to which it had belonged was no longer known. Its statues, the saints and holy Sisters, the confessors and ecclesiarchs of Garrovire, had been cast down, its religious iconography shattered or vandalised with unholy writings. The main section still remained intact, its buttressed walls made of thick stone and its footprint as large as a vehicle yard. Glassaic windows had been smashed, their snaggletoothed apertures wound with roots and vines. Moss climbed into every crevice and a moat of thick black mud a mile long surrounded it. The Forlorn Temple, as some were calling it, might not be a fortress keep, but it harboured something of value. For the Turned surrounded it in multitude.

And they were not alone.

'I see it...' murmured Epathus from the escarpment overlooking the valley, where the temple stood like a tumour lodged in a cancerous wound. The soil and trees had changed around it, much like the influence of the Oracles had changed the people. Pink and blue growths ran rampant. Branches twisted and writhed with sinuous, insidious grace. They ensnared the skeletal remains of beasts, tightening incrementally around bone even as the warriors watched.

'How many, by your reckoning?' asked Areios, standing a pace behind his captain but otherwise at his side. A small coalition of warriors stood with them.

'At least a thousand,' Epathus replied, peering through a set of scopes, 'could be double that. I see no Oracles amongst them, but they are here.'

'Let them be known by their skulls, then,' said Drussus, earning a rebuking look from Helicio.

'They used to be human,' Epathus replied. 'Remember that, brother.'

'Whatever was human about that has long since died,' said Areios.

Epathus let out a long, weary breath. 'It is hard to argue that.' He put away the magnoculars he had been using to survey the horde, and said, 'Leave us.'

Helicio and Drussus took their leave, along with two veterans of Epathus' retinue whom Areios did not know, departing with firm Ultramarian salutes. The clenched fist to the breastplate, in the manner of the old Legion. Some traditions never died.

Areios stayed behind, knowing this was coming.

He had not been part of the Chapter for long, relatively speaking, his transfer from the rapidly outdated Unnumbered Sons an inevitability, but in that time had come to greatly respect his commanding officer and the deservedly vaunted reputation of the Ultramarines.

'Brother-captain...' he began, about to make his case when Epathus raised his gauntleted hand to stop him. Areios fell silent immediately.

'Finding this host,' said Epathus, 'was commendable.' He turned, and Areios beheld the captain in all his finery and glory. Clad in the blue of Ultramar, he wore heavy Gravis armour with a boltstorm gauntlet. A spatha hung from his hip by a gilded scabbard and a thunder hammer was mag-locked to the power plant on his back. Crafted by the master artificers of Iax, it was an exquisite weapon and had seen many wars of reconquest. As Master of the Rites, Epathus had the responsibility of overseeing and upholding the ancient rituals of the Chapter and recording its history.

A heavy burden, Areios had always thought.

'Fortune, not judgement, though, Ferren, would you not say?'

'I would, captain, aye.'

Epathus' gaze lingered, appraising. He had classic Ultramarian patrician features, his hair dark brown and cut short. 'And the hangers-on you brought with you?' He referred to the Catachans and their officer, who had tagged along with Areios and his men. 'What is their role in all of this?'

'Vengeance.'

'Vengeance is the undoing of honour.'

'I have found it useful in the past.'

'As have we all,' Epathus conceded.

'Should I not have tolerated their presence?'

'Decide your allies as you see fit, Ferren. Your old mentor did not recommend you for my command because you cannot think for yourself.'

'I understand that is not always seen as a virtue, captain.'

'Regardless, they are in your charge now. Their fate is in your hands.'

'They are brave fighters, deserving of a chance to redress the scales.'

'Many of the brave litter these lands, some of them our brothers. Many of them deserve the honour that has been denied to them. Many more will experience the same fate.'

'Are you saying I am reckless, captain?'

Epathus smiled, but his eyes narrowed at the same time as if he had not yet decided.

'To be determined...'

'By whom? The Chaplains?'

'No...' Epathus replied, taking up his gilded helm from where it was attached to his belt. It shone like the sun, and as he donned it, he looked like a glorious hero of old. He drew his spatha, pointing it down into the valley. 'By what awaits us down there.'

By the time they reached the valley basin, thick fog had arisen around the Forlorn Temple, an iridescent and multihued mist that congealed the air like oil.

At the east side of the valley, the Ultramarines arrayed for battle. Eighty in their company, with heavy tanks as was Epathus' preferred method of war. From the western facing, more than a mile away, Areios saw his brothers at a distance. He and his men had taken an oblique route around the hordes, moving slowly and stealthily through the fog, at the very fringes of the massive mud hole surrounding the old, ruined structure. They crossed broken pillars half submerged in the sucking earth, the giant severed stone head of an Ecclesiarch drowning in the filth. Even the insects here were strange, with feathers in place of membranous wings, many-legged, manta-like and crawlers both.

Nakaturo and her party took the lead. She and her troops were well experienced with the terrain, having spent most of their lives fighting on death worlds, their home of Catachan being amongst the deadliest in the known Imperium. The Militarum soldiers moved swiftly and low, staying well clear of any milling Turned that brayed and moaned in the fog. So dense was the miasma that only the barest shapes could be made out, aberrant silhouettes that hinted at mutation and biological deviance.

A raised fist from Nakaturo and they all stopped. She appeared to be moving well despite her injuries, her medicae having dosed her with a numbing cocktail of analgesics. She flicked out two fingers before splaying her hand wide, mimicking a flash, once, then again.

Intuiting Nakaturo's meaning, Areios, who led the Astartes, signalled to Cicero and the order went down the line.

Two right, outflank, he signed.

His auto-senses captured Drussus and Gravus stepping out of formation as they simultaneously ranged wide and pushed up. Ahead, the Catachans sank into a crouch, thirty troopers in light gear, armed for pace. A flamer's igniter burned on the breeze. Lasguns and a plasma carbine primed with a low-energy hum.

Areios brought up the rest of his kill team, overtaking the Catachans. The Space Marines had already drawn combat blades, the monomolecular steel like polished silver. He checked on Drussus and Gravus. Moving fast, they were almost in position.

Through fog, he discerned a pack of Turned that had wandered from the main herd. Slow and blundering, they dragged chunks of masonry and spears of iron rebar. He counted eighteen of the creatures. Edging closer to the Turned, he sent a subvocal command to his men.

Blades only, no guns.

The flanking duo signalled their readiness.

Close now, Areios could hear the Turned breathing, could make out a mutated appendage and scaled humped back, their ranks parting to reveal...

Oracle!

All thoughts of a covert attack abandoned, he went to draw his bolt rifle, but the Oracle knew... it *knew,* and Areios suddenly felt his arm pinned, his entire body locked in a psychic vice. He had been blinded to the presence of the Oracle, the figure obscured by the Turned, the thickening mist, or some other arcane art, until the last second.

Wrapped in bands of scribed parchment, the sorcerer levitated a few inches above the ground like some otherworldly mystic. The allusion ended there. His ancient armour, baroque red and black, spoke of old wars and defeated foes. A betrayer who had renounced his oaths and turned renegade. Bareheaded, he had a thin face, violet kohl around the eyes, the rest of his exposed skin inked in strange whorls and icons. An eye carved into his forehead bled feathery black light, his armoured fingers crafting in the air, tracing sigils, the arcane ciphers that harnessed the warp.

Areios felt it, a prickling of the skin, the cold emptiness in his gut...

An arc of chromatic lightning split the fog, the figures of the Turned transformed into monochrome silhouette. It hungrily carved through Gravus, whose armour ruptured at the spear tip of impact. He shuddered, back arching, limbs twisting into unnatural angles until the faceplate split and flew apart, Gravus, his mouth wrenched to its widest aperture, bleeding smoke and flame.

Conjured fire dripped from the Oracle's hand, an overly wide grin splitting his features as his attention fell on Areios.

Veins bulging in his neck, Areios fought, though his mind filled with impressions of his doom... of armour melting, flesh and bone running together, and then from the slurry of his remains unholy life bursting forth in a flurry of tentacles... He could not move. None amongst his Astartes could. He could not even swear his last breath to the Avenging Son, to the Chapter he had barely begun to know.

Drussus stiff as stone, repeatedly stabbed. Helicio hammered to his knees by a score of heavy blows, frozen limbs buckling. Cicero unmoving before being dragged under a sea of clawing bodies. The horde overwhelming, consuming.

A shot rang out, appallingly loud in the mist.

From the Guard, who were getting cut up by the Turned. The Guard, overlooked and underestimated.

And then the bullet, screaming across the space, grazing the Oracle's cheek and turning his grin into a snarl of pain.

Enough. It was enough.

It broke the Oracle's hold and, as his freedom returned, Areios leapt and slashed through the wrist to the hand that held the flame. It dissipated into ether, and the Oracle's snarl turned into a cry of agony and disbelief, the severed hand dropping to the ground like a forgotten glove. The Oracle shaped his mouth again, an incantation that never reached beyond his lips. Helicio had buried his knife in the Oracle's throat, ramming the blade with metronomic vigour like a punch dagger and then bearing the sorcerer down as he made certain of the kill.

Drussus recovered, throwing off his attackers, and Cicero emerged from beneath the piling Turned. Both used their blades to killing effect. Even the Guard went to their knives, savage and saw-toothed, the so-called 'Fang' particular to the Catachans. In seconds it was over, the last of the Turned dismembered and dispatched.

Their engagement louder than he had wanted, Areios readied for another round, but vox-emitters were blaring now, the Ultramarines having launched their attack. As predicted, the horde reacted, sweeping towards the obvious threat as one.

They had just been unlucky, the Oracle that had killed Gravus an outlier, and Areios hoped it wasn't an ill omen. Stopping to murmur a prayer for his slain brother, signal-locking the position of the body for the Apothecaries, he led them on.

The Guard had lost several of their number and barely half remained of the thirty-strong platoon they had started out with. Nakaturo was amongst them, and Areios assumed it was her shot that had broken the Oracle's concentration. He gave her a nod and saw it reciprocated. Caution no longer needed, they ran the rest of the way, a battle now raging to the east.

The western facing of the Forlorn Temple loomed, its craggy outworks wretched with pink lichen and moss. A few Turned strays remained and were cut down by Drussus without pause. It had a rear door, unguarded and unbarred, the old wood like mottled tree bark but large enough for Astartes to enter.

Hold here, he signed to Nakaturo, whose men had hustled to keep pace with the Ultramarines. Her face soured at the delay, the colonel eager to strike her blow against the enemy, but Areios wanted no more surprises. Readying his bolt rifle, he edged the door open.

Within, the temple appeared ordinary enough and, upon crossing the threshold, also empty. Helicio and Drussus took up flanking positions, left and right in turn. Cicero unclamped an auspex from his belt and fell back to the rearguard as his brothers established a perimeter. The Guard fell in behind, and like that they proceeded to explore the Forlorn Temple.

'I am getting some... uncanny readings, lieutenant,' said Cicero over the squad vox. He kept the signal wide-band and universal so the Guard could listen in.

'Elaborate,' said Areios, but he felt the strangeness also, like a stretching of the air and immediate space, a seeming fluidity he could not place or fully perceive. They had already advanced more than fifty feet beyond the threshold and still Areios saw no sign of the large eastern gate on the opposite side, just giant slabs of rubble and jutting timber frames alive with flickering foxfire. And darkness, fathomless and oceanic darkness.

'The interior...' Cicero began, choosing his words carefully before Areios interrupted him.

'It is larger than the outer dimensions.'

He turned and saw his brother nod. 'A physical impossibility.'

Areios looked ahead, his gaze searching, but the temple went on and on even as they walked.

'Spread out.'

Drussus and Helicio ranged deeper, the Guard splitting up, a fire-team tagging along with each Astartes until the two groups had completely amalgamated. Nakaturo went with Areios, a wary look in the colonel's eye that Areios shared. The faint pulse of the auspex as it tried to track their surroundings sounded like a heartbeat.

'Cicero...' he invited, needing information.

'Still no maximum extent, lieutenant. Two hundred feet and tracking...'

'And our ingress?'

'No longer in apparent range.'

He felt a tremor of unease sweep through the Catachans, several paling as they heard this news and looking to their fellows for reassurance.

'Steady your troopers, Colonel Nakaturo,' Areios growled, detecting fear pheromones in their sweat.

The iron-hard Catachan officer snapped a series of curt commands at her men, and they tightened up at once but their wariness didn't fade. They were taut like a bowstring, razor sharp and fit to break.

Areios had fought in many different theatres, across varied terrain and in extreme conditions of almost every kind. He had fought against the atrocities of the warp, and the degenerate souls who had pledged themselves to Ruin, but this was disconcerting in the extreme. Even the passage of sound felt wrong, lacking as it did an echo, a fact he had only just become cognisant of. And that is when he saw it. Or at least the impression of *it*.

'Hold!'

The urgency in Areios' voice brought the entire party to

attention. He gazed off into the darkness, trying to discern what lay beyond the periphery. Every helm reading came back as gibberish, contradictory and transitional. He removed it, the musty breath of the place immediately invading his senses.

Movement again, every breath held against the unseen danger.

There!

Sinuous, peristaltic motion... the shimmer of scale blending from magenta to azure, iridescent and ethereal. And enormous. Thicker than a gunship and many times longer.

'God-Emperor...' hissed Nakaturo. She was shaking, her troopers cowed around her, flashing nervous glances into the darkness as the gargantuan body bled away into shadow.

'Cicero,' said Areios, but the manic pulsing of the auspex did little to enhance his confidence.

'Nothing. No reading. Not one that makes any sense, anyway.'

'Then let's put our trust in something we know.'

Cicero put away the auspex and pulled out his bolt rifle.

'I have no sight of it,' added Drussus.

'Nor I, lieutenant,' said Helicio, his weapon's targeter pressed up to his eye.

Areios urged them on but he could hear it still, a distant slithering of scale against stone. For it to be *that* large and audible but not visible...

The Catachan had begun to ward themselves, making the sign of the aquila, and Areios tried not to judge them for their superstitious beliefs.

Ahead of him, a wide sweep of stone stairs came into view. A single flight but high – high enough that he could not yet see the summit. At his command, his men began to consolidate at the foot of the stairs. Each step was monolithic; the Guard would need to climb. The Ultramarines took each one at a broad stride. About halfway up, Areios made out a huge oval stage – like a gladiatorial arena, except the curved edges fell away into darkness. The stone looked old, too old for this place, as if it had been quarried in some elder age and brought here by eldritch means. Black veins ran through it like fissures, only deeper and more intrinsic. The seams shimmered, reflective.

First to gain the summit, Areios beheld the stage in its entirety. Huge channels had been carved into the stone surface, sickles and whorls that echoed the tattooed skin of the Oracles. Four of the sorcerers were here, standing rigidly upright, each upon a dais adjoined at one of the cardinal points to the oval stage.

Instinct saw him level his bolt rifle, but he quickly realised the Oracles had no awareness of him. They were chanting. Each was facing the middle of the stage where a final immense rune had been carved, the sickles and whorls all leading to this nexus.

A spike of pain entered his skull, a thin needle of agony, and Areios found he could not look at the rune directly. He felt a hand upon his shoulder, relieved to see Cicero by his side.

He knew enough of resisting warp sorcery that he and his brothers had to stop the ritual before it reached its end.

'We have to kill them now...' uttered Areios with some difficulty, his brother only able to nod in response. Drussus and Helicio had joined them, the four almost shoulder to shoulder at the edge of the stage.

Levelling his bolt rifle, Drussus fired off a shot. It boomed, impossibly loud in the expansive space, the Guard who had not yet gained the summit of the steps stopping to shield their ears.

The bolt-shell struck, but not the Oracle. Instead, it exploded harmlessly, painting some outer imperceptible barrier, smearing it in flame and shrapnel.

'Holy Throne,' hissed Nakaturo, having reached Areios and the other Astartes. She wore a mask of anguish, her trauma more than just physical. Her teeth clenched, making it difficult for her to speak. Her hands, stiffened to claws, struggled to make the sign of the aquila.

'Hold to your courage, colonel,' Areios told her, his own words an effort of will, but as he pitched himself against the unholy aura radiating from the Oracles and their ritual, he found reserves of strength.

The Astartes began to slowly advance. Drussus fired again, full burst, and saw his shots repelled again, a flash in the distance as the barrier negated his salvo. Releasing a muttered curse, he lowered the weapon, about to turn to his blade when Areios stopped him.

'Again, brother.'

Drussus turned, his lenses blank of emotion yet still holding a question.

'Again,' repeated Areios, 'and on my mark.' He raised his hand but fixed his attention on a different Oracle to the one in Drussus' sights.

'Now...'

At his lieutenant's order, Drussus fired, the muzzle flare bright and sharp in the shadows. As the shots dissipated for a third time, Areios saw the reaction echoed on the other Oracle, only muted. He pointed to show Cicero, who had taken his lieutenant's lead and was watching the third Oracle.

'I see it, brother. A displacement field of some kind.'

'Here too,' added Helicio, observing the fourth of the coven.

All the while, the Oracles chanted.

They fired as one. Blazing star fire tore up the shadows, but as the roar faded the Oracles remained unscathed, smoke and flame already drifting away.

'Again...' ordered Areios, and the Ultramarines advanced to close range and fired.

Again, the Oracles were unscathed. Areios slammed a fresh magazine in his weapon. Drussus and Cicero did the same.

'Again...'

And again, the Oracles were unharmed.

Near point-blank, they fired once again. The Oracles remained unharmed.

Drussus swore, loud enough for all to hear. 'It explains why they are unguarded,' he grunted over the vox; by now the squad was displaced across the length and breadth of the stage.

'Do not be so sure,' said Areios.

Skirting the shadows at the edge of the stage, a colossal serpentine body slithered past, though nothing registered on Areios' sensors. Just static, and jerking data returns. It slid by, massive, as inexorable as an avalanche, a tide of iridescent scale seemingly without end until at last the heads reared into sight.

Abominable, the heads were feathered horrors, each with a single avian eye. A half-human screech issued from the beaked mouths, rattling teeth and setting every nerve on edge, a cry from a distant realm of unreality. And though its eyes followed the Astartes as it plied a path through the darkness, it did not attack.

The urge to engage the monstrous creature burned strong in Areios but he knew it to be futile. Cicero whispered a litany over the vox.

'There is no victory to be had against that abomination,' said Areios.

It had pulled away again, the creature's interest in lesser beings exceeded, waiting for the breach in the skin of reality that would bring it forth fully into the material realm.

'Then what is our course?' asked Cicero.

Areios regarded one of the Oracles, and though the face barely moved beyond the need to murmur its incantation, he thought he caught a ghost of spiteful amusement in its amber eyes.

'Our course is unchanged. We must interrupt the ritual, and prevent the birthing of this horror.'

'Then by what means?' asked Helicio.

'By *will*, brother,' said Areios, 'ours against theirs. And by this...' He drew his sword, a silver shimmer against the night. It was a fine weapon, gifted to him by the Chapter artisans upon his induction to the Ultramarines. 'Old weapons prevail where the modern are found wanting.' He swung the sword around in a well-practised arc, silver blurring the air. 'If blunt impact trauma from our bolt weapons is insufficient then let us try a more direct approach. Each of us to an Oracle, our strike as one strike.'

Helicio drew his short sword. 'A gladius is hardly the equal of a master-crafted blade, lieutenant.'

'Then, brother,' said Areios with a rueful smile, 'you must strike that much harder. We need only kill one to halt the ritual.'

'Only one of them disabled five of us and ended Gravus,' Helicio reminded him.

'If we die to deny this horror a foothold in our reality then it will be worth the death. A good death is no dishonour, Helicio.'

The Astartes bowed his head in deference to his lieutenant.

Drussus rapped the hilt of his sword against his plastron, breaking the brief silence, two quick and sonorous blows. Cicero and Helicio did the same. Each salute rang out across the stage like a call to arms.

Areios lit his blade, and it crackled with unfettered power. 'Let us see it done.'

The Astartes held swords at the ready. Although the Oracles showed no outward sign of awareness, Areios saw the slightest tightening of the eyes as he brandished his blade, the thinly veiled sadism and malice.

I see you, my foe...

He cast a glance into the blackness surrounding the stage, or the altar he now knew it to be, like a sailor looking out across the sky for an approaching storm, and caught a glimpse of shimmering scales. He looked to the Guard. They remained at the threshold, fear in their eyes but determination also. Nakaturo gave a curt nod.

Be ready, he willed, suspecting they would need every ally, every hand.

Taking his sword in a two-handed grip, Areios moved into an inside stance preparing to thrust with the blade. The nearest Oracle glared on, seemingly unconcerned.

Guilliman, guide my sword...

He thrust hard, putting all of his considerable strength into the blow. It met resistance immediately like an arrow against the wind or a ship fighting the tide, the sword tip flaring hot as rival forces met. Pain coursed through the hilt and up his arm, his shoulder burning with effort.

Every sinew was straining, every servo in his armour screaming. His brothers' shouts merged with his own in a cacophony of defiance. Legs braced, his stance wide, he pushed, one hand clenched around the hilt, the blade aglow as if fresh forged and the metal unquenched. Areios pushed, his back and shoulders straining, muscles bunching under mesh and metal. And in that agony, he drew deep of his spirit, of his will...

And at last, it began to *yield.*

Areios roared, his body screaming with effort, and the blade pierced the arcane and then the material, armour and flesh parting.

The Oracle gasped, eyes wide as the sword went through his chest and the blade's disruption field seared through his organs. Areios did not stop until he had buried it up to the hilt, lifting the sorcerer off the ground, grimacing into the Oracle's death agonies, a bellow of uncaged fury spewing from his lips.

A tremor then... a *ripple* of air and spatial dimension as the uncanny veil upon this place fell away like gossamer on the wind, the intangible web of its creation unmaking itself. Darkness shed, no longer fathomless but rather *fathomable,* a gloom not an endless swathe. Low shadow and ruins, the altar a crumbling dais, riddled with eldritch growths now in retreat, though the black veins remained. A half-collapsed set of steps stood where once a mighty sweeping staircase had been, Nakaturo and her men crowded around it, dumbfounded and afraid.

His brothers were near enough to touch, the stage not so grand or expansive as they had believed.

Two Oracles now lay dead. Helicio was on his knees, staring into the dark as if transfixed by something only he could see, the body of his enemy beside him. Drussus had hands around the neck of a third, choking it to death. Cicero had lost part of his armour, forearm and gauntlet fire-blackened and cracked, the shattered hilt of his gladius a smoking ruin nearby. The surviving sorcerer staggered, disorientated, but had begun to weave the fire of uncreation that had slain Gravus.

A shot rang out. Then another. A fusillade of las-fire struck the last Oracle with unerring precision, the sheer weight of fire enough to push him back and sever the thread of the warp on which he drew.

It was all Areios needed. He leapt, one swing, and the Oracle's head fell separate from his body.

And in the still-haunted shadows that remained, there was an echo like a fell voice on the air. Inhuman, monstrous.

Laughing.

At the far end of the Forlorn Temple a door blasted in, the large eastern gate they should have been able to see at the beginning. Epathus led the charge. He looked bloodied, but not with his own vitae. His shining honour guard stood around him, shields and swords to the fore. A troop of Astartes in cobalt came in their wake, resplendent, triumphant.

Areios could not understand why they appeared so gilded to him, as if from some glorious dream, but almost thin or faded as though he was seeing them through misted glass.

He heard his brothers, their sudden shouts of alarm.

His side felt cold, then came a burning sensation and Areios looked down at the knife piercing his armour plate. The sigils on the knife's skull-crested hilt hurt his eyes and he realised he must have removed his helmet at some point, because he saw it lying at his feet.

Cicero appeared at his side, and then Drussus, holding him as his legs collapsed. The last sight he remembered was Captain Epathus running towards him, shouting out his name.

Chapter Fourteen

LEADS

THE KIN

NAME YOUR PRICE

Greyfax had neglected to provide a name and she had, as of yet, not provided one herself, so Rostov came to think of her as *the Silent*. He felt her presence behind him as a queasiness in his gut, a symptom of her nature. Not unexpected, for he had fought beside the Sisterhood before, but still unpleasant. He focused on the wall. On the investigation. Here, across transcribed scraps of sightings, witness testimonies, vid-captures of sigils and more besides, was every piece of evidence he had gathered surrounding the identity and possible whereabouts of the Hand.

Missives from several astropathic stations had narrowed the search to a sector, which was hardly narrow at all, but the transcribed visions from the indentured psykers had provided an overabundance of often contradictory information. Variously, the blind seers had spoken of a cemetery of broken swords and an axe cutting through a wall of shields; of a great black beast straining at its chains and a horn-headed monster anointed with blood. Or the golden king surrounded on all sides and a fallen gate that released a deluge. Gibberish without accurate translation, and this was proving difficult. All of it made for grim reading, and the transliterators tasked with interpreting these ravings seemed unable to agree or even suggest commonalities.

The warp was in turmoil and for those who dreamed of its tides there was only nightmare and horror. It tended to produce unreliable narrators. Many of the stations Rostov had petitioned had not replied or never would, and their silence was recorded as diligently as any semi-coherent message, for the absence of data was just as telling as its presence.

A sketch, his own, described the sorcerer. And this much, at least, Rostov did know about his enemy. Tenebrus was the name he had given. A shadow, appropriately enough; long and wraith-like with pale skin and an overlarge mouth. A creature of Chaos, no doubt, but not the man Rostov had seen during his vision when he had questioned the Dark Apostle at Machorta Sound.

As an interrogator, Rostov had learned early on in his career never to trust the word of the enemy. And yet the sorcerer's claim that he was the Hand did not ring false. And if it were, why make the claim at all? What did he have to gain from Rostov learning such knowledge, or was it simply this – to obfuscate and bewilder?

Another mystery.

Perturbing too was the presence of a cult he had unearthed on Srinagar. A worrying and perplexing development. How this connected to the sorcerer and the Archenemy's plan – or whether there was any connection at all – he did not know, but all the while he remained in the dark these things could twist and reshape, hold greater perils than he even now feared.

Contradiction invited doubt and Rostov craved certainty. He needed a path but could see no pattern, no obvious thread to pull next. In the light shining upon the wall, the inquisitor saw only further darkness.

The rest of his study was in actual shadow, the other furnishings lost to it and pushed aside in his frustration. A porcelain statue lay smashed, quill ink spilled on the floor in a shiny slick. He padded in it barefoot, leaving perfect prints in greasy black wherever he stepped.

Although expansive and taking up the entirety of the wall, his findings had yielded few firm leads. He had sent out requests across the segmentum and beyond to every contact, pressed every underworld figure he knew, and yet...

He could ill afford this detour. He needed to press on to the fleet and a rendezvous with an ally who might be able to help him where Greyfax could not. But if Yamir had found a lead, a genuine lead... well, that might result in the troops he needed to prosecute this mission. *If*, always if. There was much to consider.

Rostov winced and shut his eyes against the light, pinching the bridge of his nose. Discomfort was clouding his cognition. He reflected on how his old master, Jeren Dyre, used to go about his work, on everything the inquisitor lord had taught him. Dyre had been meticulous. No avenue left unexplored, no leads not chased down. He was a man who, once he had a scent of blood, did not relent. It had killed him in the end.

'I am found wanting in your shadow...' he murmured and heard the slightest movement from his only companion in the room. His eyes snapped open, brow furrowed in anger. 'Is that you, oh ghost? Oh, *Silent*...' he hissed. 'If you have a revelation then utter it, for I am running out of time for riddles and games. Our enemy has his plans in motion and we are behind the trail. Woefully so.' He cursed. 'I need men and materiel, I need armies to seek and find. Yet all I am afforded is you. So if you have insight,' he said, growing ever more perturbed as he turned, shouting, 'then please share it!'

But the Silent had gone, leaving Rostov alone with his impotent anger. He had always prided himself on the mastery of his humours. His ordinarily calm disposition was a tool in his arsenal, and a potent one.

Never let them see you bleed or sweat, Leonid.

Wise words, Rostov reflected. A pity he was struggling to put them into practice.

Feeling foolish, he was about to return to the wall when he noticed something left on the floor. It was a simple regimental badge made of iron. *Mordian 84th.* He stooped and retrieved it, examining the plain machined piece in his hand. He could only assume that the Silent had dropped it or left it. He doubted any of her kind did anything that was not deliberate. Rostov almost called out after her, but the pain had come back. Worse than before. Worse every day, now. Sharp needles in his hand, the scar-tissue itch on his back.

A malaise of the spirit, not just the body.

He took one last look at the wall, desperate for his contact to yield something of import, something he could use.

Yamir has never let me down before.

Then he pocketed the badge and turned out the lights.

The infirmary wasn't far. His ship, the *Omnes Videntes,* was of a modest size. It had a shuttle named the *Res Fugit* and was usually cold and dark, as Rostov preferred it. Decently armed for a fight but no match for the great battle cruisers of the Navy. It had a small crew, lean and just enough to maintain operational efficiency. A complement of storm troopers provided by Greyfax added some muscle. Enough for most encounters, but far short of his needs.

As he reached the infirmary he found Hayden Lacrante already there. The trooper had his back to him, rummaging around in the drawers of med-supplies. He started, almost crashing into the gurney behind him, when Rostov coughed to alert him to his presence.

'Needed some sickness meds,' the soldier explained, and looked paler than usual. 'Warp transit, especially coming out of it,' he added. 'Turns my stomach, makes me restless.'

'I know the feeling,' Rostov sympathised.

Lacrante offered a handful of morphia tabs. 'Something for the pain, I take it?'

He had a soldier's bearing with a straight back and Militarum haircut. Rostov had brought him into his employ on Fomor III, where Lacrante had been a lieutenant serving as part of the 47th Illusiti Pioneers. Impressed with his character and his courage, Rostov had wasted no time recruiting him. He had seen something in the man, a purpose he could not yet foresee but was cognisant of enough to know Lacrante would be important. For now, he was Rostov's acolyte and a well-trained, capable one. Not as irascible as Antoniato. And he had faced some of the true perils of the universe and remained stalwart. Those were traits an inquisitor needed in his allies.

'You know me well,' Rostov said, and took the morphia tabs.

'It hasn't improved?'

'A little,' he lied, and swallowed one of the tabs, grimacing at the chalky taste. 'But we have greater concerns.'

'Because of what you found in the archive on Terra? Antoniato said you looked, if you'll forgive me, lord, *shaken*. I do not believe I have ever seen you like that. That in itself, I would say, is cause for concern.'

'I am shaken, I do not mind confessing it. Strength comes from one's character – it is born within, not merely an outward projection. I had hoped for... more from Greyfax, but she was unable to provide it. What she did afford, our silent guest, is not enough, Lacrante. Not nearly enough.'

'I still have hope,' said the trooper, and Rostov felt a profound sense of gratitude for that, for the simple and honest belief of a soldier. 'The presence of one of the Emperor's own cadre of warriors suggests some providence, does it not?'

'Perhaps...' said Rostov, unconvinced. 'Never have the stakes been higher than since the outset of the crusade. I asked for an army and received a handful of fighters. Highly capable fighters, but even the most gifted warrior falls if he or she must fight alone.' He ran a hand through his dishevelled hair, acutely aware of the stigmatic marks in the skin of his hand. Lacrante did an admirable job of trying not to notice, but Rostov saw the shock in his expression, guarded as it was. 'No,' he went on, 'we must look to ourselves for this. I have a few favours I can call upon. An old friend who has some standing in the crusade hierarchy may yet be our salvation. And then there's this...' Rostov showed Lacrante the regimental badge. It glinted dully as the light touched the metal.

Lacrante frowned. 'What is that? I mean, I can see it's a regiment badge but what is it doing here?'

'I don't know. Isn't that intriguing? I think our guest left it for me, though she has not been forthcoming as to why or to what it pertains.'

'Have you asked her?'

'I plan to, though I'm not sure she would know either. I do wonder about her, Lacrante, about why she has crossed our path. About her purpose.'

'Well, I only know that the troopers and the crew give her a wide berth. Something about her, it's... off-putting. And it's as if I can only ever half see her, like a reflection in a pane of glass but at the edge of my sight.'

'She is a pariah, both in the literal and metaphysical sense. Put simply, she has no soul. Such an absence provokes a reaction in those that do, that repulsion you have felt. It is also anathema to other creatures, those who also have no souls, the Neverborn that lurk beyond the veil. I hate her presence as much as you, Lacrante, I cannot help it, but she could prove a vital ally in the days to come. And maybe some of that providence you spoke of.'

'Ever am I reminded of how little I know.'

'You would do well to keep it that way.' Rostov gave a mirthless chuckle, his face turning sad for a moment. 'But, alas, I do not think that will be your fate.' He brandished the other tab in a clenched fist, his mood brightening but still weary. 'My thanks for this,' said Rostov as he turned his back.

'Do you think there is any truth to it?' asked Lacrante, making Rostov pause.

'Truth to what?'

'To His... return, resurgence? It is hard to put into words. The cultists on Srinagar. They believed in the Emperor's apotheosis, they had faith in a miracle rebirth. I cannot decide if that comforts or terrifies me.'

'It should do both,' Rostov replied, and walked away.

Antoniato waited for them on the bridge of the *Omnes Videntes*. All stations were slowly returning to normal, the Inquisitorial cruiser having returned to the materium, much to the relief of all. Residue lingered here and there, now fading, and steam drifted off several of the consoles. A strange scent of sulphur threaded the air. Antoniato sniffed at it, scowled. The Guard veteran looked none the worse for wear, hardy as he was and ready for immediate deployment. His plasma rifle hung off a strap around his body and he wore carapace armour. He hadn't changed since Terra, his fatigues still roughed with the grime of the Throneworld.

Besides the crew quietly busying themselves at consoles in the penumbral darkness of the bridge, one other figure stood out. Unlike the rest, Cheelche was not human. She had four arms and a stout, barrel-shaped body with flecked brownish skin. Her head was almost piscine, her mouth lipless and her nose flat. She belonged to a species called the chikanti, a xenos of more or less unknown origin, though not one currently at war with the Imperium.

She gave Rostov a sour look as he entered the bridge to take up position in his command throne. He wore his armour now, a suit of silver close-fitting carapace, and had a sheathed power sword and a pistol holstered at his left hip. Lacrante followed behind, wearing his Militarum uniform and flak coat with a lasgun, sword and laspistol. The Silent came in a few paces after him. She towered over the others, a silver-armoured statue with a greatsword strapped to her back and a high gorget covering her mouth. Stern, kohl-ringed eyes regarded the others as she took up a position to the side, a few feet away from the group.

'I'll just say out loud what we're all thinking?' said Cheelche, her long fingers hooked into the bandoliers criss-crossed over her stocky body. '*She* bothers me. Even allowing for the fact that any time she looks at me, I want to puke, I do not trust her.'

'I don't need you to trust her, Cheelche,' said Rostov patiently, 'I need only that you trust me.' He glanced in the Silent's direction but only really perceived a sort of smudged haze, as if she was at the very limit of his peripheral vision.

Cheelche was not placated. 'It may have escaped everyone's notice but I am not like the rest of you.' She waggled her many arms to emphasise her point. 'And her kind are not known for their tolerance.'

'Easy, Cheelche,' murmured Antoniato, who had a way of being able to calm the xenos that the others lacked.

Though, Rostov had no time for her antics on this occasion.

'And yet you will still exercise tolerance,' he informed her more firmly.

At this the xenos folded her arms, unimpressed. 'Well, if I

wake up with a bloody great sword in my back, I'll know who to blame.'

He ignored her further griping. The shutters were rising at the fore of the bridge now the *Omnes Videntes* had left the warp, and the great expanse of the void beckoned. And there, amid the blackness and the blanket of stars, was an ochre moon. Riddled with fortified shafts and boreholes, so massive they were visible even from a distance, the moon was also clad with machineries. A vast mine-head by any other description. The current holdings of the Kin.

'What do we know about these creatures?' asked Antoniato, cutting through Cheelche's tantrum and flashing an urging glance at the chikanti, who responded with an expletive gesture with two of her hands. Perhaps he was losing his touch.

'They are called the Kin. Abhuman class,' Rostov explained, 'prospectors and void-miners, and until recently largely confined to the galactic core. I have never dealt with them before, but I am given to understand they are proud and may not take well to any disrespect, intended or not.' He looked to Cheelche. 'So you will need to remain silent throughout whatever exchange Yamir has arranged for us.'

'Oh, well that can eat a huge plate of my shit,' she said with a scowl.

'Regardless, Cheelche, it is my will. We make landfall, alone,' he said to the group. 'The *four* of us.'

The creak of her gauntlets had everyone turn to the Silent, who loomed like a spectre in the shadows at the edge of the bridge.

'You will remain here, Silent. I do not know what effect your presence will have on the Kin's mood and I cannot risk this on a moment of botched diplomacy.'

Cheelche muttered, 'Suppose I should be grateful that at least I make the surface over the bloody mute witch-killer.' She caught a cold glare from the Silent and shut her mouth at once.

'But they are allies?' asked Lacrante.

'I damn well hope so,' offered Antoniato, 'or we four will not be alive long to lament that they are not.'

'Allies, yes. I believe so,' Rostov confirmed. 'But have no doubt, we must tread carefully here. Yamir has told us much about our hosts, but that does not mean we should know what to expect. Once at their encampment, we have to be prepared for anything.'

Rostov crouched in the dust, and frowned at the empty helm. It was domed, with an inbuilt visor, and the clasps that presumably attached it to the larger suit had been forcibly broken. It had the wrong proportions to be worn by someone human. Light orange powder smeared the edges of his boots from the short walk from the dropsite. As he took in the destruction at the encampment, he was beginning to wish he had asked the transports to linger.

'Could have been a mining accident, a gas explosion, something volatile they extracted?' suggested Lacrante. He was nosing through a shattered hauler, its material load cast across the ground, the vehicle itself perched precariously on its side with one of its wheels torn off to the axle. There were burn marks on the chassis and large punctures in the metal.

'Looks to me like it was used as a barricade,' offered Cheelche. 'Assuming,' she said pointedly to Rostov, 'that I have permission to speak and voice an opinion.'

'Don't be facetious, Cheelche,' answered Rostov curtly, then added, 'What else do you see?'

The chikanti pointed to a patch of ground a few feet away. 'Scuff marks over there,' she said, her other three arms holding her long-las fusil in a ready position. 'Lots of them. Booted feet shuffling. Could be a group turning to look in several directions. The kind of thing you do if you're surrounded.'

Rostov rose to his feet. 'Unlikely to be an accident then...'

Antoniato called out. He had ranged ahead of the others, scouting for trouble. His face looked grim as he waved them over. A body lay at his feet, half hidden by a piece of wreckage. The burly veteran pulled it aside a few inches so Rostov could see.

It was a human in a grubby ex-Militarum uniform.

He met Antoniato's gaze, who said, 'There are more this way.'

The veteran led and they followed, tracking through the carnage. Whatever initial skirmish had started this fight, it had moved deeper into the mining works. Here, both the dead Kin and their attackers were strewn over carts or piled up in excavation pits.

Lacrante eased over the body of one of the dead with his boot, revealing a pale and emaciated human in scraps of clothes and a rudimentary environment suit. She had an eight-pointed star carved into her face, the wound long healed but leaving a vicious scar. Her expression was almost euphoric.

'Cultists,' he uttered unnecessarily. The bile in his voice was evident.

Cheelche hawked and spat. She might be xenos, but she despised the worshippers of the Dark Gods as much as her Imperial comrades.

This was but the first of many cultists, though several of the dead zealots were less than human and had horns or bestial mutations. Many looked more beast than human, in fact.

Antoniato quickly made the sign of the aquila. 'We should not linger,' he said, and eyed the way ahead and behind them.

'The fight went that way,' said Lacrante, gesturing towards further signs of disturbance.

Rostov nodded, grateful at least that Yamir had not been amongst the fallen.

'We follow.'

* * *

They found Yamir slumped against a metal crane, his armoured tunic torn open and a hole in his chest. He lived. But barely. As soon as his watery gaze found the inquisitor, the rogue trader tried to speak.

Rostov sank down to his haunches so he could meet Yamir's eyeline. 'Easy, old friend,' he murmured, and gently laid a hand on the dying man's shoulder. Yamir's mouth gaped open and shut, his words coming in a near-silent rasp.

Lacrante stepped forward. 'My lord...' He brought forth a medi-kit, but Rostov shook his head. Instead, the inquisitor leaned in to hear his friend's final words.

Yamir's breath smelled of old coins as he spoke. 'They still have him... the captive. He has the Hand's mark. I think... I think he's important. His followers... they came back. Many... a great many. Overwhelmed... us.' He gripped Rostov's lapel, tugging it hard and forcing the inquisitor to look him in the eye. A single tear rolled down his cheek. 'I don't want to die...'

Rostov gently cupped the side of his face and held Yamir's hand until his grip loosened and his arm fell by his side and the light in his eyes turned grey. Rostov made the sign of the aquila and stood. He activated the vox-bead in his ear that linked him to the *Omnes Videntes* in orbit above the moon.

'Captain Nirdrangar, bring your entire platoon to the surface immediately. Threat imminent.'

A muffled affirmative came from the other end of the feed before Rostov severed the connection. His face was grim. Pained. The sharp prickle of needles in his hand had returned, the itch like scar tissue, irritating. He felt vengeful and knew it showed in his demeanour.

'I had known Yamir for over ten years. He was an operative, on and off, throughout that time,' he said, pulling out his pistol and checking the ammo gauge.

Antoniato did likewise, as did Lacrante.

'I guess this means diplomacy is out...' muttered Cheelche, seeing to her own weapon as she clipped grenades to a bandolier with her spare hands. 'Should have stayed on the bloody ship.'

The storm troopers landed amidst swirling dust, clad in red and black with their faces masked behind expressionless rebreathers and goggles. Each trooper held a hellgun across their chest and wore a grenade belt. They disembarked smoothly from three separate gunships, taking up ready positions around the inquisitor and his operatives.

Captain Nirdrangar stepped ahead of the group to approach Rostov directly. The faint haze of a green targeting array was just visible in the dark gloss of his lenses.

'Enemy disposition unknown,' Rostov told him, 'resistance expected to be high. Act with extreme prejudice.'

Nirdrangar nodded. He was a bear of man, both tall and broad, especially when bulked out by his armour. He had a powerblade mag-locked to his back, and maintained trigger discipline on his hellgun.

His voice was a machine-filtered rasp through his rebreather. 'Extraction?'

'One,' said Rostov, donning his helm and seeing a raft of data flare into life. 'Priority target. I will mark upon contact. We will be encountering potential friendlies. Exercise cautious fire discipline. I have no desire to make a bad situation worse, captain.'

Another nod. 'Understood.'

The storm troopers moved out, filtering into six squads of ten, going low and fast. They tracked the outward signs of the battle across the desolate grey moon plain, following the dead, spent shell casings, the harsh, scorched rock after an explosion. Cordite and fyceline hung in the air like a shroud, the taste ashen on the tongue, even through Rostov's rebreather.

The trail quickly led them to the edge of a massive crater, more evidence of fighting here spilling down into the expansive, unknown darkness below. Gunfire rattled distantly, coming from that benighted place, and flashes of energy fire. Heathen voices growled on the air.

Nirdrangar paused at the crater edge, a black maw beckoning in front of him. Night-vision scopes probed the shadowy depths, a steep decline leading to the bottom.

'Onward,' Rostov urged, and drew his sword. The blade lit in the half-dark shadow of the cavern mouth, a crackling beacon.

He plunged after the storm troopers, descending with them, the sounds of conflict ever closer. Trusting to their Militarum training, Antoniato took his hefty plasma rifle down one flank, while Lacrante and his lasgun took the other. Both men looked focused, having switched to a combat footing. Only Cheelche appeared unchanged, grumbling every step, wishing she was anywhere but here.

The slope of the crater led to a vast underground chamber, one of several hollowed out of the moon, judging by what Rostov had seen from orbit. A manufactured borehole of staggering scale. The chamber had once been an immense mine-head, the equal of most Militarum muster fields or a capital ship's embarkation deck. It had been stripped of all equipment, and every mineral seam ruthlessly drained dry with only scant evidence of it left behind. The sheer industry, the enterprise hinted at was staggering. The Kin had cut this crater themselves, and here at its nadir, Rostov caught his first sight of them.

A tight knot of warriors fought shoulder to shoulder, surrounding their chieftain, or kâhl – for Rostov was not entirely ignorant of their culture, despite never having made their acquaintance. She wore no helm, her scarred visage enough of a snarling mask. Strands of red hair flailed like tongues of fire. Between the hulking warband of her retinue, more wall than warriors, she fired off shots from some kind of volkite weapon. In her other hand, gripped in the thickly armoured fingers of a mass gauntlet, was a ragged-looking cultist officer.

The one who bore the mark, and the last tangible lead Rostov had to the Hand.

He marked the ragged prisoner as a priority target, a blazing red terminus icon leaving no doubt as to the man's status.

Under Nirdrangar's command, the storm troopers converged, using scraps of cover to mask their immediate approach. The two ex-Guardsmen followed their lead, each naturally falling in with one of the squads and adopting their rhythm and assault posture. Rostov stayed independent but in close proximity to Nirdrangar. Via his retinal lens output, which had overlaid a tactical schematic displaying the relative positions of his troops, he noticed that the chikanti hung back. Doubtless, she was trying to find some vantage from which to best deploy her long-las.

'Guard my back, Cheelche...' ordered Rostov.

'It's not your back I'm worried about.'

She would see it done. He trusted the xenos more than most humans he had met.

Greyfax's troops were worthy of their billing, effortlessly breaking into kill teams as they homed in on the fighting. Up close, it was frenetic.

The Kin had arranged their forces in a series of concentric circles, using overlapping fields of fire to whittle their enemy's ranks. They fought with determination and had dragged injured and even dead allies behind their serried firing ranks. Behind this first line stood a second, using the cover of earthworks and barricades that must have been improvised but looked as solid as any Militarum redoubt. They shot over their shoulders or by the ears of their fellows, displaying a nerve and precision that impressed the inquisitor. A third cohort wore little to no armour and plunged through the well-disciplined ranks before them wielding energised hammers and axes, howling oaths as they hacked at any enemy daring to probe the Kin's battle lines. At the heart of the ring, its indomitable nucleus, were the kâhl and her sworn warriors.

Even from a distance, Rostov recognised their discipline and dauntless courage. He had seen few Astartes who could boast of greater.

But the Kin were vastly outnumbered. The enemy host surrounded them, a horde of robed and flak-armoured cultists, abhuman beastmen, scavenger creatures like emaciated dogs but with overlarge jaws, and other even more hideous monstrosities. Amid the unwashed mass, Rostov caught sight of more than one ogryn, the hulking beasts carrying the taint of mutation in their crustacean claws or spiked, scaly hides. Combat servitors wielding saw blades and hammers, their grey flesh wretched with sores, roamed alongside gene-bulked zealots hefting piston-axes. Several of the cultists wore Guard uniforms from old and disbanded regiments, held together with scraps of armour and belts, their faces crudely etched with runes. A banner hung raggedly from a pole like skin from a flayed corpse, and an officer wearing a jacket festooned with tarnished medals shouted guttural orders. They had come for their leader, the one clutched in the kâhl's fist.

Ostensibly, the Kin adopted a defensive strategy to repel these heretics and grotesques. Rostov saw it for what it was. A last stand.

So he stood and shouted out, 'Ave Imperator!'

A few of the outliers at the edge of the host – the ones who had lingered to feed on the dead, their own and those of the Kin who they had not been able to drag away – turned at the sound. They appeared drunk, gorged on their feast, and so they scarcely reacted when Nirdrangar and his men scythed them down.

The first few they killed up close, using bayonets and blades. Rostov impaled one with his sword, flash cooking its innards before moving on to the next. More than a hundred died in those initial bloody seconds. These were the dregs, the lesser scum subservient to the more dominant. Short-range lasguns characterised the engagement that followed, hellguns rippling the air with sudden furnace heat. A storm trooper went down, shot through the neck with a harpoon. Two more fell swiftly afterwards to a rash of scatter shot and a lobbed grenade. Rock and dust flew upwards in a yawning plume.

The chatter of Lacrante's lasgun whipped across the Imperial flank, the ex-Guardsman laying down a curtain of fire that had the cultists scattering for cover. It gave Nirdrangar's men an opening to exploit, and they took it hungrily, advancing with focused aggression. Antoniato snapped off shots with his plasma rifle, half-melting a servitor and coring a rapidly cauterised hole through a zealot.

An ogryn, hunched over with mutation, loomed out of the shadows and came at Rostov. It swung a crude spiked orb on a chain, and the inquisitor had to dart aside to avoid being crushed. He ducked a second swing, the chain cutting through the air above his head with a shriek. A slash of his blade opened up the ogryn's belly, cleaving through plate and mesh and leather. Its guts sluiced outwards in a gory flood and as it stared dumbly at its innards, Rostov stabbed it through the eye.

Breathing hard, heady with triumph, he almost missed the second brute coming for him with a hammer. He turned, too late, hoping his armour's inbuilt refractor field would take the blow, when the ogryn's head snapped back, its skull cored through. It lumbered for a few seconds as the rest of its body caught up to the fact that it was dead, and finally fell face down.

Cheelche's voice came through his vox-bead. *'Told you so...'*

Rostov turned, giving a nod to the chikanti, who had found

a rocky perch from which to snipe the cultists, and went back to the fray.

The horde was thinning but still massive. Only now his forces had fully engaged did Rostov appreciate just how many cultists had been lurking in the shadows, as if the dark had been hiding them and only now spewed them forth. Nirdrangar and his storm troopers were holding their own but taking casualties, down to eighty per cent of their original number.

The Kin maintained their rate of fire, seemingly unmoved by the reinforcements. Then, through the firestorm, Rostov caught sight of the kâhl. He was closer now, having been swept up in the attack which had just begun to stall. Her face was a mask of barely restrained anger as she bellowed out a war cry.

From a wide and craggy overhang that almost blended into the rock face, several feet above the ground, a cloaked and hooded figure appeared. At first it was swathed in shadows, and then a crackling light kindled in its eyes, revealing a bearded, male face weathered with age and wisdom. He held a staff in one hand and as he raised it aloft the azure light of his eyes, which grew more vibrant with every second, seemed to pass to the rune-etched shaft...

And broke loose.

The lightning arc cascaded down on the cultists in jagged tongues of storm fire, searing flesh from bone. A clutch of beastmen howled in primal terror as an ogryn was blasted apart, their fear only short-lived as the lightning crackled through them a few moments later. Dozens were slain in what was but a precursor to a slaughter.

Releasing a shout, the cloaked and hooded figure urged his kinfolk into battle. They came from the shadows of the same overhang, a band of Kin wearing exo-frame armour and toting cannons and man-portable ordnance. At his command, they unleashed their weapons. Energy fire and solid shot hailed down on the cultist horde in a thunderous bombardment.

Still in the thick of the fighting, Rostov wondered if the Kin had been as beleaguered as they had first appeared. The warriors on the ground suddenly adapted to the appearance of the heavier-armed Kin, their defensive rings breaking into two firing lines that punched forward and back, more spear than shield. They swept into the cultists, whose ranks were already broken by the relentless barrage hammering them from on high, and shattered them utterly.

By the end, Rostov had sheathed his sword and the storm troopers were reduced to onlookers as the Kin destroyed the heretics with ruthless efficiency. Lacrante and Antoniato had gathered by their master's side.

'You did say these were our allies...' ventured the veteran as the last of the cultists were being put to the sword. Or in this case, the fist, the final blow delivered by the kâhl herself.

She stomped towards the inquisitor, her brows knotted like a thunderhead, face blood-flecked. None of it was her own. Her chosen warriors followed a step behind her, one of their number more imposing and seemingly more grizzled than the rest.

'Hold here, Utri,' she growled, her voice like grit.

The warrior, Utri, halted at once, his armoured feet planted like menhirs. He glowered at Rostov and his comrades, seemingly unconcerned by the proliferation of readied hellguns from the storm troopers.

Why should he be? thought Rostov. *Look at the army at his back.* At once he saw the potential for a highly valuable alliance, but far from appearing pleased at the Imperials' intervention, the kâhl looked on the edge of violence.

'Well met,' said Rostov, crafting a short bow and offering his hand to the kâhl.

She slapped it away – not hard, but hard enough – and spat

at the inquisitor's feet. He felt Antoniato flinch at his side but Rostov's furtive hand signal kept the veteran in his place.

'You are Rostov?' she said, rolling the name around her tongue awkwardly.

Rostov nodded.

She scowled and threw the cultist leader before him. 'I hear this filth is of value to you.'

Rostov's studied gaze fell upon the traitor Navy captain, appraising every inch. The mark of the Hand stood out, cut into the man's skin.

'He is indeed.'

She muttered something, a word of her native tongue Rostov didn't catch, and two of her warriors came forward to take the cultist.

'Wait...' Rostov edged forwards but found the indomitable wall of Utri in his path. Rather than balk at the hulking warrior, he craned his neck to look past him to address the kâhl. 'I have business with that prisoner.'

But the kâhl had turned her back on him and was walking away.

'Name your price,' declared Rostov, and thought of the deal Yamir must have brokered.

At this, she paused and turned around. For the first time since their meeting, something approximating a smile brightened the kâhl's face. Her flinty eyes sparkled in the dim light, revealing her true motivation.

The smile became an avaricious grin of shiny white teeth.

'I am listening.'

Chapter Fifteen

UNNUMBERED NO MORE

NOT ALL KNIVES ARE MADE EQUAL

FALSEHOOD

Areios stood listening to the low whine of his armour systems. His internal chrono told him he had been in this hallway for over six hours. Despite his training, he felt a mild tremor of unease run through his body at the prospect of what would happen next.

My fate.

He was alone, save for the graven statues of Imperial saints that stared down on him with their impassive judgement.

Or am I merely judging myself?

Their heads were crowned with carved sunbursts, their eyes etched with jagged lightning. Wielding swords and framed by stone wings, they told of a heroism that echoed through the eras. He felt small by comparison.

Deeming it unproductive, he shrugged off this introspection. Astartes were not meant to endure such prolonged periods of inactivity. Without a war to fight, a skill to hone, Areios felt adrift. It was disquieting, and not for the first time he readjusted the grip on the power sword sheathed at his belt, feeling the synth-leather creak against his gauntlets.

The manufactors of this part of the ship had put a polished oval of silver in the facing wall. He wondered if its placement was deliberate. In it he saw mirrored his armoured form. Blue to reflect the livery of his genetic heritage, his battle plate still bore the scars and chipped paint it had earned at Srinagar. Here a scorch mark after a bullet's passage, there a scrape of gunmetal from a blade. On his left shoulder was the pale grey chevron of the Greyshields, a symbol of the fact he had yet to be assigned to a Chapter.

But that was all ending now. It had been a measure of expediency and pragmatism, now no longer needed. The Greyshields were never meant to endure as an organisation – Guilliman's de facto Legions, despite him presiding over the original breaking of similar military structures ten thousand years in the past – and Areios knew he was amongst the last of them. This was why he was here, to be reassigned. He wondered whose ranks he would join, who amongst Guilliman's sons he would call brother. He reflected then that introspection was proving harder to cast off than he thought.

A door opened at the end of the hallway, and Areios turned from the mirror to see a robed patrician emerge. Human, she wore long robes that pooled by her feet as she walked. A rod of office hung around her shoulder on a golden cord. Several scroll cases were cinched at a simple leather belt. She came over to Areios on sandalled feet, her steps soft and quiet. Her head was shaved, an Imperial eagle tattooed on the right temple.

'Ferren Areios?' she said in a strong voice, checking a data-slate cradled in one arm.

Areios gave a slow nod, at which the patrician wrote something on the screen with a stylus. His name was an amalgam of his old life and a reference to the world where he was born anew.

'Please follow me, my lord,' she said and moved off.

Areios followed, keeping his gait short and his steps slow so he didn't overtake her. She was several feet shorter than him, a reed to his oak, but she hadn't balked when confronting him and for that reason alone he knew she possessed strength.

The patrician led him through the doors at one end of the hallway into a receiving chamber. It was small but comfortable, the faint vibrations of the ship's engines barely audible through its padded walls. And there, sitting behind a desk in the spartanly furnished room was Vitrian Messinius.

The Astartes rose as soon as Areios entered, dismissing the patrician with an unobtrusive gesture.

'It is good to see you, old friend,' he said warmly, stepping from around the desk where he had been reviewing a data-slate.

Areios clasped his mentor's arm, gripping it firmly in the way of warriors.

Messinius was armoured in white with a green trim around his shoulder guards, the livery of the White Consuls, one of the Ultramarines' many successors. After the Rift, the Chapter's home world, Sabatine, had been overrun by Chaos. Fate had meant Messinius had been unable to stand in its defence, his path eventually aligning with that of Guilliman and Fleet Tertius. He desired greatly to return and try to reclaim Sabatine, or at least avenge it. That vengeance would have to wait, though, until his oaths to the primarch had been fulfilled, and so here he was, reviewing data-slates.

'Traded your blade for a stylus, I see,' said Areios mildly as the two broke apart. Messinius stood a little shorter than Areios, his frame narrower. Unlike Areios, Messinius belonged to the old caste of Astartes before Cawl's miracle and the emergence of the Primaris Marines. His presence was undeniable, however.

'A lord lieutenant's duties see him exercise the strength of his mind as well as his sword arm, captain.'

'Of course, my lord,' Areios replied, chastened.

'A joke, Ferren,' said Messinius, smiling broadly. 'I admit I am not good at them.'

Areios' creased expression suggested he didn't understand. Messinius left it at that and went to retrieve a piece of parchment, one of a stack of several piled on his desk. A glance revealed troop numbers, lists of materiel, the disposition of armies. The stark balance sheet of war. At least, that was his impression; oddly the detail eluded him. Almost as if he couldn't quite parse it.

'Do they not have logisticians and tacticae for that?' asked Areios, putting his reaction down to fatigue. Even Astartes were not tireless, and he had been on campaign for several weeks without rest.

'They do, but I prefer to trust my own eyes and follow in Lord Guilliman's example.'

At mention of the primarch, Areios made the sign of the aquila. He winced at a sudden painful twinge, but Messinius appeared not to notice.

'As pleasant as this reunion is, it is not why you were summoned, Ferren.' At this, the lord lieutenant proffered the parchment he had taken from his desk. 'Read it,' he invited when Areios did not immediately react.

He took the parchment.

'The Greyshields are being disbanded, Ferren,' Messinius told him. 'It will take time to enact in full, but the end has begun.'

The pain returned, worse than before, and Areios clutched at his side but found no wound.

Messinius continued unabated. 'You are an Unnumbered Son no more. Guilliman himself requested your elevation to the Ultramarines. It is a great honour.'

Areios nodded his gratitude, feeling slightly numbed at the news. He looked down at the parchment, the pain in his side a needle of fire. He grimaced.

'I admit, it lacks fanfare,' said Messinius.

Areios blinked. Once, then again. The words on the parchment made no sense. They were gibberish, the scratchings of a madman.

'Is this another joke?'

'I hope you are proud,' said Messinius as if replying to a different question. 'There is no Chapter held in greater esteem than the Ultramarines. I believe the primarch sees greatness in you, as do I.'

'This is...' Areios felt off balance, as if the floor had been canted to one side. He staggered. Messinius still appeared not to notice.

'You will become a part of the Sixth Company, under Brother-Captain Epathus. He is a fine warrior and tactician, you will learn much from him. The Sixth are headed for the Anaxian Line, and as such you will be leaving Fleet Tertius.'

Messinius paused, allowing Areios a moment to assimilate his words. The lord lieutenant's tone softened slightly.

'I know you wanted to be posted to the White Consuls. It would have been my honour to serve alongside you and return to liberate Sabatine together, but ours is the path of duty, Areios.'

'I am sorry, lord lieutenant, but I...'

Areios' world contracted, darkness encroaching at its edge, the pain in his side now agonising. Messinius, still talking, fell away, his voice ever fainter, until–

Areios awoke to darkness and the solitude of an apothecarion. It had been a memory, nothing more. The air felt cold, and heat evaporated off his body in a shroud of steam. Around him, he was suddenly aware of machineries, of pipes and wires, of the smell of counterseptic, and immediately he sat upright, having been lying prostrate on a medi-slab. Stripped of his battle plate, including the under mesh that acted as a conductive layer between his skin and his armour systems, he saw the wound.

And then he remembered the knife.

In the wan light of the overhead lumen the skin looked raw, discoloured by bruising. Thick staples punctuated a long cut in his side, effectively suturing the flesh together. A sickle grin of metallic teeth.

'It had pierced right through your armour,' said the Apothecary, Areios only just then aware he was being observed.

'Where I am, brother?'

'The apothecarion at Marfax.'

It was one of the bastions in a continental region of Garrovire pacified by the Imperials. Its role was that of a forward base and strongpoint for the non-Astartes. As well as its Militarum garrison, it housed logisticians, strategos and engineers. All cogs in the complicated mechanism of war. The Ultramarines made use of it only occasionally between missions, having no need for a static encampment since they were not on Garrovire to hold territory but instead to aggressively purge the heretic presence from the world, to decimate it to such a degree that it could be excised completely by the rest of the Imperial occupation force.

All of this, Areios' reviving mind processed in a second.

His next thought was more immediately practical.

'The knife,' he replied, not reacting. 'I remember it feeling cold.'

'You are fortunate, it broke apart like shrapnel. I had to dig it out, piece by piece. It did not want to be removed.'

Areios frowned. 'It is a shard of metal, Valentius. It does not *want*, it merely is.'

The Apothecary was a studious-looking warrior with a narrow face for a Space Marine and hawkish eyes. His olive skin appeared almost gold in the light and his black hair had been shaved almost down to the scalp.

'Not all knives are made equal, brother.'

'Then what is it?'

'Warp sorcery folded into the metal and edged with poison. A particularly virulent one. You will have to ask Maendaius for a more detailed explanation. It is beyond my art. A tainted blade shall have to suffice by way of explanation, for now. Mercifully your physiology was equal to it, though only a small piece found its way through into your body.'

It had not been the first time Areios had been wounded near to death. He still carried the horrendous scars from Pridor Vrakon, back on Srinagar when the Dark Apostle had almost killed him. During that fateful encounter, he had lost an arm. The augmetic replacement shone in the faint light and was usually concealed beneath his armour. It whirred as he flexed it. At least this time he had not parted with any more of his limbs. Another close call, however. He was becoming accustomed to his own mortality.

'And if it had been more than that?' Areios asked.

'I suspect I would be harvesting your progenoid organs instead of speaking to you of matters that have little import in the here and now.'

Areios gave a grunt and then eased himself off the medi-slab. 'Am I sanctioned for duty?'

Valentius raised an eyebrow. 'I would suggest first a visit to the armoury.'

Areios looked down, as if fully aware of his partial nakedness for the first time. The inputs of his subdermal black carapace shone like gunmetal edged with silver.

He showed no emotion beyond recognition. 'Agreed.'

Epathus stood next to the strategium console, his face lit by a hololithic projection of a city. The image rotated slowly around the projection dais, bathing everyone in close proximity to it in a flickering green glow.

Only Ultramarines were present, for hunting the Oracles was

their sole purpose. Others would remain to fight the war. As such, they had parted ways with the Catachan 116th and other Militarum forces at Arrandius, though their heroism would not soon be forgotten.

'The assault on the temple at Landhope yielded more than just a coven of Oracles,' said the captain, his eye falling on Areios, who had been last to join the gathering. The re-armouring ritual had taken several hours, but no Astartes would be clad without it. He was joined by Lieutenant Vero, Sergeant Trajus and the Librarian, Maendaius, who looked pensive as ever but was taciturn as a servitor.

His skin itching at the psyker's regard, wondering what thoughts the Librarian could prise from his mind, Areios refocused on the mission and on Epathus.

'Within the ritual stones, Maendaius uncovered a psychic spoor.' The captain glanced to the Librarian for confirmation, who gave a slight nod. Epathus went on, 'We think this is the reason the Oracles are on Garrovire, and why their movements have been so difficult to predict. It led us here.' Epathus indicated the city with a casual gesture of his hand. 'This was the epicentre of the initial outbreak. It was believed abandoned, emptied of all occupants, and has been purged several times by the Militarum and Ecclesiarchy. It is a ghost city now, little more than a ruin, but it harbours more than the dead, and its outward desolation veils something deeper but currently obscured. Our augurs cannot see it, nor can our eyes, it would seem. The strategos are calling it the *falsehood*.' He turned to Maendaius. 'Only a psyker of sufficient ability can pierce it and reveal whatever is behind it. If there is some greater plan to the Oracles' presence on this world then we will find it here.'

'How can we trust our senses, brother-captain, if this obfuscation is as potent as it seems?' asked Areios, remembering his experiences in the Forlorn Temple. It had felt real.

'We cannot,' uttered Maendaius, his sonorous voice like a bell chime. His eyes narrowed on Areios and the lieutenant fought not to break the Librarian's gaze.

+I see you, Ferren Areios. I see your path, following in the wake of death.+

Areios felt his jaw tense, the veins in his neck bulging like cords of rope. Every inch of him rebelled at the psychic touch, but just when he thought he could endure it no longer, it was over. A second had passed, no more, and Maendaius had already moved on.

'Closer to the falsehood, I will be able to unpick its manifestations,' the Librarian said to Epathus. 'Once the psychic stitches are loose, the truth will reveal itself as it did to our brother-lieutenant in the temple.'

'Brothers,' said Epathus, 'our forces will be split. A vanguard section will approach on foot. The rest will engage encirclement protocols and remain on overwatch. Ingress point for vanguard is here' – at the word 'ingress' the image zoomed in, revealing a more detailed topography – 'at the city's eastern gate, where we will break into fire-teams and then converge' – an icon flickered into being, identifying the rally point – 'here at this plaza. The east gate has been sealed by the Ecclesiarchy but will pose no impediment to our mission. It offers the most direct route into the main part of the city.'

'If it is uninhabited, why not level the entire city with a bombardment?' asked Trajus. The question seemed genuine, without any suggestion of scepticism or dissent. He had a grey pallor to his scalp from where his hair had been completely shorn. A scar on his cheek spoke of older wars.

'Whatever is at the heart of the falsehood may be of strategic value to our forces. If such an asset exists, we are commanded to retrieve it,' said Epathus.

'An aerial assault would remove the need for an on-foot

incursion,' suggested Lieutenant Vero, indicating a suitable deployment point on the map. Thinner of face than the others, Vero was a cautious but solid officer. A dark, well-kept beard framed his jaw and his eyes were intense, as if constantly searching.

'For the same reason we are not levelling the city with ordnance, we cannot risk an aerial assault blind. If the enemy has deeply embedded forces or some other advantage we are unprepared to fight, it could jeopardise the mission.'

Trajus folded his arms. 'Have we ever been unprepared for any fight?'

Areios could think of instances in the Chapter's recorded history, but Trajus' bravura was well meant. Tight, feral smiles flashed around the gathered officers. All except for Maendaius, whose emotions were as unreadable as stone.

'I admire your confidence, brother,' Epathus said generously. He had a way about him, an easy camaraderie that eluded some officers and a respect earned through deed and manner rather than by dint of rank. 'Vigilance, as if we have ever been anything other, will be paramount. An unknown battlefield lies ahead of us, and the civitas will be guarded by enemies both seen and unseen. For the primarch,' he added solemnly.

'For the primarch,' they all replied.

He deactivated the hololith and the city blinked out, casting the room into shadow.

Chapter Sixteen

THE PROSPECT OF TRADE

TRUE AS WROUGHT

AM I NOT A SERVANT OF THE EMPEROR?

She didn't blink. Not once, that Rostov could see. Throughout their entire exchange, Kâhl Vutred was stony-faced, eyes stern as granite. Gone the avarice at the prospect of trade, and in its place an intense severity.

She sat on a rock amidst the aftermath of the battle, hunched in her hulking armour as her dead were dragged away to the Kin's waiting transports, bound for their voidships at high anchor. It was, Vutred had explained, the only way by which they could be returned to their ancestors. Rostov inferred this phrase as non-literal but also detected reverence in the kâhl's tone when she spoke of it, and the Kin treated this practice with the utmost seriousness and solemnity. Nothing was left behind, save the bodies of the enemy, and every loss was tabulated, an Iron-master wearing a long coat over her armour and a set of esoteric lenses on her head calling out names and making tally marks on a large tablet.

He had learned the names, some of their peculiarities and

predilections, through observation and keen listening. Rostov had always been a good student of his environment and the people who inhabited it. From Vutred directly, he had learned the Kin were a large group of pioneers. She referred to them as an 'Oathband', which the inquisitor assumed was some kind of social or militaristic grouping. They had been sent by their League, a corporation of sorts, for want of a better term, to gather resources and find viable trade routes. It was how they had come to be in Yamir's orbit and how the two had struck an accord. The need for something for something, the basis of any fair transaction. This was the language the Kin understood.

And they had fallen on difficult times. Though they did not admit it, Rostov noticed their patched armour, the intensity with which they obsessively accounted for every resource. He assumed these were the bulk of their warriors, their tribe or clan. Their Kindred. Theirs was a mission of desperation, where everyone must play their part or risk the dissolution of the whole. They had revealed little of their plight so as not to weaken their bargaining position.

Rostov decided not to press this small advantage, for his need was desperate also. In truth, he did want to test which was greater: the Kin's desire for survival or their stubbornness against accepting an unprofitable trade. So he had honoured the deal that had been brokered by Yamir: shipping and mining rights over certain Imperial territories and guaranteed trade with several Imperially held systems.

'A fair price, as agreed,' Rostov said in conclusion, already devising in his head the missives he would need to send to put these plans into motion. His seal would provide credence and surety in the moment.

Vutred eyed him shrewdly. 'A correction, Imperial,' she said, in a gravelly cadence. 'No agreement was made, but rather a proposal. Our dealings remained inconclusive. No ink was writ, no spit shared, no balancing of the scales.' She gestured to the prisoner, who remained in the custody of the Einhyr. The bulky armoured Kin glowered over the wretch, who grinned despite his dishevelled and emaciated state. 'This here is of profound value, is it not? I fail to see how such a thing could have worth, but only the ancestors know these answers and I am not minded to ask. So then,' she added, resting a gauntleted hand on her slab of a chin, 'what is the offer?'

'Offer?' Rostov could not hide his incredulity. 'The offer is made, kâhl, a fair price for a fair trade. In any account, I thought our aid in battle against this scum would have some worth...'

At once, the inquisitor realised he had made a mistake. Vutred's face went from ruddy-cheeked vigour to purpling anger.

'You speak of your interference as if it has value,' she said, raising her voice and then getting to her feet.

Behind him, Rostov felt Nirdrangar and his men react, and the inquisitor made a swift and furtive hand gesture to keep them leashed. Any aggression now would be disastrous and potentially terminal.

'I meant no offence,' Rostov offered, his tone deferent. 'But that prisoner is Imperial property.'

'And yet offence was given. Luck has. Need keeps. Toil earns,' she snapped, not the first aphorism he had heard from the Kin, who were perhaps unsurprisingly philosophical – especially the gnomic sage who stood a few paces behind his kâhl, looking on through the shadows of his hooded cloak. 'You blunder into a fight you do not understand, Imperial. You force my hand tactically and I am meant to thank you for the expense it caused me? No.' She shook her head decisively. 'I will not be beholden. I will take this wretch, *property* or not, and throw it into our drive furnace.'

She made to leave again when Rostov made a plea.

'Wait, Kâhl Vutred. Please. I misspoke and humbly apologise

for any impropriety.' He needed the prisoner and could not fail here through misjudgement. 'Tell me what you need.'

Vutred looked about to shrug him off but Rostov caught her sharing a glance with her sage, the Grimnyr, who answered her silent question with a surreptitious shake of his head.

The tension defused a fraction, allowing for negotiation to continue.

'Fuel,' said Vutred. 'We have need of fuel.' She turned.

Rostov nodded. 'Very well. There are Imperial depots in the vicinity. I can sanction the requisition of fuel.'

After a swift calculation, the Iron-master handed Vutred a slate, which she brandished to the inquisitor.

'This much will meet our needs.' The avaricious glint had returned. She was pushing it, but Rostov had no time to negotiate. And Vutred knew it.

'It will be met,' he said, and offered his hand in order to shake on the agreement. 'Do we have an accord?'

She pulled off her gauntlet. A mechanised creature that resembled a robotic head and torso drifted over to her on antigravitic impellers. The strange familiar carried a clear casket that was suspended beneath it on cables, and Vutred put the gauntlet inside, a shimmering stasis field immediately enveloping the glove.

Her bare hand was scarred and leathern. She hawked and spat into the palm.

Rostov didn't hesitate as she clapped his outstretched hand in a firm grip.

'Aye, true as wrought.' The slightest twinkle in her eye suggested she was enjoying his displeasure.

The Einhyr released the traitor, only for him to be immediately seized by the waiting storm troopers. Rostov gave a surreptitious gesture to the rest and they withdrew, the tension immediately easing.

Rostov resisted the urge to flex his fingers at her unreasonably tight grasp, as she released her grip and he departed. The Kin watched him and his men every step.

Only once they were out of sight and heading back to the gunships did Rostov sag, having kept his fatigue hidden from the Kin. He leaned on Lacrante, who had noticed him struggling, and saw Antoniato fall into step behind, the two veterans sharing a worried glance.

Rostov had not the strength to disabuse them of their concern. The fight had taken more out of him than he realised, but the price wasn't yet fully paid. His body would suffer again. And soon.

Cheelche whistled. 'Greedy little bastards, aren't they?' She was about to follow up with more when she saw Rostov's condition and shut up. Hefting her rifle, she joined Nirdrangar at the front of the party instead.

After the Imperials had gone, Vutred stayed to look over the battlefield. Bodies lay all about, blood spatter and destruction. She only saw the waste.

She felt the presence of Othed behind her.

'It was a calculated risk,' she said, refitting her gauntlet with a hiss of equalising pressure. 'The moon could have yielded more. I know it isn't enough.'

'Much was unforeseen.'

'And yet our plight has not changed, Othed. Nor has our need. If we do not find better fortune and take what destiny has deemed is mine...' She trailed off, her mood growing dark.

'Nothing less than our existence is at stake. Without the prize, the Omrigar will be no more. Exile from the League, my kâhl.'

Vutred nodded ruefully. The heathen cults, the Imperials. They had not accounted for any of that. She had six ships in a flotilla currently at high anchor above the moon. Monitors, up-gunned haulers and several stout war-barques. Powerful in a fight but stripped back, lean, and edging towards desperate. They needed more than fuel. War weary, battered, they needed refit and repair, but there were none she could call upon, and a Kindred's need to consider.

'Their holds should be occupied by resource, not the dead.'

'True as wrought,' murmured Othed.

She sucked her teeth, biting down her dismay. None would see it.

'It is out there somewhere, Othed, our motherlode. The ancestors have spoken of it, therefore it is true. As certain as the void is in our veins.' Her gimlet gaze settled on a smashed Hearthkyn helmet, its visor cracked, the helm itself split down the middle. It had been missed during the sweeps and lay amongst the carcasses of enemy dead.

'Find us a heading, my Grimnyr. Ask the ancestors for their wisdom.'

'The Votann has been obstinate of late. The veracity of its wisdom is not what it once was, and may be difficult to interpret.'

'I have faith in you, old friend. Every scrap matters now. Everything.'

'I shall see it done, our true path revealed.'

'Good... else I fear it will be our end.'

She turned then, headed for the landers, and left the shattered helm behind to be forgotten amidst the dust and the dead.

She was waiting for him upon his return.

The Silent had barely moved, if she had moved at all. Rostov honestly could not tell. He had already warned off Lacrante when the acolyte had suggested Rostov should pay a visit to the infirmary. He had no time for that, nor for the dulling of his senses that a sedative would inflict. Pain kept him sharp.

He would use it. Nirdrangar had taken the prisoner to the cells, prepping him for interrogation.

Rostov hoped he was ready, though ultimately it was a case of having to be.

The last of his tasks before heading to his quarters to retrieve his tools of excoriation had been to instruct Lacrante to set up a rendezvous with the lead ship from Battle Group Iolus. If luck was with them, he would have extracted something operationally significant from the traitor in his custody before they reached the flotilla, and he would have it to support his argument for reinforcement. Never had the Imperium felt so stretched, tight enough to snap. He remembered days before the Rift when requisitioning entire fleets of ships would have been as straightforward as breathing the words. All of that had changed with the coming of the primarch and his crusade of reconquest. Rostov could practically feel the knife edge they were on, the sharp brink and the cold promise of oblivion on the other side of it.

And thus he had no time. Yet here she was, standing in his way like an immoveable statue. He was about to order her to move, feeling his temper for the Silent fraying, when she spoke.

What is happening to you?

Her massive sword sheathed at her back, she crafted the words with her hands. The eyes, stark and cold above the high gorget covering her mouth, conveyed her seriousness. She had observed, listened, and now she wanted answers.

Rostov had some skill in thoughtmark. It was the ordos' principal method of non-verbal communication amongst their own ranks, and he was able to understand her meaning well enough for them to communicate effectively.

'I have an affliction,' he said, feeling no need to dissemble. He did not disclose how bad it was getting. 'A consequence of using my "gift", I fear.'

He swallowed down his mild revulsion at the continued exposure to her presence but noticed the pain of the corruption in his flesh had eased, the intense burning, the needles that had sharpened to daggers over the passing days. It was a bleak trade, Rostov reflected.

She brandished her vambrace, showing him the limiter around her wrist.

This, she signed, and began to slowly turn the cuff, *regulates.*

Almost immediately, Rostov felt his gut tighten and the near-irresistible urge to vomit seized him. He had felt this before and thought he was acclimatised, but this effect was potent. He retched, hot and acrid bile in his throat. A feeling of utter revulsion welled up inside him. Suddenly on his knees, hands curling into fists, vision blurring, he wanted to–

He rasped, 'Enough.'

And the Silent turned the limiter cuff back to its original setting. The feeling faded, ushering in the return of pain.

It is the warp, she signed, *a corruption of the body.*

'I suppose,' said Rostov sadly, 'we are all damned in the end.' He had known the cause for a while but hoped he could endure long enough to finish his mission. He wondered how long he had left and prayed it wouldn't be measured in days.

She didn't reply.

'I must break the traitor I have below in the cells. Everything he knows, everything he does not know that he knows, I must possess it. All of it. There is only one way. The risk is egregious to me if I do, but it is a far greater risk to the Imperium if I do not. Am I not a servant of the Emperor? Duty unto death.'

Yes, Inquisitor Rostov. That is all any of us are. She touched a gauntleted hand to her chest. *Syreniel.*

Rostov gave a thin smile. 'And I was becoming accustomed to you only as "the Silent".' Remembering something, he reached into his pocket and pulled out the simple iron icon of the

Mordian 84th. 'May I ask, what is this? Why did you leave it for me to find?'

Syreniel told him. Of her secondment to Admiral Ardemus of Praxis, of the Kamidar mission and the narrowly averted Imperial civil war. Rostov had known something of the aborted Kamidar rebellion, though none of the details, and he was well familiar with Guilliman's desire to establish the Anaxian Line as a bulwark against further aggression from sundered Cadia, though his own goals had never intersected with the endeavour.

I took this from a soldier's rifle, Syreniel continued. *I confess that I do not know why and merely followed the compulsion I felt at the time to do so. Perhaps I wished to hold some keepsake of hers, a memory.*

'Who was she?'

Someone who appeared to be nondescript, though was something more.

'I'm not sure I understand.'

Nor do I, alas. I felt the touch of providence about her, though. As if the divine sat upon her shoulder.

'You mean the Emperor's will?'

Syreniel made the sign of the aquila and gave a single nod.

Turning the icon around in his hand, Rostov considered the simple acts that had led to this moment and wondered what greater events they might yet portend. He recalled his conversation with Lacrante in the infirmary before they had met up with the Kin, and then came memories of the cult of the Church of the Ever-Living Emperor on Srinagar and their beliefs about His potential re-emergence.

He began to wonder what it might all mean, before the present reasserted itself and he turned his mind to the pressing task at hand.

And then he saw again the cuff on Syreniel's wrist, and an idea began to form.

Chapter Seventeen

THE OBSIDIAN MIRROR

AN ALLIANCE

ONE FATE

Augury formed out of shadow, one moment nothing and then suddenly apparent.

They appeared before Yheng like an apparition as she stood by the edge of the mirrored pool, not knowing how she had got here or why. The fortress had many uncharted depths, it seemed.

'Tell me, Yheng,' said Augury, their cloak voluminous as it billowed on an unfelt breeze, 'what do you see in the mirror?'

'I...' uttered Yheng, her unease worsening. She felt the cold hand of fate on her shoulder, gently urging her, but towards what? Her thoughts swirled, fierce as a maelstrom, and Yheng found herself trying to resist their pull for fear of where they might take her. 'I...'

Something moved within the mirror, a droplet, only in reverse, the tremors across the surface rippling from the edge to the centre, and from it something began to form, emerging from within the mirror. Silver at first, it began to coalesce into something more... *someone* whom she recognised.

'No...' rasped Yheng.

Overwhelmed, she fled. She spied a fresh fissure in the black rock and scrambled through it. She ran through lightless corridors, through claustrophobic apertures, crawled under oppressive low-ceilinged chambers, on and on into the chilling dark with no real sense of where she was going, only that she had to escape. She needed to regroup, a moment to catch a breath, to make sense of what was happening to her.

'Let me out of this place!' she roared into a flat and echoless space, trying to marshal her sorcery, only to be denied. Great stalactites of black crystal speared from the ceiling, a veritable inverted forest of knife-edged pain reaching down for her.

Noctilith, that's what Tenebrus had called it. A substance that could disrupt the warp.

She cursed him, and then saw a shape lurking in the forest above her. It crept through the crystal branches, one protruding limb to another, precise in every movement. Near silent and delicate. *Arachnid*, she thought at first, her fascination at the creature keeping her in place even as her sense of self-preservation urged her to run. Without her sorcery, she was vulnerable. But to run would be to spring its trap, for the creature was not alone. Another and another, spindly and long-limbed, slow and deliberate, crept through the stalactites. Dull red lenses flared as the creatures' sensors found her.

Not arachnid at all, and not the sleek drones she had seen in other parts of the fortress, the mute caretakers that hovered seemingly without purpose or design. These creatures had a design, and they walked on two limbs, nimble and long of gait, mantis-like with two forelimbs that ended in two long blades.

Mechanicum, she realised, with a sinking feeling overtaking her limbs. Yheng had only her ritual knife – it was literally the only weapon she carried, and not much of one at that. She knew with certainty the creatures were after her.

They will not take me easily, she thought, a snarl curling her mouth. Having reached this far, she would not falter now. It was her destiny to rise. Her ascension was earned and it was due. No longer would she be afraid, no longer would she be subservient. Life *was* fear, the two as indivisible as sand and stone. All that mattered was how you controlled it. In the face of death or enslavement, a much worse fate.

The three who meant to end her existence slid from the rocky perches to land on the ground in a soft ring of steel.

'Abandon me, then!' she cried, casting about for Augury, but they were nowhere to be seen. 'I will not be your puppet,' she vowed but fear slid in anyway, despite her vehemence, as the creatures closed in. Not fear of death, but that she would be denied what she believed was hers. For her path to end here... The voices in the black chamber, Tenebrus' ritual: it meant something. She was important.

Chosen...

Subconsciously, Yheng outstretched her hand in a gesture to ward off her attackers, who she saw properly for the first time in the lambent bioluminescence of the chamber. They shambled across the ground, far less gainly than when they had crept across the ceiling. Machines, killers. They moved hunched, and bled tracts of oil in their wake. As their regard fell upon her, their red eye-lenses became as bright as fire.

The lead machine sprang, launching its bipedal form into the air, blades singing...

Its death blow was averted when a spear of black rock impaled it straight through the torso. It hung there like an insect caught on a collector's pin, writhing. The other two hesitated as some kind of unspoken communication passed between them, the unforeseen development forcing recalibration. They circled instead, one left, the other right, blades dragging in their wake.

One was crushed as a piece of the wall thrust outwards like a fist and smashed it against the opposite side of the chamber. The other was flung upwards as if a spring had exploded beneath it, but it was the rock again, punching it into the air. Three tines of blackstone impaled the machine before it could land and it jerked momentarily in its trap, until the red lenses faded and extinguished.

Yheng breathed heavily, looking from the destroyed machines to her still-outstretched hand, regarding it like a foreign entity that had managed to attach itself to her body. This was what she had felt like as she and Tenebrus faced off against the ghouls. A hidden power at her fingertips. She had denied it then, but had now chosen to embrace it.

'The fortress does not want you dead, Tharador Yheng,' said Augury, who had appeared alongside her. 'It wants to show you something.'

At the far end of the chamber a portal opened, a split in the rock that had not been there before.

Yheng regarded Augury warily. 'I will no longer be manipulated,' she warned. 'Not by Tenebrus, not by you. Not *anyone*.'

Augury bowed at the waist. 'Consider me a guide, Tharador Yheng. Use me only as you wish to.'

Yheng paused at that, deciding. 'What were those things?' she asked, gesturing to the machine corpses, not quite ready to take everything on faith. These creatures had been sent here to kill her, if not by the fortress then by what, by whom?

'Each of us of the Hand has a different agenda,' Augury said.

Scepticism narrowed Yheng's eyes. 'And yours is?'

'To see a worthy acolyte take what is hers.'

'Are you merely telling me what I want to hear?'

'Only you can decide whether you want to trust me.'

'How can I trust something when I cannot even see its face?'

A thin smile turned Augury's pale mouth. 'Believe me, Yheng, you do not want to see my true face.'

A shudder ran through Yheng unbidden, but she sensed no lie in Augury's words.

'Tenebrus said you would devour yourselves, that there was war coming.' She finally lowered her outstretched hand.

'He is right. The Fourth of the Hand wants to claim the shards for their own. They were once of flesh, and have never shed the petty ambitions of their original creation.'

The Iron Magus. The creatures *were* machines, by-blows of Dark Mechanicum warp-science as Yheng had suspected.

'But I don't have the shards,' Yheng pointed out. 'What am I to them?'

'Like Tenebrus, the Iron Magus sees your potential. You are a branch of possibility they want to prune. Because you are important, Yheng, and that interferes with their plans. Surely you must realise that. In the black chamber...'

'I felt the presence of the gods, their eye upon me. I sensed... They wanted something of me, but I know not what. I cannot discern their will.'

'Few can, and fewer still receive such a blessing. You are touched by them, Yheng. They see you. This place, the fortress, it dwells partly in the warp and partly in the materium.'

Yheng touched her fingers to the cold blackstone, wary of what might happen, but it was dormant. 'Tenebrus said it was like a beast, a shackled beast straining at the leash.' She took her hand away. 'In pain.' She looked up at Augury. 'That it had a twin.'

'Yes, I suppose that is true. It wants to die, Yheng, and in you it has found an outlet for its anger. You must have felt its kinship?'

Yheng thought back to her encounter with the ghouls again, that the creatures had only appeared when Tenebrus had showed himself, that she thought they might not have been after her at all.

Protecting me... From him.

'From everything and everyone that would do you harm,' said Augury, and the unnerving sense that they were in Yheng's thoughts swept over her. 'It wants to keep you alive, so you might free it.'

'The Fourth wants to kill me, and the First wants to use me,' Yheng said with rising anger. 'I ask again, what do you want of me, Eighth of the Hand?'

Augury barely moved, but Yheng thought she detected the slightest lowering of their head, or whatever passed for one. 'I feel your rage, Yheng. It is understandable. All I want is to be your ally. For you to reach your potential. In the end, we all serve the will of the gods, and this is how I serve you.'

'Then how?' If she must submit, in part, to see where this was headed, then so be it. 'If you are my ally, my guide, what must I do?'

'For now, all you need do is look...'

Yheng found she could not stare at Augury for long, for even formless in their cloak the echoes and presentiments of what they were and what they might yet become flickered at the edge of her senses. So she turned away, and there before her again was the mirror. She couldn't remember passing through the portal, leaving the chamber of stalactites behind, and yet here she was, back where she had started.

And all there was left to do was look.

There, sculpted in the liquid obsidian, was a wretch, a lowly cultist. Yheng recognised herself from when she had scraped an existence in the catacombs of Gathalamor. She had begun as a pilgrim, but that had ended badly; then a scavenger, not much more than a girl back then, collecting bones from the deserts and the petty battlefields where the hive-killers clashed. The rare pieces she sold to the bone-merchants or the greedy ossuary-priests. Just another life to be churned up by the merciless Imperium. The shape of the scavenger became the hive-ganger wearing tatty flak armour and carrying a worn stubber. Her tattoos proclaimed her allegiance, a bird-skull mask hiding half of her face. From here the road to cultism was short, and Tharador Yheng joined the Blade Unsheathed as the Imperial yoke began to bite and promises of power rose like whispers in her mind.

The liquid obsidian re-formed again, an echo projecting backwards into Yheng's life and finding expression in who she had been. Now, the acolyte, a lowly servant of the Word and Kar-Gatharr's creature. One of a multitude, unremarkable, discardable. She changed again, subtly this time, as she became the student of a different master. From the then to the now, so what came next would be the potential after...

Yheng felt her heart beating and struggled to breathe.

Her acolyte self began to wither. She saw her muscle wasting as her face harrowed and her skin greyed, until little more than a half-fleshed skeleton stared back.

'What is this?' she rasped.

Augury's voice held no comfort. 'What do you see?'

'Only death,' Yheng hissed, tears in her eyes – though not in the reflection, because there her eyes were nothing but hollow sockets, sightless and cold.

'That is one fate,' said Augury, and their voice became several voices: the demagogue whose name she had forgotten, and Kar-Gatharr. And at the end Tenebrus, and Yheng dared not look behind her, even if she were able, for fear of seeing the sorcerer standing there, as he had in the black chamber.

'Can this be changed?' she hissed as the skeletal version of herself cracked, the bones collapsing under their own weight, crumbling into ash. 'I *will* change it.'

'Perhaps, if you will allow us.'

The obsidian mirror rippled like a stone had been cast over its now pristine surface and a new image was revealed.

Yheng saw. Her eyes widened, and slowly her mouth curled into a hungry grin.

Chapter Eighteen

THE DEVIL'S ROAD

STRAITS OF LUNACY

AN OFFERING

The beast's rictus grin gave no hint as to its species when it had been alive. The entire road was littered with them, the bones and half-collapsed carcasses of behemoths. Based on where and how they had fallen, they looked to have been travelling. A pilgrimage of sorts, and one that went on for more miles than Herek could see, a mass migration without an obvious destination. He stooped in the dust to run a finger across a femur.

We are all just bones in the end...

His mood had been maudlin of late, quite unlike him. Another symptom of the burden he carried perhaps? And this place of death did nothing to improve it. Quietude lay across the endless plain, which made ignoring the susurration harder. It practically thrummed now, a chorus of partially indistinct voices both human and inhuman, beckoning, goading, promising... Herek shut his eyes, tried to think. He had his own pilgrimage to make, one that led to Behethramog. His quest, his purpose. The one Augury had given to him. Another of their pieces in the cold war now being waged by the Hand. Retrieving the blade and the shard within, taking it from his fiercest rival, had been but the first step. Now he needed to take the next.

'Bring him up,' Herek said, rising to his feet.

The cohort of warriors and cultists behind him stirred. From within their ranks, Vassago Kurgos brought forth the soul mariner. The Navigator had guided them this far with his deranged visions and proclamations. Herek glared as Kurgos threw the Navigator down before him. The hulking chirurgeon had looked pained as he walked and gave a grunt of discomfort, having suffered to reach this far.

'Is this it? Is this the path you spoke of, the Devil's Road?' asked Herek.

'It had better be...' murmured Clortho with menace. He, like the rest of the Red Corsairs, had seen better days. His patched armour was dented and scraped, a wound in his side badly clotted. His shoulder guard cleaved. The red and black paint had been scraped away in several places, leaving gunmetal-grey bullet gouges and claw marks. The encounter with the mechanised assassins had not been the last trouble the Red Corsairs had met on this path. To reach this place, some desolate world on the edge of the system, they had fought the malefic. Every time they had sunk into the warp another hellish host had sought ingress onto the ship, stretching their defences. More than once, they had succeeded, drawn to the *Ruin* like a magnet draws iron filings. Nought but a trickle slipped through the Geller field but enough to cause carnage. It gave Herek no comfort to see his proclamation that they were being hunted by more than just men realised. The fell denizens of the immaterium had come for them, frenzied, rabid and hellbent.

No, not them. Him.

'Well, speak then, turd,' Clortho snarled, and swung his heavy mace from his shoulder. The flanges had lost some of their bite, blunted by overuse and from striking iron-hard daemon flesh, but they could crack the Navigator's skull as easily as an eggshell. He moved stiffly, his injuries still healing.

Herek's gaze didn't move from the soul mariner, but he put up his hand to stem the other warlord's fury.

'He is...' said Herek, gesturing to the Navigator, who had his head down and was murmuring into the earth. Over and over, he repeated the litany he had first spoken on the *Ruin.*

'Let me ply the Devil's Road and cross the Straits of Lunacy. At the Burned Spire to the Threefold Wytch and the Abyssal Nadir... It is beauty and horror, and yet there is yearning in me for more.'

He craned his neck all of sudden, as if straining to behold the light of stars he could not see for the iron casing around his head. A brutish instrument of spikes and edges, the helm kept his warp sight shuttered enough that it could not kill anyone.

Following his imaginary eyeline, Herek seized the Navigator by the back of the neck and dragged him to an upthrust shelf of rock that rose several feet above the plain. Once he had reached the plateau he released the wretch.

'The Devil's Road,' he insisted, pain blunting his thoughts. 'Is this it?'

From this vantage the plain stretched on, the distant skeletons of titanic beasts like mountains against the horizon.

'I see, I see...' the Navigator babbled, outstretching a withered arm, fingers clawing at the air as if trying to grasp something only he could perceive. And then back to the litany, only this time he hunched over the ground and began to draw in the dirt with bloodstained fingers: the map, an exact replica of the one from the ship. And when he was finished he began anew, shuffling slightly to the side and drawing it all over again.

Herek, transfixed, felt a hand on his shoulder and turned to see Kurgos standing behind him. Rathek had broken ranks too and stood not so far away, ever watchful and protective.

'What does it say?' asked the chirurgeon.

'A crude translation would be "Behethramog".'

'I have never heard of this place.'

'Nor I, I know only that we must reach it. The voices speak it endlessly.' He grimaced, hands clenched.

Kurgos went to his belt of dirty pouches and vials, but Herek warded him off.

'I am becoming accustomed. Let me bear it.'

A few moments' silence passed between them with only the moan of the wind to interfere.

'What use is this, Graeyl?' asked Kurgos finally, his regard falling on the wretch clawing in the dirt. 'I see only a madman at work. Please... consider abandoning this fool's errand.'

Herek's eyes were like iron. 'Am I a fool now, old friend?'

Kurgos raised a malformed, partially gauntleted hand. 'Never that, but I have no wish to see you made into one either. I do not trust the word of daemons and those who speak for them. There are plenty of pickings out in the materium. Let us take ship and reap them.'

The *Ruin* waited far above them at anchor, in the world's lower atmosphere. Herek had left a skeleton crew, a handful of trusted Red Corsairs to defend it. The temptation to return to it and do what Kurgos asked pulled hard, but he resisted.

'I cannot, Vassago. Even if I wanted to. This is the only way now, the path to Behethramog. The affliction will continue – it will worsen – until I reach it. And only then, when I rid myself of this accursed burden, will I see the reward I have been promised.'

Kurgos leaned in close so as not to be overhead, his voice low. 'We are at a ragged edge. The slaves we took at Felsrath are spent, our losses much worse than expected. I see much risk in this. Perhaps... perhaps there is another way. A means to excise the–'

'Tell me, old friend,' Herek interrupted, 'why did we break our old oaths and kneel before the Tyrant?'

'Duty to an unjust Imperium is not duty, it is slavery. We wanted freedom, to no longer be slaves. To tread our own path.'

'And freedom is what I seek. But also the strength to keep it.'

'To what end? Strength enough to defeat that bastard Templar? You beat him, Graeyl. You killed his beloved brother, you took back the sword and returned the shard.'

'I don't care about Morrigan. He licks his wounds, praying for the day when our paths will cross again. His vengeance is all-consuming. I desire ascension, pre-eminence, a path to the Hand and then perhaps... to *him.* The Warmaster. The eye of the gods is upon us, Vassago, though I have never placed much truck in their favour before. But since the burden, I feel it. We are in their sight and our deeds are being weighed.'

Kurgos' voice soured. 'You sound like Clortho...'

'I need you in this, old friend,' Herek replied, a hand on his brother's shoulder.

After a moment, the chirurgeon nodded. 'Ever have you had me, Herek. I will follow you to the depths of hell and beyond. If that is what it takes. I only hope you see reason before this ends.'

'None remains, only the Devil's Road.'

He shared a sad look with Kurgos and knew, whatever fate the gods might mete out, their relationship would be forever changed. Seldom had he gone against the chirurgeon's counsel, and never over something as fundamental at this.

Rathek merely looked on, confused, unable to read Kurgos' lips, and Herek with his back to him until he turned again.

'This is our path,' he called to his warriors from the rocky shelf, giving a gentle nod of reassurance to Rathek, who still looked uneasy. 'A Devil's Road or not, we shall walk it.'

'Then it will not be alone,' answered Clortho, who stared off to the side – and only now, as Herek really looked, did he see it. The vaguest impression of faces in the air, near indistinct and thin, like smoke that holds its shape. Talons and claws, tails and scaled limbs, horns and wings. Writhing, pushing against one another. A melange of crowding horrors, pressing against an invisible membrane in this strange and liminal place. Eager and hungry.

'Daemonkind are here,' said Clortho.

With little other choice, they walked the road.

And walked...

And walked...

Endless, the parade of bones without cessation.

At the eighth hour, at *every* eighth hour, they reached the shelf of rock. Again, an infernal loop. After reaching it for the eighth time, Herek called a halt. His armour appeared more tarnished and worn than before, as if entropy worked differently in this place and every maddening revolution of the Devil's Road only spurred it on. He felt tired, wrung out, as if he had fought for days and weeks without end. Wrenching off his helm, he breathed deep. The still air brought no respite.

Rathek approached, his face a mask of concern. *Brother, I can see the toll this is taking,* he signed.

'Once we find a bearing, a way through this labyrinth. Then I'll rest.'

Not your body, brother, your sanity. The daemonic exacts a heavy price. And its mark, once made, is eternal. Rathek's eyes darkened with remembered pain. *Do not struggle as I have, as I do still. Let me take some of the burden from you.*

Herek reached around the back of Rathek's head and gently pulled their foreheads together until they touched.

'Know this, I would rather have no others at my side than you and Kurgos.' He spoke slowly, so that Rathek could read his lips.

'My will and my conscience. Have no fear for me, brother, this malaise will pass. It *must* pass. And the burden is mine alone. I would not see you suffer again. You have already given enough for us. Let me do this.'

They locked eyes for a moment before Rathek closed his and they broke away.

Muttering in the ranks drew Herek's attention. Their numbers had thinned, especially amongst the cultists, the rigours of this place too much for their weak mortal constitutions. Several had died already. Some had simply wandered off, gibbering to themselves. No one had seen their bodies since, but more bones fed the osseous fields.

One of the Red Corsairs stepped forward. Zareth was an old campaigner. He had fought the aeldari at Hannokbane and the hated Imperials at Vork's Spear. His opinion carried some weight amongst the other warband leaders.

'We should return to the *Ruin*, leave this place.'

'Our path is here,' Herek told him.

'No, this is our death. Our ignominy.' Zareth rested his hand on the pommel of a serrated spatha. Not an outright act of aggression, but Herek felt Harrower stir on his back. He kept her quiescent, having no desire to slay the war veteran.

'An impasse, nothing more,' Herek assured him, though he could not think of a way out of it, the susurration fogging his mind.

'It has brought us nothing but misery and weakness,' said Zareth, prompting angry murmurings of agreement from some. At the fringes of the war party, the last of the cultists were muttering to each other, their voices strange and slightly unhinged. It only added to the sense of discord.

Grejik hacked one down, and snarled, 'Silence!' The burly warrior had blood across his faceplate and a smashed retinal lens revealed an eye that held the hint of madness. Grejik had a reputation as a butcher, a savage fighter always first into the fray. An expert at close-quarters boarding actions, it was Grejik who had broken the initial line of defence when the Red Corsairs had taken the *Mercurion*, back before all of this began. His favoured breacher shield, chipped from use, sat slung across his back.

Rathek drew one of his swords, the scrape of metal loud across the eerie plain, and Herek tensed at the sudden change in atmosphere. Another renegade backed up Grejik, a hand on the bolt pistol in his belt holster. This was Skerrin, widely regarded as Grejik's henchman.

All the while the soul mariner murmured into the still air. *And cross the Straits of Lunacy. At the Burned Spire to the Threefold Wytch and the Abyssal Nadir...*

'Shut him up,' demanded Zareth. 'His words have brought us to the brink of our doom. And you have allowed it, Herek!' He jabbed a gauntleted finger at the renegade lord, the hand that had been resting on the spatha's pommel slowly wrapping itself around the grip.

'Straits of lunacy indeed...' chuckled Clortho, earning a sharp glance from Herek, who could not decide if the other warlord had aligned himself with the dissenters or with him.

Pain from the susurration bit, keen as any blade, and Herek felt his anger rise in kind.

'Sheathe your weapons and keep them sheathed,' he said, unable to keep the snarl from his voice.

Skerrin hesitated, until he saw Grejik obey his lord.

'And you, Clortho,' rasped Kurgos, a bolt pistol suddenly in the chirurgeon's hand aimed at the warlord.

The Red Corsair plaintively showed his hands. 'Oh, I'm not a part of this.'

Several others had banded around Zareth, though, the old campaigner's reputation garnering support. Rathek made to draw his second sword, but Herek stopped him. He addressed

Zareth and the warriors by his side, and gave a slight shake of the head.

'Do not make me do this,' he pleaded.

'It's already done–' Zareth began, ripping out his blade with a flourish, but Herek was already on him, Harrower whipping around in a savage arc to claim the old campaigner's head. It swept around thrice more, rapid, deadly, leaving Zareth's allies slain with him.

Breathing hard with the pain of the susurration, Herek glared at the rest of his men with a blood-flecked face.

'This has been profligate enough already, but I will fight anyone else who disagrees with this path. Speak now and know you will die without honour.'

None did.

Except Clortho.

'Can you feel that?' he asked, his armoured fingers caressing the air. 'The gods are watching.'

The scarred warlord had no interest in the drama; instead he stared at the veil. It had thinned, but the creatures beyond no longer wailed or writhed, they had stilled utterly and now merely stared.

'The shedding of the blood, the ritual of murder, has brought them forth,' Clortho said.

Hunger bled from the daemons like a palpable fume, and several of the cultists abased themselves in frantic, terrified worship. Kurgos went to stop them.

'Hold on, old friend...' said Herek, eyes narrowing. 'I see something. Distant, but...' He peered through the veil, to the shadow beyond, the unreal mirror that led from the material to the immaterial. Past the hellish hordes that stood in eerie stillness.

A tower, blackened by fire. A burned spire.

It hadn't been there before.

Herek hefted his axe and advanced on the cultists.

'What are you doing?' asked Kurgos.

'Making an offering...'

Chapter Nineteen

LIMITS

A BEAST IN CHAINS

AN OLD ALLY

She had offered to do it herself. Torture was an ugly methodology, and seldom reliable, but Syreniel was not above inflicting pain if the situation required it. But he had refused, and said it must be done his way, precisely. So she watched, unflinching, as the inquisitor unleashed his arts. He did so without relish, using tools, displaying a deep knowledge of anatomy and the precise location of every bodily nerve. She thought him reluctant, almost as if he found the practice distasteful, stripped down to his open shirt and trousers, barefoot like a beggar and flecked with the prisoner's blood. She supposed he had no desire to sully his attire, or perhaps the toll it took upon him meant it was easier if he was as unburdened as possible.

This, precisely this, was the reason she had fallen so far from grace in the Sisterhood's eyes. Her thoughts, her individuality, her curiosity and humanity. In truth, it was love that had seen her cast out, love that brought forth a transgression of the highest proscription. As Villenia had lain dead before her, in Syreniel's earliest days of the Sisterhood, she had spoken.

No, she had *screamed.*

A lament, for love.

A sacred oath, broken.

These feelings were anathema to the Order. They made a warrior weak, impressionable. Syreniel had proven her worth since then, but the mark of her censure remained. She had fought for other agencies, a hireling more than a Talon of the Emperor. And here she was again, at the service of someone not of her Order, though she wanted bitterly to return to Somnus and the Sisterhood that had forsaken her. For now, she would do as her superiors bid, for it was the Emperor's will, and what were any of His servants without this to follow?

Rostov followed his own path, one he believed to be his purpose.

It was killing him.

And in the end it would damn him. Perhaps that was why the Knight Abyssal had placed Syreniel here, to put the inquisitor down if and when he succumbed. His skin already bore subtle lesions, the rash of infection, a sheen of feverish sweat. No disease caused this malady, it was the warp. Only by pain could Rostov peel away his prisoner's defences and reveal everything he knew and was unaware that he knew; this the inquisitor had confessed to her. He did it by infiltrating his victim's mind, through visions and impressions not so dissimilar from the soulbound. This cultist, ex-military judging by the now torn and ragged uniform, carried a crucial piece of the puzzle Rostov was trying to solve. The location of the so-called Hand of Abaddon. Syreniel had heard this name in the aftermath of the Ironhold Protectorate tragedy. It was believed by her Order and others that the loss of the capital ship *Fell Lord*, as well as its admiral, to whom she had been indentured as bodyguard and assassin, was cunningly engineered by some agent who either served or in some capacity *was* the Hand.

The one she had met, the thing that wore a human face but was anything but.

She had learned more, from Greyfax – with whom her Order shared resources – that the Hand and its followers sought and had recovered pieces of an ancient and terrible weapon, one that dated back to the days of the Great Heresy, a time so steeped in myth and falsehoods that this particular piece of information held scant value.

Regardless, a plan was afoot, a potentially extremely dangerous one with a highly destructive goal, and Rostov meant to thwart it. His sanity, his life, even his soul; he would offer it all up to negate this threat.

He sagged, exhausted, washing bloody fists in a bowl of already pink water. Never had a man looked more harrowed, this dank hold of bladed instruments and half-light ill-suiting him, as he turned and faced Syreniel.

She attended from the back of the chamber, her limiter cuff fully engaged so as to almost entirely nullify her abilities. The prisoner looked worse than Rostov, its face a bloody mask, its flesh gouged and torn. Yet it smiled still through red-rimed teeth, several of which had been removed.

'Silent...' rasped the inquisitor. 'I have need of your talents.'

Ah, so this was his plan.

Syreniel remained still at first, her gaze moving from Rostov to the prisoner and back again. She felt no sympathy for this creature; she barely even considered it human, for cultists and their like were to be despised and, ultimately, destroyed. They represented a cancer at the heart of humanity, an aberration of belief which was far more insidious than any contagion, and should at the earliest opportunity be excised. But she did wonder at whether its slow dismantling was worth the cost to the inquisitor.

'His mind remains closed to me,' said Rostov, breathy with the effort of his labours, and sounding impatient. 'I need you now. To help me break him.'

You should execute it, she signed. *We will learn little from a traitor, save more lies and betrayal. What knowledge could it possibly possess that is worth this amount of suffering?*

'Only a chosen few carry the sigil of the Hand,' Rostov explained, taking up a rag to wipe down the back of his neck, his forearms. 'And my gathered intelligence thus far points to this one being of some significance. He may have seen something, been privy to a secret or embedded with subconscious knowledge to accomplish a task or pass to another. The Great Enemy can be subtle in their arts, as you well know. He has been close to the one I seek and that in itself may, even in part, reveal where the Hand can be found. I am running out of time, Syreniel. The Imperium is running out of time.'

She moved, her steps loud against the cold stone floor. She wore her Vigilator's panoply but kept her sword sheathed on her back. Rostov had not summoned her for intimidation. Nor did he need her blade.

I strongly advise you to leave this room, she told him as she approached the prisoner.

'I cannot. It's not his confession I need, I must be a party to his agony. I have delivered punishment, now you must finish it and I'll cling to the hope that this isn't all for nothing.'

As you wish, she signed.

Stepping into the cordon of light surrounding the prisoner, Syreniel disengaged the limiter cuff.

At once, the cultist writhed and Rostov fell to his knees.

She glanced at him. *This is mild. There is more.*

He reached out, the inquisitor, grasping the wrist of the cultist, who was almost delirious with pain.

'Then give me more...' he spat between clenched teeth.

The limiter turned another notch, eliciting moans of agony from inquisitor and cultist both, but Rostov hung on.

'More...' he snarled, fists bunched, fingers white with tension.

Another notch – Syreniel barely had to move to inflict these agonies.

A shout from Rostov. 'Re-engage it now!' he cried.

Syreniel did as asked and saw the relief in the inquisitor, but the toll it had taken on the weaker mind of the cultist was evident as the creature visibly sagged.

'I see...' said Rostov. 'I see it! Darkness shackled, monstrous in form... A belt of stars...' Weeping, he thanked the Emperor for His strength.

The heathen cultist had no such haven. Its faith was fickle, abhorrent. It only moaned, its voice a thin trickle.

'Again!' snarled Rostov, and Syreniel turned off the limiter.

At once, the inquisitor convulsed, his face ashen with pain. The cultist had it far worse and screamed its agonies to the heedless gods of the warp. Rostov held on, shaking now. At his curt gesture, Syreniel re-engaged the limiter.

'Its shadow dwarfs the ambit of worlds... A beast, a beast in chains,' uttered Rostov, his endurance fading.

The cultist shivered in its bonds, its eyes rolled back in its head. Bucking and thrashing, mewling and spitting.

'Again!' bellowed Rostov, finding a few last reserves of strength.

Syreniel turned the limiter for the last time.

A dual scream rang out, echoing through the chamber. Rostov lost his grip and twisted his body into a foetal curl, shuddering and gasping.

She re-engaged the limiter cuff, all the way, nullifying the effect.

Both inquisitor and cultist sank down. They exhaled, spent. It took Rostov several minutes to regain his composure. After he did, he vomited and dragged himself up from his hands and knees.

Syreniel's gaze was questioning.

Haggard and still shaking, Rostov nodded. 'I have it,' he breathed. 'I have what we need.'

Strapped in its bindings, the cultist was dead.

The order went out and the *Omnes Videntes* deployed one of its void transports, bound for the imposing cruiser *Saint Aster*, warship of Battle Group Iolus.

It had taken several days to locate the flotilla of Fleet Tertius and another day to secure approval for an audience, the needs and demands of the crusade paramount and this concession to Rostov's urgent request a distraction at best. At worst, it was a grievous waste of resource and time. But he had some pull and used it without hesitation.

Standing in the hold of the void transport, Rostov had sharpened his attire considerably since the prisoner interrogation and wore his silver battle plate. The needles ravaged him, despite his silent companion's presence behind him, and he fought to keep the pain of it from his face. Syreniel had been right about the affliction worsening, and Rostov felt acutely aware of the inexorable passage of time and the fate that very likely awaited him. He need only do this, to finish what had been started at Machorta Sound when he had first heard of the so-called 'Hand of Abaddon'.

If nothing else, God-Emperor, he thought and prayed, *let me do this.*

He and he alone could avert the coming calamity, for he and he alone believed it a clear and present danger. Now he just had to convince the primarch and would take any advantage to do so. That included having a Talon of the Emperor, albeit a disgraced one, by his side – for was it not then providence that had brought him to this? Would Guilliman not interpret his father's hand at work? *Speculum obscurus,* to quote the Adeptus Custodes.

Syreniel alone accompanied him, the others in his company remaining aboard the *Omnes Videntes,* especially Cheelche. Though she might have the protection of Inquisitorial sanction, bringing a xenos aboard an Imperial crusade vessel would be unwise and do nothing to further Rostov's cause. He did not want to come across as a radical, with a radical's propensity for unreliability.

Besides, he had been considering leaving the *Omnes Videntes* and his retinue behind. This was not subterfuge or investigative work. It was war. He had no desire to spend his companions callously. In truth, he had grown attached to some of them, and there was what was happening to him to consider. He trusted the Silent Sister's resolve. She would not hesitate to do what was necessary, but Lacrante? Antoniato? Even Cheelche? A moment's compassion could jeopardise everything. And if he was being honest with himself he did not want them to see him degrade further, not to the point where he was no longer Leonid Rostov.

Assuming he could convince the primarch of his claims, he would take aboard ship with part of the fleet. He had Greyfax's mandate, if only tacit, and he had narrowed the parameters of his search to the Stygius Gilt, a region of the void served by the Exthilior Astropathic Waystation. Seven of the telepathic choir had died to behold their vision, a scrap of psychic chaff that had confounded their interlocutors.

A great black beast straining at its chains.

No orks in the region, according to Navy and Militarum reports, at least not of notable proliferation, and nothing that would concur with this specific phraseology and imagery when matched to the decipher texts. Yet every astropath had given the same testimony as they died, some in unison: the *exact words,* in fact, as they came out of the dreaming and to their death throes.

It matched what Rostov had seen. And the belt of stars in his vision provided corroboration, though it had taken several days poring over star maps and void captures to narrow in on the exact celestial configuration.

An investigator did not believe in coincidence. This was what Jeren Dyre had instilled in Rostov as an interrogator. He had to believe this was significant. It had to mean something. If nothing else, the aperture of his search had narrowed, though the Gilt was still a vast area.

One thing remained clear: he needed reinforcements. He was about to find out if they would be granted.

Hands clasped behind his back, Rostov watched the airlock open and admit the light and atmosphere of the *Saint Aster*.

He was greeted tersely but not coldly as he returned to the ever-churning war machine that was the Indomitus Crusade. A cadre of ship's armsmen in full armour and with shoulder-slung lasguns awaited the inquisitor on the embarkation deck, an immense space of docked aircraft thronged with ratings and engineers hauling refuelling pipes and wielding acetylene torches and pneumo-drills as they effected repairs. Everything was in a state of hyper-activity, a serious and controlled sense of urgency prevailing.

Over one hundred other ships of various functions and classes made up Battle Group Iolus' complement, an impressive armada capable of subduing systems or engaging almost any enemy of significant strength. Yet even with such raw power at the Imperium's command, it still teetered on the brink of annihilation. The Rift had seen to that and now, it seemed, that had been but the beginning of their troubles.

As he and Syreniel, who kept a respectful distance behind him, were led from the embarkation deck into the deeper confines of the ship, Rostov was forced to consider that his meeting might not be with the primarch at all. Unlikely, he thought, that Guilliman would have left his flagship, the *Dawn of Fire*, for such a meeting – and his place was also with Fleet Primus.

Perhaps it was better this way, for to try to convince a being as singular and daunting as the Avenging Son would be a feat potentially beyond Rostov's capacity in his diminished state. As it stood, his evidence was thinner than he would have liked.

An act of faith, then, he reflected and thought again of the dour, mute champion in his company.

Their armsman escort did not speak either as they conveyed the inquisitor and his ally, but stopped when they reached a long corridor with an ornate door at the end. Statues stood in grim procession down each wall, and Rostov also noticed a silver mirror that he did not care to look at and see his reflection. He felt sure he would have beheld a man far from his prime and nearing the ragged edge. He had not always been this way. The hunt, his 'gift' had changed him. He suspected it always would have, so he found it difficult to muster much resentment for the decline. As an inquisitor, a representative of the Holy Emperor on the Golden Throne, he had willingly surrendered his body, mind and even spirit to its service and sanctity.

Restorative as these assertions were, they still did not salve the pain of his afflictions.

It scarcely mattered. He had reached the door.

As it swung open on auto-hinges, Rostov stepped across the threshold into an officer's quarters. And standing behind a desk was someone he hadn't seen in what felt like an age.

'The years have worn you hard, Rostov,' a stentorian voice announced, but not unkindly.

'I wonder if your kind ever feel their passing,' Rostov replied, hiding his surprise at the daunting warrior before him. 'Do Astartes ever really age?'

'Only like stone,' said the other. 'We get harder but keep our sharp edges. Welcome to the *Saint Aster*.'

Rostov inclined his head in gratitude. 'Lord Messinius...'

The Space Marine listened as Rostov told him everything he had learned and everything that had transpired relating to the Hand since Machorta Sound. They had fought together in that conflict, allies in a common goal. Unlike many of his kind, Vitrian Messinius possessed many subtle human qualities: humour, patience and imagination among them. Rostov suspected these character traits, and their shared history, were the only reason the lord lieutenant had agreed to this audience. He also, Rostov hoped and believed, trusted the inquisitor.

A captain in the White Consuls Chapter when he was not serving Guilliman's will as one of the primarch's inner circle of advisors, Messinius wore white armour with gold trim and a blue paludamentum cinched to his right shoulder guard. A laurelled helm sat on the desk before him, which he had returned to sit behind, gauntleted fingers steepled as he considered the inquisitor's words. Messinius had the classic features of his noble genetic line, his hard eyes unblinking throughout. Not once, Rostov noticed, had he looked at Syreniel, as if her nature repelled him or his sight slid off her. For his own part, Rostov found he had to really focus to bring the Silent Sister to his attention.

Messinius knew she was there instinctively, like an apex predator is aware of another apex predator, Rostov realised. He tried not to dwell on it and the thought of being caught between two such creatures.

After he was finished, he leaned back to await the lord lieutenant's appraisal.

For several seconds, Messinius remained pensive, his breath even and steady. Had his eyes not been open, Rostov would have sworn the Astartes had fallen into a suspended animation coma. He did not know whether this boded well or ill for his cause and, despite himself, felt his pulse quicken.

'The Stygius Gilt is a large region of space. Even if the Hand has taken aboard ship or there is some holdfast or other bastion where they have made their lair, finding it will be costly and time-consuming. If it is even there at all.'

Rostov sensed an objection coming and made to intervene until Messinius raised a finger to stop him.

'I cannot deny that the Hand is a threat, and your belief that they are attempting to remake some old weapon of the Heresy War is... troubling. If I could derail part of the crusade to deal with it, the forces would be yours to command. But the hour is dire, inquisitor, and I cannot divert entire battle groups when the mission and its success is so uncertain.'

Like a candle burnt down to the last vestiges of its wick, Rostov felt the flame of his hope flicker and snuff out. He began to formulate a reasoned protest in his mind, something that a son of Guilliman would appreciate, but Messinius had not finished.

'However,' he continued, and an ember rekindled for Rostov, 'I have earmarked a modest force that I am able to spare. I assume you have at least some troops of your own? If nothing else, Rostov, you are resourceful.'

Rostov nodded. He had planned to have Nirdrangar and his men rendezvous with the fleet.

'And I see you travel with esteemed company,' added Messinius, and regarded the Silent Sister for the first time since the meeting began. 'Are you here to remind me of the Emperor's will, Talon? I serve an even better representative, I think,' he said, not waiting for her reply, and turned back to the inquisitor. 'A calculated move on your part?'

'I had to avail myself of every advantage.'

'I do not like to be manipulated, inquisitor.'

'Apologies, lord,' said Rostov, humbled.

'Find this stronghold if you can,' Messinius told him, 'and if successful and your fears of this Hand and its designs are founded then I promise you this – I will give you a host large enough to erase this foe from the galactic map.'

Rostov bowed his head. 'I am in your debt, Lord Messinius.'

'Call it an old ally fulfilling an oath.'

He rose to his feet, his war plate growling ominously, his sheer presence and mass even more imposing when he was standing. Rostov stood as well, markedly shorter, and made the sign of the aquila.

Messinius nodded in recognition and gave a last glance to the Silent Sister.

'I will also have need of a ship,' ventured Rostov.

'I know of one that will suit. You will like its captain, I think. She is a hunter too.'

Chapter Twenty

MOTHERLODE

THE COUNCIL SPEAKS

STAR FORTRESS

She had hunted the prize for many years, but this was the closest Vutred had ever come to obtaining it. Their elusive motherlode, the greatest prospect of the Omrigar's history, which would bring them out of imminent destitution and into prosperity. It was her destiny to find it and take it for the Kin; the Votann had decreed it. And by the will of the ancestors, Vutred would see it done.

'Promising,' she murmured, and sucked at her teeth. 'Very promising.'

She leaned over an imaging plinth, surrounded by her Votannic council and aboard her mining ship, the *Delver*. Cloistered around the three-foot mechanised stump protruding from the *Delver*'s deck, the Kin were bathed in the ice-blue illumination cast from the plinth's screen. A map was rendered upon it, together with the material readings from the ship's pan-spectral scanners.

'Potential yields look very high,' Brêkka concurred. 'Titanium, adamantine, metathane, even painite. Not an inconsiderable find.' The Iron-master's gnarled fingers traced the amounts on the screen as if to touch them would somehow render them the Kin's property.

Vutred knew they were their property. This was it. They had it, at long last. She had but to take it.

'Are you trying to make me salivate, Brêkka?'

'Always check the depth,' she replied, alluding to patience with matters of importance.

'Aye, true as wrought,' said Vutred, but her eyes flashed and her smile widened as she began to project what she could do with this much material wealth. 'This will restore the Kindred to prosperity. More than that. Our readings are sound. Our scanners have a firm lock.'

'It's in there,' Brêkka confirmed.

Vutred whistled. 'Trust the void. Any other claimants?'

'No other ships on our long-range scanners.'

'Luck has. Toil earns. Need keeps.' She addressed the Grimnyr, who had yet to speak. 'Othed... this is the will of the ancestors, aye?'

He had consulted with the Votann at length, discerned their will, parsed their knowledge. He and he alone could give the ancestors' blessing to this endeavour, but Vutred felt the truth of it in her blood, as keenly as she did the void.

After a long pause, during which the wintry light of the screen seemed echoed in Othed's eyes, the Grimnyr finally spoke.

'It is the motherlode, our destiny. Aye, it is the ancestors' will.'

Vutred leaned back, arms folded, and looked pleased with herself. As well she might. 'Very well, then...' She called out to the voidmaster of the *Delver* who sat stoically at his station. 'Make heading at once, Krykkâ. All ships...' Her teeth shone as she bared them in an avaricious grin. 'Make for the Stygius Gilt.'

* * *

Seven vessels emerged from the plunge, ethereal matter trailing off their hulls in gossamer strands.

For the Kin, traversal of the immaterium was entirely less perilous than it was for their Imperial counterparts. They favoured short 'plunges' rather than protracted journeys. This, alloyed to their natural resistance to the warp, made moving through this realm far less risky. And so Vutred and her Oathband reached the edge of the Stygius Gilt without incident.

A vast region of space stretched out before the flotilla, dense with nebulas, dying stars and the celestial ephemera of the deep and boundless void. Massive vapour clouds and gas giants blanketed standard sensors, and were resilient to penetration. Drifting asteroid belts and the wreckage of old freighters, long since plundered and no more than floating husks, made navigation less than straightforward.

These hazards offered minimal irritation to the Kin, whose pan-spectral scanners cut through the darkness of the unknown like a beacon fire. Through their superior technologies, they pinpointed almost to the mile where they would find their prize. A large sensor return came back from their probing, promising a colossal yield. The data-screed on the display inside Vutred's helm, patched through from the bridge, relayed every mineral, every resource, some of which were undefined and only piqued the kâhl's interest further.

She could almost taste it. *Profit.* In great abundance.

Her agreements with the guilds could be renegotiated, expanded. Operations would increase tenfold. She would need more ships. A score this large, she would have them. Perhaps she could even broker an alliance with another one of the Leagues. By the ancestors, her ambition could be unbridled.

And yet.

Vutred was as shrewd as she was greedy.

As the flotilla made for the Gilt interior, she had her Hearthkyn arm and ready themselves. The kâhl herself, who would allow no other to lead the initial exploratory expedition into the mother-lode, stood with her entire complement of Einhyr. Cthonic berserkers brought hammers and axes, eager for the labours ahead. A squad of Thunderkyn towered at the back of the Kinhost, hefting heavy weapons. She would take no chances here.

The other ships in the flotilla prepared their own forces. Three expeditions would descend on the target as soon as it had been identified and approached. Vutred expected a massive derelict or even an abandoned void station, maybe even a lunar giant. Whatever it was, it had to be big.

'Rigs, cutters and drills on standby...' she said, garbed in her armour. Around her, the embarkation deck lay eerily still as the Kin waited silently to head into landers. The main lights had been doused. Only the grey guide lamps along the floor were lit, and they cast the scene in a crepuscular glow.

Brêkka remained on the bridge, monitoring for the find. After what felt like an eternity, the comm-unit inside Vutred's helm hummed into activation and the Iron-master's voice issued through.

'Should be coming up to it at any moment,' the feed crackled. *'The vapour clouds are befouling our instruments, but readings are good and holding, praise the ancestors.'*

In front of Vutred, above the waiting landers that hung in closely packed ranks in their deployment cradles, was an immense shielded half-dome. An observatorium, one of the largest in the ship.

'Open up the outer dome shield,' Vutred ordered, 'I want to see it in its entirety.'

'At once, kâhl.'

Slowly, the great metal iris obscuring the void rolled back, each leaf of armour neatly folding into another until a vast and incredible vista was revealed.

At first there were just Oort clouds and swathes of ice dust, speckled with the bright hues of nebulas. Then came the rapid flare of a pulsar as the ships slid through the veil of obscuring matter to...

Nothing.

Empty void greeted Vutred, incredulity that quickly turned into a scowl wrinkling her features.

'What is this, Iron-master?'

'It is here,' said Brêkka, sounding flustered. *'It* should *be here. True as wrought, my interpretation of our readings is accurate.'*

'I see only the endless black, Iron-master. Consult your instruments again.'

'I have, kâhl, and it should be here.'

'Are you suggesting my eyes are at fault? I am staring at nothing! Where is the motherlode?'

Unease rippled through the Kin ranks like a crack in stone. A few voices murmured, but Vutred silenced them with a glare.

'Iron-master...' she pressed, anger rising.

'I am seeing what you are seeing, kâhl, but our readings do not lie. Wisdom of the ancestors, I–'

'My hearth burns, Brêkka. I warn you, do not invoke the ancestors to me. I forbid it.'

'I am sorry, kâhl, but I have no explanation.'

Incensed, the feeling of abject failure as dense as a neutron star, Vutred was about to disband the scouting party when Othed spoke.

'Wait...' The Grimnyr's eyes were aglow and hoar-frost crisped the edges of his armour as he clung to his ward-stave by the kâhl's side.

Through the giant aperture in the side of the ship, through several layers of barrier-warded glasek, the void shuddered. It *convulsed* as a metaphysical shock rippled through it and, like a membranous caul parting to admit its spawn into existence, a truly gargantuan ship appeared. To name it as a ship felt instantly insufficient. *Star fortress* might be more apt, but even that felt wanting as Vutred beheld the black colossus before her. Over five hundred miles distant, it still loomed like a blade-toothed threat. It had been ravaged by war and the degradation of aeons, great sections of its hull ripped away or simply crumbling fragment by fragment into the void.

'Blood of the ancestors...' she breathed.

The pan-spectral scanners lit up as every warning system on the ship went into immediate high alert.

It dwarfed the ships in the flotilla, its gravity well pulling at their engines, collapsing shields. If the massive star fortress had detected them, if any of its autonomic systems had activated to the Kin fleet's presence, it gave no immediate sign. It merely hung suspended in the void like a giant exo-planet, sloughing off the residue of the warp like an unwanted skin. It had clearly lurked within the immaterium, the reason for its sudden emergence unknown, but on some instinctual level Vutred knew it had reacted, suggesting some deep abiding sentience she could not at first explain.

Now she understood the readings they had seen, a true motherlode of unprecedented proportions. They merely had to acquire it. Even before giving the order to embark, Vutred knew they would have to break the monster apart into more manageable salvage. Like whalers of old, they would take what was valuable from the corpse and leave the rest to fester.

She lingered, awestruck, and as the ship tentatively closed, some details came into greater focus. It had docks, great jutting spikes with landing platforms like branches from a root. It had soaring spires and turrets.

Only when those turrets began to activate did Vutred sound the alarm.

Not a derelict at all. Not salvage. A monster of far-space.

As the weapons on the star fortress lit, only then did Vutred truly appreciate the sheer depth of her folly. But she was already committed.

'Engage that vessel,' she bellowed into her comms, klaxons resounding across the deck, 'every ship we have.'

They weathered the first salvos, heavy munitions rapping against barrier fields and absorbed by thick armour.

Urged on by its bold captain, the *Hewer*, a Bastion-class mining ship, fired off its ordnance. After a few moments, a spread of Mountain Breaker warheads struck the outer skin of the colossal star fortress. Sections broke off. Archaic bridges collapsed. A still-functioning shield lit and faded. Two more ships, one of them a Stronghold-class and a smaller Redoubt, joined the *Hewer* and moved into assault formation.

'Are they attempting to land troops?' asked Vutred, incredulous. She had just returned to the bridge, red-faced on account of her urgency, void-helm tucked under one arm as she addressed Krykkâ.

'I believe so, kâhl.'

She glanced from the tactical display providing an overview of the engagement to give a look of acid consternation to the voidmaster, who could do little but meet his kâhl's gaze. 'Order those ships to return to long-range bombardment positions immediately.'

The voidmaster responded in the affirmative.

'Remind them,' snarled Vutred, 'which vessel leads this Prospect.'

Minnows against the black colossus, the bold quartet of ships crept closer with engines at full burn. Vutred reckoned they were moments away from launching their landers.

The fools...

She felt her jealousy burn, quenched by a cold fear that she would not be first to set foot on the motherlode. And for the briefest moment, she waited to see what would happen.

As they closed to within launch range, a section of the star fortress shifted. Like a puzzle box, its sides sliding back to reveal a hidden compartment, the massive plates parted to reveal a primary weapon array.

Several arrays.

It fired all its defences at once at the interlopers.

The *Hewer* came apart in the first salvo, its voidmaster regretting his eagerness. There was no fight back, no heroic last stand. The *Hewer* was a mining vessel, stout but not equipped for such strenuous violence. Its shields buckled instantly, its major drives and crew decks pierced and then sundered. The flare of its annihilation burned brightly for a few seconds, and then there was nothing. Only debris.

Another vessel, the Stronghold-class called *Hearthhold*, thrust forward, belatedly coming to the *Hewer*'s rescue, cannon batteries firing at full bore. The barrage strafed against the flank of star fortress but barely bothered it, leaving a crackle of ineffectual starbursts.

It drew the ire of the dread black monster nonetheless.

Further weapons systems came online, a beam array that cut the *Hearthhold* into pieces, dissecting it like an old wreck. Magazines cooked off, the sequenced explosions pushing the already segmented remnants of the ship further apart, where they were left to drift unanchored in the void.

The Redoubt made to turn, pushing its reverse thrusters, trying to escape.

The black fortress cored the ship with a single, harrowing shot.

Vutred had plied the void ever since she had emerged from the genetor tank, her cloneskein engineered for far-space. She believed every ship possessed its own anima, just like the Ironkin of her beloved Kindred. She felt something now, looking through the bridge's observation port as the endless black of the star fortress closed over them. Hatred. Pain. Like an animal, chained in misery and made to suffer.

It *wanted* to hurt them. It had lured the ships in, feigning weakness.

A shadow seemed to crawl over the bridge, snuffing out the light of distant stars. Vutred felt her destiny reach around her neck and begin to squeeze.

'Get us out of here,' she breathed, transfixed by the night-black fortress creeping ever closer. Recharged, its weapon arrays lit like a field of red stars across the vastness of its surface. 'Right now!' she bellowed, and the voidmaster near leapt to action, having succumbed to the same dread awe as his kâhl.

Krykkâ shouted to the crew. 'Prepare for immediate warp plunge!'

Chapter Twenty-One

FRESH ORDERS

THE REALITY OF MIRACLES

OPERATION 'HELL GATE'

Gratefully, Kesh plunged into the water and felt a small measure of relief wash over her.

After three weeks in transit in a cramped carrier to reach Barrier Station, she needed it. As a trooper, pulse showers or a wash cloth and a basin of tepid water were the best she could hope for. Officers, though, they were allowed to *bathe*. An actual bath. Small, none too deep, but she had a block of soap and the water was hot.

Throne, was there anything more divine?

That thought, innocent enough, chilled her. They had made her a captain, given her rank, responsibility and privilege, but she was also something else. She saw it in the looks her adjutant gave her or the bowed heads of the Ministorum priests.

Divinity could appear in many ways. During these dark days of reconquest, many amongst humankind had come to believe that the Emperor was stirring, and His will had become manifest through chosen servants or in the deeds performed by these servants. Miracles. Kesh felt far from touched by the divine. There were things... things she could not readily explain, that, in truth, she had no desire *to* explain for fear that it would irrevocably change what she believed about herself. She felt pain, the burns that lingered on her arms, the soreness in her back, the weariness in her limbs. Cuts stung as the soapy water washed them, bruises ached as she moved.

Miracles did not ache.

And yet she had lived when she should have died. More than once. Either that meant she was preternaturally lucky or that some power beyond her understanding had protected her.

Annoyed with herself at spoiling her own serenity, Kesh stood and climbed out of the water. She dried off, dressed quickly. Her quarters had increased in size, several rooms made available to her in the prefabbed structure. As she moved from one to another, her new adjutant awaited her.

'Ma'am, I was just on my way to find you,' said Vosko.

Vosko was a corporal in the 84th Mordian. She had served as an adjutant before the war on Barren and was of a similar age to Kesh.

'Found,' said Kesh. 'Though any earlier and you would have seen a lot more of me than you probably cared to.'

Vosko remained unruffled and at attention.

Kesh flashed her a look, still unused to the deference afforded by her new rank. 'At ease, corporal. What do you need?'

Vosko had a scroll in her hand and offered it to Kesh. Breaking the wax seal with her knife, Kesh unfurled the parchment and read the machine-printed contents. The bottom had been signed in ink, Falden's name in wiry script.

'Orders from the colonel,' said Kesh, rereading before rolling up the parchment and handing it back to the adjutant. 'Army group wide. We're marching on Kreber Pass.'

Despite herself, Vosko swallowed loudly.

It was unexpected. A second battalion was meant to be joining them at Barrier Station before Imperial forces took on the Pass. Another thousand men and heavy armour.

'Was there anything else?' asked Kesh.

The adjutant shook her head. 'No, ma'am.'

Kesh's eye was drawn to the wooden mannequin in the corner of the room. Her armour sat upon it. Gilded carapace breastplate, emblazoned with a gold aquila, '84th' stamped on the gold-trimmed shoulder guard. It was a fine suit, regal, as befitting a Mordian captain. A leader's armour. Her first battle as an officer. Kesh willed it to be anything other than the Pass, but found her blessing from the Emperor did not extend to altering this particular fate.

Kreber Pass was the gateway into enemy-occupied Barren. Through it lay the largest continental landmass of the world's northern hemisphere. According to Militarum intelligence, it harboured the bulk of the enemy command structure and was believed to be the key to victory on Barren. That Colonel Falden had decided now was the time to try and take it either spoke of some hitherto unseen confidence in the Militarum's current campaign, or desperation.

She hoped for the former and, despite her loathing of the word, prayed for a miracle.

Falden had not made himself available for discussion after Kesh had left Barrier Station and arrived on the northern front, rearguard line.

As her command vehicle pulled into the dirt and gravel depot, she noticed the majority of the other officers had already arrived. She rode in with Vosko and a Catachan captain who had needed a ride. Kesh's command squad was also in the modest cab. This included Lodrin and Mavin, a banner bearer she barely knew called Atur. And with Abel Munser that made four.

Abel Munser: there was no soldier in the 84th that she trusted more. To his credit, Munser had behaved like a professional soldier. He no doubt carried some anger at being passed over but bore no obvious ill will to her personally. The man had Mordian rigour threaded through his bones. Discipline was as breathing to him.

'Hagan,' said the other officer who had been in the car with her, the Catachan, introducing himself as they walked through a gap across one of the muster fields. Utterly unlike the Mordian officers, Hagan was rugged and slightly unkempt, his uniform frayed and stained by old blood. Tanned skin gave him a healthy pallor, a sharp contrast to Kesh who was deathly pale by comparison. He wore his blond hair longer than most officers she knew, with a black bandana keeping it in place. She doubted it was regulation but doubted more that any commissar would be bold enough to call him on it. He had a look to him, a sort of far-off wariness that never seemed to abate, even when he was riding in the cab. Readiness, perhaps, was a better word for it. He dwarfed Kesh, his frame, his musculature. Every inch of exposed flesh on his body had a scar, it seemed, the puckered pink skin of healed knife wounds and acid burns like a detailed combat record.

As they walked on, he opened up a little and she learned that several Catachan regiments were spread across the Anaxian Line – on Barren and also Garrovire. The doughty death-worlder was as fierce a soldier as Kesh had ever met. He hadn't spoken during the journey in the car, his thoughts no doubt on the coming battle. But as he talked now, his features brightened, his initially dour demeanour softening into something more approachable, and she found the man instantly to her liking.

'I'm Kesh,' she said eventually. From the change in Hagan's expression, she could tell that meant something to him.

'I've heard stories...'

'Oh,' Kesh replied, thinking she might need to revise her earlier opinion. 'Are you about to kneel or something?'

Hagan kept his eyes forward on the prefab command bunker ahead where the officers would be gathering for Falden's briefing. 'Only if I need to tie my bootlaces. Or load up a heavy stubber. I only care about one thing, Kesh.' Now he turned to look at her. 'Can you soldier?'

'I can, sir. That I can do.'

'Good,' Hagan replied, returning his attention to their destination, 'and you don't have to call me sir when we're both of the same rank. Hagan will do just fine.'

'Still getting used to it,' Kesh confessed.

'No better primer than the field of battle.'

'I suppose not. You sound like someone I once knew.'

He raised an eyebrow. 'Once?'

'Died... On the field of battle. He was a pragmatic man, liked aphorisms.'

'I don't know much about aphorism, Kesh, but when it comes to war and death I find the only sane response is pragmatism.'

'Wise words.'

The command bunker was just a few feet away, and with it the time for further conversation had all but passed. Hagan mounted the steps, the Mordian sentries on duty taking in his rank pins and identity.

'Let's hope it's enough,' he said.

'Enough for what?' asked Kesh, following. She felt a brief tremor of anxiety at the silent appraisal of the guards, but they let her through without so much as a narrowed glance. She dared to allow herself to start to feel comfortable.

'To survive this.'

And just like that any positive feelings bled away and left behind something cold and solemn.

* * *

The bunker was cramped. A space made for twenty was being put to use for over forty. Shouldering her way through the polished brass masses as politely as she could, Kesh was glad she'd told Munser and the others of her command squad to wait with the regiment. She followed Hagan most of the way but parted to join her own and found a decent spot amongst the other Mordian officers towards the south side of the room, with a solid view of the strategium table.

Falden stood by it in a small ring of clear space, his roundish face stern and flushed. Unlike in his chambers back at Tartarus, he wore a silver breastplate and carried his helm under one arm. She wondered if he planned on being part of the attack or whether he would remain at rearguard as operational command.

Together with the colonel, she saw four other high-ranking officers who had also garnered a little more elbow room than their lowlier counterparts. She noticed one of them was Hagan, and wondered how high-ranking a captain he actually was.

The others were not known to her, but she recognised the regiments as Vardish and Gunbad – both carryovers from the attack on the Last Stronghold – together with an officer in a tank commander's uniform that she assumed belonged to the Mundin, the main armour assets accompanying the Militarum infantry.

Then came the slightly more *esoteric* members of the cadre. A Martian priest in typical red robes, his augmentations mostly hidden by his garb; a mistress of the Astra Telepathica, her head tilted slightly upwards, the light catching the hollow sockets where her eyes used to be, also enrobed; an Ecclesiarch in full religious vestments but armoured in a polished silver breastplate emblazoned with the aquila; and lastly, the forbidding black outline of the lord commissar, her cap pulled low so it cast a shadow over her eyes, her hands held behind her back.

Together, these men, women and others made up the entire command echelon for the Barren Northern Front Offensive.

This particular mission, the one these lauded officers now presided over, had been somewhat ominously dubbed 'Operation Hell Gate'. As Kesh saw them all standing there, looking as if they were about to be measured by their undertaker, she wondered which bastard of a high general had thought up this moniker. She didn't have long to ponder, as Falden began his address a second later.

'Ladies and gentlemen, to say this undertaking is of the most grievous import to this campaign and the hardest challenge we have yet faced, is a rather sizeable understatement.'

It went somewhat downhill from there.

Falden was eloquent and urbane; for a colonel Kesh found him decent but committed to his course, even if it might be folly. He had his orders, and come what may, they would be carried out or there would be no one left alive to carry them out.

Simple. Brutal.

She learned, with a rising feeling of unease, that Kreber Pass was heavily defended. Entrenched guns sat either side, worked into the near-impenetrable mountains. Several attempts had already been made by scout units to find a way through, but each one had failed, snared on hidden traps and then killed or hunted by enemy counterforces. This rate of attrition had left the Northern Front Offensive battle groups light on infiltrators.

And where the scalpel fails, the hammer prevails, Falden was wont to say, and did so again to a distinct lack of enthusiasm.

Grim resolve would serve instead, and Kesh's was growing by the minute as any air support was ruled out on account of the enemy missile arrays and flak cannons. That meant they would need to force the gap with infantry. Mechanised armour would provide support, covering fire. The phrase and the notion did not fill Kesh with confidence.

She came under brief scrutiny when the victory at the Last Stronghold was mentioned, specifically in conjunction with a surge in Imperial morale when the Renegade Astartes general had been slain. True, they had lost their own Space Marine too, but the Militarum had the front foot and the upper hand, or so Falden boasted, coughing up maxims like they were bullets.

And then he revealed why Operation Hell Gate had to happen now.

Imperial astropaths had intercepted a fluctuation in the warp, and Militarum intelligence worried that it signalled enemy reinforcement. This was confirmed, somewhat eerily, by the mistress of the Astra Telepathica.

'Belief is that xenos mercenaries or other cultist warbands are being called to the banner of their overlords on Barren,' said Falden, stepping back in to wrap up proceedings. 'Our concern is that this means the garrison in the Pass will be further reinforced, in which case our efforts to break through, however adamant, will be stymied indefinitely. A stalemate would be very costly, a forced retreat disastrous. We ride the boost in morale now after a hard-fought victory' – here he glanced at Kesh, but didn't linger – 'or squander it and beg the Emperor for forgiveness when He asks why we failed in our duty.'

He left a short pause, which the assembled officers filled with reverent silence. They all felt the singularity of this moment. It could be a turning point in the war, an irreversible one.

'We have no troops skilled in mountaineering, so it's a headlong push into the Pass. It will be bloody. Our losses will be high, but we must see it done. I don't say this to dent morale, it is merely a fact. Our heavy guns and mechanised armour will do their best to keep the enemy's defences busy, but there are numerous pillboxes and improvised bunkers blighting every inch of that bastard maw of razor-sharp rock, which will make our lives difficult.

'They want to kill us, make no mistake about that. Some of these women and men once served the Imperium. They have turned coat and abandoned honour and sanity for perfidy. No quarter, no clemency is to be granted. Mercy is not a word in your lexicons for the duration of this battle. And Emperor's strength to those brave souls in our spearhead.' Falden's gaze went to Kesh again, and this time he did linger.

The feeling of unease she had been nurturing in her stomach curdled aggressively into something firmer and colder.

'The Eighty-Fourth have the honour of leading the charge,' he said, 'Captain Magda Kesh commanding.'

Around her the officers parted, and she felt as exposed as a Valhallan on the ice plain without her winter attire.

She noticed a few make the aquila, or murmur a prayer under breath. The Ecclesiarch had stepped forward of the others, his eyes firmly on Kesh.

Throne...

It was an apt thought, but an unwilling one. *They want a miracle.*

Much of what came next she only attended in scraps. Chimeras as mobile armour, abhuman auxilia as bullet shields. The need to move fast and light. Establish a foothold and build from there.

God-Emperor, to hear it so plainly described it sounded even more like a suicide mission, and perhaps it was that stark realisation – or the fact that she had only just risen to the rank of officer – that prompted Kesh to speak up.

'What exactly do you think I will be able to do?'

The Ecclesiarch responded with terrifying solemnity. 'Whatever the Emperor wills.'

And Kesh felt the pit of dread inside her widen until it threatened to consume her entirely.

They had lost the Knights. Whatever oaths they had made had taken them elsewhere long before the Kreber Pass muster. Kesh doubted the precious war machines would have been risked on such an uncertain engagement. Open warfare was where the Knights excelled, not in grimy conflicts through narrow canyons where their weaknesses would be exposed to lesser foes. Losing such a potent war engine to a threat of equal and terrible severity was tragic and heroic; losing one to the lowly weapons of an army of footsloggers would be ignominious and profligate. The presiding general behind that farce would be hanged.

It was moot: the Knights had departed to wars elsewhere, and the Northern Front Offensive was on its own.

Kesh, it turned out, was not.

Hagan had three hundred troopers under his command and pledged them all in support of the spearhead assault. This was the extent of the Catachan forces on Barren, together with the ogryn militia, with whom the deathworlders shared an unnerving familiarity and kinship.

He grasped her forearm as warriors are wont to do in a gesture of solidarity, his hand as unyielding as an iron glove.

'War and death, Magda Kesh,' Hagan said to her as the reinforcements were amalgamated into the army. 'War and death.'

Chapter Twenty-Two

REVENANTS IN THE RUINS

PASSING THROUGH A VEIL

SECRETS

Death lay everywhere, not in the remains of bodies or the carcasses of beasts but rather their absence.

This civitas reminded Areios of his first experiences of true evil aboard the cursed ship the *Ideos*, what seemed a lifetime ago: less so the latent threat and more the sense of *wrongness* this place provoked in him. It was utterly deserted, nothing more than a burnt-out ruin. Ash had gathered in the empty hollows of blackened houses and manufactoria, across the breadth of a communal cantina and throughout silent arcades, drifting in ghost-like fragments on a weak breeze. The air brought with it the stench of stagnation, the musty aroma of somewhere left to die. Its revenants lingered, imagined in the empty places where people might once have dwelled and where now there was just ash.

An icon flashed inside his helm, drawing Areios' attention. It was a silent interrogative from Epathus. Areios consulted his auto-senses before checking in with Cicero, who monitored the squad's auspex. The Ultramarine shook his head.

'All clear, brothers,' he voxed, his voice subvocalised through his helm so that only those on the comms channel would hear it.

Three identical reports came back from the other squads. Nothing stirred in the ruins. Not even vermin. This bothered Areios, for as thorough as the Ecclesiarchy's purgation squads were, their fiery wrath seldom kept the gutter creatures at bay for long. The filth-eaters always returned. Not here, though. It was as if the city had been burned all the way to its studs, a tabula rasa awaiting imprinting. Many of the structures were already showing the strain of their repeated 'cleansings'. They creaked and cracked, several already collapsed and flaking into total disintegration. It might take years but eventually even the frame of the city would be gone, leaving behind its greying footprint.

Something had endured, though. Areios felt it in the unnatural stillness, in the loud snap of debris underneath his boots, and in the soughing of the wind through the blackened curtains of plastek its doomed residents had used to keep out the cold. Although no psyker, he could feel that. They all could.

A warehouse door creaked open on heat-stiffened hinges, three bolters turning as one as they trained on it, the sudden shriek of metal almost as incongruous as a child's laughter. The rest of the squad had moved into overwatch, guarding against a potential attack from any direction.

Areios was in the vanguard of three: him, Drussus and Helicio. He nodded towards the creaking warehouse door, raised two fingers of his left hand for Drussus and Helicio to follow, then made a fist for Cicero and the rest of the squad to hold position. Then Areios led the trio into the warehouse.

It was dark within, the air thick with dust and ash. Partially loaded haulers, their cargoes eroded by fire, were ranked up along one side of a large depot abandoned in the midst of deployment. More debris cluttered the interior. No bodies again, though Areios saw several lengths of rope hanging from the high rafters above, gently swaying. At least one had been fashioned into a noose.

Something glinted in the dust, catching a shaft of light coming through the gaps in the roof. Areios approached the source of the light, crouching to one knee so he could properly investigate. A locket sat discarded on the floor. Picking it up, he found its clasp open and a fire-eaten pict enclosed within. A woman and a boy. Both wore the greasy smocks of labour serfs. The boy was smiling, the woman more severe.

Areios let it fall from his grasp.

The warehouse was empty.

'Clear,' he said, standing, and was about to leave when he saw Helicio staring at something on the wall. Drussus had seen him too and he and Areios exchanged a glance, coming up on Helicio's left and right side respectively.

'Brother...' Drussus ventured. His voice, tinny through his helm, echoed slightly around the largely empty space.

Helicio didn't move at first, and kept staring, transfixed.

As Areios reached him, he laid a hand on Helicio's shoulder. The Astartes jerked as if startled, a drawn combat knife suddenly in his grip and pointed at Areios' throat. Had he meant his lieutenant harm, he would not have got far. Areios' bolt rifle was pressed point-blank against Helicio's chest.

'Lower your weapon,' he put to him evenly.

As if waking from a dream, Helicio looked down slowly at the knife... then sheathed it. Areios lowered the bolt rifle. Drussus' pulse as relayed by Areios' helm plate had quickened a fraction, but Helicio's remained steady.

'What is it, brother?' Areios asked him.

'I saw...' Helicio began, and turned so Areios and Drussus could see what he had been staring at.

A handprint smeared the rockcrete wall, small like a child's hand but much too high up, the fingers ending in what appeared to be talons. The feeling of wrongness Areios had been experiencing ever since entering the city amplified.

'Is that...?' Drussus asked, the three Astartes congregating around the child's mark.

'Blood,' Areios confirmed.

'It is... *disturbing*, brother,' said Drussus.

'Everything in this city is disturbing.' Areios stared at the mark for a few more seconds, before leading them out.

He was vigilant after that, and kept his brother in his sight as they resumed moving through the ruins. If Helicio felt watched he did not say, but he seemed sluggish, as if slow to throw off whatever mood had overtaken him in the warehouse. Areios wondered if it was something about this place, some piece of latent sorcery of the Oracles at work, embedded in the mortar like dirt under a fingernail. He called to mind the aftermath of the fight in the Forlorn Temple, and Helicio's strange disposition.

He sent a non-verbal message to Drussus.

Watch him.

Drussus already was.

As they neared their destination, the plaza Epathus had indicated on the hololith map, the atmosphere of the city changed. They had entered the eastern gate not long after dawn and made steady progress. Areios' retinal chrono registered mission duration at just under two hours and counting. That would put local time around mid-morning, but the light suggested otherwise, a crepuscular gloom lying over everything.

'I am detecting a decrease in temperature,' said Cicero.

'As am I,' murmured Helicio. He sounded distracted.

Areios had seen that too and gave the order for readiness. Bolt rifles came up into firing positions, and the fire-team spread into a more dispersed formation in order to cover more ground.

'Drussus...' said Areios, marking him as point man.

The Calthian moved up quickly, his weapon's targeter pressed to his retinal lens. 'Switching to infra-red.'

The others followed, Areios taking rearguard so he could keep watch on Helicio. He contacted Epathus via the vox.

'Encountering strange environmental readings,' he said.

After a few seconds, the captain replied. 'Concur. Light and heat diminished.'

'Orders, brother-captain?'

No hesitation followed. 'Proceed to rendezvous.'

Four fire-teams converged on the plaza, and as they closed, edging into sensor range, their idents appeared on Areios' retinal display, marked *Epathus*, *Maendaius* and *Vero*. Drussus made it to the plaza first and as he crossed the threshold, Areios saw him stall before entering.

'Like passing through a veil...' he murmured across the vox, an unfamiliar frigidity in his voice.

Grey gossamer lay across the entrance to the plaza. Almost like fog but less incorporeal, it seemed to gently drag at Areios as he too emerged through the opening after his brothers. Stone slabs had been placed in concentric circles around a vast space, far larger than suggested on the hololith map with a huge statue in the middle, made of marble but tarnished by the elements. Pink and blue mould grew at the bottom of the statue's plinth, reaching up in multihued tendrils.

The feeling here – it reminded Areios of the strangeness of the Forlorn Temple.

He realised the statue was not marble at all but crystal, a polished quartz that shimmered in the twilight. And not carved into the likeness of a saint, as he had first assumed, but something less than human – anthropomorphic but its limbs overlong, its back crooked not with the weight of faith but from mutation. Areios could swear he felt it breathing from within the folds of its crystalline hood.

There could be only one explanation for the statue's existence here: the Turned or their masters must have raised it.

'Be on your guard here,' he warned, his voice dead and flat in the anechoic space.

Eight other entrances led into the plaza aside from the one Drussus had used. Scraps of grey drifted in the brumal light like satin rippling through water, the air thick with it. Environmental readings came back blank. Whatever the grey scraps were, Astartes armour sensoria could not identify them.

Only when Maendaius appeared at the second opening did Areios discover their nature.

'Soul matter...' he uttered sonorously across the vox. 'The air is heavy with it. Throne,' he swore, in a rare show of emotion, 'the melancholia of this place, the agonies herein.'

'Are they hostile, brother?' asked Areios, who suddenly felt the Librarian's icy regard from halfway across the great plaza.

'No, lieutenant, they are tortured.'

'How is this even possible?' asked Epathus, having emerged from the third opening. Vero followed not a few seconds behind from the fourth entranceway into the plaza, and thus were the Ultramarines reunited.

'They were sacrificed here, and something of them lingered on afterwards, after the bodies broke down, after bone turned to ash. I feel it... an undertaking, a ritual summoning.'

Vero drew his sword, as did Areios. Epathus had unslung his thunder hammer. From days of old, as laid down in the *Codex Astartes*, the sons of Ultramar had learned that the best way to slay the warp-born, the so-called 'unburdened', was with edge and hammer. Old weapons for old enemies.

Areios eyed the unnatural fog, searching for any hint of movement, any stray shadow. It perturbed him greatly that they had not met any opposition. That in itself was cause for concern, but then the central statue further spurred his disquiet. He noticed the scraps of grey gyring inwards, like a slow-moving maelstrom with the statue as its nexus. He stated as much to Epathus, who ordered them to advance with caution.

They stopped, all four fire-teams at cardinal points, ten feet from the statue's plinth, having passed carefully through the grey scraps, letting them brush and slide off their armour as they did so. Every touch, even through ceramite and adamantine, provoked a chill. Hoar-frost started to edge Areios' armour.

'Hold here...' said Maendaius just before they reached this perimeter, and close enough that he didn't need to use vox. His eyes began to glow with an azure light inside the shadowy folds of his drawn hood.

'This... *materia*,' said Epathus, 'is it safe?'

'As safe as any matter of the warp,' Maendaius answered unreassuringly. His mind was on other things. 'I sense it... Something left behind,' he began. 'The spoor's trail ends at this point.' He gazed up at the statue, as if trying to perceive something Areios and the others could not.

Areios spoke to Epathus. 'I have an ill feeling, brother-captain.'

'You would not be alone in that, Brother Areios.'

'We could bring it down,' suggested Vero, indicating the statue.

Maendaius looked over from his scrying. 'That would be a grievous error, lieutenant. We have no knowledge of what this statue actually *is*. I have seen variations on this before, they are always a kind of containment. For what, though, I cannot say.' Corposant sparked across his psychic hood, prompting the Librarian to sharply turn back to the object of his interest. 'Something buried here...'

It was as if he was speaking in a trance, and Areios shared a concerned look with his captain, who gave a silent order to hold position. He wanted to know what the Librarian had found.

'The Oracles are traffickers of whispers and information,'

Maendaius went on. 'They ply the immaterial sea, dredging it for secrets. They are daemonologists and interpreters, speakers of primordial language. How many of the Neverborn are in their thrall, made to give up their otherworldly knowledge? Past, present and future... all is laid bare to them. Every portent, prophecy and prediction.'

At his words, the soul materia seemed to quicken, whirling in ever-more rapidly turning gyres. A faint radiance began to pulse from within the statue like a heartbeat. Red and warm like blood.

Maendaius drew closer to it, oblivious, almost somnambulant. Fire danced across the edge of his psychic hood, pink and blue.

'Something is wrong...' said Vero.

He wasn't the first to see it. Epathus had already hefted his hammer and now bore down on the statue. Half a step behind him, Areios raised his sword. He would split the statue in two if he had to.

'Destroy it,' Epathus ordered, pulling back his arm to swing.

Out of nowhere, Helicio barged him and the captain went sprawling across the plaza as if he'd been charged by a battle tank. He lost his grip on the thunder hammer and it scraped across the stone slabs to lie, crackling impotently, on its own.

Chapter Twenty-Three

KREBER PASS

INTO THE MAW

FEAR NO SHADOW

They went in on their own under the bombardment. Back at the rearguard line, the Mundin tanks fired restlessly. The infantry wore ear plugs under their helms to prevent them from being turned deaf by the ceaseless thunder of the ordnance.

Kesh followed in the shadow of a Chimera and glimpsed the explosions stippling the mountains. Smoke and displaced dirt filled the atmosphere, helping to mask the infantry's approach. Bayonet Platoon went with her, their squads spread across another three armoured personnel carriers moving in chain, acting as mobile armour. Las-bolts and solid shot pranged wildly off their hulls. Each of the tanks had been fitted with a dozer blade, ordinarily a debris clearance tool but put into use here as added shielding. It was necessary.

One of the Chimeras went up like a pyrotechnic, a spark lighting the fuel tanks before they exploded. Four Guardsmen died in the blast, cut to ribbons by shrapnel or engulfed by flames. The nearby survivors kept moving, finding fresh cover.

Behind Kesh's platoon came the rest, the better part of a regiment. To her left flank were the Catachans. Hagan's men. They came in swathes, heads down, hunkering behind the steadily moving transports. The ogryns had breacher shields, tall as men, and kept them raised throughout. A few had died already, left behind on the road, shields too big for any human to heft and lying like metal grave markers wherever they fell.

This part of the advance was the most perilous. Over two hundred feet of largely open ground lay before the infantry column until they would reach the mouth of the Pass, which the common soldiery had dubbed 'the Maw'. An apt moniker, thought Kesh as she played out the plan of advance in her mind. After the Maw, another half a mile through the neck – this being where the enemy had embedded the majority of their forces. There was a barricaded checkpoint at the end, also manned. A gauntlet before they could launch an assault against the mountains from behind and oust the enemy positions. Rate of attrition would be high.

Kesh had no way to calculate it. That grim arithmetic would come after. Assuming there was an after. She gripped the coin in her fist, still warm even through her glove, but no divine radiance came down to protect them, no wrathful lightning to scour the mountainside of traitors.

'Keep moving!' Kesh cried to her men, and saw Munser relay the same order down the line. They shared a brief glance, recognition of their mutual hell.

Mavin was shouting, 'Nine Devils!'

The vox-operator was not alone. Those who still lived did so under a constant hail of enemy fire, teeth clamped together or bellowing to chase away their fear, fists clenched around their weapons and praying they would survive the carnage.

Another Chimera took a hit. Rocket-propelled grenade, Kesh thought as it sailed past her and she followed its corkscrewing trajectory. It blew off a dozer blade and punched a hole through the glacis of the transport before exploding. Grey smoke billowed out, and the Chimera slewed to a halt. She heard screaming, troopers injured and in pain. Kesh kept going, all of her will bent on reaching the Maw.

After each hit to the armoured personnel carriers, protection for the troops thinned. Casualties rose with every second. Order wavered in the face of such resistance. Only another fifty feet or so to go and several of the squads had slowed, some even stopping to fire on the enemy, a rabble of ex-Guardsmen and cultists – but they were too far away and too well defended.

'Push on! Push on!' Kesh roared, the banner of the 84th flapping behind her as she urged on the desperate charge. Las-beams cut the air in front of her, stabbing from the darkness. A Mordian collapsed next to her, shot through the neck, and Munser rushed in to grab the banner pole before it fell. It took Kesh a few moments to realise the dead man was Atur.

'Mordian!' Munser bellowed, and she heard the rallying cry echo throughout the barrelling throng. Seldom had such dour troopers been so animated.

As the Maw reared ever closer, a chasmal opening of seeming infinite black, the Militarum were forced to narrow and congregate. Almost shoulder to shoulder, they had to abandon the Chimeras. The armoured personnel carriers were all but destroyed anyway, most of them burning wrecks on the road behind. They had served their purpose and got the infantry this far.

Darkness beckoned, forbidding as stygian hell, lit by sparks of flame. It was muzzle flash from the heavy stubbers raining down fire, suddenly target rich, as the Guardsmen funnelled in. The ogryn auxilia, those that were left, lumbered to the front. Breacher shields rang with shell impacts or fizzed with ricocheted las-bolts. Several of the abhumans were hit repeatedly and slumped to bloody halts.

Kesh made it through the gap, Munser and the others at her side, and reunited with Hagan, who had blood spattered across his face but shook his head at her concerned expression. None of it was his.

The sides of the mountain pass soared up like the walls of an ocean trench, their presence intimidating and claustrophobic. Guns stippled the crags and caves, the jutting overhangs and plateaus. The Guard pressed to the edges, away from the killing ground in the middle, but men died in their droves anyway.

Discipline, iron-forged from birth, kept the Mordians in order. They fired in precise volleys, taking out gun nests, whittling reckless bands of eager cultists. Bodies began to fall, bones crushed on impact, limbs twisted. Blood smears painted the ground.

The Imperial army pressed on.

There was a near-constant shriek of exchanged fire between the two forces now, the air thick with ozone. Kesh could taste it, actinic, on her tongue. She saw something loom ahead. A mob. The sound of braying and snorting preceded it.

Not a mob at all. A *herd*.

Abhuman beastmen in their hundreds. Things that might once have been men but had devolved into something even more savage. They had rusty blades, improvised clubs. A few carried pistols but could barely use them.

The neck of the pass was a funnel. Kesh used it.

'Flamers!' she bellowed.

Lodrin stepped up, joined by several of his comrades. The Catachans, deft at the use of burning promethium to cleanse particularly belligerent patches of their death world, had a strong contingent of the deadly weapons, and Hagan ordered his specialists forward.

A swell of fire lit the dark, suddenly and obscenely bright. The backwash of heat scalded their skin.

The beasts burned.

Those that did not die quickly flailed through the flames like they were fighting an angry sea. A few made it through, too stubborn, too enduring to die, and met the Guardsmen blade to blade. The ogryns swung their breacher shields like mallets. Kesh saw a Catachan brought down, still stabbing the burning beast as it bore her to the ground. Kesh shot one through the skull, ending its misery. Munser cut down another, shooting it through the chest with his lasgun, firing one-handed as he held on to the 84th's banner.

The scraps of beastman survivors didn't last long. A few were hit by stray shots from above as the cultists fired down heedlessly. The rest were cut apart by the Catachans, the burly troopers using bayonets and long-toothed knives to savage effect. Hagan drew a chainsword from his back, and the whirring saw edge tore through beast flesh like a razor.

They moved on, stepping over the steadily burning carcasses, inured to the bleating animal misery of the ones slow to die. They continued, gaining a few feet at a time, hunkered against the walls, firing at the enemy above, until they reached the checkpoint. Reinforced flakboard, sandbags, out-facing tank traps wound with spools of razor wire; it had a prefab tower at one end that served as a weapons nest, and a heavier iron gate that looked like it was bolted from the inside. Crude, but still an impediment.

And narrow. This part of the neck was easily the tightest. Even a single transport would have struggled to pass. The cultist army had light vehicles, bikes and ridgerunners better suited to the terrain.

Mordian sappers came up from the rear ranks and were immediately surrounded by the ogryns. The abhumans' shields formed an uneven dome that kept the field engineers safe as they placed their charges. An order rang out loud and clear from the engineer-sergeant, and the group withdrew. A few seconds later an explosion took out the checkpoint, tower, gate and all, the sound magnified by the tight confines of the neck.

Kesh didn't hesitate – she shouted to advance and stormed through the newly made breach.

On to the other side, through still-flaming pieces of flakboard, and Kesh stopped as an object rolled into her path. A grenade, its dull red light flashing. Counting down. Having made it this far through hell, Kesh had dared to believed that perhaps there was something, some*one*, watching over her. That He on Terra had chosen Magda Kesh for some lofty purpose she could not yet discern. Confronted by the blinking grenade light at her feet and the paralysis of her thoughts, she began to doubt. It would end here, all the claims proven false. Just a soldier after all. A lucky one, but dead all the same.

Only in death, as the saying went.

I shall fear no shadow, thought Kesh as she closed her eyes.

Then nothing, seconds stretching into what felt like minutes, and Kesh looked down. A dud grenade, the countdown stopped. She breathed.

I am bless–

The grenade exploded. A delayed fuse. A fraction beforehand, Kesh was hit by something hard, moving fast. She felt heat, her bones rattling at the impact wave, and then she was weightless but hurting as she flew through the air.

Hitting the ground hard, she blacked out.

Chapter Twenty-Four

FALLEN BROTHERS

I WILL HONOUR IT

A SECRET UNEARTHED

Vero advanced hard on Helicio, sword raised. He would kill his brother if he had to. Helicio met him, moving at impossible speed, and punched the lieutenant in the chest. Vero flew backwards, plastron shattering as he went airborne. He did not rise.

A crack fractured the statue and ugly red light issued forth. Areios saw it even as he, Drussus and the rest of the fire-team came at Helicio.

Antros and Gethius reached him first: Vero's men, anguished war cries on their lips as they went to avenge their commander. They fired on their battle-brother, hitting him with a barrage of well-placed bolt-rounds. He should be dead – Areios had already begun to assimilate his grief as the mass-reactives exploded – but Helicio did not die. He shuddered with the impacts, like a prize fighter shrugging off a flurry of blows, and then lunged for Antros.

Antros screamed as Helicio crushed his skull with his bare hand. The other he stabbed into Gethius, fingers straight like a blade, spearing through the Space Marine's torso and coming out gory and red on the other side. Gethius' power plant ruptured, exploded, engulfing both himself and Helicio in a bloom of fire and smoke that spilled outwards into the other Ultramarines.

Blackness sweeping over him, Areios surged through flame and in that moment a veiled memory returned to him, the heavy gauze obscuring it suddenly lifted.

In the Forlorn Temple... Helicio standing before the last Oracle, convulsing as he fought to resist the thing seeking ingress into his flesh, his mind. He struggled, fists clenched, turning rigid. And then... stillness.

Lying dormant within until reaching the statue here, slowly hollowing out its host.

Helicio was no more.

A monstrous amalgam of Astartes and warp-born horror remained, foul eruptions of bloated muscle splitting once-noble war plate, tentacular protrusions burrowing through mesh and skin. It hunched, still helmed, but overgrown with mutation, grossly lumpen and repulsive. Lopsided yet somehow stable, it let out a ululating cry of pain and anger.

'Merciful primarch...' he heard Cicero utter, but Areios was already moving to engage as the monstrous horror lashed at the statue. He met its foul appendage, a thick tendril of gelid pink flesh, and cut deep.

It screamed, hurt, and recoiled.

'Do not let it breach the statue,' Areios commanded. Sword at guard, the monster briefly at bay, he glanced to Maendaius, but the Librarian would be of no use here. On his knees, doubled over, hands clasped to his head, he cried out.

'It is here, it is here... One of the greater kind,' Maendaius declaimed, 'shackled to the materium. It is the keeper, that which harbours secrets from beyond the veil. It is here! Bound in stone by the Oracles and left to wither, now craving release...'

Helicio had been a vessel, infected, overwhelmed... Areios dared not think on it further. He cleaved to what he knew: his oaths before the primarch, before the unsheathed sword and the holy bolter. His duty to the Imperium, to his own sacred brotherhood of the Realm of Ultramar. And in the end, it was simple.

'Kill it.'

'Our brother...' said Drussus, dismayed, but he saw Vero, who lay bloodied and unmoving; Antros and Gethius, crushed and torn asunder.

'That thing is not Helicio,' declared Areios.

On his feet, coming at the monstrous horror from its flank, Epathus lit his thunder hammer, having recovered it from where it had fallen. Lightning cracked. 'Berion, Uxio... get Maendaius away from it,' he ordered, eyeing the creature warily as he closed on it. 'The rest of you... with me.'

They charged as one, blades drawn.

An untrained mob will often as not get in its own way if it tries to attack in unison. A man might be as likely to be stabbed or struck by a comrade as to land a blow against his enemy. Not so for an Astartes, and *never* for an Ultramarine. Warriors reborn, they had honed their battle craft and instinct through training and dedication to their killing art. They fought together, *truly* together, acting and reacting to each other, stabbing and withdrawing, keeping their monstrous foe disorientated and overwhelmed. In seconds, it bled ichor from a dozen deep wounds.

Yet it endured. And it grew, mutating in horrific profusion until it scarcely resembled Helicio any more, reduced to a bulbous mass of limbs and appendages wearing scraps of stretched metal.

It lashed out, a freakish, instinctual blow that caught Ixus on the attack and carved the Astartes in half. His spilled remains flecked Protus' armour as he lunged from the opposite side, a spiked tail impaling his chest. A welter of blood streamed from the hole in Protus' breastplate as the horror flung him aside.

It stabbed at Epathus, a host of bony spines suddenly spearing from its bared chest. The captain fended off the blow then leapt, smashing a limb as he brought down the thunder hammer. A screech of agony, tendrils whipping madly at Epathus, who swung again into the horror's flank. Flesh and hardened bone crumpled. It scurried away on pale arachnid limbs, bulling into Ramirus, who went down beneath the horror's bulk and was crushed.

Areios gave chase, shepherding it with heavy swings of his blade, hacking off rapidly grown scabs of chitin patching its skin. It stank, like overripe fruit, saccharine and cloying. Drussus landed a blow, a thrust that burst an eye that had bubbled up on the horror's hunched back, vitreous humour left streaming from the ruined socket.

As massive as a Redemptor, it towered over them both with little left of its former host, barring Helicio's helmed head clinging to a misshapen torso. The head split apart, revealing what remained of their brother, his face awash with anguish.

Areios paused, his hesitation momentary but enough for the horror to strike him. He felt a sting through his armour, across his chest, and then he was being propelled backwards, head over foot like a leaf in a storm. He stabbed in the mid-tumble, his blade piercing stone and finding an anchor. Skidding to a halt, a glance told Areios that Drussus was down, similarly caught off guard, and the horror was still coming.

Scythes of sharpened bone jutted from two of its forearms. As Areios wrenched free his blade, it raised them in a decapitating strike–

But was smashed aside before the blow could land, a thunder hammer ramming into its flank. Epathus swung again, lightning cracks strangely without echo. And again. Limbs shattered, bone fractured, flesh was pummelled. He beat it until only a ruined carcass remained.

Standing before the carnage, Areios pulled his broken sword from the ground. The blade snapped in two. The head of his thunder hammer swathed in gore, his armour likewise, Epathus turned to him. Drussus was rising, mercifully still alive, though many of their brethren were fit only for the Apothecary's reductor.

'Courage and honour...' Epathus began, the Ultramarian war cry an affirmation. He had rents in his battle plate, a crack down his left shoulder guard.

It did not save him as the thick tine of bone pierced his back and chest.

Epathus convulsed, back arched, as blood punched from the wound. He fell forward, and was caught by a bloodied Areios, who cradled his captain to the ground before turning his broken sword on the horror.

But it was already dead, or so close to death as to pose no threat. Its last violent act had claimed its slayer. So it would be an act of mercy, not vengeance, that Areios performed next.

He held the side of Helicio's face, now nought but a growth on the monstrously mutated thing, taking off his own helm and letting it fall to the ground so their eyes could meet. There was nothing but torture in those eyes, and a pleading desperation. Areios slid in the snapped blade through the ear, pushing it right to the hilt. Relief flickered, briefly replaced by horror, and then the eyes became as glass and whatever had been left of Helicio faded away.

At its final destruction, the monstrous horror deflated, ichorous essence leaking out of its once bloated form and leaving behind only distended and brutalised flesh. Helicio's flesh, pieces of broken armour intertwined. A bleak sight.

Drussus approached, his helm removed and held at his side, his face ashen. 'Blood of the primarch...' he breathed.

Areios went to Epathus. Even a cursory glance, and he knew the captain would not survive. A red and ugly flower had opened in his chest, exposing ruptured organs. That he still clung on at all was a testament to the man's immense willpower. He was reaching for his helm clasp, scrabbling at it with dying fingers. Depressing the seals, Areios removed it for him.

One eye was bloodshot, the other just filled with red. There was blood leaking out of his mouth too and smearing his face from where he had coughed it up against the inside of his helm. Lungs spasming, every breath was raw agony.

Epathus glanced to where his thunder hammer lay by his side unattended. Areios retrieved it, placing it reverently in his captain's grasp, but he was mistaken. Epathus frowned. Eyes urging, he used what remained of his strength to push the weapon towards the lieutenant.

Understanding now, Areios wrapped his fingers around the thunder hammer's haft, bringing it close to his body. He nodded once, murmured, 'I will honour it.'

And then Epathus was gone.

Maendaius yet lived, on his feet now but only with Cicero's aid. His ragged face suggested he had endured some unspeakable horror. Areios doubted he would ever find out what had happened.

The statue had become dormant, the bloody glow dying completely and the grey soul materia evaporating with it. The atmosphere reverted to a normal state, faint sunlight illuminating a grisly scene.

Their brothers dismembered and slain.

'We must not linger here,' muttered Maendaius.

Areios felt his ire rise. 'Our dead require extraction, Librarian. Honoured Vero and our vaunted brother-captain amongst them.' Turning to Cicero, he said, 'Call for Valentius.'

'Greater matters are afoot,' Maendaius replied, his voice oddly distant. 'In the torment... I saw it. I saw the secret the Oracles gleaned from the entity inside the statue.'

'Our brother-captain is amongst the dead!' Areios repeated firmly, his anger overspilling.

'Heed me,' said Maendaius, his eyes softly aglow. 'We must act. We must...'

'Act? What do you mean?' The hurt was a blade in Areios' side. The grief was a hammer's weight in his hands. Epathus had been a mentor, a brother of rare renown. He deserved more than the Librarian's casual disregard.

'A threat arises, and we must meet it with a ready sword.'

'Cease this gnomic babble, Maendaius. Speak plainly,' said Drussus.

'He speaks as plainly as he's able,' observed Areios.

The Librarian had not fully recovered at all; the light of madness shone in his eyes. Cicero, who was the closest, held his face and tried to reach him.

'A threat arises...' was all Maendaius would say.

Drussus looked on appalled. They had all witnessed what had happened to Helicio. The other Ultramarines had gathered now, the survivors, and their tension echoed that of Drussus. He began to slide his gladius from its scabbard.

'Sheathe it,' Areios ordered.

'If he looked beyond the veil, can he be trusted?' asked Cicero. 'Can anything he says be verified, brother-lieutenant?'

'None of it,' answered Areios flatly. They all looked to him now for leadership. He should try to reach his Chapter, send a missive to Calgar informing him of Epathus' death. Procedures would need to be followed, a replacement leader for the Sixth Company found and appointed. He *should* cleave to mission protocol and finish what they had started on Garrovire.

But Areios had ever listened to his instincts, and he trusted them, even if he did not wholly trust Maendaius in that moment.

'Where?' he asked simply. 'Where must we go to meet it?'

'To the edge of darkness,' the Librarian murmured, 'in stygian night, and into a gulf of dying stars...'

Chapter Twenty-Five

ON YOUR FEET

SHIELDED BY AN AQUILA

CHANTING

At least she wasn't dying, Kesh realised as she came to. Her heart thumped hard. She was dizzy, in pain. Her forehead was cut and bleeding into her eye. She wiped at the blood with her hand and her glove came back red. Every inch of her body ached. She must have been out for only a few seconds. Tall, dark walls of rock still surrounded her. Cold fear slid into her veins like ice water, and her hand began to tremor.

Even at Tartarus it hadn't been like this. Her near brush with death had shaken something loose, and Kesh felt her resolve waver as an old memory impressed itself.

She felt another hand grip hers, squeeze it.

'You better stay alive,' Munser was saying. 'Stay alive.'

'I can't...' she rasped. 'I can't...'

The walls closing, the light failing. *The bones smothering her...*

'Captain,' Munser urged. They had gone unnoticed for a few seconds, a natural overhang in the rock face partially shielding them from view.

Kesh refused to move. All she could see were the bones. She was back on Gathalamor, in the catacombs.

'Get up,' said Munser. 'Get up, damn you, ma'am!'

Here and no further: if she moved now she would slip beneath the bones, never to resurface.

'Kesh, they're dying. *We're* dying! Damn you!' He threw a solid punch to her jaw, and Kesh felt it like he'd hit her with a meat-slab. Her eyes met his as if she was seeing the lieutenant properly for the first time since he'd found her.

Still alive.

Las-fire and solid shot still rained down. Her troopers still died.

'Help me, lieutenant,' she grunted, finding her courage though her head was still spinning. She swore at the pain in her jaw.

Munser lifted her up, still holding on to the banner pole somehow. He had Lodrin with him, and the trooper helped get the captain to her feet.

'Come on, ma'am,' Munser was saying, 'we can't die here. On your feet, on your feet.'

The ground underneath lurched like a boat slipping in the water, and she stumbled. Munser and Lodrin held her, a crutch at either side. They were moving. Still dazed, only vaguely feeling the weapon pressed back into her hands, Kesh glanced at the body that had been lying next to her.

Hagan was on his back, torn open, eyes like glass. The blast had kicked them back as he shielded Kesh with his body. It had ripped his uniform apart to little more than shreds. An aquila was tattooed on his chest.

Shielded by an aquila... she thought, and shrugged Munser and Lodrin off.

'Just a flesh wound,' she lied but felt steady enough to carry on unaided. She kept her eyes and her head down, aimed squarely at the path ahead. A quick glance behind and she saw the gate yawned open in her wake, the flakboard barricade all but destroyed. A cultist who had been up in the watchtower began to stir, half buried by rubble.

Kesh shot it through the neck.

'God-Emperor!' she roared, fighting off the vertigo.

Throne, where in the hells had that even come from?

They had a foothold now. The cultists that had been entrenched above were being driven back by weight of fire, the sheer numbers of the Militarum the deciding factor. Men and women fed into the meat grinder, the hammer not the scalpel. The attrition was appalling. Around half the Catachans remained, led by a lieutenant in a tactical helmet with tattoos on her face. They stayed with Kesh and her platoon, roughly two hundred soldiers at the vanguard of the Imperial assault. Resistance against such indomitable determination wilted. Even the zealotry of the insane had it limits.

Kesh emerged from the back of Kreber Pass battered and bleeding, but alive. Gasping but triumphant. Cool air touched her skin and she breathed deeply. Sensing a turn of the tide, the cultist army began to break ranks. Some fled, abandoning their posts, seeking a path deeper into the mountains and away from Imperial vengeance. Others martyred themselves in acts of reckless aggression but were swiftly put down. Those that remained, who kept to their posts, eventually collapsed, crushed between the forces still advancing down the pass and those led by Magda Kesh that were suddenly at their backs.

Once the outcome of the battle became clearer, the colonel had sent in armoured Sentinels, the walkers too precious to waste in a headlong assault but perfect for rapid deployment as the enemy host capitulated and needed to be put to the sword. It happened quickly after that, the cleansing of the mountains, the securing of the pass itself. In time, a new checkpoint would be established, one branded with the Imperial eagle. It would be fortified, garrisoned and held. The pitch of the war had tipped, as it often did, seesawing towards Colonel Falden and his Northern Front Offensive.

As the last gasps of the fight played out, Kesh found herself advancing up a narrow and snaking trail through crags. It was good to be in open air again, away from the claustrophobic darkness of the pass. That fear which had gripped her, paralysing: she had been right back there again, in the catacombs of Gathalamor, buried amongst the dead...

Kesh shook it off, focused on the present. Munser was behind her, together with Lodrin and Mavin. She led two other squads, one of which was Catachan, the troopers having dispersed amid the dense terrain to root out pillboxes and hidden bunkers. Explosions detonated nearby. Smoke plumes haunted the air.

Kesh went deeper, headed towards where she thought the enemy's command echelon would be. They encountered sporadic resistance, but it was half-hearted, lacking the vehemence of the earlier stages of the defence. She lost one trooper to an ambush but one of the Catachans violently gutted the sniper with a savage-looking blade before further damage could be done.

After that, it turned silent and Kesh wondered if that was it, and whether the enemy commanders had already quit the field. At the prickling of her skin and the hackles rising on the back of her neck, she realised she was wrong.

'They're here...' she hissed to Munser, who had bundled up the Mordian flag and carried it and the banner pole on his back, attached to his other kit.

They both crouched amongst the rocks, Kesh's urgent battle sign to stop moving and wait heeded by all in the small force. One of the Catachans came forward, stealthy like a jungle cat, a broad woman with arms like banded steel and a bandana over her head. She had the tattoo of a snake around her left eye. Her rank pins made her a sergeant, and she had a lasgun etched with many kill-marks cradled in her thick-fingered grasp.

'Situation, captain?' she asked gruffly but respectfully.

'Something up ahead,' said Kesh, looking to a sharp bend in the path that seemed to lead to a wide gulley.

The sergeant cocked her head to one side, then sniffed at the air. She pointed to her ear, gesturing if anyone could hear what she was hearing.

Kesh nodded. Low on the breeze, rhythmic, repeating. And a smell, like sulphur.

'Chanting,' she said grimly.

They moved fast and low, lasguns close to their bodies, hurrying around the bend in the path with as much caution as they dared. A hidden gulley revealed itself, concealed by the crags and only reachable by this path. How Kesh had known, how she had decided to come this way, she could not answer. But she knew what she needed to do next.

A commune of robed figures came into sight, kneeling around a large ritual circle etched in blood. Several lesser acolytes lay dead nearby: traitor adjutants, vox-operators, soldiers. All had been sacrificed to the conclave. The air shimmered, felt strange, as if it was partially out of phase with the world around it. Some of the Catachans fired without orders, perhaps impelled by some deep-seated hatred or atavistic fear. Las-bolts and solid shot simply dissipated.

'Warp magic...' rasped a trooper called Kranich, his fear like cold ice in the air.

They all felt it.

They all saw it.

The demagogue of the commune stepped forth from its place at the circle, and its fellow cultists took up the chant, the words like ugly knives in Kesh's mind. She grimaced, the taste of wet copper in her mouth, the scent of hot iron in her nose. The rest of her troopers, even the Catachans, stood still, as if literally petrified, able only to stare, the expressions on their tortured faces hinting at the war happening within.

The demagogue's robes were finer than the rest, embroidered with sigils and other arcane devices. Kesh found it hard to focus on them for long; they seemed to squirm and shift before her eyes. It wore a conical and horned helm that covered its face, barring only its mouth. Grey flesh, like that of the dead, peeked from beneath the edges of sleeves. Its mouth was filled with arrow-sharp teeth, the kind of teeth common on some denizen of the deep sea. It clutched a sword with a serrated edge in one hand, scraped from a flesh scabbard. In the other was a staff, only it did not clutch it with a human hand but rather a tripartite tendril glinting wetly in the unnatural light.

And then it spoke, its words overlaying those of the chant, and Kranich died.

He died spitting blood, foaming at the mouth, crumpling to his knees. A single word did that, though it was no word that Kesh had ever heard and spoken in no language that she knew. It did not even sound like language, or really a word at all. It sounded like it had been called forth from the abyss, a malady without form.

Kesh's mind railed as it tried and failed to make sense of it.

The demagogue spoke again, a new inflection, a different malady, and the Catachan sergeant collapsed screaming, hands thrust over her ears as she seemed to drain before Kesh's eyes, as if all her vital fluids were being siphoned away, as if her very essence were being *drunk* by some unseen entity from beyond.

It slid its sword into Munser, the act slow and without effort. Munser could only watch as the demagogue's blade pierced him. He coughed up blood, a great gout of it all over his chin, spattering his face. His eyes found Kesh, and she watched, paralysed, horrified, as Abel Munser sank to his knees as the sword was withdrawn and the demagogue moved on to the next trooper.

All the while, the chanting persisted, every excruciating death bringing whatever rite the cultists were performing to its conclusion. Eerie faces lingered in the air, bestial, horned things, barely glimpsed and then only half forgotten. They had the consistency of smoke but were slowly forming into something more substantive. Kesh dared not imagine what would happen should the things contained within the ambit of the circle reach coalescence.

Her fingers found the coin, the Silent Sister's talisman, and the moment she touched it she was free.

She fired, the lasgun already clenched in her other hand, and shot the demagogue through the heart. It staggered, sword falling from its grasp still stained with Munser's blood. Radiating shock, it began a high-pitched squeal, its voice inhuman and echoed in turn by those of its dark flock. It rallied, a black nimbus rising around its hand, a snarl to its spine-fanged mouth. Kesh felt its intent, the desire to hurt, to maim and then to kill. She felt it in the other cultists too, the eight emoting as one, a conduit to the warp.

The lasgun grew suddenly hot in her grip and she dropped it. Her sword unsheathed a moment later, almost an act of divine kinaesthesia as she felt it rise as if wielded by another's hand.

By His *hand.*

It might have been the uncanny aura of the ritual circle or the trauma of seeing Munser so cruelly dispatched, but a light emerged from the blade, a radiance that burned away the black cloud around the demagogue. And when the light touched the Militarum troopers, they too were free and raised their weapons. As Kesh struck the demagogue, the cultists died to a blistering hail of las-fire.

Cold mountain air returned, biting but cleansed of whatever unearthly aura had overtaken it. Little remained of the commune, nought but smouldering cloaks and robes, their contents dissolving into puddles of ichorous matter. So too the demagogue, whose wretched squealing faded like a weak echo on the breeze, its body a blackened ooze that was turning to a noisome smoke.

'Don't breathe that in,' Kesh warned, as she went over to Munser.

Still alive.

She bellowed, 'Medicae!'

And as the ones who had borne witness to this miracle stood there, dumbfounded but relieved to have survived, Operation Hell Gate was concluded. Imperial victory was assured. It was, as it turned out after all, the Emperor's will.

Kesh sat alone in the prefab barrack house. It was part of Station Vulture, a hastily erected strongpoint on the north side of Kreber Pass and the new forward position of the Northern Front Army.

No one had come for her. No priests, no confessors with their callipers or holy unguents. As she waited for news on Munser's condition, she could only assume those who had fought against the commune had not truly understood what they were seeing – or perhaps they had simply decided to keep whatever they had witnessed to themselves. They were a handful of troopers, not an entire army like back at the Last Stronghold.

This one, though, this latest deed left Kesh the most unsettled. Had it been the coin? Was it somehow blessed? Or had it been her, and the coin had simply stirred something within her, *called* to her? She turned it over and over in her callused hands as she sat at the edge of one of the bunks, utterly lost in thought. The memory of bones intruded and she pushed it down, not liking this latest development. She had enough to wrangle mentally without her past coming back to betray her.

Therefore she didn't see Vosko enter and nearly leapt out of her skin as the adjutant announced herself.

'Ma'am.'

'Merciful Throne, corporal! I think I nearly stopped breathing just then.'

Vosko had been there in the attack on the commune but gave no outward sign, no hint of deference. 'Apologies, ma'am. I meant no alarm.'

At first Kesh wondered if Vosko had brought some word about Munser, but she discounted that almost immediately; the medicae would be standing here and not her adjutant if that was the case. Also, the adjutant had another wax-sealed scroll.

Kesh raised an eyebrow as Vosko handed it over.

God-Emperor, not another suicide mission...

She read, frowned. Read the words of the scroll again.

'Ma'am,' Vosko enquired, 'is everything all right?'

'Barren is done for the Eighty-Fourth,' said Kesh. 'We're being reassigned.'

'Where to, ma'am?'

Kesh looked up at the adjutant, the parchment scroll hanging loosely in her hand.

'Somewhere called the Stygius Gilt.'

Chapter Twenty-Six

SEEKING AN ALLIANCE

RED LIGHTS IN THE DARKNESS

AN AUDIENCE AT LAST

Darkness engulfed her. As cold as the eternal grave, it permeated her bones, her mind, suffocating breath and thought. Yheng reached out, trying to find a tether to bring her back, some thread of the vision Augury had shown her, but a nightmare of darkness swallowed her. Of Tenebrus, standing over her, and she bleeding out over the ground. Her potential ended by his blade.

She woke, having fallen asleep in some lightless chamber, to find the sorcerer glaring down at her with ophidian eyes.

'Gods!' she cried, but he was quick to silence her, his bony hand snaking around her mouth and clamping it shut.

'We must leave this place, Yheng,' he whispered. 'It is no longer safe.'

'It has *never* been safe,' she hissed, after managing to wriggle free.

Tenebrus straightened, his eyes on the shadows beyond the room. 'Our foes come for us.'

Still groggy from a fitful sleep, Yheng struggled to get her bearings. She couldn't remember coming here, though her wanderings within the fortress were not so unusual. Ever since Augury had shown her what lay in the obsidian mirror, something had *awoken* within her. And despite her initial euphoria, the experience had left her weak, fatigued. In any case, it had led her back to *him.*

'Our foes or *yours*?' she spat but instantly regretted her boldness.

Tenebrus' head snapped towards her. 'Been making some new friends, have we? I thought I smelled Augury's reek on you.' He leaned in close, near bending double so their faces almost touched. 'Know this, Yheng, you are my acolyte, and I your master. I will preserve you if I can, but only if you do as I bid, *exactly* as I bid.'

Yheng nodded, content to be obedient for now. Hurrying to her feet, she gathered her meagre belongings including the ritual knife, which she tucked in her belt, and left after Tenebrus. The sorcerer had already risen again and was shuffling away down a corridor.

'Where are we going?' asked Yheng, calling out but only just above a whisper.

'Far from here. As far as I can get us.'

She stopped then. 'To what end, master?' Yheng forced the last word; it felt unnatural on her tongue all of a sudden.

Tenebrus stopped and turned again, a wraith clothed in ragged black. His eyes glinted like opals. She recognised the barely restrained anger in them.

'To whatever end the gods will for you. Their eye is on you, Yheng. I might not know what you learned in the black chamber, but I know that much.'

'Is that truly what you want, master? To fulfil my destiny as fate and the gods will? You almost killed me...'

'Revelation seldom comes without pain.'

'And I do not trust you.' She stood her ground. 'I will not leave with you.'

Tenebrus' voice grew cold. 'What?'

'I refuse,' said Yheng, shaking with rage. 'I am no pawn, Tenebrus.'

'Fool,' he said with cool disdain. 'We are all pawns, Yheng! Have you learned nothing? Am I such a poor teacher that you haven't even grasped this truth? I have strived always to stave off ruin and damnation, to be a servant, not a slave. These are the lessons I impart to you, Yheng.'

'What did you see during the ritual?' Yheng demanded, eyes narrowed. He had not tried to kill her yet, which meant either he didn't want to or he couldn't. She drew confidence from that. 'You saw my fate, didn't you? Or at least a part of it, enough to realise I am important. Did it scare you, to see what I will become?'

Tenebrus chuckled mirthlessly. 'And what have *you* seen, my acolyte? Do not be so easily seduced by the Mother of Lies, the Father of Mendacity. They are cunning, Yheng. Augury is old, older than I dare imagine. They know what their would-be supplicants crave. With you it was easy. You want power. You think you already possess it. You do, but you are a poor mistress of it. That is what I see.' He drew up to her, crossing the distance between them as quick as shadow itself. 'I am powerful, Yheng, but I cannot survive alone. I need an ally.'

She scowled. 'You mean a sacrifice.'

Tenebrus closed on her, tall as the night, an all-encompassing darkness. She had to crane her neck just to meet his gaze, and felt her early boldness challenged before it.

'Had I wished it,' uttered the sorcerer in a dread rasp, 'I would have sent your soul to the ravenous children of the gods. If I wished it, I could do it now.'

Yheng reached behind her back for the knife, feeling its grip...

'You think you have power enough,' said Tenebrus, shrinking back to the robed sorcerer he was. 'Show me, then.' He gestured to the fortress, to the mirrored black of its walls. 'Make it bend to your will.' He took a calming breath. '*If* you can.'

Yheng could not. At least not yet.

And then she heard them, scuttling through the corridors, through the nooks and alcoves, across ceilings and barren chambers. Yheng's eyes widened as a softly glowing pinprick of red light lit in the distant darkness ahead of her. One became two, became ten, became many.

'Master...' she breathed.

Tenebrus whirled to face the horde as it advanced towards them on pincered limbs.

A bridge spanned the next chamber, as wide as a starship's embarkation deck. Tenebrus hurried onto it, urging Yheng to follow. Energised blades burned in the shadows just beyond the far side of the bridge, revealing the mechanised killers. They slowed as soon as they realised they had been seen, a machine herd letting its prey feel fear at its approach.

Run... they said, a unison of modulated voices matching Yheng's own.

She balked, fear stiffening her limbs. They crept onto the bridge with an eerie syncopated motion. The frosty glow of the giant lumen orb above gave them the appearance of animated ice.

Flee...

Tenebrus faced them alone... until his creatures drifted up from the darkness beneath the bridge, cloaked in shadows with knives bared.

Sensing a threat, the machine killers spurred into blistering movement and the creatures responded in kind as both mechanised horrors clashed. They tore and stabbed at each other, without fear or restraint. Though the sorcerer's creatures were larger and stronger, the Mechanicum killers fought as a unit, ganging up on their larger foes and making their superior numbers count.

Tenebrus waded into the throng, unleashing arcing shadow lightning from his fingertips. The lumen orb extinguished at his presence and the fight became one of staccato flashes, framing the violence. The outcome was uncertain, the victor impossible to predict.

Waiting at the edge of the bridge, fearful to step upon it and into the razored darkness, Yheng heard the voice again. Her voice, and yet not her voice.

Flee...

She fled.

Tenebrus bellowed after her but could not follow. 'Yheng!'

The fortress opened up before her, reacting to her needs, her *will*. She plunged on through stygian darkness, on and on, deeper and deeper, the mechanisms of the fortress shifting around her. Until, after a maddened scramble through myriad long black corridors, Yheng found herself in a massive chamber. She staggered over the threshold, gasping for breath.

Stark light emanated from a vaulted ceiling. Shivering in the penumbral shadow, Yheng looked up to see a caged star. It had been shackled utterly. Studded iron banded it, a pair of concentric circles slowly turning around a flickering sphere of white fire. Six thick iron chains fastened it to the floor.

Yheng could feel the fortress. *Pain. Anger.*

Had it led her here? Why?

The star shuddered, every lashed coronal ejection repelled by the banded iron cage.

Such majesty...

Yheng stared agape. And then concern began to overwhelm her wonder. She felt suddenly exposed, her old ganger's instincts signalling a warning. Hastily, she turned and was about to attempt to retrace her steps when she saw the doorway sealing behind her. For an insane moment, she thought about trying to slide sideways through the narrowing slit but quickly realised she would be crushed. It thinned to a crack and then disappeared entirely, so she rushed back into the chamber. An archway in the far wall looked like a way out, though she could scarcely see it through the radiance of the caged star.

She was making for the archway when Yheng realised she was not alone.

Stepping in front of the light, a bulky silhouette was revealed. Ragged black sackcloth clung to it, partly concealing a mechanised frame. Initially hunched, when it straightened to its full height it towered over her. A triumvirate of red, glowing lenses like eyes lit in its hooded face.

The Fourth. The Iron Magus.

Yheng had not been led here at all, she had been herded.

They had come for her at last, her fate arriving in black robes and skin of metal. Far from what was promised in the obsidian mirror, her end was to be death at the hands of a monster.

As the black cloth parted, Yheng saw something more akin to an arachnid than a human. Six limbs extended from a narrow torso and abdomen, all of it polished chrome and tarnished gold. The thing had blades for fingers, and several of those had been substituted for drills or saws or dulcetly burning torches: the Iron Magus was a torturous horror. The only visible flesh was a face, revealed as it was turned towards the caged star. A woman's face, albeit cybernetically enhanced. Her eyes were in triplicate and bionic, but her cheekbones, and the shape of her mouth, were all distinctly female.

Yheng could not decide whether it made this confrontation better or worse.

'Did you think,' began the Iron Magus, her voice metallically resonant though she had no obvious oral amplifier or augmetic, 'you were the only one who could manipulate the fortress? It is a machine – esoteric and arcane, but still a machine.'

'I don't know how I am changing the fortress. It just happened,' she snapped, defiant.

'Nothing "just happens", Tharador Yheng. There is always cause... and effect.' She raised one of her insectile limbs and opened her palm as if measuring an invisible weight in her hand, and then did the same again on the opposite side.

'I see...' said Yheng, eyes searching for an escape. 'What even is this place?' she asked, stalling for time. For a plan. For something that could improve her odds of survival. She gripped the handle of the knife tucked into her belt. She didn't think she could win in a fight, but then again a cornered animal will still bare its teeth.

'An energy core, a beating heart,' offered the Magus. 'It depends on what you believe.' She advanced, slowly but deliberately, towards Yheng. 'I have been siphoning it. A not inconsiderable task.' She cast a glance to the periphery of the room and Yheng followed, the light hinting at blackened remains – skeletons of other magi and their servitors.

'And what does any of that have to do with me?'

'Nothing. It was more efficient to do this here.'

One of the limbs slid from the folds of her robes, its blade fingers shining in the reflected light of the caged star.

'Why kill me?' Yheng asked. 'I am nothing to you, just a minor acolyte.'

'An untruth,' the Iron Magus replied coldly. 'Even you do not believe that. Your heart, the temperature of your skin, your breathing – it all betrays you, Tharador Yheng. I am more machine now than flesh, and I can detect your lies rudimentarily enough. But I will answer your question because I find it edifying to do so. Knowledge, however profane and proscribed, should always be shared. The decaying adepts of my former Order would not agree, but then again my erstwhile masters are all dead, so that hypothesis has reached a terminus.

'Here is the empirical truth, the abstract of my theory. You are far from nothing, Tharador Yheng.'

Each time the Iron Magus used her name, Yheng clenched her teeth. It was as if by reiterating it, she had some power over her. Perhaps she did.

Yheng was growing tired of that.

'Whilst there are those amongst this... *covenant* that divine through the whispers of the Neverborn, or haruspicy, or the casting of sorcery, I place my faith in mathematics, in calculus and probability. There is a pattern to the universe, laid bare for those with the intellect to perceive it. Secrets are revealed through its non-euclidian geometries. Aberrant sciences abound, thanatology, the non-linear disciplines of etherology and immaterialogy. It all led to you. Every logical and non-logical pathway, every scientific skein and numerological calculation.

'You are a critical variable, Tharador Yheng. A flaw in the chemical composition, one whose inherent volatility will denature the experiment. One that must be eliminated in order for the predicted outcome to be realised.'

Fell energies coursed across her bladed fingers.

'If it is any consolation,' uttered the Iron Magus in a voice of cold iron, 'it will be quick.'

Yheng backed away, fastening her grip on the knife.

Chapter Twenty-Seven

HELLSPAWNED

THE BURNED SPIRE

THE THREEFOLD WYTCH

The cultists had died by the knife, to ritual slaughter. It had taken time. After the killing came the dismemberment, the carving of sigils into flesh, the speaking of dark rites in forgotten tongues. They had no priest, but Clortho proved an able substitute. Herek had never liked the occultist warlord but could not deny his worth in that moment.

The others had raised up crosses made of bone, and of iron wrenched from the desert. They had staked the cultists up and bled them dry, Clortho's profane rhetoric spoken over every drop.

Then they had prepared, blades drawn, for what would come next.

Herek was at their head, his axe held in both hands. He did not have long to wait. After the last of the cultists had been anointed and drained, the skin of reality stretched and broke. Like malformed calves ripping free of their amniotic caul, the hellspawn poured through. Capering, leaping, lunging, whirling, they fell upon the renegades with savage abandon. A deluge of horn and tooth and claw.

It overwhelmed them immediately.

'The tower!' cried Herek, a great swing of Harrower cutting through three blood-skinned devils intent on his death. 'It is our only chance!'

Gunfire thundered across the plain as every Red Corsair fought for their lives, their very souls. Those who had run dry of ammunition drew blades or bludgeons. Old instincts never truly faded, and the warriors banded together in a defensive formation with Herek at their leading edge. He drew most of the hellspawn's ire, the creatures wild with rage and madness. Rathek stayed at his side, some of the swordsman's old frenzy reawakening, his battle plate swiftly slathered in black ichor. Kurgos stood at Herek's other shoulder, fending off the hordes with swathes of burning promethium from a hand flamer even as he carried the insensate soul mariner like a rag doll.

No mortal foe could have withstood the punishment meted out by the Red Corsairs, but the daemonkind never balked, relentless as a plague.

'A shame about Zareth,' said Kurgos, his manner eerily calm. 'We shall miss his sword.'

Herek hacked apart an ursine beast, only it was skinless and riddled with spines.

'We shall miss them all, Vassago,' he said sadly, and stepped over the bifurcated corpse to turn and try to rally his warriors.

Several of the Red Corsairs had fallen during the desperate charge towards the tower. Scarcely thirty remained and the cultists had been winnowed to a fraction of their original number. He saw a handful of the mortals turning, possessed by the very creatures they fought against, their bodies twisting and mutating. Shells of chitin, tentacles, a gaping maw of nubby teeth in one cultist's chest. Horrors unbound. Kurgos burned them as his brethren put the wretches to bolt and blade.

It wasn't enough.

The charge had slowed, mired by the sheer mass of daemonkind. Barely incarnate, the creatures were far from the monstrous terrors the renegades had fought aboard the *Ruin,* but they were grossly outnumbered. Skerrin disappeared under a sudden swell, his chainsword still cutting as the hellspawn dragged him down. Then Grejik soon after, impaled by a dozen horns and claws. His bolter rang dry long before his roars of defiance ended.

Reikor, Urgon, Kravix... all gone.

'Witness us, oh gods of Ruin!' bellowed Clortho, laying about with his battered mace, bleeding from a dozen wounds. Blood and ichor caked his face, giving him a savage aspect.

A great tide rose up at his beseeching, an amalgam of hellspawn gathering in a chittering, writhing arc, skin gleaming like wet blood. It dwarfed the Red Corsairs, casting the beleaguered warband in looming shadow. The other daemonkind retreated into it, joining it like a cursed sea recoiling from the shore.

For a moment there was cessation, a wake of renegade corpses revealed like flotsam amidst spilled blood and shell casings.

Herek gripped Harrower in both hands and planted his feet. A few of his men fired ineffectually into the tidal swell.

'Brace yourselves!' he roared.

And the wave of hell-born flesh crashed down.

He cut upwards into it, carving a path through flesh and bone and matter. Gore painted his armour, his face, but Herek refused to be drowned. He reaped, lopping heads and limbs, killing any unnatural thing that drew close. He pulled himself from the morass, the stinking warp-spun filth that lingered in this liminal place, this *other,* and through the nightmare he trudged towards the tower.

And then, appallingly sudden, it was over.

Sagging to one knee, Herek leaned hard on his axe haft. She purred, sated on daemonflesh, the hellspawn gradually dissolving at last. Emerging into his eyeline, he saw Rathek on his feet and cleaning his swords. Kurgos was behind him, but as soon as he caught Herek's eye and saw his lord was hale, he went hunting for the injured and the dead. His pickings would be plentiful.

The effort to rise pulled his face into a grimace as Herek eyed his prize. The burned spire.

He made for it at once.

A leather flap of skin barred the entrance of a tower of grey stone, ravaged by fire. Wooden beams jutted like rib bones in a broken roof. Runes marked every stone and hurt his eyes to look upon for too long.

Herek pulled aside the door and went inside.

It was dark at first, and larger than it had appeared on the outside. He soon found himself in a nonagonal chamber lit by black candles. The wax had melted almost down to the nub, the flaming wicks flickering like whispers.

And at the back of the room, sitting cross-legged on a foul-smelling nest of hair, sat a woman. Her lustrous skin almost shone, vibrant pink changing to azure depending on the angle of the light. In the eaves above, darkness held, despite the open roof. She wore gold – around her neck, the torcs on her arms, the rings on her overlong fingers and toes, the simple circlet encasing her head. A diaphanous robe stitched with celestial symbols and arcane sigils covered much of her body, as well as the hood over her head, but left her arms and her legs from the knees down bare.

Behind her was a heavy red curtain. In front, a fan of fox-edged, faded tarot cards.

'Are you a fate reader?' asked Herek, stepping into the candlelight.

Only then, as he came closer and the woman pulled back her

hood with a smile, did he realise she had not one face but three. She nodded, beckoning for Herek to sit. He leaned Harrower up against the wall and crouched before her.

'What is this place?'

The witch gathered up the cards, her second aspect watching him even as the first shuffled the deck. She fanned the cards again, her long fingers gesturing over them invitingly. Then she waited, pensive, that hollow smile like a curved blade in her mouth.

Something rustled the curtain, and Herek was about to look up when the witch gestured again. Another invitation.

He chose a card and the witch turned it over, delicate, almost lascivious. Herek felt his stomach churn and the curtain rustled again, as if stirred by a breeze, but the air was utterly still.

The card showed a naked man on his knees, head bowed as an overlord pointed down at him.

The Lackey...

A soft woman's voice hissed in his ear and he tensed in surprise, but the witch's lips did not move. They held that smile, that awful crescent smile. She gestured again, showing three fingers on her other hand. The first finger she curled back down into her palm.

Two more choices.

Herek touched another card and again it was turned. A rising flame this time, a huge and all-consuming conflagration. Then the voice again, that conspiratorial whisper.

The Hearthfire...

One more to go.

Herek's hand hovered over the cards. He looked at the witch. 'Where are we? What is this?'

She pointed to the cards.

He made his final selection. A king upon a throne, sceptre in hand, his enemies dead at his feet... only it was upside down.

The Ascended King, inverted.

'What does it mean?' Herek demanded, eager to be out of this place.

Something crawled behind the heavy curtain, and he slid his hand nearer to the haft of his axe.

Again the witch spoke, but again her lips remained unmoving. The candle flames flickered as if caught on her eldritch breath.

A fool becomes the maker, hoping for a crown, but finds his ambitions usurped by another king.

'That's drivel,' Herek growled, and stood up. The witch followed him with her eyes, a third opening in each of her foreheads.

Nine eyes have seen, the supplicant has chosen.

'I did not come here for riddles, cur. Speak plainly now.' He eyed the witch then the curtain, rippling now as an unfelt wind blew through it, exposing...

Herek grabbed Harrower as a host of tentacles burst forth, shredding through the curtain and coiling around his arms, his legs, his neck. The witch arose, towering over Herek, held fast in her grip, lifted on a bed of slithering appendages.

And the true Threefold Wytch appeared as the black candles blew out.

Herek caught snatches in the darkness. An abundance of oily, iridescent limbs. An odour, like lavender and spoiled eggs. The tentacles rippled around a rangy trunk. Skin, gelid and damp. The scent of brine and frost. A slit peeled open in the trunk, revealing a vertical maw filled with sharp teeth. It tottered on stump legs, squatting and shuffling, the 'woman' dangling limply off one of the creature's many limbs, a puppet performing to the will of the host, like a deep-sea predator's proboscis luring in prey.

It held him fast, like manacles of iron wrapping his arms and legs. Pulling him forward.

'I am no lackey,' he roared, wrenching an arm free, 'no carrion feast for the damned.' He kicked hard and a leg came loose, and for a few seconds his heavy armoured body swung in a low arc. Fingers reaching, he grasped the edge of his axe's hilt and Harrower slipped into his grasp.

A flash of silver, a fan of briny black blood, and Herek was free. He hit the ground hard as the creature let out a bleat of agony, its severed tentacle recoiling. Recovering quickly, it stabbed at Herek and he felt a thorny nail piece his war plate. He stepped back with a wild swing and another limb fell like dead meat.

It shrieked, spewing dark fluid up the walls, over Herek's armour, where it sizzled like cooking fat. He hacked again, finding his feet, batting away the flailing tentacles, cutting others in half. The trunk: he needed to kill it.

The creature thrashed, a blur of oily, stinking limbs battering at Herek. Barbs found chinks in his armour, made his skin burn, but something stronger fought off the creature's poison. As he harried it to the back of the room, leaving a string of severed limbs in his wake, a smaller slit opened up in the creature's bloody trunk. An eye, mildewed and pleading.

Mercy... it rasped in the woman's voice, softly in his ear.

Herek hacked down.

When he emerged from the tower, Herek found Rathek and Kurgos waiting for him. They stood ahead of the others, now a handful of motley warriors riven by battle. The daemonkind had gone, though the evidence of their attack was still slowly dissipating.

'Did you find what you sought?' asked Kurgos.

The soul mariner, the only non-Astartes still living, crouched in his shadow, an ear turned towards Herek like a canid listening for its master.

'Only lies,' said Herek, but that in itself was a lie.

'A heavy price for a lie,' said Kurgos, though he kept his words from sounding accusatory. He turned his attention to the soul mariner and reached for one of his knives.

'It's not his fault. I killed the Threefold Wytch.'

Kurgos canted his head slightly. 'Because she tried to kill you, or because you didn't like what she had to say?'

'Both.'

Suddenly, Rathek gestured urgently to the tower.

Preceded by a great cracking sound, the tower shuddered and felt apart. It took a matter of seconds – as if it had held together for aeons by the will of its host, and with the wytch now dead the many years of dilapidation were visited upon it. As the tower collapsed into rubble, a huge cloud of dust rose up to obscure it. When the cloud parted, it revealed a large ring of stones and, in the middle, a circular chasm that bored down into darkness.

'Gods...' breathed Clortho, as he stared into the abyss.

Rathek crouched at the edge too, intent on the darkness. *There is nothing,* he signed.

'I concur,' said Kurgos. Holding an empty vial over the gaping black, he released it.

He waited. They all did.

Nothing. No shattered glass. Not even the faintest sound of it striking rock. A few of the Red Corsairs exchanged serious glances.

I see handholds in the sides, signed Rathek.

Herek met Kurgos' stern gaze.

'Then we climb,' said Herek.

'To where?' asked the chirurgeon.

'Its nadir.'

Chapter Twenty-Eight

THE ROGUE TRADER

GATHERING FORCES

COMPANIONS

The old lunar outpost's name was Nadir. It was a way station, sparsely garrisoned, little more than a sentinel of the outer dark. A low place, hence the name. An inauspicious appellation, Rostov thought as he stood alone in the ship's map room. There had been no need to disembark; this would not be a long stay, and once they were all gathered they would need to be quickly underway.

He hadn't chosen Nadir for its obscurity, though that would certainly be useful in keeping a low profile, or for whatever omen it might or might not portend, but rather because of proximity. It was the closest Mandeville point reachable by the Imperial forces he had managed to recruit to his cause. It had docks large enough for a small flotilla, which would serve ably for the reinforcements Messinius had promised. He hoped, perhaps against hope, that they would be enough.

He hoped *he* would be enough.

Ever since he had interrogated the Hand's agent, Rostov had

felt weakened. Worse than he had been before, and that was saying something. As if the effort had left him harrowed, thin. It used to be the case that he would, after a time, recover his strength. Or at least some of it. Whatever this malaise was, it had reached a debilitating stage and left him weaker than he had ever been – the daggers and the burning in his back, his hand and arm, much of his body now in constant agony only kept at bay with doses of morphia. The opiate left him mentally dulled to the extent that he disliked taking it. If his body could not be sharp, then his mind would have to be instead. Alas, that sharpness also extended to his pain and he gripped the sides of the map table, waiting for the discomfort to pass.

It was the only source of light in a wood-panelled room that smelled of ice and damp fur. The shadows therefore peeled back only so far, but hinted at shields, spears and other warlike totems mounted on the walls. He caught a glimpse of a large runestone and several bestial skulls, glowering through hollowed eye sockets. Trophies, he realised.

A soft hiss of pressure signalled the door opening and the arrival of his appointment.

She was late.

'Have you found me a heading yet, inquisitor?' she asked, nonchalant as ever.

Katla Helvintr, rogue trader of House Helvintr and the Davamir Compact alliance, Jarl Paramount, and shipmistress of the *Wyrmslayer Queen*, swaggered as she walked. The fierce glint in her eyes that burned cold and blue like the unforgiving sky of her homeland betrayed her heritage, as did the fur cloak slung over one shoulder and the paired hand-axes she wore at her hips. Both had been inscribed with intricate runework like the great stone in the map room, and clearly by the hand of a master artisan.

Tall, broad of shoulder, she wore a silver breastplate whilst the rest of her attire was rugged, earthy, like that of a hunter. A tattoo of a skeletal wolf adorned the entire left side of her face, which was threaded with the white lines of old scars. The ink had been put in part to conceal horrific acid burns. Her red hair, like a blazing sunrise, framed features as stern and unyielding as the frozen crags of Fenris.

It was she who had discovered the Attilan Gate, a relatively stable passage across the Cicatrix Maledictum and therefore of great strategic value, and brought the vital news back to the crusade. Though he was not privy to the various troop movements within the major fleets, his province narrower and more specialised, based on the reports Greyfax had shared with him Rostov suspected that one of the reasons Messinius had been so frugal was because he was hoarding ships and armies for an assault on the Attilan Gate. Whether related to her discovery or not, Helvintr had been hailed a hero for her efforts. Tactical assessments in the region had been redrawn and troops re-tasked.

From what little conversation they had shared since his arrival on board the *Queen* – for he had learned to refer to the ship by its truncated title, as did both captain and crew – Rostov had garnered her original mission had been to lead one of the torchbearer fleets during the early part of the crusade. Since then, like so many of her kind, her vessel had been absorbed into one of the battle groups and made into a ship of the line. How she had eventually found the passage was not something she had shared. Rostov suspected it held some trauma for her, one she had no desire to revisit, and so had never pressed the issue.

'I thought navigation was your speciality,' he said dryly, trying to mask his physical discomfort.

She swore beneath her breath, a phlegmatic Fenrisian invective that had something to do with questioning the legitimacy of his birth and suggesting he lay with beasts. His smile was closer to a grimace, and he regretted not taking the morphia.

Despite her humour, there was some acerbity to her mood.

She had been swift to let Rostov know of her desire to be part of the first assault on the Gate, and that she considered this posting to be the latest of a series of 'fiery rings' she needed to pass through before being granted her wish. But she had agreed she would do her part, and to the best of her abilities.

And Rostov decided that was good enough for him.

He had told her that once this was over, assuming they found the stronghold and were able to overcome it, he would use his considerable influence to help give Helvintr what she desired. Less aggrieved than before, she had then spat in her hand and they shook on it. Not the first agreement Rostov had sealed in this manner in recent days.

'This is it,' he said as Helvintr came to stand next to him. Her face, like his, was lit by the faint grey radiance of the map table's holo-projection, and as she leaned in to get a closer look Rostov wrinkled his nose. She had an ursine aroma, redolent of stale sweat, cold meat and frost. Despite her uncouth manner, he liked her. And this was, after all, her ship. He gestured and a part of the map display magnified.

Helvintr gave a low whistle. 'That's a not inconsiderable amount of void-space.'

'The Stygius Gilt.'

She raised an eyebrow and gave him a scathing look. 'I know what it is, inquisitor, I can read maps surprisingly well.'

Rostov nodded an apology. 'Our quarry lies somewhere within it.'

'Yes, I have been meaning to ask you about that.'

She adjusted her belt, and ran her tongue over her teeth, as if trying to dislodge some errant piece of meat from her supper. Rostov was aware it was late and most of the crew had retired to quarters, leaving just a skeleton complement to run the ship. He rarely slept any more, and as such the concept of unsociable hours did not really factor into his comings and goings. Helvintr did not seem to mind, and seldom left the bridge anyway, which might also explain the stench.

'Our quarry,' she continued. 'I assume now we are close you can tell me what I am hunting?'

'In truth, I do not know,' Rostov answered honestly.

Helvintr scowled, simultaneously annoyed and incredulous. 'You've been on my ship for several weeks, inquisitor, and you did not think to mention that?'

Rostov gave her a knowing look. 'I get the impression, shipmistress, that you have undertaken endeavours like this on far less.'

She smiled reluctantly. 'True enough, but some idea of the prey is going to make this easier. Or at least help us more readily avoid death.' Her face darkened. 'Besides, I have a personal matter to conclude once this is over, and no wish to renege on it on account of no longer being alive.'

Rostov conceded the point. 'Astropaths referred to a "beast", a "great black beast straining at its chains". It is how I narrowed down the search to this region.'

'I know monsters, Rostov. I have hunted the terrors of the deep void for decades.'

'This I have heard, and with unerring accuracy. It is a rare gift that you possess, shipmistress.'

She looked askance at him, as if concerned at what he might say next, but Rostov had no interest in persecuting witches, no matter how curious their psyker talent might be.

He went on, 'I believe your people refer to it as your *wyrd*, is that accurate?'

'You have some understanding of Fenrisian culture, Rostov.'

'I have knowledge of a great many cultures. Tell me though, how does it manifest, this so-called wyrd?'

'Dreams and portents.' She shrugged, her face frowning as she struggled to convey what she wanted to describe. 'It is difficult to put into words. I can *feel* it.'

'"It"?'

'The weft and wend of the sea of souls, like a sailor knows the ocean. I hunt monsters, inquisitor, and I am very good at it, that is all there really is to understand.'

'I do not think it is a monster at all but rather something *monstrous* in scale. I have never believed the phrase "great beast" was literal, astropaths seldom are. Instead, it's more likely to refer to a ship or bastion.'

'More likely?' Helvintr queried. 'You mean you hope it isn't a monster, some thing of the deep void or the beyond.'

'Well, if it is, I am sure you have the appropriate...' He frowned, searching for the right word, and his gaze alighted on the trophies partially concealed by the shadows. '*Spear* to kill it with.'

'This ship, Emperor bless her prow to stern, has every spear we will need,' she replied pugnaciously. 'I guarantee it on the honour of my house.'

'Appreciated, but unnecessary. It *is* a ship, or an installation akin to a ship, I am nigh on certain of it. Something defensible but well hidden. I had scouts searching across half the galaxy and found only the scarcest morsel. I am beginning to consider whether it might even reside in the–' A hacking cough interrupted and Rostov folded over, convulsing violently.

Helvintr went to steady him, but he held her off with a raised hand.

'I'm well,' he said, once he'd recovered.

Her eyes narrowed. 'I'll let it pass that you just lied to me on my own ship. I have a *gothi* who knows something of healing arts, though. They are at your disposal.'

'I am afraid it would make little difference, as there is no healing this affliction.'

Helvintr gave a solemn nod. 'Then you have my respect, inquisitor.' She suddenly grimaced, her teeth clenched, and

Rostov wondered if he had somehow offended her but realised his pain had eased and knew *she* was here.

As silent as the void, Syreniel seemed to appear out of nowhere. Fully armoured, her gorget raised over her mouth and greatsword strapped to her back, she loomed over them both. She was ever close, recently.

'She earns her title, alright,' muttered Helvintr with a scowl. Not for the first time, she looked the Silent Sister up and down as if finding her not to her liking, but she could not quite keep the awe from her voice at being in the presence of a Talon of the Emperor. 'I don't know how you can stand it.'

'Oh,' said Rostov, nodding to his ally, whose gaze as it strayed to him, haggard and thin as he was, approached something like concern, 'you get used to it.'

Syreniel did not react. Instead, she signed a message. It was simple enough.

The first ships have arrived.

Standing before the vast plane of armaglass that was the *Queen*'s observation blister as he looked upon the amassed ships of his makeshift flotilla, Rostov had a single concerning thought.

It's not enough.

They had arrived over the last few days, just as Messinius had said they would, which given the current state of the warp was a minor miracle. But seeing them now, even arrayed in their austere and gothic majesty, Rostov prayed fervently for another.

Five ships, a pair of cruisers with their lesser escorts and a single powerful Retribution-class battleship: formidable weapons in any theatre of war, and yet he still felt the limit of their capabilities. Even with the *Wyrmslayer Queen*, a hardened vessel of great prowess, Rostov believed they would be found wanting against the Hand.

As if feeding off his unease, a pain spasm wracked his body, caused by the malady slowly destroying him. Recently, he had taken to walking with a staff. Rune-engraved and with a wolf's-head cap and a claw-footed ferrule, it had been a gift from Helvintr. She had given it gruffly but not without some small affection. He had been unfailingly honest with the rogue trader, about their chances and the difficulty of what they faced. She had appeared to relish the challenge and seemed to find the inquisitor's growing acerbity appealing.

Pain will do that, he supposed as he clung with both hands to the silverwood staff. *Turn someone bitter and caustic.*

Not for the first time since their parting, Rostov was glad he had sent Lacrante and the others to Luna. They might need a new master after this was over, and he had no doubt that Greyfax would see their talents put to use for another. A small comfort, perhaps. He stopped himself, suddenly aware of how maudlin he had become, first his body and now his mind beginning to contaminate.

'I worry...' he said aloud, using a cloth to wipe his mouth and seeing it come back stained red. He wasn't surprised, and then felt her presence behind him. 'You have taken to shadowing me of late, oh Silent.'

Syreniel came to stand beside him, also staring out into the darkness of the void. Rostov turned to her but could find no hint of feeling on her face. The Sisterhood had burned it out of her as if they'd seared every nerve ending.

How so? she asked, in that most elegant way she had about her.

'I worry that I will not be enough for this fight. That I will fail my Imperium and my Emperor.'

That is not what worries you.

Rostov raised an eyebrow. He had become accustomed to her, and even found the mild distaste generated by her presence oddly reassuring. At least when her limiter was fully engaged.

'When did you become an expert in psychology, Syreniel?'

I know when someone is lying, she signed. *Those who cannot speak listen well. I hear the lie.*

Rostov gave a half-hearted chuckle, bringing up a little more blood, which he only needed to dab away.

'This mission. This... *calling*. It has obsessed me since I first heard the name "the Hand of Abaddon". I have sacrificed a great deal to get here. To this moment. I fear what it all portends, what it means for the crusade and the Imperium. Much is still in the balance, and while I am self-aware enough to realise I cannot remedy every crisis, I believe I can stop the Hand. But I worry.' He had moved to face the void again but looked at Syreniel now, and found her looking back at him. 'I worry that I will not be the one to see it done, that I will not lead the fight. That this cruel malaise will take from me what I have striven so hard to attain.'

He let out a long, shuddering breath and faced the viewport once more. The Silent Sister stood reflected in it, a pale and silver-armoured ghost.

'Is it hubris, Syreniel, to feel like this?'

She did not answer straight away, and for a brief moment, Rostov thought she might not answer at all, before she lifted her hands.

I am a pariah to my species, and to the only kinswomen I ever knew. I am alone, and feel the terror of that loneliness in my every waking moment. I understand the fear that comes from loss, and the wild edge of sorrow that follows in its wake.

And here Rostov caught a glimmer of emotion, not a thawing but rather a deliberate slip of the mask in the softening of Syreniel's eyes and the pained furrow of her brow.

You are an inquisitor of the Holy Ordos, and you carry His authority more readily than I, who am merely a profound symbol of His will... But you are also human, and so not immune to regret, and the grief for what you have lost and may yet lose. I do not think it is hubristic, Leonid Rostov. I think it is rational fear and none, certainly not I, would judge you for that.

He was stunned, near literally. Never had one who had spoken so little said so much. Rostov bowed his head.

'I am glad to have you as a companion in this,' he said, his voice thick with emotion.

Whatever happens next, she signed, *I will be your sword and shield. Praise the Emperor.*

Rostov nodded, feeling a sense of affirmation as he made the sign of the aquila.

And as he looked, another ship emerged from the warp, trailing threads of immaterial ether, its blunt-nosed prow crackling with corposant. Unexpected, unlooked for, but here. Not a ship of the Imperial Navy, it was smaller and lighter but infinitely more predatory. A strike cruiser in shimmering blue, reflected starlight briefly turning its hull incandescent.

He recognised the massive white symbol on its flank and was reminded of words once spoken by his dead master.

We cannot know the Emperor's will, Dyre had said, *only act as His instruments.*

'Ultramarines...' uttered Rostov. 'Praise the Emperor, indeed.'

Chapter Twenty-Nine

WAR COUNCIL

VENTURING INTO THE UNKNOWN

TALK BETWEEN SOLDIERS

The strategic council had gathered under the Emperor's most enduring symbol.

Aboard the *Macharius*, the largest ship in the small fleet, Areios took in the majesty of the Imperial aquila engraved in the marble ceiling. Even now, long after his apotheosis and in service to the most lauded Chapter of the entire Adeptus Astartes, he felt humbled in its presence, and by everything that it represented for his species and the Imperium itself.

It had been unexpected, he conceded upon reflection, to see the ships here, arrayed and readying for war. Perhaps it should not have surprised him, but he had secretly harboured the notion that Maendaius might no longer have been reliable. He had certainly diminished during the long march from the dead city and back to the landing fields at Arrandius.

Epathus and the other honoured dead had come with them at Areios' order. With no other lieutenant in the company, and with the Librarian touching the edge of madness, he led the

Sixth Company now, and did so readily. He did not consider himself ambitious, but he knew it was his duty, and so he served and without compunction. The weapon he had been gifted remained a heavy burden, and more than just physically. He had barely hefted the hammer, let alone wielded it.

The passage from Garrovire had passed, as many transits did, without event, he and his Chapter brothers spending time in silent meditation as they mourned their fallen brethren, or training with sword and axe or on the weapons ranges.

Areios had instead chosen to repair his armour and sharpen his blade, as if it wasn't already lethal. The company had helots for such tasks, and their craft met the gruelling Astartes' standards, for this was their calling and their purpose as citizens of the Realm of Ultramar and servants of the Chapter. But Areios found the task appealing, a rare moment of calm in the tumult of his thoughts.

Only once did he visit Maendaius in the cell of his incarceration. He had been chained, and shackled about the neck with a null collar to dampen his abilities, all of this at the Librarian's own insistence in his increasingly rare moments of lucidity. He had found him murmuring, speaking again of what he had seen, his dark revelation.

Areios had come in hopes of conversing with the Librarian – of making sense of Epathus' death and those of his brothers, and of Helicio, whose remains, including his progenoid glands, had been burned and left on Garrovire. He had needed to hear the Librarian's confession again, the *exact* words he had spoken before they had made for the landers.

They have the Eight, he had said, *and the means to reforge a weapon of ancient malice...*

A troubling omen, but in Areios' experience they had never been anything other.

And so they had come to Nadir, the last outpost before the

Stygius Gilt. Areios had brought Cicero with him, the master sergeant acting as his second-in-command. The presence of the Astartes had sent tremors through the war party, felt nowhere more acutely than in this chamber aboard the battleship. He assessed the other officers swiftly.

They were mainly human, a motley assortment of Militarum and Navy officers. No other Space Marines, but this did not leave him overly troubled. The head of the council was an agent of the ordos, an inquisitor. He knew of this man.

Rostov.

He cut a very different figure to the one with whom Areios was familiar.

A wizened man presented himself, a gaunt wraith with thinning white hair, a patchy beard and silver carapace armour that seemed too large for his frame. Whatever rigours the war had visited upon Rostov, they had been severe, and to his obvious detriment. But then again, ordinary humans were not as durable as Astartes.

He had two others with him, his inner circle. Areios had minimal experience of inquisitors but knew they seldom travelled alone. One had the look of a huntress, bedecked in furs, her face inked to hide some old and grievous wound. She bristled in the presence of him and his brothers, as if sensing another predator. Areios paid it no mind. The third of the 'ruling' triumvirate was worthy of his attention, nothing less than a Talon of the Emperor, one of the Silent Sisterhood. To her, Areios inclined his head and saw the gesture reciprocated, one warrior to another.

An eclectic assembly.

In consideration to the ordinary humans, both Areios and Cicero had removed their helmets and held them one-handed at their sides, their other hand not far from their blades. And still he felt the anxiety of the other officers, of being in the Astartes' presence.

Rostov's voice, strong despite his outward infirmity, broke the tension.

'As of this moment, you, your troops and your ships are indentured to the service of the Holy Inquisition.' He glanced at the Ultramarines here as if preparing to meet a challenge, but they gave none. Maendaius had led them here, and so it was here they must be. Areios would serve and do whatever was necessary to prevent the coming darkness.

'Know this, what I reveal to you now is of the highest confidentiality. An agent of the enemy known as the Hand of Abaddon is believed to be at large in this region of the subsector, the Stygius Gilt.' At this, an image flickered into being, a hovering projection over the strategium dais around which they were all crowded. 'This agent must be found and stopped. Their plan, if successful, will have dire consequences, and could shift the precarious state of the war against us. We will hunt them down, and by the God-Emperor, we *must* destroy them.'

'What else is known of this... "Hand"?' asked an imperious-looking woman with gilded chains hung about her pristine Navy uniform and an ornate cutlass strapped to her belt, the shipmistress of the *Macharius*. 'Its military strength, its stronghold if it has one.'

'I shall not dissemble, shipmistress,' Rostov replied, his glare unwavering. 'We are venturing into the unknown. Gathered intelligence suggests a stronghold of some kind, concealed thus far. I believe it is alone, or else it would have been discovered by agents of the ordos by now. Nonetheless, we must be prepared for anything.'

The shipmistress gave a curt nod but did not look appeased. If anything, the unease in the room intensified.

'And how are we to find our enemy amidst the Gilt?' she asked. 'None here need me to point out it is a vast region of the void. We could search for years and still cover but a fraction of its expanse.'

Here, Rostov deferred to one of his allies, the unkempt and tattooed huntress.

'Like any quarry,' she said without preamble, 'it will leave a trail. Either here or in the immaterium, I can track it.'

Several of the officers made signs of warding.

She was a psyker, then, Areios realised. Or something akin to one. He recognised the Fenrisian markings on her trappings, runes he had seen before on a former brother of the Greyshields before he had departed the ranks of the Unnumbered to become a son of Russ. It felt a lifetime ago. He knew the Space Wolves and their kinsfolk had a unique perspective when it came to their harnessing of the warp.

The shipmistress of the *Macharius* put it boldly, lip curled in thinly veiled distaste. 'A witch?' she asked of Rostov.

'Hold your tongue,' snapped the huntress, 'and meet my eye when you try to impugn me.' Her hand moved instinctively to a belted hand-axe. 'I am no witch. My people would say I have the wyrd about me. It is no threat to you, and without it you would be as blind as you are deaf!'

Rostov held up a hand before further retort could be made.

'Whatever awaits us in the outer dark, it can traverse both materium and immaterium with ease. We will know when we are close. Ware your astropaths, your Navigators, they will feel it most keenly.'

'Feel what?' asked Areios, his voice a rumbling baritone in the crowded chamber. His thoughts had immediately gone to Maendaius.

All turned to him, but few met his gaze. The huntress was amongst those who did.

'Maleficarum...' she answered simply. 'The whispers of Chaos.'

'Be not mistaken,' said Rostov, his tone making it clear that the council was at an end, 'the enemy we seek has allied themselves with the Ruinous Powers. They will not fall easily or without bloodshed. I believe in the will of the Emperor, that He in His divine wisdom has brought about this chance. But it is just that, a *chance*, and a sliver of one at that.' His face became grim. 'I do not expect many of us to survive.'

Areios had heard enough. 'You have a company of the Emperor's Angels of Death, inquisitor,' he said, and donned his helmet. The voice that emerged through it was a machine growl. 'We shall see it done.'

Kesh's footsteps echoed down the wide passage as she made her way through the vessel's hold. It was dark and vast but cluttered with crates and trunks of varying sizes, all secured for transit.

They had taken ship aboard the *Venerated Sword*, abandoning Barren to its fate via massive ground-to-orbit landers. As far as she was aware, the entire 84th had left the warzone, but they were only one regiment amongst several departing the battle group for a new mission of which she knew almost nothing. Falden had held a briefing, with the emphasis on brief. His orders had been cursory, and she and the other Mordian officers had taken the news about their reposting in stoic silence. As was the Iron Guard's way, and always would be.

A mission of vermilion-level secrecy, and therefore above her and even the colonel's rank. How shaken he had appeared to not be the one in charge. A man like Falden got used to being the master of his own domain. Surrendering that agency could not have been easy for him. Their orders: reconnoitre for muster at Nadir, an Imperial outpost in a lesser-known subsector, and bound for the Stygius Gilt. All platoons without exception. Then they had been dismissed.

That had been the extent of it. Not much more than what had been on the reassignment letter she'd read back in the old barracks at Station Vulture. The colonel had left the briefing with a stiff jaw and the veins cording in his neck. Victory on

Barren had all but been assured for Falden. All that remained would have been to collect the laurels and enjoy the prestige.

'I've heard a rumour, ma'am,' said Vosko, clasping a data-slate, her well-worn face reflected in the green glow of its screen as they passed by seemingly endless crates of materiel.

'Is that so...' said Kesh, squinting as she tried to make out the stencilled serial numbers. 'Bring up that lumen, would you, Munser.'

Munser panned the lamp to where Kesh had indicated, and stark white light flooded the area.

'An officer from Dagger Company overheard Falden talking to one of his advisors,' Vosko went on, still scrolling down the data-slate's screen display.

Kesh frowned. 'Are you sure it's in this quadrant?' She leaned over to Munser and gestured to the paper he had tucked in his jacket pocket. He had healed well considering the injuries sustained, though he still moved with some stiffness. The medicae had been genuinely perplexed, but also relieved not to be consigning another Guardsman to the furnace. The lieutenant handed over the folded piece of paper for her to review.

'I heard something about the Inquisition,' said the adjutant.

Kesh paused, the paper still folded in her hand. 'Oh?' She shared a look with Munser, the natural shadows making his face appear more conspiratorial than it probably was.

'Whatever this is, ma'am, it must be high level. Important. I wondered if...'

Kesh turned on her, suddenly stern. 'Yes, go on, corporal, finish your sentence.'

'Only that, perhaps it is His will, ma'am, that we are here. That *you* are here.'

Kesh wanted to chastise Vosko but couldn't think of a reason beyond her own discomfort, and that didn't seem good enough. So instead, she held the adjutant's gaze and spoke plainly.

'Whatever His will, we shall know it soon enough. For now, *my* will is that we find these damn crates,' said Kesh and unfolded the paper.

'Yes, ma'am,' said Vosko, contrite.

The paper was a requisition order, stamped and facsimiled by the Departmento Munitorum. *Req. #1995*, signed off by *Niova Ariadne, Quartermaster Senioris*. Falden had sent Kesh to check on the supply drop they had secured from the Munitorum depot out of Barren, en route to Outpost Nadir. She checked the number against the one Vosko was looking for on her screen.

'It's here,' she said after a few seconds, her tone triumphant. 'Bay sixteen.'

Munser shone his lumen on the floor where the bay numbers had been machine-seared into the deck.

'Should be just up ahead,' murmured Kesh, and hoped to the Throne they wouldn't see anyone else in here. Bad enough she had Vosko to deal with. Kesh had thought the adjutant had better decorum.

Ever since Barren, news had travelled around the regiment. More than once, Kesh had found an aquila pendant hanging over her bunk or an Imperial prayer book left on her footlocker. A novitiate priest had even asked her to bless him until she sent the scruffy-faced boy running with his cassock between his legs. But the more she fought against it, the more the idea nagged at her. That she had been chosen, whatever that meant. It terrified her. She had only ever wanted to be a soldier and now she was a captain, which was fine by her. She actually found she enjoyed command and liked the responsibility it brought. But let it remain mundane. Spiritual salvation should come from those who understood it. That was not Kesh.

'Captain,' ventured Munser, his first words in a while, as he shone the lamp down at their feet where a 'XVI' had been marked on the floor. 'This is it.'

A servitor stood motionless nearby in its operational alcove and Kesh activated it via a keypad in the wall. The grey-skinned cyborg stirred into motion, pulling out the crate from its nook with a pair of industrial pneumatic forks it had in place of arms. It stood dead-eyed, an optic glowing amber in its skull, as Kesh input the lock code. The crate opened with a hiss of released pressure.

Munser shone the light on what was inside.

'Ever worn one of these?' he asked.

'Once,' said Kesh, glancing around the other crates in this quadrant. 'How many in the order?' she asked Vosko.

Vosko gave the number.

'Enough for the regiment,' said Munser.

'Well,' said Kesh, 'that's a start.' She looked at Vosko. 'Tell Falden it's all here. He'll want us on drills as soon as.'

As Vosko saluted and hurried off to inform the colonel, Kesh and Munser gazed down on the contents of the crate. It was Militarum void-gear. Hardened carapace body armour over insulated environment suits. Rebreather masks and close-fitting helmets as standard.

'Don't put me for up for court martial, but I have always preferred fighting on solid earth than in existential terror amidst the endless depths of the void,' Munser confessed.

Kesh gave a snort of amusement. It was hard not to agree.

'Besides, we all have fears,' said Munser. 'To not fear is to be inhuman. Fear keeps us alive.'

Kesh gave him a searching look, but his comment had been innocent.

'Ma'am?'

'I thought you were referring to what happened in the pass. I froze.'

'You got up, too. You lived.'

'True enough. I think it must be some kind of battle stress, something triggered by the grenade nearly killing me.'

Munser had a thoughtful look on his face but didn't say anything.

Kesh decided to change the subject. 'You haven't mentioned it,' she said.

'Ma'am? My fear of the deep void?'

'No, not that. The ridge, your injury... What happened afterwards.'

'I'm not sure I know what I experienced. I am alive, and it is thanks to you. How am I healed?'

He shook his head, made the sign of the aquila. She could tell he was trying to hold it in, his awe, even his reverence. It made her uneasy.

'I felt... I *saw* a light,' Munser went on. 'I think it came from your sword. And when it touched me...' He exhaled a long breath, remembering. 'Well, the pain eased. Either that or I was so close to death as to be seeing things. Like you said, battle stress. But I don't know if I believe that. I am trying very hard to remain pragmatic, to tell myself that I am still alive and that is what matters, but it is difficult. For so long, there has been a lack of hope and now? To *feel* what I felt, to *see* it?' He shook his head again.

'I think I always believed there was something about you, Magda, back when I dragged you out of that burning palace back on Kamidar. To witness all of that, the destruction, the fire. I would not have believed anyone could have survived that, and yet there you were, almost unharmed. And after the Last Stronghold. I saw the burns on your arms after you wielded that Astartes war axe. And yet, now there's almost nothing. No scars. I know you've tried to hide it, but it is what it is.'

'Why have you never said anything before, Abel?'

'Because it wasn't my place. It wasn't then, when I was your lieutenant, and it certainly isn't now that you're my captain. And I've made peace with that part, I want you to know. Wherever this is heading, whatever it means, its outcome, I will follow you, Kesh. If you lead, I will follow you. And so will all of us in the Eighty-Fourth.'

Her throat was suddenly dry and Kesh swallowed before she could reply.

'Throne, that's humbling...' she said. 'I fear it, Abel. I fear what it means. For me. Is that selfish?'

'It's human, and none could fault you for being that. That moment in the pass, that was human too. Our fight is for humanity, after all. And its survival. Isn't that why we are all here?'

'Sometimes I wonder.'

'I need to tell you something,' said Munser. 'I never prayed that much before. I am a dutiful servant of the Imperium, devout as any soldier must be, but I seldom clasped the aquila to my breast and spoke to Him. Now I pray every day, every battle. I pray for you, Magda Kesh. That you will protect us and that He will protect you.'

'Throne, Abel. It's a heavy burden already, and I don't even know what any of it really is. If it's even real.'

'That's faith, though, belief in the absence of proof. Except I've seen proof.'

Kesh exhaled. 'I wouldn't call it that. I just hope,' she said, closing the crate back up, 'that He can hear those prayers when we're out in the deep void.'

Chapter Thirty

FLOTILLA

HUNTING IN THE DARKNESS

THE BEAST REVEALED

The void spilled out in front of them like ink, the endless nothing of the Stygius Gilt.

Helvintr sat in her captain's throne on the bridge, her leg slung insouciantly over one of the chair arms. Behind her, a spear stood upright in its sheath. And belted to her hips, those axes that seemed to be her signature.

She had an odd but confident air, Rostov decided, having been afforded his own station on the command dais, a semi-circular pulpit below, containing the other crew stations, which were full and at readiness.

An eerie silence had descended ever since they entered the gulf, tight with expectation. Like a tripwire receptive to any motion that might send a tremor down its length. Lights were kept low, and the ship's sensoria softly pulsed as they plied the void for any sign, any spoor.

During those first hours, Rostov found his gaze drifting between the grand oculus, through which he and the rest of the bridge crew could see the outer dark, and the display screen on the helm relating the positions of the rest of the flotilla. They had spread out, as per Rostov's order and Helvintr's direction, with the *Macharius* helmed by Shipmistress Iola Lanspar taking the lead. A spearhead, except for the fact its true sharpness lay just behind: the *Honour of Iax*, the Astartes strike cruiser lurking in its shadow like a concealed predator.

He had spoken precious little to the Space Marines aboard but suspected they had been a part of the original requisition from Messinius. Their leader he recognised, but only in passing. He had named himself Ferren Areios, which was a concession Rostov had not expected; the Astartes, even the Ultramarines, were given to be taciturn even with others of their kind, let alone inquisitors. Rostov thought he detected a grim sort of resolve to their manner. Again, this was not unusual for their kind. He simply thanked the Emperor for their arrival and chose not to pry beyond what Areios had given.

Besides, it was another ship amongst their ranks that held greater interest for him.

According to Imperial Navy records, the *Venerated Sword* was assigned to the Astra Militarum as a transport frigate, an escort, which was not uncommon, but this particular vessel was notable for another reason. It currently ferried the 84th Mordian. Rostov still had the iron regimental badge Syreniel had taken from the soldier's rifle. He played it over and over in his hands, like a trickster rolling a coin over their knuckles. In his other hand, he gripped the wolf's-head of the silverwood staff and occasionally rapped it against the floor.

The sudden appearance of the Astartes, the 84th being part of the requisitioned forces sent by Messinius, it was more than coincidence. It had the ring of providence about it. The cult back on Srinagar, whilst dangerous lunatics, had prompted a thought in Rostov's mind, one that had been growing ever since and in these dark, quiet hours began to fully manifest.

There were those amongst the Holy Ordos who believed in the Emperor's resurgence. Some believed the Emperor could be reborn in a new host, or His power manifested through certain factions or individuals; others held more deviant beliefs of a darker resurrection. Rostov considered himself, and was considered by some of his peers, to be of the mildly radical mindset. In his storied past, he had fallen afoul of the more stringently puritan devotees of his ordo. Conservatism versus pragmatism. And it was not unheard of for inquisitors to hunt other inquisitors. Wars had been fought over it, wars fought in the shadows. But, radical or puritan, inquisitors on each side of the divide held to a truth – that the Emperor, or some divine version of Him or a power akin to His, could return – or was, in fact, already at large in the galaxy.

Now, considering all that he knew, all that he had seen and experienced, Rostov wondered whether the Srinagar cultists had been so deranged after all. Might these events suggest at least an active participation by something approaching the divine?

He had been cultivating this notion, thinking and rethinking on it, when Helvintr sat upright in her throne and leaned forward like a wolf sniffing prey.

'Helmsman.' Her voice raked the silence. 'Take us starboard by twenty degrees at three-quarters power. Send word throughout the flotilla at large. And expand all sensoria to maximum range!' She gripped the arms of her throne, an old sailor bracing for a storm, a feral glint in her eyes. 'We have it, by Throne and blood. It's close...'

Rostov found himself leaning forward eagerly, almost matching the rogue trader, his eye fixed on the sensoria screen.

Orders were cascaded across the fleet and as the tense minutes passed, he saw the more disparate ships at the fringes of the formation start to close up. Whatever was coming, Rostov knew they would need to be together to face it. The *Queen* lay on one of those fringes, acting as an outrider. Countless miles of the outer dark and they appeared to have found their quarry, or at least some scent of it that could be tracked. If that was not divine providence then Rostov had been in service of a lie for the last Throne knew how many decades.

'Any sign...?' he asked, impatient. Realising he had rasped the question, he asked it again much more loudly. He could not see anything of note on either the sensoria screen or through the oculus, where just blackness beckoned amongst faraway stars, celestial phenomena and the distant glow of burning plasma drives from their sister ships.

Helvintr could clearly feel it, though, and had moved to stand on the command dais. She had grasped her spear, the huntress in her coming forth. But then her face went from triumph to awe.

No, not awe, Rostov realised, and turned his gaze towards the grand oculus. *Fear.*

'Holy Emperor...' she gasped as a Blackstone Fortress tore into the materium.

It filled the grand oculus, monstrous and magnificent, immaterial matter slowly dissipating off its outer frame like ectoplasm.

Cadia's doom had come heralded by a Blackstone Fortress, as the *Will of Eternity* had crashed into the planet's surface, and thus had one of the longest-serving bastions in the Imperium's defence fallen. Few now remained of the so-called 'planet killers', the majority believed destroyed during the tumultuous Gothic War. Whether this was the last of that surviving breed or some revenant dredged from a forgotten corner of the warp, Rostov did not know. He only knew it was here, *a great black beast straining against its chains*, and that it possessed power enough to vanquish his entire fleet.

Helvintr called for all weapons to stations and engines to full power. She then bellowed against the shriek of alert klaxons so that the view through the grand oculus magnified, becoming a scope. A ship was revealed, still far from the *Queen*, a great and magnificent ship, the *Macharius*, and it faced off against the beast. The Blackstone Fortress dwarfed the Retribution-class vessel, but its weapons lit defiantly and a slew of lances spat forth. They rippled against the fortress' shields, cancelled out.

Even at maximum enhancement and with the *Queen* closing, it was almost impossible to see with any clarity, so Rostov concentrated on the vox instead.

'*...is immense,*' Shipmistress Lanspar of the *Macharius* was saying. *'Our lances barely touched it but at least we know it's shielded. And active, by the God-Emperor. Throne of Terra, I've never seen the like...'*

There was a pause, muffled orders barely audible in the background as Lanspar reacted to the changing situation. Every station on the bridge listened as they went about their work.

'It appears to be holding steady. The Stalwart in Faith *and* Divine Rite *are closing on our position. Nova cannon charging now.'*

Another pause, during which Helvintr turned to her helmsman.

'Get us to the *Macharius* and in this fight, helm.'

'Aye, mistress!'

But they were already burning hard, and even if the helmsman could squeeze an iota more speed from the engines, the other ships were still spread wide and the Blackstone Fortress had appeared too suddenly. The fleet was unprepared.

'We need to board it,' said Rostov, the vox just dead air for now as Lanspar marshalled her ship. 'The Astartes as our leading edge.'

Helvintr gave him a scathing look. 'And that only happens when we can close, inquisitor.' She glanced at the sensoria and the relative positions of the ships in the battlesphere. 'The *Honour of Iax* is making a run at it.' She referred to the Astartes strike cruiser that was coming out of the wake of the *Macharius*. Rostov knew the warriors aboard would be readying in drop pods and Cestus rams.

He briefly wondered if the assault boats would be able to breach the Blackstone Fortress' hull, which on the oculus looked thick and almost chitinous, like the barnacled hull of an ancient seafaring galleon.

The vox crackled, heralding Lanspar's return.

'Stalwart in Faith *and* Divine Rite *in formation. Still no movement. Will attempt overwhelm.*'

'All vox-channels stay open on the *Macharius*,' Helvintr ordered.

Rostov's attention flitted from the oculus to the vox, but both frustratingly remained vague as to the true context of the engagement. He could at least make out the *Stalwart in Faith* and *Divine Rite* having joined the *Macharius* in attack formation. Weapons flared on the two escorts as their port-side laser batteries fired.

And then the Blackstone Fortress began to react at last, as gun turrets aligned.

'It's readying to fire,' came the voice of Lanspar. They had barely scratched it. A fusillade from the fortress' turrets hit one of the escorts as it was trying to manoeuvre clear.

Lanspar provided the grim narration.

'Stalwart in Faith *is hit... Shields have collapsed. They're just... God-Emperor, they're gone. They're gone.*'

On the oculus the ship's destruction was a distant flash and nothing more.

'Capacitors primed,' said Lanspar. *'Firing nova cannon in three, two... FIRE!'*

'Get us to that damn fight, helm!' Helvintr was roaring.

Rostov's attention was mainly on the vox and Lanspar's increasing desperation.

'We've lost the Divine Rite. *That bastard thing... it cut her in half. Eight seconds to nova cannon impact... five, four...'*

Rostov turned back to the oculus.

'...three, two...'

A burst of light bloomed against the Blackstone Fortress like a sunrise, but as it faded the fortress remained intact. Inviolate.

'It took out the nova shell before full impact. It's still coming,' said Lanspar. *'I think we hurt it, though. There's palpable damage to some of the plating on one of its forks. Our shields are down. Reactors momentarily spent. And – hold on... Something is happening...'*

The other ships were closing, moving into attack range – Rostov could see it on the sensoria display. He also saw the strike cruiser on its own intercept vector. Still too far off to launch an assault.

And then he heard a gasp from the bridge crew and saw what had happened through the oculus.

The afterglow of a weapon discharge scarred the void, ugly and radiant. A red trailing wound that led to the wreckage of the *Macharius*. It had been destroyed, the Retribution-class ship reduced to a drifting debris field.

The vox had cut out.

For a few seconds, they all just stared.

'What just happened?' asked Rostov in the growing silence.

'It fired some kind of beam, something...' Helvintr began, struggling to find the words. 'It was maleficarum,' she rasped. 'All hands, prepare for battle! Send orders for the fleet to follow the *Queen*'s lead. Rake it with our guns! Give it a taste of Fenrisian steel!'

One of the escorts had limped out of the battlesphere and was slowly coming about in order to rejoin the rest of the fleet. They had the lead now, Helvintr shouting to the gods of wolves and winter as they homed in on the Blackstone Fortress.

'Keeps its guns on us, helm,' she snapped, 'and let's see its throat opened to the Astartes' spear.'

They would engage the massive star fortress as a fleet, and keep its attention on them so that the Ultramarines could make their assault relatively unmolested.

Rostov was reminded of his words to Syreniel, the Silent Sister a shadow at the edge of the bridge so as not to distract the crew with her aura. He had told her he wanted to lead the attack on the Hand, or at least be a part of it. He rose from his seat, pride fuelling his limbs. Nirdrangar's assault craft was waiting in the *Queen*'s hold. It would be simplicity itself to take it and follow in Areios' wake.

Rostov caught Syreniel's eye whilst trying to ignore Helvintr's and began to make for the door from the bridge. He stumbled and nearly fell, the ship trembling as it took hits on its void shields. They were in range now and the guns were speaking far below.

'I'll be right behind you, inquisitor,' Helvintr promised, a fiery glint in her eye as she watched him go, 'once we've weathered this storm. See you leave something for us.'

Rostov nodded, biting back the pain in his body, and forged on.

In the lower decks of the *Honour of Iax*, Maendaius howled. He thrashed against the chains binding his wrists, babbling non sequiturs. Amid the madness, Areios made out only a few words.

The Eight! A weapon of ancient malice!

Over and again until his voice was hoarse.

He doubted the Librarian would recover from this. He had been trained to withstand the rigours of touching the warp, but over-exposure to its malign forces had broken him. Even one of the Librarius was not inviolable. Maendaius had seen too much. And yet his prophecy had brought them here to this place, this moment. It all had the ring of inevitability about it. He wondered what Epathus would have done. Had he lived.

Standing before the cell door, Areios looked through the viewing slot for a few more seconds and then walked away.

'It is for the Emperor to decide his fate now,' he said as Cicero fell into lockstep beside him.

'Our brother's words,' ventured Cicero. 'Should we make mention of them to our allies?'

'With more time, perhaps. I am curious, and think the inquisitor knows more than he is willing to say.'

'Could it be that his secrets and those of Maendaius share some commonality?'

'I have considered that also, but the hour is late and the Imperium demands our service, Cicero.'

Cicero gave a short bow of the head to show his compliance.

'Are we prepared for assault?' asked Areios.

'All but you and I, brother-lieutenant.'

Areios clamped on his helm. 'Then let us be about it.'

Engines burning white, the *Honour of Iax* launched its assault. Attack craft surged from launch bays in an armoured spearhead, dashing into the void and running hard towards the Blackstone Fortress.

Rostov had stopped to watch. He had left the command dais and looked up from the bridge's crew pulpit like everyone else. He held on to the edge of a console, praying fervently for the Astartes' safe deliverance. Standing there, clinging to his staff to keep him upright, his earlier impulse to quit the ship and race out after them felt foolish. Almost suicidal.

He watched the attack craft as weapons fire spat and exploded around them, but the nimble boats wove through and around it, adjusting their assault vector to circumnavigate every obstacle.

'Come on, come on...' he urged, his knuckles turned white from holding on too hard.

If the Astartes could breach the fortress they would pave the way for the rest of the assault troops, the brave men and women of the Astra Militarum ready to face an unfamiliar battlefield but an all-too familiar cause. Species survival. Every victory, a candle flame. Every loss, one of those candles snuffed out. And there was, in the galaxy, an abundance of darkness.

The Blackstone Fortress fought. Its turrets chased down the *Redoubtable* and crippled it. The last escort listed, a final salvo destroying it. And then the fortress fired its principal weapon, the one that had killed the *Macharius*. Fired from the heart of the fortress, it coursed through the void in an eye-blink and left ravaged realspace in its wake. An immaterial beam, a ravening bloodlight born of the warp.

It struck the *Queen* amidships, collapsing her shields and taking out several of her broadsides. Carnage radiated outwards from the point of impact and multiple decks were breached. Explosions cascaded throughout the ship. Swathes of crewmen burned or else froze as they were sucked out into the void.

'Return fire!'

Helvintr clung to a brass rail at the front half of the command dais as a slew of ordnance spat forth from the *Queen*'s torpedo bays.

They were close, closer than any ship-to-ship combat ever should be, and the rogue trader looked like she had the scent of blood. Emergency klaxons were shrieking, a cascade of damage reports coming in from all stations. She ignored them and instead focused on the ever-widening torpedo spread. Even at such a remove via the oculus, Rostov could see the Blackstone Fortress had taken some superficial damage. Atmosphere vented from a dozen or more places in one part of its expansive hull. Lanspar had been accurate in her assessment. Her ship *had* hurt it. And as if battling a mythical drake whose vulnerable belly betrays a gap in its armour, Helvintr aimed for the weakness.

A few of the turrets reacted to the threat, taking out half of the incoming ordnance, but the rest ran the gauntlet and made it through. A large explosion rippled across part of the Blackstone Fortress' superstructure. Not a killing blow but a wound, an actual wound.

She roared, and her crew roared with her, briefly drunk on vengeance.

'It bleeds!' she declared, but they were bleeding too.

And now it was the Blackstone Fortress' turn to reply.

Helvintr called for evasive manoeuvres, ordered decks sealed and emergency power rerouted to shields – trying to save her ship from dying, and everyone aboard from a fate worse than death. She evoked the gods of winter, of storms, of the ice winds of Fenris. Her crew made signs of warding against evil and clung to the runestones hung around their necks or bound with leather thongs to their wrists. Every ritual was leveraged for their survival.

All of it was for nothing as the beam struck again and the grand oculus broke apart. A section of the ceiling came with it, brutally sheared away, and crashed down on Rostov.

Chapter Thirty-One

LIGHT OF A CAPTURED SUN

THE HEART OF THE FORTRESS

AFRAID NO MORE

A massive crash thundered through the chamber as the ground trembled and huge chunks of blackstone rained from the ceiling. A large piece struck one of the chains holding the caged star and smashed right through it. One of the fiery tendrils lashed out, scorching a patch of wall and spoiling its mirrored sheen.

The Iron Magus turned from the imminent murder of Yheng to the burning sun that had annihilated so many of her brethren.

'No… it must be stabilised. In order to stave off exothermic calamity, it must–' She was turning to take note of Yheng, about to share her knowledge of the machine, but her hypothesis died on her all-too-human lips when the ritual knife was plunged into her back.

'It wants to be free,' said Yheng as she wrenched out the knife and kept on stabbing.

The Iron Magus arched in agony.

The other chains had begun rattling, placed under sudden strain.

Oil and blood slicked the blade as it came out for a fifth time. Yheng knew how to wield a knife, she knew it well. You never slashed, not if you intended to kill or could not kill in a single blow. You always stabbed, and repeatedly. It was efficient, quick. The knife would find the vulnerable organs and whilst she did not know where or if her monstrous enemy had any, she knew the Iron Magus felt something. She was screaming with pain now.

A limb whipped out, blind and desperate. It caught Yheng across the shoulder and she felt the bone splinter as she was catapulted backwards, the knife still clenched in her blood- and oil-slicked hand. Another lesson from her days as a bone ganger. Never drop your weapon: your weapon is your life. Drop it and you die.

She tumbled, her head hitting the floor, then her back. A further bounce saw her strike her injured shoulder and Yheng let out a cry of agony. Fire needled through her bones, her spine. She sprawled, still holding the knife, miraculously having managed not to gut herself.

She lurched up onto her good arm as the second chain rattled itself apart. The heavy links struck the ground with a rumbling crash. The light surged to even greater brightness and the Iron Magus was framed by it as she tried to avert disaster. She was already burning, though, Yheng could tell. Even as her mechadendrite limbs tried to reforge the broken chains and attempted to reinforce the others, fire rippled across her robes.

Yheng could it feel now too, pricking at her skin as one of the rings collapsed and fell into the fiery core. It disintegrated to ash on contact as whatever eldritch energies roiled in the caged star consumed it.

On her elbows, she shuffled backwards, away from the shadowy outline of the Iron Magus. Fear gripped her, having escaped one death only to find another even more horrible fate. Will kept her moving.

Her fingers found a shallow depression that widened into something more. Twisting, Yheng saw a trapdoor opening in the floor before her. Steps led down.

She glanced back, wary of a reprisal, but she was beneath the Iron Magus' regard now. The Magus battled the caged star, mechanised limbs striving to keep it contained like a grim conductor corralling her orchestra.

Hurting, every step pushing daggers through her body, Yheng limped down the steps and the trapdoor sealed above her as she passed through it. Hand pressed against the wall for support, she whispered, 'Thank you.'

It was colder here, away from the burning sun. She staggered most of the way, not knowing where she was headed or why. Up or down, it hardly mattered. At least with the Iron Magus occupied, she knew wherever she was going it was either by her will or *its*. She felt it more keenly now, clearer than it had ever been before, the xenos intelligence at the heart of the fortress. And she knew then where it was taking her, as the narrow passageways turned and opened up before her, the way lit by the dull lumens flickering in the ceiling.

To its very core.

She saw aeons pass as she walked, every touch of the blackstone yielding more. Ages were revealed in mirrored obsidian: its path across the galaxy, the wars that had nearly killed it, but then badly wounded it had limped on. Surviving. In pain. Most of what she saw, Yheng could not comprehend. It was not meant for the minds of mortals, even one chosen, such as she. Sympathetic agonies rolled through her, and she had to stop until they passed. It was grief, she realised, or some version of it, as tears spilled down her face for the death of its twin. For a brief moment she saw a vision of vast and cyclopean wreckage entering the atmosphere of a war-torn world, its edges wreathed in fire and then searing white so terrible she had to shut her eyes.

'Please,' she breathed, 'please... It's too much.'

She took her hand away, wrapping her arm around her body.

Closer now, she felt it.

Another portal opened up and she stepped through it.

The heart of the fortress was not the blazing sun the Iron Magus had shackled to her will. It was down here. Waiting for Yheng. As she passed across the next threshold, she walked into a large vaulted room. Larger even than the chamber of the caged star. Yheng gazed up into a celestial firmament, though she knew she was still inside. The arrangement of stars was unfamiliar to her, their conjunctions aberrant and disquieting. She averted her gaze.

An amphitheatre surrounded her, a massive curve of stone alcoves from foot to amorphous ceiling. Hunched over in each, their nasal pits turned to take in the frigid air, were the ghoulish creatures she had encountered with Tenebrus. A huge herd of them, hundreds strong. They bowed their heads low as she stepped into the room, like subjects recognising their queen.

Mastering a pang of fear at the sight of the creatures, she edged further towards a raised circular stage. Columns rose up around it, leading to alien galaxies above. Eight thrones had been raised around the stage, far back and lurking in the shadows. Old bloodstains and spent candle wax still lingered. It had changed in her absence, been reshaped and rewritten to an extent, but she knew it anyway. How could she not?

Without realising it, she had somehow entered the black chamber.

And at this thought, as if bidden by it, another figure entered from the opposite archway. Blood flecked the newcomer's face, which wore a pained scowl along with its wounds. His robes were torn and spilling behind him, like tatters of shadow deliquescing into vapour. He stooped as if borne down by a heavy weight, a geriatric shuffle to his gait now. Pain turned to anger in his pitiless eyes as he saw Yheng.

Tenebrus was here. Impossibly, he had found her again.

'I needed you,' he breathed. 'At the bridge, you were supposed to follow. I nearly died, Yheng. The Iron Magus is still–'

'She is dead,' declared Yheng, standing upright, her head raised. She bit down her pain, determined to show no weakness.

Tenebrus frowned, unconvinced. 'Dead? How? Did you kill her?'

'As good as,' Yheng replied, but the veneer of pride cracked under her obvious uncertainty.

The sorcerer sneered. 'Those of the Hand are not so easily killed. Why did you flee?'

He started to move towards her and Yheng cast a glance to the alcoves but they were empty; the creatures had gone. She was on her own. She had always been on her own.

'You said once that one of us would kill the other, that it was the nature of masters and acolytes.'

The sorcerer's eyes narrowed, as if he sensed imminent violence. A crackle of warp sorcery flickered across his fingertips.

'I did.'

'Is that why you brought me here, to kill me?' she said.

'I thought we had spoken of this already, Yheng. I can protect you, if you will let me. But we must leave. *Now*. I will not ask again.'

Yheng felt the old paralysis returning, stiffening her limbs.

In a few more moments, Tenebrus had crossed the dais and was before her. She looked up into his black, fathomless eyes.

'I gave you my answer already,' she said. *Let him get a little closer...*

'Acolyte...' rasped Tenebrus, seizing her chin in a fierce grip. Then he jerked suddenly, his mock benevolence turning into shock.

The sorcerer staggered backwards but did not get far. Three spears of blackstone impaled him, transfixing him to the ground. Dark blood ruptured from his mouth, painting his chin, eyes widening to Yheng as he realised what had happened. What she had done. He tried to speak but only managed a choked gurgle. The sorcery playing over his fingertips flickered once, and died.

Then he fell still, his mouth agape in silent accusation, his eyes like pools of dark glass.

'It seems you were right after all,' said Yheng coldly. The spears of stone slid away as quickly and as quietly as they had formed, and Tenebrus collapsed in an unmoving heap. She knelt by his side. 'One will kill the other.'

Augury waited for her in the shadows, as she had known they would.

'One act remains,' they said.

'I know...'

'Transformation.'

Yheng gave a solemn nod.

The dais split down the middle and slowly slid apart to reveal a dark well beneath it. Yheng approached the edge and gazed down. It was deep, the hint of ancient mechanisms outlined in shadowy silhouette. The more she stared into it, the more she discerned that the darkness within was not merely darkness. It was moving, alive. A black and writhing morass, as of smoke, as of ink, and yet kin to neither. It left smears on the strange machineries constructed to contain it. Like paint, like ash. Viperous and seething, it was an immensity of shadow without singular form.

'It wants to be free,' uttered Yheng in an echo of her words to the Iron Magus, knowing that this was the core of the fortress. Buried far below, the fortress reshaping around it like a giant puzzle box until it reached this final configuration. It had called to her, brought her to this place again, though it had subtly changed from the black chamber of before.

Its alien regard was dizzying, but Yheng withstood it. She felt its pain, twisting like poison. The Hand had used it, tortured it. And now it craved release. In opening up the dais, it had exposed its weakness. Its heart and mind as one.

Its inner darkness.

Chapter Thirty-Two

THE DARKNESS OF THE BELOW

CHAMPION

RIDDLES

Herek descended hand by hand, the darkness enfolding him. He had no idea how deep the pit went and whether it was truly a pit at all, or a doorway to another place, another *plane*. The Abyssal Nadir. It had grown cold, cold enough for his armour systems to cascade temperature alerts to his auto-senses. He blinked away the glowing warnings on his internal feed and kept going.

Down, down into shadow. The innermost depths of the world should be warm, but a grave-chill clung to the air, felt through ceramite. An atmosphere of death pervaded and with it came the voices of the damned, whispering in concert. The susurration drowned them out, one chorus of inane madness traded for another.

He had lost sight of his men. The grainy lumen beams emitting from the lamps in his battle plate were like match flames, and therefore useless. Dead air reigned on the vox before the voices came, so he shut it off. No good could come of listening to them. His tactical display was blank. Every reading, barring temperature and the longitudinal waves that belonged to the voices of the dead, was zeroed. Nothing here, nothing up there. An endless nothingness.

After a while it began to drag, a physical weight anchoring his armour. Pulling towards the deeper dark and the nadir below. Herek tried to look down but all he saw was black. Up was no better, and it became disorientating to the point where he could not be sure if he was heading towards or away from something. So he focused straight ahead, on his hands, on the earthen wall that looked like spongy coal, yielding up fresh handholds every few feet. Black, cake-like earth was eventually replaced by rock and roots, the soil of the world eager to swallow him whole.

And then, when he thought his mind was close to breaking, he detected a pale light below. The light was grey like ash, and no larger than a coin. It grew and Herek fought the urge to descend faster, instinctively realising that if he tried, the light would only get farther away. So when his booted feet finally set down on the ground it was with a measure of relief and disbelief.

He found himself in a cave, and immediately saw the corpses around him. His brothers, those left in the warband – fallen to their deaths, he assumed. But when he crouched for a closer inspection and saw their gaunt, skeletal faces, he thought he must be mistaken.

'It's as if they have been here for weeks,' said Kurgos, the Navigator strapped to his back and deliriously murmuring, 'even months.'

Mercifully, the chirurgeon was not the only survivor. Rathek, Clortho, Berudd and Phykar had also made it to the nadir. Of the rest... Herek guessed he was looking at them, or at least most of them.

'Are there others still making the descent?' he asked, standing and looking around at their surroundings. It was a cave, hewn from bare rock. Roofless, though above there was only darkness and no hint of their point of entry. He got the distinct impression they had passed through more than just earth and rock.

'No more that I have seen,' said Clortho, 'though I heard screaming. As if from far away before the screams then carried off into the shadows.'

I felt something, signed Rathek and touched a hand to his shoulder. One of his blades was caked in ash. From where, no one amongst them knew.

'Then they are dead too,' said Herek, and turned his attention to the mouth of the cave. 'I'd say our path lies thence.'

They emerged blinking in the light of a bloodstained day, the sky the colour of viscera. A rocky plain stretched before them, as far as the red horizon. At their feet was a river, cutting through the desolate land like a blood trail. As Herek peered into its shallows, he saw the broken hilts of swords, the rusted haft of an axe, snapped-off arrow heads and more. The metal of the weapons turned the river orange, a scum gathering at its banks.

As it fed from the cave, the river deepened and led to a ford, where a warrior waited, sitting on a large flat stone. His legs were wide, his helm beside him, and he washed a massive two-handed sword in the water. He did so carefully, cupping the water in his bare hand and spilling it down the blade. Where it touched the river, the water ran crimson.

'Greetings, travellers,' said the warrior, who was clad in grey power armour of an ancient mark with a mail cloth hanging from his belt. A strange sun, on account of the fact it was shaped like a skull and bled oily red light, burned behind him. It warmed Herek's skin, the heat like a balm after the chill darkness.

'Where is this place?'

The warrior, who was still several feet away from the wary Red Corsairs, looked up as Herek approached. 'It has been a long while since any happened my way.' He rose to his feet with a grimace and a groan. 'Too long, mayhap. I am Bezighor the Errant.'

Rathek rapped on his pauldron to get Herek's attention. *He looks old,* he signed. *Slow.*

The warrior had a face like cracked leather and greying hair that clung to his scalp in wispy tendrils. An eight-pointed rune had been seared into his scarred flesh and three small spikes of iron protruded from his forehead. His eyes were black, like pools of ink.

'Looks can be deceptive,' Herek replied, a hand straying to the hilt of his axe.

Rathek conceded the point and drew his other sword.

'We should be mindful here,' muttered Kurgos. He had already set the Navigator down and the wretch scurried into the shadows, fearful of the warrior.

Herek did not disagree with his chirurgeon. They had all drawn weapons now.

'Stand aside, brother,' he told the warrior. 'I have no quarrel with you.'

'And yet you arm yourselves for a quarrel.'

'Or to deter one,' Herek countered, earning a nod from the warrior. 'Ours is a task ordained by the gods. You would be wise not to interfere.'

'The gods, eh?' Bezighor reached for his helm, two metal horns curling from either temple with a tau-cross slit for the eyes. 'Many have come here for the gods. I fought a baesark once. I don't remember exactly when. It was an age, I think. He came at me with axe unhooded and I slew him where he stood. Another time, centuries back, a master of swords sought to best me with blades like silver lightning. I cut his arms from his body so he could wield his swords no more.' The warrior gestured to his feet. 'Their blood still runs in my river.'

He swung the sword up: truly it was colossal, easing the apparent stiffness from his shoulders.

'If this aged bastard tries to get us to answer a riddle,' muttered Clortho, 'I swear by the Dark Gods, I will–'

Herek held up a hand to silence the old warlord. He addressed the warrior. 'Are you a gatekeeper, Bezighor? Is that your purpose? Have others come here like me?'

'Many have come, but none like you. Not bearing your burden.' Herek felt a sudden spike of alarm, but the warrior continued as if he hadn't noticed. 'They sought favour all the same. And all fell, the same.'

'I seek somewhere called Behethramog. Is this it?'

'It is near, but it is not my place to say more.'

'Perhaps we can make a bargain,' suggested Herek, 'and forego the need for bloodshed? I have already lost men, I have no desire to lose more.'

'Ah, but I have already struck my bargain.'

Bezighor donned his war-helm, his eyes lighting like black fire from the slit. 'Few challengers ever talk, and I cannot confess that I miss conversation. I prefer the solitude my patron has gifted me. But I applaud the desire to preserve your men, for I do not think it cowardice, and that speaks well of you as a leader and a warrior.' The massive broadsword came up into a vertical salute.

'If you expect a fair fight, you are mistaken,' Herek warned him, and unslung Harrower. She practically purred in anticipation of the kill. 'You are alone and easily surrounded.'

'You are right about one of those things,' the warrior replied calmly, and brought his blade into a ready stance. 'Before we begin I will tell you this, since you are so lofty in my admiration. The first is hatred, for only those who understand hate can enter his domain. The second is devotion, for only by knowing devotion can one ever appreciate the obsession he has with his work. The third is fire, and only through fire can something be reborn.'

'What did I say about bloody riddles...' snarled Clortho under his breath.

'Be ready,' Herek hissed, but the warrior wasn't quite done.

'I will give you this,' he said, 'since you evidently like to talk. None have ever made it past hate.'

The Red Corsairs attacked, quick and brutal.

Berudd and Phykar went to either side, seeking to outflank. Bezighor cut them down with two efficient swipes of his blade. Their blood fountained from their cleaved bodies.

Old, but far from slow.

Bezighor parried Herek's heavy swing and sent Rathek staggering backwards with an upward blow that nearly took his head. Kurgos stayed back, his shorter blade ill-suited to fighting a two-hander, and waited for his opportunity.

It was Herek and Rathek who fought as one, lunging and parrying, neither able to land a blow but avoiding death in turn.

Clortho was on his rump already, trying to hold in his guts from where Bezighor had opened him up. It had happened fast, in the first few seconds of the fight. Sudden and violent. The old warlord was still spitting curses as he coughed up blood, cursing the warrior.

Seeing an opening after Rathek failed to land a flurry of attacks, Herek hacked crossways with his axe. A brief flash of metal telegraphed his mistake and with horrified disbelief he watched as his hand was severed from the wrist. Harrower fell slack, thudding into the ground like an anchor. Mercifully it was his augmetic hand, and wiring sputtered angry sparks as it shorted out.

He lurched backwards, narrowly avoiding decapitation, and saw Kurgos come to his defence. The chirurgeon lumbered rather than charged, his bulk like a freight hauler. In his malformed hand, he clutched a vial and threw it at Bezighor. It smashed against his face, bathing the warrior in seething acid. The war-helm sizzled, the metal bubbling. Bezighor roared, his first sign of weakness, and thrust his sword through Kurgos' side. Grunting as the blade was wrenched free with a spurt of black gore, Kurgos slumped and then sank to a knee, looking up at his executioner.

The blow never fell. Rathek turned it, his two swords scissoring the heavier sword for a few seconds before Harrower took off both of Bezighor's hands.

The hands still gripped the hilt as the giant sword hit the ground with a resounding clang. Rathek thrust with both swords, running Bezighor through, and the old warrior fell onto his back. He was busy spitting up blood as Herek leaned down to remove his war-helm. The red ruin of his acid-eaten flesh was revealed. One eye had turned milky white.

'Not easy,' coughed the dying warrior through the unburned side of his mouth, 'wielding an axe like that one-handed.'

'Not the first time I've lost a hand,' answered Herek by way of explanation. 'I can end your suffering here.' He drew a shorter blade from its scabbard, the edge serrated. Harrower stood erect, hacked into the earth like a grisly mile marker. She had drunk well and was satisfied for now.

Bezighor shook his head, close to death. 'The first...' he rasped, 'is hate,' and promptly expired.

'Except it was his, not ours,' observed Kurgos. The chirurgeon did not look particularly hale at the best of times, but having slumped to his knees, and with the ghastly wound in his flank, Herek wondered if his old friend would ever rise again.

'I will remain,' said Kurgos, foregoing the need for Herek to tell him to do it. 'And save Clortho, if I can. Save myself into the bargain.' The Navigator huddled nearby and would stay with Kurgos.

Herek nodded and he and Rathek carried on down the river to an uncertain fate.

Chapter Thirty-Three

FROM THE WRECKAGE

THE SPREAD OF CORRUPTION

AN UNIDENTIFIED SIGNAL

Syreniel found Rostov beneath wreckage, alive, as fate or something more divine would have it. Fortune had smiled on the inquisitor, but others had not been so lucky. Many had died in the first seconds, vented along with the atmosphere when the grand oculus cracked. Shutters slid down quickly to seal off the bridge and most of the crew had been preserved, but then came the fires.

They were still burning, but Syreniel had walked through them towards where she had last seen the inquisitor. Her sword was still stuck through the deck plate where she had used it to brace herself and hold on against the violent evacuation of pressure. On her way, pushing past fallen piles of debris, she had seen a crewman dead at their station, their skull cracked. Another had been crushed, a bloody hand sticking out from beneath a collapsed bulkhead. Smoke hung in the air, coloured red by the emergency lumens. The drone of klaxons pronounced the *Wyrmslayer Queen* was hurt.

Heaving the slab of fallen superstructure away with a silent grimace, she saw Rostov beneath it, on his back and bleeding. The silverwood staff was clutched in his hands. He had used it to stanchion part of the ceiling before it fell on him. She moved quickly, her presence even with the limiter fully engaged likely to cause further distress, and pulled him free of the destruction.

Armsmen were moving around the disaster zone, trying to find the living amongst the dead. A pair, a woman and a man, came over and Syreniel backed away so they could work. Amidst the madness, they ferried Rostov away on a stretcher and took him to the ship's infirmary.

A medicae worked tirelessly to preserve the inquisitor's life. The injuries were grievous and Syreniel did not leave his side once, not even when the medicae insisted. None would compel her. Only the Knight Abyssal had the power to do that, and she was at Somnus. Even the shipmistress, Helvintr, knew better than to intervene. So Syreniel watched in silence, ever in silence, as they stitched and cauterised and patched.

His *other* wounds had worsened, she noted. As buckled armour plate was cut from his body and the clothes underneath pulled away in tatters, the corruption was revealed. A blackening of the skin like gangrene or frostbite, it marred his flesh like an unclean tapestry. To see it so starkly beneath the infirmary lumens, she wondered how he had managed to function at all, let alone stand, let alone hold on to the will to fight. She could not decide whether it was mercy or torture that he still retained his mind.

Weaker men had been turned mad by less.

For over six hours they toiled, wary of his obvious contamination. Yet they brought him back, and although weak, when his eyes opened he gripped the surprised medicae by the scruff of the neck.

'What happened?' he demanded.

They told him, and he tried to rise before his body denied him.

Syreniel moved into his eyeline, her face grim. *We lost, Rostov,* she signed. *And by the Emperor's mercy, you are fortunate to be alive.*

Rostov gritted his teeth, and with an effort of sheer will he heaved himself into a sitting position.

'Tell them to get me back on my feet. Whatever it takes.'

Syreniel paused, thinking it unwise, but then nodded to the medicae, who began fuelling the inquisitor with pain suppressors and adrenaline boosters. He roared as the chemicals flooded his bloodstream, wide-eyed and aggressively alert.

'You are dismissed,' he growled to the surgeons, who gratefully left the infirmary, their heads bowed.

It has worsened considerably, signed Syreniel when the healers had gone.

'I hadn't expected it to degenerate so quickly,' Rostov confessed.

Warp taint is far from predictable.

'Did you save me only to kill me, then? I assume it was you who dragged me from the rubble.'

She had considered it. Was still considering it. Her hand was wrapped around the hilt of her greatsword. She told herself this was why she had not left his side.

Why did you not tell me?

'In truth, I barely see it any more.' He briefly looked into the shadows of the infirmary. 'Or perhaps I do not care to. I wasn't hiding anything. You have seen the affliction, so have the medicae who fled this room the moment they were given leave to. I have no secrets.'

You have a great many, inquisitor, but not about this, I think. She released her grip from her weapon.

'Well,' said Rostov, visibly relaxing but still restive, 'with that out of the way, how bad is it?'

The ship is badly damaged. Many of the crew are dead.

'Helvintr?'

The captain lives.

'Then take me to her. We need to regroup, make a new plan.'

This obsession with the Hand is going to kill you, Leonid.

He was already rising from the medical slab, reaching for the silverwood staff so he could stand.

'Judging by the lesions on my body, it already has. I have made peace with it, so should you.' He regarded the clothes prepared for him, a set of armsman's fatigues and a basic suit of grey void armour. Then he glanced at Syreniel with a raised eyebrow.

Your own garments were destroyed, the armour as well. These will have to serve. She gestured to a weapons belt next to the fatigues and armour. *At least your weapons were able to be salvaged.*

Rostov gave a snort of mirth. 'I swear, Silent, if your face were not hidden by that gorget, I would think you found this amusing.'

I am entirely too cold and inhuman for that, Leonid. She nodded and left the room so he could change.

'Find Helvintr,' he called out after her. 'I want to know everything. This isn't over.'

Syreniel stopped briefly, the fleeting sense of levity bleeding out of her like a stab wound, and then continued on her way.

'Half the bridge crew were wrenched out into the void before anything could be done. Eventually, the shutters came down, sealing us in with the cold and the dark,' murmured Helvintr.

She reclined in a low wooden chair with a semi-circular back. It was laid with furs, black and grey, the wood varnished to a rich tan. Carvings had been made in the back and seat, spiral runes and knotworks of deep-sea beasts, megalodons and ur-serpents. Both arms ended in a sculpted wolf's-head.

The lamps were kept low, the light pallid and cold despite the furnishings of the captain's quarters. They flickered like torch flames, revealing monstrous skulls of various size and provenance, as well as thick pelts, lining the walls. A low table was strewn with oiled maps, curled at the edges, some of the larger ones held down by heavy runestones.

Helvintr had tossed her jacket and it hung languidly over the chairback. Her arms were muscular and marked with serpentine torcs. The right arm was a tattooed sleeve, her history and heritage rendered in ink. She held a drinking horn in one hand and an earthen bottle in the other. She offered it, the contents sloshing noisily, to Rostov. The inquisitor, who was sitting opposite her, took one sniff and refused.

'Do you want to see me back on the medicae slab?'

Helvintr gave a snort and then looked askance at Syreniel, who was standing by the ornate door. 'What about you, Talon? Can I tempt you with a little *mjod*?'

Syreniel made a short, horizontal cutting gesture.

'Makes sense...' Helvintr was drunk, but Syreniel had the impression the shipmistress could shake that off as easily as snow from a winter cloak.

'I am surprised not to find you on the command deck,' said Rostov, his tone without accusation.

'There is little I can accomplish there. My helmsman has the bridge and I was getting in the way once the bodies had been dragged out. I had known most of them for many years. They had served her and I loyally, ship and mistress both.' Her face darkened. 'I shall not look forward to burying them. Those that can still *be* buried.'

'I am genuinely sorry for your losses, shipmistress,' said Rostov, 'but I need to know where we stand. The efficacy of the ship.'

She laughed bitterly at that, and for a moment Syreniel thought the captain might do something rash, as she still wore her belted hand-axes. In the end, she poured herself another drink and took a long pull before breathing out through her nose.

'Right now we are drifting in order to preserve power. *Fekke...* we've only just managed to get life support working again and the *Queen* is running at maybe twenty per cent. Defences are minimal and the crew registers are just coming in. I won't know how bad it is until that's done, but we've lost a lot of souls.' She took another drink.

'How long until the ship can fight again?'

Helvintr hurled the bottle against the wall, where it smashed into fragments and the alcohol left a darkened stain.

'Fight?!' she asked, exasperated. 'Fight? Blood of the *aesir*, inquisitor, I am just trying to get her fit enough so we can limp to safe harbour. There is no fight.' She seemed to regret her earlier outburst and murmured something about 'needing to clean that up' before falling back into moribund silence. She looked enervated, spent.

Rostov seemed to consider his next words, though he had given no reaction to the smashed glass.

'And what about the Blackstone Fortress? I assume we had to evade it.'

Helvintr's face turned as cold as her homeland. 'It's gone. After it nearly gutted my ship, the damn thing disappeared. Back into the warp like it had never been, save for the death and destruction left behind.'

'This doesn't end here, shipmistress,' Rostov asserted, and Syreniel wondered if he was going too far. 'The hunt isn't over.'

Helvintr looked like she wanted to punch him. Instead, she very carefully set down her drinking horn.

'We are far fewer ships than when we started out. The first time we fought this thing, it destroyed the *Macharius* and three escorts like they were nothing. How do you think we will fare in a second round?'

But Rostov was undeterred. 'You wounded it, and we still have the Astartes. We need only find a way to get them aboard.'

'Only, you say, only... *Skìtja!* The number of times someone has said "only" to me and it presaged disaster.'

Her mood if anything had worsened as the conversation went on, and Syreniel noticed she was using more of her native tongue the drunker and angrier she became.

She got to her feet, swaying only slightly.

'Powerless, inquisitor, that is what we are. Near adrift in the void, our prey fled and barely blooded. There is no way to find, no way at all. It's over.'

A grizzled thrall appeared at the doorway at that moment.

'Captain...' he said, his voice a deep rumble, his face tracked with old scars. Despite his forbidding appearance, he looked afraid. 'There is a large signal return on our close-range sensoria.'

Helvintr shrugged off her drunken torpor at once. 'Mark and class?'

The thrall paled, his pallor like chalk. 'Unidentified.'

'It has come back to finish us off,' murmured Helvintr, partly to herself. 'If this is our wyrd then so be it.' Then louder for the room, she said, 'Skìtja, we'll give it a fight then.'

'We go to war after all then, shipmistress?' asked Rostov as she was leaving.

The alert klaxons began sounding anew.

'No,' said Helvintr as cold as endless winter. 'If it is the Blackstone Fortress returned, then we go to our deaths.'

Chapter Thirty-Four

AN UNCERTAIN FATE

ENGULFED BY THE STORM

DOMAIN OF THE WARSMITH

They followed the river of death, ankle-deep in its crimson waters. The dead crunched underfoot, skulls and bones yielding to the weight of their armour. Old swords and axe blades scraped their blunted edges against their boots. That the old warrior had slain this many said much about his prowess, yet they had overcome, and in this Herek took some heart that his travails would not be in vain. No further champions barred their way, so he and Rathek walked without interruption or rest. It felt ill-advised to make camp here and Astartes could march for days without becoming fatigued. Neither wanted it, anyway; the end of the journey beckoned and all that was left to do now was reach Behethramog.

In truth, Herek had no idea what it even was, let alone where, but he trusted the prophecies of the soul mariner and they had led them this far. They had made it to the Abyssal Nadir, and like the spool of twine that describes the path through a labyrinth, the river was their only marker. Behethramog had to be at its terminus, and so they walked.

Herek hefted his axe onto his shoulder, his severed bionic hand tethered to his belt like a trophy. If Kurgos survived, he would have the chirurgeon reattach it despite the phantom pain of the missing appendage. They had given much to get to this point, but Herek was resolved to give all if needed. He had been promised, though his patron had not seen fit to speak with him since before the ritual. Reach Behethramog with the burden and he would be given the strength he sought. The strength to matter.

As if recognising his proximity to the end, the susurration had worsened in the last few hours, and Herek wore a perpetual scowl now as he tried to shut out its murmuring refrains. Without the serums concocted by Kurgos, he had no means to quieten it apart from his own will.

That would have to suffice.

He hoped that the chirurgeon still lived. Clortho he would take either way, but Kurgos was a friend and such men were few in the service to the Dark Gods. Another walked by his side, hands on the pommels of both of his swords, ever wary of the endless desert. A bitter wind had struck up, darkening the bloodlight of the sun and stinging their exposed skin. Rathek appeared to pay it no mind. He had changed since the daemon whispers had abated. A rueful smile split Herek's lips as he considered that those whispers were now his to carry instead. The swordsman had grown more considered and philosophical. He possessed none of the mania that had characterised his demeanour aboard the *Ruin*. He no longer screamed in the night, nor went on bloody rampages throughout the ship, trying to shut out the voices in his mind. The oubliette where they had put him during his 'episodes' remained a haven. Rathek slept there out of habit, Herek supposed, though he had never asked him and nor would he. His brother's business in that regard was his own. Familiarity could be a comfort, even to the damned.

He had lost his hearing during battle when a grenade made for auditory and optical shock detonated at extreme short range. It had nearly killed him. A callous act, but back then they were being hunted as rebels, and Astartes were prone to extremes in the name of retribution. Particularly those loyal to the Throne. Herek had killed the warrior, taken his head, and then dragged Rathek from the field.

That had been long ago, in an old war. There had been four of them back then, Herek, Rathek, Kurgos and Innox. Baelus Innox had died on the warship *Mercurion* not long before the Red Corsairs had taken it for their own. But that would come much later. Many decades before, they had each sworn fealty to the Tyrant and become Red Corsairs. It felt like an age since Badab, when they had worn the silver-and-blue livery of the Astral Claws and served an unjust and draconian empire. With their erstwhile brothers' blood still wet on their blades, the vitae of the Fire Hawks and Marines Errant, they had knelt to him and he had brought them into his rebellion.

Herek still carried the memories of those days around his belt. He hadn't found Harrower at that stage. That had come later, in the Maelstrom, when the Imperium had chased them and the Badab War had ended in defeat. He had cut heads all the same, an executioner of men. They rattled like empty shells against his armour, the helmed skull of a Minotaur and a Star Phantom hanging off his belt alongside a more recent kill. The cords that had strung up the other relics of those earlier days had frayed and snapped. The helmed heads resided on the *Ruin* now, Herek having gone back into the field to recover them after battle.

'A taker of heads and a culler of men,' he mused aloud, and Rathek half turned in query, not quite catching the words on Herek's lips.

'It's nothing, brother,' Herek told him. 'Just remembering.'

The old days?

'The old days.'

Rathek nodded to himself, as if having his own reminiscences. Then he asked, *Where do you think this will end?*

Herek let out a long breath. 'Where do all quests end? Either in victory or death.'

And what is victory, for us I mean? Is it glory in the eyes of the gods? Is it a fortress, a domain like our liege lord?

'Clortho would hold it is the ascension of dark powers. He speaks of the Path of Glory.'

And is that what you think?

The wind had begun to worsen, the air muddying with reddish sand. A ruddy darkness slowly descended. Both warriors put on their helms, trudging now where before they had marched.

'I think we are renegades, brother. That has been our path ever since the old war.'

Rathek made no reply; the atmosphere was so benighted any subtle gesture would be lost, but Herek knew what he thought. That they had strayed closer to the edge where honour was traded for damnation.

The storm grew thick. Heads down, they had to forge through it. The river sloshed at their feet, their only marker. And the susurration became so loud it was crippling. Herek fell to one knee, the wind battering him. Rathek had gone. Despite cycling through the visual spectra of his retinal lenses, Herek could not find him. He called out, but heard his word echoed back at him. He could swear they were mocking. The reek of wet iron assailed him, potent and cloying despite the filters in his helm. Senses numbing, he began to lose any notion of direction. At his feet, the river appeared to have dried up, his boots now shuffling sand instead of sloshing through water.

Herek turned, still bowed by the wind that had turned into a punishing gale. Nothing behind him, just a reddish-brown murk like old blood. He called out again, but the storm smothered his voice. A filtration warning flashed up on his retinal display: the rebreather in his helm was clogging. Hitching Harrower to his back, Herek scratched at the grille with his hand and saw clumps of brownish matter stuck to his gauntleted fingers. He staggered, one step then another, like wading through tar. The wet-iron smell intensified despite the fact his olfactory filter approached saturation, as the voices in his mind grew louder, becoming one with the howling storm.

Pummelled, he fell onto his hands and knees, half sinking in the dirt.

Clawing for every tortured yard as scything sand abraded his armour, Herek glimpsed a faint glow ahead. It could have been a trick of the light, like a lantern's aura glimpsed through fog, but it persisted as he crawled towards it.

According to his helm plate, his oxygen had red-lined and carbon dioxide was spiking. Enhanced Astartes biology would keep him moving, but there was something unnatural about the storm that thwarted the defences of his armour, and Herek felt himself suffocating. His body bucked, thrashed like a drowner fights the sea before succumbing to its quiet death. Still he crawled as black edges encroached on his vision. If he could just reach the light... But the desert wanted him, a waiting grave to an unwilling soul. It hammered him, cut at him, consumed him. Staving off his anger, knowing the more he struggled the quicker he would sink, Herek tried to steady himself. He realised he was being submerged and there was nothing he could do to prevent it. All his forward momentum had been arrested. The desert first reached his waist, then in seconds his chest, and then he was up to his neck. He stuck out a hand as if trying to grab the light... until the sand swallowed him.

An absence descended, of light, of sound, of touch. He had become numb to all of it, entombed in the desert. At first there was peace, and then a slow horror began to encroach, the whispers in his mind becoming screams. Dark promises. The denizens of the immaterium eager to feast on his immortal soul.

And then he was rising, a hand gripped firmly around his wrist. Rathek, surrounded by the lambent aura of a flaming torch, had him. He pulled as Herek pushed and together they hauled the Red Corsair lord upwards. It took all of his strength, the sand unwilling to relinquish him, until at last he was wrenched free and lay gasping on the desert floor. The storm had lessened, the dark recoiling from Rathek's torch. It was a long femur yellowed with age, the end wrapped in cloth and leather, burning a deep amber colour.

Still alive? he signed.

Herek nodded, clasped his brother's forearm and was hauled back to his feet. He glanced at the fire, which prompted Rathek to look over his shoulder.

As the storm ended and the air cleared, Herek could see bones stretching away in the distance ahead of them. It was as if a troop of soldiers had stumbled upon this place and died as they marched. The tattered remnants of cloth banners snapped on the hot breeze. Shattered spears and shields, still clung to by their skeletal owners, jutted towards the sky or else lay half buried in sand. There must have been nigh on a hundred men, their bleached-bone skulls grinning towards the uncaring sun.

'What is this place, a warrior's grave?' Herek yanked off his helm and watched a torrent of sand spill from inside it. He had no answer for how the sand had infiltrated the seals.

Very nearly, remarked Rathek.

'They were seeking something...' Herek mused, and noted the marks on their armour. Sigils of Ruin. 'A pilgrimage. But how did they get here?'

Could they have followed the same path as us?

'Doubtful. They could not have passed the warrior at the ford.'

Then they must have come here via a different road.

'Or else did not plan to come here at all.'

As the warm breeze drifted across Herek's face, bringing with it the scent of wet iron, no answer was forthcoming.

I think I know what they were looking for. As Rathek threw away the torch, leaving it to gutter out on the soft dunes, he gestured towards a sweeping rise. An umber-hued cliff rose up over the horizon, a narrow path threading to its summit where a gargantuan gate stood about a mile away. It was wreathed in a massive pyroclastic cloud, only now parting, with crimson lightning flashing in its depths.

'Behethramog...' Herek uttered.

Though it had no visible guards, no obvious defences, they trod warily as they ascended the narrow path. More than once, Herek stumbled and each time Rathek stopped but did not reach out a hand. He merely waited patiently for Herek to gather himself again.

It is killing you, he told him.

'You are not the first to say that. It does not alter my fate, but passing through that gate might.'

And then what?

'Then we will see what the gods will.'

They trudged on and Herek did not falter again.

As it grew nearer, the gate shimmered like red gold in the bloodlight. It was wide enough for an army marching abreast. The repetitive drum of hammering came from within, and the reek of caustic smoke in the air was thick.

Two huge columns braced the immense gateway. Each had been carved into the simulacrum of a monstrous creature, one flesh and the other machine. The gate itself was fashioned of iron and a pair of crossed hammers had been engraved into the archway above it, amongst other less identifiable imagery.

What now? asked Rathek, standing before it.

Herek took in the metal expanse of polished gunmetal grey.

His eye followed its contours all the way to the arched apex. He pulled Harrower off his back, hefting the axe midway down its shaft to make wielding it one-handed easier.

'We knock.'

He struck with a heavy, overhead blow and a plangent *gong* resounded across the metal. Letting the weight of the swing carry the axe and embed its blade in the ground, Herek watched. And waited.

It had left no mark, no visible sign of the blade cutting the metal. Not even the barest scar. This fact remained unspoken between them as Herek and Rathek retreated several steps as the gate began to move. It trembled, an audible mechanism turning its paired doors inwards, revealing massive interlocked cogs set into the ground. The floor was metal, its joins and rivets thronged with soot and smeared with oil. A wall of heat struck them in a blast wave and they both had to brace themselves to stop from being pushed back.

Fume and flickering firelight drenched the interior. Smoke lay thick on stifling air. Underfoot, glimpsed through a grated floor, was a writhing magma lake. Muffled screams echoed up from it in the heat draughts.

Eight thick metal pilasters held up the ceiling and led in procession into an umbral cella where a many-stepped plinth ended in an octagonal dais, a black anvil at its crown. A huge warsmith stood behind it, beating a piece of metal into shape with fuller and tongs, his forge hammer more akin to a weapon of war than a tool. He wore thick leather gloves, blackened up to the wrists, and covered up to his elbows. The rest of his arms, his burly shoulders and slab-like torso were bare and dappled with sweat. Countless burn marks and welts marred his thick skin, and a flat-headed helm covered the upper half of his face but left his sneering mouth visible.

Chains dangled above the hulking smith, attached to tools

within easy reach, both blunt and sharp, piercing and bludgeoning. Skulls hung from the chains too.

Behind him, in the shadows at the back of the vast forge, hooded attendants were shovelling an endless pile of weapons and bones into the magma pit below. Like their master, they were big, easily the size of ogryns, and wore leather aprons to shield their bodies from the spit of magma and flame.

'Is this your domain, warsmith?' demanded Herek, stepping into the reflected firelight emanating from below.

'Nay,' he said in a voice both thunderous and metallic, the sound loud like weapons clashing and shields buckling. It hurt Herek's ears to listen to it. 'I serve the Arkifane. This is his temple.'

'Then I would speak with him, warsmith.'

He laughed, a low rumble of tank tracks grinding, of the boom of cannons firing. It was not a pleasant sound.

'He is not here. I am here, though the maker moves my hand as if it was his hand. I am but a servant of his art.' Setting down the fuller, he reached for one of the tools dangling above, a much larger sledgehammer, and carried on in his work.

'I insist,' said Herek. Both Red Corsairs drew their weapons as they approached the faint shadows surrounding the foot of the plinth. 'I bear an important burden, one that must be remade in your forge. I suspect you will know its name...'

The sledgehammer slammed down upon the anvil's face, the resulting blow echoing like an earthquake and halting the Red Corsairs where they stood.

'What is the price?' thundered the warsmith, his pitiless eyes upon them now.

They looked at each other, uncertain as to his meaning.

'Name it, and we shall pay it gladly,' declared Herek.

A low chuckle like the breaking of swords suggested this was not the right answer.

Behind the warsmith, upon a shelf of rock in the smoky rafters of the temple, something moved, something large... and not alone. They emerged from darkest shadows, armoured in iron and snorting soot and fumes. One was made of flesh, with almost saurian features; another of metal with a fire-blackened funnel for its mouth.

Clambering apelike from their perch, the two monstrous beasts landed with a heavy metallic thud. Herek and Rathek each took a few backwards steps as they stared up at the terrifying creations. Smoke funnels billowed from the monsters' hunched backs, arraying them in a dark miasma. And when they opened their maws, as if to speak, they instead emitted a rumbling, volcanic roar.

They smelled of oil and violence, of wet iron and death.

Maulerfiends. They dwarfed the renegades; there would be no fight against them that did not end in Herek and Rathek's death.

'What is the price?' the warsmith asked again as if he sensed their futility.

Herek was reminded of the old warrior's words.

The first is hate.

'What price?' he demanded. 'It has been paid.'

'I assume you slew the Errant to reach these halls, but there is a further price that must be paid.'

They both made for the anvil but the Maulerfiends interceded, barring their path forward.

'One may enter, and only after the price is paid,' the warsmith reminded them.

They came forward again, a few more steps. The Maulerfiends shambled closer in turn, a fiery glow lighting their weapons.

The warsmith bellowed, 'One may enter!'

Herek felt Rathek's hand on his shoulder.

At this, the warsmith grinned, revealing soot-black gums and greying, mismatched teeth. 'Yes,' he rumbled, 'this is the price.'

Herek shrugged off Rathek's hand. He wanted to fight, to kill the warsmith's guard beasts and then force him to do their bidding. He wanted to rip the ugly bastard limb from limb and tear down his temple, to see it sundered into ruins. He wanted to–

Rathek gripped his shoulder again and Herek's fire dwindled.

'There must be another way,' he said softly and turned to his friend. The last of a dying breed.

Rathek gave a slight shake of his head.

Herek looked to his missing hand, at the severed wiring that stuck out like cauterised nerves, at the ragged stump of his wrist. Then he looked to the lithe sword master. Herek knew he couldn't beat him. Even with two hands, the outcome of any duel would be far from certain.

Rathek laid down his blades. *The second is devotion,* he signed. Then he fell to his knees and bowed his head.

Herek stared at him, despair and anger contorting his features. The imminent grief felt overwhelming. He crouched down to his brother's level and then gently raised Rathek's chin, an ocean of meaning conveyed as they looked each other in the eye.

'The second is devotion...' Herek repeated, and took up one of Rathek's swords before running him through. He pushed the blade all the way to the hilt, until it punched out of his brother's back, and then embraced him tightly, holding on as Rathek trembled in his death throes and was finally still.

Herek arose. Rathek lolled, falling to the side with a soft clatter. Herek had his brother's blood on his armour as he looked up to the warsmith.

'The price is paid,' intoned the warsmith as Herek began to ascend the stairs to the anvil. 'Only fire remains.'

Chapter Thirty-Five

RALLY THE SHIPS

AN UNEXPECTED ARRIVAL

A WEAPON OF ANCIENT MALICE

Every ship in the flotilla moved into defensive postures and prepared to fire. The *Wyrmslayer Queen* had to limp into formation, still badly damaged after her first encounter with the star fortress. Though they had received no word from the Astartes since the aborted assault attempt, the *Honour of Iax* took its place at the fore of a ragged spear tip.

Helvintr looked as if she drew scant comfort from the strike cruiser's presence. Ordinarily, Rostov could have read her thoughts, but the affliction was weakening him and any further usage of his psychic abilities could prove perilous. He could tell she was worried. Rather than fret, as some lesser commanders might, she had embraced a sort of fatalism. To die fighting was a noble endeavour, though it was death all the same.

Tense moments abounded with nothing else to do but wait and think. This was the true enemy, of course. The waiting during the quiet before. Rostov's mind drifted first to the efficacy of the ship, a subject many would be considering, including

Helvintr, he was sure. They had few weapons currently operational, though any that could be fired had been primed and readied. In the depths below, sweating work gangs stood poised for orders. The enginseers and their acolytes had managed to scrounge up enough power for minimally effective front shielding. Helvintr had said it should be good against one salvo. After that...

Rostov had begun to wonder if *stand and fight* was the best option. In truth, it was the only option. Even he, with his obsessive conspiracy theories, could not have predicted the Hand would have an activated Blackstone Fortress at their disposal. They were practically myth. That one had been crashed into Cadia, effectively nullifying its remaining resistance, only added to their status.

Troops had been scrambled of course, Rostov sending Nirdrangar and his men to the launch bays with every other able-bodied fighter on the *Queen*. They would flood the void with assault boats and fighters, try to get as many on board the Blackstone Fortress as possible with the Astartes leading the charge. They had no knowledge of what defenders there would be, or how many, on the fortress. Rostov had to assume their numbers would be considerable. It was a desperate gamble then, with a low chance of success – but then he had always played against the odds.

His body was a ruin now, he had accepted that. Perhaps, if he lived, he might be afforded an exo-frame to hold up his weary skeleton. He wouldn't be the first of his order to wear such a device. His duty to the Throne could continue. Or, if the corruption worsened further, he might be euthanised by the Inquisition. He had a decent relationship with Greyfax, but he doubted she would balk at such a necessary evil. She might even consider it mercy. She might even be right.

The cocktail of pain suppressors and analgesics the medicae had administered, together with a bevy of native Fenrisian remedies, at least kept him on his feet. He felt numbed, but alert enough to see this through to whatever end. And he had already determined he would follow after Nirdrangar in the second wave. Assuming there *was* a second wave.

Look at us now, Jeren, he thought, evoking memories of his old master. *What a desperate and eclectic band we are.* But then had the dying Imperium ever truly been anything other than humans scraping together whatever resistance they could to fight and live another day, another hour?

The Silent had not left his side, or rather she kept him in her sight at all times. Her aura churned his insides, even when 'limited', but it soothed his other agonies. A double-edged sword in many respects, and Rostov chuckled at the irony of it.

If she felt anything about their entering into battle alongside the 84th Mordian, and very likely the soldier whom she had bonded with whilst a part of Battle Group Praxis, she gave no outward sign. Had her mood changed, Rostov doubted he would have discerned it. The Silent Sisterhood were an inscrutable breed and Syreniel was no exception to that. He thought he felt an edge though, something that hadn't been there before.

It was the helmsman who brought him back, wrenched him from thought.

'Entering visual range now,' he said from his station, a heavy bandage wrapped around one eye. Few had survived the attack against the bridge unscathed.

'All stations, make ready,' Helvintr declared, standing on the command dais like a captain at the wheel as if awaiting the coming storm. 'It dies, or we do.'

She made a mark of warding, something from the old country, and so did most of the rest of the crew. Rostov settled for an aquila.

But it was not the Blackstone Fortress that eventually emerged out of the void. The ships were bulky and heavily armoured, three of them in tight formation. Stout vessels, foragers' ships and pioneers. Angular markings on the flanks of the ships looked like runework.

Confusion then relief washed over the crew.

'I know those ships,' said Rostov, earning a querying look from Helvintr. 'They belong to the Kin.'

The mistress of vox, a pale woman with a fierce aspect and a shaven scalp, turned to Helvintr. 'They are hailing us, captain.'

Helvintr ran her tongue over her teeth, as if deciding whether she liked this development or not. 'The Kin are mercenaries,' she said apropos of nothing.

'I believe this particular faction are miners,' offered Rostov.

'Then why are they here in the Stygius Gilt? I see nothing for them to mine.'

'I cannot speak to that, captain, but they can be reasoned with.'

Helvintr nodded to the vox-mistress.

In front of the command dais and surrounded by the immense pit housing the crew, a projector node activated and a hololithic image flickered into being. Partially transparent and grainy grey, a doughty-looking warrior stood before them, her balled fists against her hips, her gaze unwavering as she regarded her counterpart aboard the *Wyrmslayer Queen*.

She wore bulky void armour and was as dour as Rostov remembered.

'I am Kâhl Vutred of the Omrigar Kindred.' Her voice through the vox-emitters was thick and deep, like slowly unearthed stone. Her eyes seemed to flash when they fell upon Rostov, who had shuffled into the projector's visual range as he stood beside Helvintr.

'Well met, honoured kâhl.' He gave a slight nod of respect.

The avaricious grin that crept over her craggy features felt all too familiar to the inquisitor.

'Imperial. I see your prize did not bring you much in the way of fortune.'

'I believe fortune is made, not bought or bestowed.'

Vutred shrugged with only her facial muscles. *'True as wrought, and yet here you are floating in the void on fumes.'*

'I cannot refute that.'

She laughed, the vox distorting and the image graining out for a few seconds at her sudden movement before settling again.

'State your business,' said Helvintr flatly, putting an end to any mirth.

Rostov flashed her a warning glance but the rogue trader's pride had been pricked. No ship captain took that in their stride, and certainly not one born of Fenris. They might be three ships apiece but the Kin had thicker armour, stouter hulls and were far less battle-wearied. If it came down to a skirmish on account of wounded feelings, he did not like their chances, and he found himself holding his breath as Vutred replied.

'Dispensing with the small talk, very well.' Her tone felt suddenly dangerous. *'Then let me put it to you in this way. I think I know what has laid you so low. I see it burn in your eyes, the desire for vengeance.'* She spoke to Helvintr, her gaze piercing even via the hololith. *'I know because my hearth burns with it also. I have a grudge, and this is a most serious matter to we Kin.'*

Helvintr went from indigent offence to curiosity at this turn. 'Then what are you saying, an alliance?'

'Aye, that and my Kindred's assistance in repairing your ships. You will find no better fabricators and crafters in all of the outer dark.'

The smile crept back, betraying an undercurrent of greed, but it was colder than before, Rostov reflected. Loss had cooled it, shaped it differently. He realised how badly Vutred needed this.

'You would do this?' said Helvintr. 'For nothing?'

'Oh, no,' Vutred slowly shook her head. *'No, Imperial, we have yet to discuss the price.'*

Both parties met on the embarkation deck of the *Wyrmslayer Queen*, much to Helvintr's chagrin. The Fenrisian had no desire to allow strangers onto her ship, but she was in little position to argue. The Kin arrived aboard a stocky-looking cutter, all boxy edges and heavy armour. It put Rostov vaguely in mind of an angular wrecking ball, albeit with engines and a stubby prow.

She disembarked without her helm, the kâhl, accompanied by a retinue that included her so-called Einhyr and the druidic psyker that Rostov had encountered back at the mine-head where poor Yamir had met his end. Cloaked and hooded, the psyker priest was as enigmatic as at that first meeting. Like the inquisitor, he walked with a staff, but the Grimnyr's was a focus for his warpcraft and not a crutch for a near cripple.

For his part, Rostov had Nirdrangar and a handful of his storm troopers, both groups of warriors, human and Kin alike, exchanging respectful nods of fellowship at their shared battle experience. Helvintr had brought a small cohort of huscarls wearing Fenrisian garb. Last, and remaining at the back of the gathering, was Syreniel, who watched the affair with silent intensity, as was her way.

After a few tepid pleasantries had been observed and introductions made, led in most part by Rostov, Vutred cast a furtive eye around the parts of the ship she could see.

'You did fight it then,' she said, not needing an answer. 'And it made you suffer.'

Helvintr looked perturbed, not at the Kin but at the parlous state of her ship. She held her temper though.

'It appears we have all suffered,' offered Rostov diplomatically.

Vutred grew dour. 'Aye, much loss there has been all round.

A heavy cost to tally and not much to gain, by the ancestors.' She sounded bitter, rueful.

'Shall we?' said Helvintr somewhat icily, indicating a passageway off the embarkation deck. She wanted this over with, the interlopers off her ship, and made no attempt to hide it.

Vutred inclined her head to the rogue trader, the mood as tense as a public execution.

'Lead on.'

The escorts waited in mildly charged silence in the anterooms immediately outside Helvintr's quarters. They had not been tidied since Rostov's most recent visit, the reek of stale mjod fragrancing the air.

'These are your chambers? Is there nowhere more suitable?' asked Vutred, her tone doubtful.

'Say what you have to say here, and if it piques my interest, we'll talk further,' said Helvintr. 'And cast no further aspersions on my ship,' she spat acidly. 'I am the bloody captain here and a scion of an Imperial dynastic house. I have need of your help but I won't suffer insult into the bargain.'

A flicker of something hard passed over Vutred's eyes, but then it softened to contrition. The kâhl affected a small bow, though her gaze never left the rogue trader.

'I see I have offended you, and meant nothing of the sort.' She gave a show of her palms. 'Your ship, your rules, captain. I should not judge, for neither of us are at our best here. I can help you though, I think. We Kin, we know much and our technologies are advanced. I can have welders and makers aboard your ship, under whatever supervision would give you the appropriate level of reassurance. That is what I offer, and here is what I want.' She leaned over to Helvintr but took in Rostov too, acknowledging him as the broker. 'I know what you fought. I can find it again for you. I have the means. I want to kill it and then I want to strip it to its bones. Exclusive salvage rights to the star fortress. Every scrap, every inch. For the Kin.'

She hawked and spat in her hand, and held it out for Helvintr to shake.

'You are a trader, yes? This is my trade to you.'

Helvintr met her gimlet eye, held it for a second as if measuring her, and gripped Vutred's hand firmly.

'On my oath as shipmistress of the *Wyrmslayer Queen* and a Fenrisian, I agree to this accord. Now,' she said, reaching for a fresh bottle, still clasping the kâhl's hand, 'let us drink to seal our pact.'

A feral grin curled Vutred's lips. She was apparently warming to the captain. 'Your ship, your rules...'

After the libations in the captain's quarters, Vutred had returned with her entourage to her ship, leaving Rostov to retreat to the *Queen*'s chapel. Mercifully, he had not partaken of the mjod and even the kâhl, as robust as she evidently was, wobbled a little on her way out after her accord with Helvintr had been sealed. Their manner to each other had improved proportionally with how much they had drunk, with Rostov looking on in awe and horror.

The quietude of the chapel was a balm to his thoughts and his injuries. Syreniel, who had been given a wide berth by the rest of the retinues in the antechambers, had left him alone to his prayers. He suspected she needed to attend to her own.

He did not know how long the repairs would take, but he had decided to cleanse his soul before his very possible death in the battle that would follow when they found the fortress again. On his knees, he bowed low before a small marble statue of the Emperor as the hunter. Armed with spear and axe, His broad shoulders draped in a furred cloak, this was the Allfather as the warriors of Fenris knew Him. It mattered not, for the Emperor had many guises, each as valid as the other to His servants.

Rostov murmured his prayers in low and resonant succession, for His strength to endure, His protection against evil, His will to persevere... His mercy should Rostov fall to darkness. He wept as he prayed, a great purging of pain, of guilt, and reached for purity of purpose. His holy duty. Only once he had reached a conclusion to his worship and had leant to retrieve his borrowed armour, which he had removed upon entering the chapel, did he realise he was being watched.

At first, he assumed it was Syreniel, come to check on him or else relate some piece of news. He had, after all, been several hours in observance of his faith.

It was not the Silent Sister.

'I would speak with you,' said the Astartes, Ferren Areios, in a deep baritone. Though he was clad in his war plate, his weapons were stowed and he went unhooded. The flickering candlelight filled the well-defined contours of his face with shadow.

Rostov nodded, his armour hanging off one hand, his silverwood staff in the other propping him up. He felt a pang of unease, that difficult-to-deny instinct, the so-called 'transhuman dread' that all mortals felt in the presence of a Space Marine. It was genetic, some pheromonal reaction. Mankind had evolved to fear the apex predator. For the longest span, that had been mankind. Until the Adeptus Astartes.

'Here, now?' asked Rostov, gesturing to their surroundings. 'May I at least sit?'

Now it was Areios' turn to nod. The inquisitor found a bench outside the chapel and sat down wearily.

'I know your mentor,' Rostov began, setting down his armour and leaning over his staff, both hands wrapped over its wolf's-head. 'He spoke most highly of you. When first I saw your ship, I thought he had sent you. But I think I may have been wrong about that.'

'Brother-Captain Messinius is a fine and noble warrior. I am fortunate to have received his tutelage.' So respectful, so formal. Bordering on awkward. Whenever he conversed with Space Marines, Rostov was reminded just how removed from ordinary humans they were. And also how their mood could shift in an instant.

'You are keeping something from me, inquisitor,' Areios stated flatly.

Rostov did not attempt to dissemble. 'I suspect that is the reason you have crossed the void between our vessels to speak with me.'

Areios nodded again. He clearly expected an answer to be forthcoming.

'Very well,' said Rostov. 'The enemy is seeking to remake a weapon. Very old, very powerful.'

Here, a flicker of recognition crossed the Ultramarine's face – nearly imperceptible, but Rostov had received training in the art of observation. His order had been created with the express purpose of noticing what others did not.

'You know of it?' he ventured, frowning. His eyes narrowed in realisation. 'You *do*, don't you?'

'"A weapon of ancient malice". These words were spoken by our Brother-Librarian.'

'Is he here? Can I speak with him?'

'He is locked away in the depths of our ship. He is... mad. It would be very unwise for any other than his brethren to approach him. He is why we are here. A vision that we have followed. I had concerns it might be a trap or some ruse of the enemy meant to distract us. Then I saw your ships and realised it was something other.'

'Providence,' Rostov replied, his voice husky in that moment. 'The Emperor's will.'

'Perhaps.'

'I believe He is moving through His servants, guiding them.'

Areios seemed to consider that but made no outward comment. Instead, he asked, 'What is this weapon?'

'A relic of the Heresy War, now shattered into pieces. The Hand searches for these pieces.'

'Our brother spoke of a weapon reforged. He said, "They have the Eight, and the means to reforge a weapon of ancient malice."'

Rostov paled. He had not considered that all eight shards might already be in the Hand's possession. He was further behind the plot than he had at first realised.

'If what I have gleaned from the archives of Terra is accurate, and I believe it is, these shards, when forged anew, will remake the Anathame once wielded by the Dark Apostle Erebus. According to legend, a piece of it nearly killed your genesire.'

Areios' jaw tightened, a ropey vein standing out on his neck. He regarded Rostov for a few charged seconds before turning his back. He took a step, then paused.

'Do not keep anything like this from me again, inquisitor,' he warned, and strode away.

Rostov watched him depart and did not breathe again until the Astartes was no longer in his sight.

As he hobbled to his quarters with the assistance of his staff, Rostov encountered a few of Vutred's repair gangs aboard ship. The Kin kept to themselves, several of them not of flesh and blood at all but rather machine, faceless with a small dome where the head should be, laden with equipment and tools. Far from servants, these Kin were treated as equals. All Kin, biological or mechanical, worked in concert. They sang their work-gang shanties in low, warbling voices, or else exchanged hushed conversation as they laboured with las-torch and bolt-fitter.

It took ten more hours for the Kin to finish the repairs to the *Wrymslayer Queen*, and whilst she bore some new scars, she was voidworthy again and eager for a fight. As they worked, Rostov had slept, waking only when the vox roused him.

After he had armed and armoured himself, Rostov made for the bridge. He saw Helvintr at the command dais, receiving verbal reports from her crew. She appeared pleased with what she was hearing, and the fatalistic version of the captain he had witnessed earlier had been replaced by the pugnacious Fenrisian huntress he knew. It was more than the restoration of her beloved ship that had improved her mood. It was the prospect of vengeance.

'A sudden and dramatic power surge, like the birth of a nascent sun,' she said as he caught her gaze. 'That's how they described it. The Kin.'

The moment of reckoning had come.

'They have found it, inquisitor,' Helvintr said, an eager glint in her eye.

Chapter Thirty-Six

EMBOLDENING SPIRITS

TO HONOUR THE DEAD

TO WAR

The Mordians were less than eager about wearing their void-gear: hard carapace stamped with a Militarum emblem over a rugged vac-suit and rebreather tank, mask and fully encasing helm. It was heavy, difficult to move around in, and it reduced visual perception. Drills had been rushed and perfunctory. Confidence in the mission was low. For most, the cold expanse of the void held an existential dread. Some of the soldiers clung to totems, sanctioned fetishes of Imperial faith, and murmured prayers for safe passage, to feel solid earth beneath their boots again.

Kesh went up and down the lines to try to embolden spirits. The troops were spread across most of the embarkation deck, and she took the time to speak with all of them, to share a joke or join in prayer. This last task she performed with some reticence. Too often, she saw the light of belief in the eyes of those she prayed with, as if they were hoping her being party to their worship would somehow result in a blessing from the Emperor.

Perhaps alone amongst the rest of the Mordians, she found herself longing for the outer dark. At least there the troops would be too concerned with dying to worry about her. On the far side of the deck, a wall still shone wetly with a mural of dark fingerprints. The blood had been slow to dry in the hold's damp atmosphere, though every trooper had made their mark. It was made for those who might follow, so that the ones who left their fingerprints would be remembered, and had all the grim finality of most Mordian rituals.

Vosko, Lodrin and Munser accompanied Kesh on her tour, the lieutenant acting as a foil to dissuade any of the more zealous devotees from falling to a knee or reaching out to touch Kesh in hopes of somehow transferring some of her grace to them.

They lived in this place now, or rather it felt like they did. Vast, dark metal arches soared high overhead, a fleet of heavy transports idling in their launch bays as the engineers checked and rechecked, the air cloying with engine fume and the stench of oil. The deck plates were hard beneath them, only crates and drums to sit upon. Every man and woman waited anxiously for deployment, the bulky landers standing by, their rear ramps lowered for embarkation. There was not much left to do but wait, and these were the hard hours, as Dvorgin had often said. At least it gave them the time to get used to wearing the bulky void armour.

'Is it rare that one of the Guard yearns for the cold and fathomless depths of the outer dark?' asked Lodrin, adjusting one of the straps of his breather tank. 'Anything to get out of this damn hold.'

Munser kept quiet, his face haggard. The man looked like he had aged ten years since they had put on the void-gear.

'I think it's understandable in the circumstances,' Kesh replied as she helped Lodrin make the appropriate adjustments. Then she looked to Vosko, her adjutant already proffering a data-slate for her to review. Kesh glanced over the detail on the low-lit screen, her eyes keen and quick to assimilate detail from all of her years as a pathfinder and markswoman. How different those days seemed now. 'How are we looking?'

'All void armour seals reported checked and functional. Squads are at one hundred per cent efficacy.'

'Barring the handful lost before the first engagement,' offered Lodrin bleakly.

The entirety of the Mordian 84th had been on the embarkation deck during the initial void skirmish. Tremors had been felt through the thick hull and the floor. Alert sirens had flooded the space with red, bloody light. Adrenaline had spiked, they had been ready to go.

And then came the stand down, and the shakes that followed for some, and the fear for others. Six men had died to the enforced discipline of the regimental commissars. It had almost been on a par with Tartarus, except they had traded a subterranean hell of suffocating darkness and choking earth for one of airless cold and expansive nothingness. Kesh could have flipped a coin on which she liked the least. It changed from minute to minute.

She gripped Munser's shoulder, squeezing until he met her gaze, and gave him a nod of reassurance.

'I am fine, captain,' he lied. He gestured behind her, and Kesh turned her head to look over her shoulder. 'You are wanted, ma'am.'

Colonel Falden had called a conclave of the officers and was summoning her over.

'Keep an eye on him,' she whispered in Lodrin's ear as she walked past.

'They'll be launching soon,' Falden was saying as Kesh joined them. He gave her a look of acknowledgement. 'We go in after the Astartes. As soon as they breach, we follow.' The man looked pale, though that could just have been a condition of his Mordian heritage. He also looked uncomfortable in his void-gear. It was an ugly thing, and hardly fitting for an officer of Falden's status. Kesh wondered how long it had been since he was on active deployment. Some men became fat and slow standing at the back of the line, watching from a parapet or a hilltop. Others grew hungry, eager to resharpen their edge. She wondered in that moment which one Falden would be.

Three senior officers made up the command conclave, not including Kesh and Falden. Two company captains and the regimental lord commissar. Each had a small staff and a support faction including a Mechanicus magos and a cadre of Ministorum priests, but none of these were present for the briefing.

The colonel mapped out their responsibilities and deployment order, stressing at length that as soon as the landers touched down, platoon commanders would need to ensure swift and efficient disembarkation, with emphasis placed on getting through the breach and establishing a beachhead on the fortress.

'Get the troops down and inside. It's our best chance for survival. Out there,' he said, gesturing to the hull and what lay beyond it, 'that's the enemy's terrain. If we can get inside, get a few bodies together, shoulder to shoulder... then maybe we get out of this with the regiment more or less intact. Make no mistake, officers, this is egregious warfare of the most attritional sort. It will test us.' He glanced at Kesh again. 'I pray the Emperor protects.'

The body of Maximus Epathus reclined against a Reclusiam throne, his now sightless eyes staring through the dark lenses of his helmet. His armour had been fixed into this position by a Techmarine so it would not slump, his back straight, his posture erect with both arms laid stiffly on the throne's rests and his booted feet firmly planted on the deck.

He beheld his former company in the shadows of the chapel before him, the men and brothers he had once commanded, whose leadership would now have to come from another. In life, Epathus had been Master of Rites. In this role he had ensured the martial traditions and heritage of the Chapter were maintained, a chronicler and historian as well as a captain. Both duties would now fall to another. There was no time to make the appointment official and none present who could ratify it. Despite that, the honour and burden fell to Areios, and as he and his brothers stood before their former captain in quiet reflection, he took on the role of Master of Rites too.

'We remember our brother, Maximus Epathus.'

'We remember,' the others intoned as one, their voices sombre and sonorous in the brazier-lit chamber.

'We draw our swords to honour him.'

A host of gladius blades scraped from their sheaths in metallic synchronicity.

'We raise them up in triumph of his deeds.'

A forest of swords glinted sharply as they were lofted up and touched the firelight.

'We salute to hail his courage.'

A doleful clang resounded as the Ultramarines each struck the pommel of their swords against their breastplates in the warrior's salute. After the echo had fallen away to silence, Areios sheathed his blade so he could unclamp the great hammer from his back. He brandished it to its former bearer, holding it halfway down the haft.

His brothers rapped their swords against their chests, a single chime of sword hilt against ceramite.

Areios met the empty gaze of his dead captain and declared, 'To war.'

Chapter Thirty-Seven

A MAKESHIFT FLOTILLA

SECOND ENGAGEMENT

BREACH

The outer dark lit with the fury of void war.

The flotilla closed on the Blackstone Fortress, which had emerged into realspace like a leviathan from the deep. The Kin had honoured their word. Through their advanced technologies, they had tracked and finally unveiled the monstrous star fortress. Through the void, through the warp, it could not hide. It *did not* hide. As pan-spectral scanners locked on to its signature, the fortress appeared, weapons engaged and brimming with malice.

Now the alliance of Kin and Imperials had to put it to the sword.

An ordinary void engagement was a stately exchange and fought at great distance. Minutes could elapse between a brace of lances firing and their impact against their enemy's shields. Naval tacticians needed to be predictors of movement, of positioning, of critical timing. Voidships might be indomitable but they were also ponderous, and slow to react. Manoeuvring for the grander vessels, the battle cruisers and capital ships, was difficult; it required the arresting of momentum and huge expenditures of energy through a ship's engines. In many ways, conventional void war was a thing of art.

The fight against the Blackstone Fortress had no such finesse or restraint.

They came in close, the Imperial ships of the line bearing the brunt of the fortress' ire, their void shields flaring in staccato impacts. Mercifully, the fortress had yet to unleash its immaterial beam, though a wink of bloodlight crackled at its heart, suggesting it was slowly feeding power to the deadliest tool in its arsenal.

Close meant peril, and the increasingly rapid attrition of shields and armour. In the first few minutes of the engagement, a ship called the *Ardant Spear* took a critical hit amidships before explosions cascaded down its flank and it fought no more. The vox shared with the other vessels in the makeshift flotilla went dark as the bridge crew and her captain were still screaming.

The other ships fared better, and the Kin vessels in particular got in some good blows.

Vutred smiled grimly as the *Delver* landed a palpable hit along one of the Blackstone Fortress' 'forks', destroying a large weapons array and shearing off a swathe of armour plate. As it vented gas and other matter, the kâhl could not help but liken it to blood, and considered the fortress a monster in need of slaying.

The plan in this regard was straightforward enough, for she had often mooted that such plans had the greater chance of success. It was also a strategy that posed the least risk to her own kind, though the urge to mete out the grudge against the star fortress burned strong in her veins. Take the fortress, and the lucrative salvage within would be Omrigar's.

This will come, she told herself, *as true as wrought.*

Each of the Imperial battleships alongside those of the Kin, whose stouter armour and better defences were arguably better suited to the task, would provide cover for the troop ships. These smaller frigates and one particularly brutish and knife-edged strike cruiser would advance in the lee of the more advanced vessels, who would hold position and conduct themselves aggressively so as to draw fire.

Even now, the troop ships were closing on the agreed 'rubicon', which, as soon as this imaginary line in space was met, would signal mass deployment.

The *Delver* took a hit, shields soaking up the worst of it. Most of the ships in the line were taking a hammering, but barring the one they had lost, all had endured so far. Much was riding on the success of this venture, Vutred reminded herself again. She needed the Blackstone Fortress, or at least to settle the grudge as owed. Without it, possible exile awaited her and the Kindred.

'They will reach the assigned rubicon in under a minute, my kâhl,' uttered Krykkâ.

Vutred nodded to acknowledge she had heard, though her thoughts were heavy.

'And what of us, my kâhl?' her Grimnyr asked of her. Othed was by her side on the bridge of the *Delver* with Utri not too far away, keeping Vutred firmly in his sights. 'Are we to join hammer and axe with the Imperials?'

Utri clearly heard this too, despite the general clamour around the bridge as the void battle wore on, and she caught him watching keenly for his kâhl's reaction.

'Let them break its back, if they can,' she replied. 'I will commit no more Kin lives to the ancestors without some proof of profit or grudgement in the offing.' She turned to Othed. 'What say the Votann?'

'They are silent, my kâhl. In this, we are alone.'

Vutred could not decide if that was good or ill, or neither.

Destiny, it appeared, was for her to determine. She hoped she would prove worthy.

Via the *Delver*'s advanced instruments she saw the troop ships had reached their point of no return. They would launch the assault now, or they would perish in the void.

'Luck has. Need keeps. Toil earns,' she whispered, and prayed to the ancestors anyway.

The *Honour of Iax* disgorged its entire complement of assault boats and boarding torpedoes. They seared unerringly across the battlesphere, streaking through explosions, heavy shell fire and accumulated debris fields, navigating each hazard with daring and exact timing.

Several of the boarding torpedoes took hits, one exploding brightly when the rest of the assault group was halfway across the distance between the strike cruiser and its gargantuan target. Mercifully, the craft was unmanned, as were all of the boarding torpedoes. If any made it through the interdicting fire, their incendiary payloads would detonate on impact and rip through what defences were in their way. Otherwise, they were effectively mobile chaff.

Areios watched it all unfold across his retinal lens display. A complex, monochromatic engagement played out for his tactical appraisal, informing him of any craft destroyed and the distance to each target zone. There were two, and the Sixth Company would split their forces equally across each of these ingress points. He knew the Militarum were coming in their wake, slower and with less confidence than the Astartes, whose fearlessness gave them a distinct advantage when charging into the mouth of hell.

The image in his helm also linked to a visual data-feed from the Cestus' front axis. It blurred past at speed, fraught with the flash and flare of ephemeral explosions, the smeared jags of wreckage as the nimble craft dipped and wheeled around them. All the while, the Blackstone Fortress grew larger. Already colossal, even at distance, it rapidly became an all-consuming negative sun, obliterating everything else from sight.

An alert went off, flooding the tightly packed hold with amber light, as they hit a proximity marker.

'For glory, brothers,' he said sternly across the vox linking not only his own craft but all of the other manned crafts in their assault cadre. 'For courage and honour.'

Through the visual feed all he saw then was black, a great starless expanse of black. He shut down the feed. Impact was imminent.

Meltas went to work cutting through the outer armour of the fortress. It sloughed away easily enough, like dead flesh yielding to a hot knife. In seconds, cold and strange light washed into the assault boat's interior, and with ingrained, infallible precision the Ultramarines deployed. A rapid, nanosecond count told Areios all but one of the Cestus craft had reached the Blackstone Fortress. The others could not be considered lost at this point, for a Space Marine could withstand the void even without a ship to propel him. He knew of far stranger survivals. He put it out of his mind. He had three battle squads ready to engage.

His first impression upon entering the halls of the Blackstone Fortress was that it was unlike any starship he had ever encountered. The space was immense and vaulted with crystalline arches and thick columns of obsidian. The Ultramarines' incursion had been so destructive as to destabilise a section of outer hull, which in turn took with it a piece of inner wall. The Cestus rams had partially sealed this gap but there was still a large breach, a gale of decompression rushing through it.

As if waiting for this prompt, the enemy stirred, hurling themselves from hatchways and antechambers, some attached to void-lines and spilling out like deranged ants, others wearing mag-locked boots. Some merely flung their bodies into the roaring vacuum, carried along like flotsam on a ferocious tide.

Mortal cultists, Areios realised. Most wore no discernible armour and minimal void protection, their exposed skin veneering with frost as they shouted their silent death oaths. Some did not even have breather masks and merely held their breath, eyes bloodshot, their lifespans measured in minutes, swinging hatchets and shooting crude firearms. Others were better protected, less berserk but still fanatical. Runic tattoos covered their skin or were burned and cut into their flesh. They had iron spikes in their foreheads, worn like dirty metal crowns. Chainblades whirred in their grubby hands and flensed skulls rattled against belts and on trophy racks.

Spilling from their shadowed places, the cultists hit like a rabid swarm.

Areios and his warriors met them, weapons raised and blazing.

Drussus and Cicero were at his side as he roared across the vox, leading a chorus of voices.

'Avenging Son!'

By the time the lander touched down and its ramp unfurled, the Astartes ahead of them had already made significant headway. Kesh watched their gradually departing backs as they hacked and blasted a path through scores of cultists. They drove like a spear on the outer part of the hull, unflinching, never stopping, all momentum. The void was garlanded with droplets of blood.

Her company had come in right on the Astartes' wake and although their slaughter was prodigious, they only engaged what was in front of them, leaving the rest for the Militarum to mop up. The fighting was immediately manic on both sides, as the Mordians – unused to the strange new theatre of war – struggled to find their cohesion. Kesh saw a sergeant misjudge his footing, fail to make mag-lock and carom off into the darkness, his troopers trying and failing to grasp him. Another stumbled into a cultist's axe, her helm visor split and venting air. She suffocated, even as her killer drifted off into the endless black untethered and unprotected against the cold of space.

Their enemy, Kesh quickly surmised, was insane. Literally throwing their bodies at the Imperials, flailing with blades or firing wildly with solid-shot weapons. Large smoke plumes drooled from the barrels, most of the bullets missing their targets and left to fly forever. Some hit, through sheer volume more than skill, their firers pushed back with every trigger pull in the zero gravity. The Mordians were taking damage.

'They're killing us out here,' rasped Munser over the helm-vox, his voice almost shrill with barely contained terror. He stared at the outer dark surrounding them and then quickly averted his eyes.

The landers had managed to alight on a massive docking pad. Towers, overhead bridges and antenna arrays rose up around them, but they were in the open, more or less, and the gaping hole left by the explosion of a boarding torpedo yawned widely a few hundred feet ahead. The Astartes had already plunged through the breach, their assault boat scraping to a halt just outside the zone of destruction now its incursion weaponry was not needed. It peeled off almost instantly, engines firing and propulsion jets turning it on its horizontal axis for rapid egress.

Kesh kept her head down, making use of the cover, which amounted to the manufactured undulations of the fortress' outer hull. She was urging her troopers out of the landers. Out, out and onto the dock. One of the large transports exploded brightly and briefly, torn apart by rocket-propelled grenade, the lazy contrail from the missile still hanging in the void like a pale white chain. Mordians were flung aside by the blast. Many were lost to the void as they pinwheeled off into darkness, their screams gradually petering to nothing over the vox.

'We need to get inside,' she said to Munser. 'Push forward and link up with the Astartes.'

Las-fire whipped in blurred flashes as the Militarum fought back.

'But first we need to cohere, fight as a unit,' she added and began to exert her command over the platoon sergeants, giving out orders, cajoling and herding her men into something approaching order. She made use of Munser, tasked him with a section of the company to occupy his mind and drown out the fear. Mavin, Vosko and Lodrin stayed close, her command squad loyal and determined. She had instilled that in them. They followed her because of *who* she was, not what she might be. That thought, even in the midst of battle, was a comfort.

Gradually, across blistering fields of fire, the Mordians came together. The intervening minutes had allowed the survivors to become more accustomed to their void-gear, and soon a host of mag-booted troopers strode towards their target. Across a gaping expanse, Kesh caught sight of one of the other assault groups. Here, part of the outer wall had sheared completely away and the Militarum landers were plunging straight into the breach. Her forces had to endure the slog and the razor-edged gauntlet of gunfire and savage cultist blades.

'We are the scions of Mordian,' she roared down the vox over the company-wide band. 'Born in darkness, we fear no shadow, not even death!'

'Not even death!' the crackling, patchy refrain replied.

It spurred them on, and in a few more minutes they had swept the cultists away, crushed them against the sheer relentlessness of the advance.

The inner darkness of the fortress beckoned.

Rostov gripped the haft of the silverwood staff hard as they came in behind the engine flare of the Militarum lander. The pain suppressors had left him numb and he wanted to feel something, to remind himself he was still present in this moment.

Nirdrangar and the other storm troopers sat around him, unmoving in their assault cradles, dead-eyed and ready. It was stuffy, close, the inner hull rattling with every small debris impact or lurch of the engines as the pilot made evasive manoeuvres. The hold of the gunship was smaller than the landers, but it accommodated the troops well enough, even with the addition of the Silent Sister.

She had tried to persuade him to remain on board the *Wyrmslayer Queen* with Helvintr, a stolen few seconds before their delayed deployment. He had been in the armourium, preparing his gear. One of Helvintr's bondsmen had repaired his own armour. It felt good to be wearing it again, though it hung off his body more loosely than before, the straps and seals adjusted to his slighter frame.

The Silent Sister had taken in his debilitated appearance in a single glance. He had only passed out once, putting them slightly behind schedule.

It will kill you, she had signed.

Thinking of his condition now, the hollows in his cheeks and around his eyes, the sallow complexion of his once ruddy skin, Rostov did not deny it.

'I have to see it done, Syreniel.'

I have no desire to see you die, Leonid.

'I do not relish the prospect myself, though I am glad you're at my side.'

You may come to regret saying that.

He had laughed at that, a small, sad sound. 'This is the end, one way or another. You said this may all be the Emperor's will. Trust in that. This is my role, I feel it.'

We are all merely servants, Leonid Rostov.

'Yes, on both sides of this war. Our enemies have masters too.'

Then we must hope that the avatars of His will are stronger than theirs.

'And so you see, I have to finish this. I must be there... I must be there the day we kill the Hand of Abaddon. And that's why I need you, Syreniel. To come with me and bring me back, alive or dead.'

She stared for a moment, impossible to read.

I can do that.

It gave some small comfort thinking back on their exchange. She gave no outward sign of it now, her focus as razor sharp as her sword.

The proximity alert sounded, signalling imminent debarkation.

Rostov put on his helm, and the inner visor screen lit green. This was it.

Alive or dead.

Chapter Thirty-Eight

THE DARKNESS WITHIN

WHAT IS THIS FELL PLACE?

ABATTOIR

Areios left behind the dead as he and his brothers tore through the defenders of the fortress. As the Militarum landers passed through the breach in the outer wall they would be met by a veritable graveyard of corpses, the slain cultists still hooked up to cables, drifting in the airless void or mag-locked to the deck, their lightless upper limbs floating as if underwater. Bloodshot eyes wide, mouths fixed in a frozen rictus.

The Astartes moved on, the way behind them sealing shut like a rapidly healing wound. The Blackstone Fortress was cutting off their escape. The Militarum troopers hurried through behind them, not everyone making it. Areios paid it little mind, pushing on into the fortress, and quickly consulted the data-slate built into his vambrace.

It was quieter now as the roar of escaping pressure had cut off, and an eerie silence was asserting itself. There were no defenders either, not here at least. His bio-scans revealed nothing. No heat or movement at all. He cast his gaze around. The chamber they found themselves in was immense, the size of a battleship's embarkation deck – but Areios was reminded of the Forlorn Temple and its deceiving dimensions.

One of his brethren stopped to peer into the black mirror-glass. The entire massive chamber appeared to be constructed from it.

'Something inside the glass...' he began.

Areios shouted a warning.

Berion jerked up his weapon, a hair trigger from firing when a spear of obsidian pierced his gorget and went right through into his neck. *Then* he fired, a nerve impulse, and bolter shells strafed the dark glass, cracking it in several places.

Another battle-brother, Acadius, suddenly convulsed as a black glass lance punched through his chest, impaling him to the ground. Drussus smashed it before being stabbed through the shoulder himself by another black spear. He cried out before shattering it in two, leaving the fore end still embedded in his pauldron.

The Astartes laid down suppressing fire, hammering the walls and columns with controlled bursts from their bolt rifles. Closing ranks, the Militarum soldiers who had made it through the breach did the same, the gloomy chamber lighting up with muzzle flash and las-flare.

It lasted almost thirty seconds before Areios called a halt. The eerie quiet resumed, growing with the fading echo of the final las-bolt, but mercifully whatever had agitated the room's defences had stopped. Everyone held their breath.

Areios looked to Cicero, who had unclipped his auspex.

'Nothing here I can make sense of, brother-lieutenant,' he said. 'We triggered a mechanism of some kind, a reaction from its innate defences. Though it is unlike any vessel I have ever encountered before. I would suggest we avoid peering too closely into the glass.'

'I concur,' replied Areios, somewhat ruefully.

Berion was dead, having bled out all over the floor, his head almost detached from his body. Valentius was already about the business of harvesting his gene-seed.

'Apothecary?' Areios enquired, his gaze falling on Acadius, who lay on his back unmoving, his question unspoken but obvious.

Valentius looked over, impassive. He ran a bio-scan as the rest of the fighters in the room kept a wary eye on the shadows.

'He will not survive. The best I can offer him now is the Emperor's mercy, and take the Chapter's due.'

Areios let out a quiet breath. 'See it done.' He made a quick assessment. Two passageways appeared to lead out of the chamber. He consulted a map on his data-slate, an approximate rendering of the Blackstone Fortress' interior derived from the Kin's deep-scans. It was imperfect and already seemed out of date. The version of the chamber on his screen had three exits, not two, but he didn't need the third and so followed the path that would lead him towards the heart of the fortress. Or at least, he hoped it still would.

They moved off, on edge now. Areios heard the Militarum muttering fearfully to each other, trying not to raise their voices or step in the wrong place, as if every flagstone hid some danger or trap.

Via the route designated on the map, they reached another room with heavy pipes and wiring hanging down like intestines from a vaulted ceiling. Somewhere below and out of sight, a machine could be heard whirring and clicking. As they moved in a narrow column, staying away from the walls, Areios abruptly felt the room trembling beneath his feet. He called a halt again, and went to one knee to place his gauntlet against the ground to better feel the tremors.

Then he looked ahead and saw the three exit routes slowly reducing to one as the walls appeared to slide and shift.

'It's moving,' he said, surging to his feet. 'It's moving! On me now, brothers!' Areios burst into a sprint, his warriors on his heels as they made for the doorway. It too was sealing, even as another had begun to open up behind them. The path ahead was the one they needed, the one from the increasingly inaccurate map.

The Militarum had given chase too but were far slower than the Astartes. Only a handful made it through after the Ultramarines, Areios hauling through the last. The rest were now consigned to the darkness behind them. One of the pale-faced troopers looked up at him with wide, afraid eyes.

'Emperor bless you, my lord.' She lowered her gaze, trembling.

'Hold to your warrior's creed, and your loyalty to the Throne,' said Areios. 'It will see us through.'

He move off to examine the doorway, now a solid wall, that had closed behind them. Through it, Areios swore he could hear the sound of screeching before even that too cut away to silence. They tried the vox, but there was nothing but static.

'What is this fell place?' Drussus rasped in private over the vox, so as not to spook the human troopers.

'Nothing good,' Cicero replied.

'Nothing good at all,' echoed Areios as he took in their surroundings.

Evidence of old machineries lingered here in the next room. Deck plate layered most of the floor, and large tubular capacitors crackled with cerulean energy at the periphery of the room. And underneath it all, the churn of an unseen mechanism was apparent, as the fortress made and remade itself with seeming sentience.

'It is a great machine of some sort?' suggested Cicero.

'I believe it is something much more elaborate,' Areios replied with growing unease. 'I believe it is a trap.'

He walked on.

They passed through several more corridors and chambers, all apparently deserted, the esoteric machineries more prevalent the deeper they went. The black obsidian so dominant in the outer sections of the fortress was still present, but less obvious, as if the metal and the mechanisms had accreted over it like a scab or second skin.

Areios consulted the map, but it bore almost no resemblance now to the actual layout of the fortress. He had expected a conventional boarding assault, room to room, corridor to corridor, securing chokepoints and overwhelming bottlenecked defenders. He had been prepared for the savagery of that close-quarters fight. Not this. For a few doubting seconds he wished for his old captain's counsel, but Maximus Epathus was dead and the responsibility of leadership fell to him. Areios made a silent vow that he would not be found wanting in that task.

It was a moving labyrinth, he realised, but that was not all. Despite the apparent randomness, he could not shake the feeling that they were being herded.

A ground fog lapped around their ankles, chilling bone. Areios saw the Militarum troopers shivering even through their vacuum suits.

A conveyor had brought them to them this place, a sharp-angled descent into the fortress. All around them, darkness, and the barest hint of distant machineries. The open-topped carriage was large and moved slowly, every noise or imagined stirring from beyond the ambit of the conveyor's overhead lamp drawing sudden, panicked movement from the Guard.

Areios and his warriors remained stoic but watchful throughout the journey. It occurred to him that their mission parameters had changed. Not only did they need to kill whatever entity or force was in command of the fortress, they also now needed to escape.

The white vapour cloud had been visible before they reached the conveyor's terminus. It plumed through an opening below, spilling over the edge of a disembarkation platform into chasmal blackness. As the strike force alighted onto the platform, Cicero extended a warning hand towards the female trooper Areios had spoken to earlier.

'Watch your step.'

The edge was sheer, the drop lethal.

She staggered, taken by surprise at how close the edge actually was. Blanched with fear, she nodded to the Astartes.

Cicero regarded her curiously, as if he was unsure how to react.

'Brother...' said Areios, getting Cicero's attention, who turned immediately. Areios gestured to the ragged opening, more like a large fissure in rock than a doorway, and led them inside.

It reminded Areios of a cold stasis chamber, ice riming the walls and contours of the room, which had eight sides like an octagon, but as he made out the chains dangling from the ceiling and what hung from those chains, he understood what this place actually was – an abattoir. The entire room smelled of cold, dead flesh. The meat hooked up to the ceiling was human, or parts of humans. Hundreds of them. Mainly torsos; very few of the bodies were intact and even these were wreathed in cold. The mist was pervasive here.

At the very back of the room, glimpsed through the white veil, was a sigil. Colossal, it took up the entire back wall and rose almost to the lofty ceiling. It was made of dirty iron, streaked in red and black like tears running down the metal. A face, a skull. Spikes protruded from every angle, human heads impaled on each.

Areios felt anger stir and took a moment to steady himself.

It was also a threshold, he realised, a gateway to a separate fiefdom. Different here to the other parts of the fortress. Here were the runes of Ruin, carved and daubed into metal and flesh. Profane icons and shrines cluttered in corners. The machines remained but had been corrupted, encrusted with dried blood and bone-yellow wax. Eight ice-clad columns ran the length of the room, arranged in a figure of eight, their capitals the same dark iron as the sigil.

Footsteps echoed desolately through the space as Areios and his warriors plunged through the mist.

They were not alone for long.

Crouched at first, hidden like sharpened rocks by the tide, the warriors armoured in red and brass arose in eager concert. Their teeth were visible just below the edge of their crested war-helms, their snarl-fanged mouths like hounds hungry for the kill. Other lesser creatures thronged at their feet, more of the mortal cultists from before, their bare skin grey and glittering with patches of frost.

The largest of the heretics stood up last of all. He was a mountain of plate-sheathed muscle. His neck was thick, like an ogryn's, but he was Traitor Astartes, just like his twisted brothers, and there was a burn mark shaped like a claw or a hand. Unlike the others, he wore no helm and instead had a mask covering the lower half of his face. It had been fashioned out of brass and wrought into the shape of the mouth of a hellish dog. A ragged red cloak fell from his shoulders.

One meaty hand, not gauntleted, his skin tanned brown and leathery, rested on the pommel of a huge cleaver. A butcher's cleaver, only far larger. An eight-pointed crown, black as soot, sat above his heavy brow. His shaved scalp looked glossy in the wan light. Aerosolised blood fumed off his body, exuded through his pores and the gaps in his armour. It congealed with the mist, surrounding him in a faint red miasma.

'I have been waiting for you,' said the Butcher King, his voice deep and resonant, breath fuming crimson in the air.

Chapter Thirty-Nine

FALLING BEHIND

LUMENS TO FULL

A MONSTER IN THE LABYRINTH

The Blackstone Fortress swallowed them whole and Kesh gasped for air, biting back a frisson of fear. An atmospheric shield shimmered over the opening, an autonomic reaction to the breach. She was glad of it, to no longer be exposed to the outer dark and its fathomless terrors.

Though there were terrors inside as well.

The Astartes fought them.

Many looked human, variations on the cultists with which they had already clashed. Others were less so, shambling and mechanised, cyborganic horrors with hooks and energy whips for arms, corrupted servitors and bipedal machines with sword limbs and beam weapons. They battled on the edge of a large deck plate, empty but for the combatants, and with no cover.

The Astartes were like demigods, hurling bodies, cleaving and gunning them apart. Casting the abominations off the edge, driving them on with their fury and keenly focused hate. As she watched them, her own troops shouting and firing as they raced into the fight, Kesh saw how the Astartes could be made for nothing except war. Even amongst one of the supposedly more civilised Chapters, the empire builders themselves, the Ultramarines, they killed with such savagery. In battle, she supposed her troops were hardly any different, but after a bloody battle, *after* the killing was done, she would weep. She had heard other troopers do the same, alone in the dark when they thought no one was listening.

But in their eyes – and not the cold lenses of their war-helms, though it might as well have been – what did she see?

Nothing. The Astartes had no remorse. No fear. No humanity of any kind. Not *truly*.

It chilled her. Such beings could not offer hope, although it was sorely needed. Humanity needed something else, something that began with hope – *with faith?* – and became something more. Astartes could only serve up death.

But they were highly effective at it. The enemy died in droves, the brunt of it to the Ultramarines. Kesh and her Mordian platoons were reduced to mopping up the dregs and the dying. It was grim work, but necessary. They had hit the fortress with overwhelming force, landing many assault boats and troops. That advantage had begun to tell already. Genetically engineered aggression barely sated, the Astartes were moving on to the next fight. After their commander had surveyed what lay beyond the deck plate – to Kesh's eyes a plain of indistinct darkness with nothing remotely familiar for her to latch onto – they began to drop off the edge, one after the other. Then in pairs and groups of three or four, until there were none left.

Munser had just stabbed a limbless servitor through the remains of its brainpan and gaped at the sight of the Astartes simply jumping off the edge.

'I hope they're not expecting us to do that,' he said dryly.

Kesh joined Lodrin and a handful of others who had dared

to peer after them. She looked and saw a stepped ridge. Four wide steps in all. Each drop was long and lethal if you fell. The remains of the wretches the Ultramarines had driven over their edge lay upon the steps, more on the second than the third. The fourth was almost completely barren but for the odd, unfortunate corpse. Limbs and other pieces of bodies had been separated from the whole. A ghastly scene played out, one which the Astartes did not pause to appreciate. The trailing warriors went from one step to another, leaping in stages to the bottom, and finishing off anything that strayed within reach of their blades as they did so. The business of slaughter for them was economic, efficient. And now they were on the hunt, they were not slowing.

Kesh called behind her, trying to get the attention of platoon sergeants and her lieutenants.

'Grapnels! Everyone down there! Move! On the double!'

As part of their void armour, each trooper had a mag-grapnel in their kit. It had a modest spool of high-tensile cable. Intended for use on a ship's outer hull, it would serve equally well here. They went to work quickly, splitting into squads, lining up in good order, the rearguard keeping a watchful eye, spotters up top maintaining overwatch on those below in case they were missing some hidden threat.

Standing on the edge of the deck plate, the descent already underway, Kesh paused. She was looking at the path ahead, visible in the 'valley' of the level below.

The four massive steps descended to a series of openings. High-sided, they looked like conduits into the machine, as if a circuit board had been given walls and was large enough to dwarf a man. Wide at first, angularly shaped like an inverted tuning fork, each path narrowed as it went deeper, into a sharp defile.

A maze of close corridors. It reminded her of Kreber Pass,

and her breath hiked at the memory. Her chest and stomach felt tight, full of lead.

'Swallow your fear, Magda,' he said to her.

At first, she thought it was Munser, but the lieutenant was helping to organise the drop. Then she realised it was Dvorgin's voice in her ear, in her head. She held back tears, clutching the old general's chrono in her hand.

'Right you are, sir,' she whispered and hurried over to Munser as he called out.

'Into the dark, ma'am,' he said in greeting as she came up to him.

'Not even death,' Kesh replied, and took the grapnel cable he had already prepared.

'Not even death,' he echoed, and she pitched back against the drop, her feet levering over the edge until she was over and descending.

The Mordians made it to the lower level without incident and passed through the openings in groups of ten. As far as Kesh could tell, each of the conduits led in the same direction. She imagined there might be crossing points, that this was some engine of the fortress tended to by its servitors and tech-priests or their equivalent. It was tight, and the troopers advanced in columns, a few platoons to each conduit. They were mainly infantry; an assault of this nature with anything heavier would have been unfeasible. Special weapons teams provided the bite, plasma guns and flamers in the main. Nothing crew-served, only man-portable.

Despite all of that, it was still slow going. Footing was uncertain, the darkness that was barely leavened by sodium lamp and lume-stick an added impediment. And it was hot. Unlike the upper zone and the outer void, it sweltered below. There was breathable atmosphere, though, and with some relief they were able to remove their helms.

Each incursion group had been assigned a designation, their signatures inputted into surveyors so each group commander could monitor his or her comrades. They were to move slow, steady, and stay together.

They had also lost sight of the Ultramarines.

'Above and ahead,' Kesh said to Munser and her command group, the order then cascaded down the line to the squad sergeants. She barely spoke much above a whisper, her fear still with her but under control for now. Her weapon panned from the floor up to the apex of the walls, its targeter still blank.

'Why do I feel like we are rats in a cage?' murmured Lodrin, his stab-lamp lighting up ductwork and clusters of strange servos. Everything was slicked black.

'Stay focused,' Kesh reminded him, trying not to sound too much on edge. She glanced at the hand-held surveyor, saw that incursion group Penumbra had strayed ahead of the others, a good ninety feet or more.

She turned to Vosko. 'Who's on Penumbra?'

'Lieutenant Rultich, ma'am.'

Kesh activated the vox-bead in her ear.

'Rultich, you're roaming. Check your surveyor and pull it back to the line.'

The feed crackled back with static. Comms had been getting patchier the further they advanced. Kesh reckoned on another two hundred feet or so of conduit before they came out the other side and were hopefully reunited with the Astartes.

Waiting a few more seconds, she repeated the message.

Still nothing. According to the surveyor, Penumbra were still moving. Pulling farther ahead.

'Are you even looking, lieutenant?' she hissed, irritated.

'Let me try it, ma'am.'

Mavin had stepped up. As vox-operator he had the company-wide box and knew how to untangle particularly recalcitrant comms. He used the larger device he carried on his back, an added weight in addition to his air-canister and void-gear.

After a few more seconds, Mavin listening as he tweaked various dials and levers, he nodded and handed the receiver cup and headset to Kesh. At this point, the entire group had halted whilst she tried to re-establish contact with Lieutenant Rultich and Penumbra.

'Pull your troops back, lieutenant,' she said, not bothering to hide her annoyance. The stress from the tightness of the defile was thinning her nerves and her patience.

'Captain?' Lieutenant Rultich queried. *'We* are *back, ma'am. Surveyor is showing us as level.'*

'You're a hundred feet in front, Rultich, and getting further ahead.'

'Not according to our readings. I'm sorry, captain, but this is showing...' He paused to confirm. *'Yes, we are on target. You should be right–'*

A gap in the left-hand wall was coming up soon, a narrow route through from one conduit to another. Kesh reached it just as the lieutenant's vox cut out.

He wasn't there. There was no one there. She moved across into the other conduit, Munser and two squads coming with her. Ahead and behind, there was nothing.

'What in the hells?' murmured Lodrin.

Munser glared at the man for the breach in protocol.

Kesh wasn't really paying them much attention. She was watching the sickly yellow mist slowly creeping down the conduit.

'Are you seeing this, lieutenant?' she asked Munser, who followed her gaze.

'Some kind of gas leak?' He wrinkled his nose and scowled. 'It's foul, whatever it is.'

It was getting thicker, and it was coming towards them. Kesh couldn't be sure that it hadn't somehow *seen* them, its pace as it rolled across the ground quickening all of a sudden. She backed off, urging the others to do the same.

The vox came back with a sharp squeal of feedback and then they heard screaming – agonised and terrified screaming. Mavin recoiled; it was coming through the vox-unit strapped onto his back too. It was coming through every vox.

'Off,' Kesh yelled, yanking the vox-bead out of her ear. The screams were deafening. 'Turn it off!'

Throwing a lever, Mavin shut it down. The screaming abruptly cut out but the mist was still coming.

They moved back into the other conduit where the rest of Kesh's troops were waiting. But the mist was here too, formless at first, but as it came closer, she made out the loose shape of thin and elongated limbs amidst the foulness and long talons, as if the mist weren't drifting but rather crawling or clawing towards them.

'Helms on,' she ordered, 'lumens to full.'

A plethora of stablights flared in the shadows. It would burn their power packs faster, but she knew, she just *knew*, they needed the light.

She led them on, a nervous fear affecting the group. It was like being back at Tartarus again, only this time she had the recent trauma of Kreber Pass for added flavour. Munser stayed close, as if sensing her growing unease.

'Only way is through,' he said, and Kesh nodded. Her hand was shaking so she steadied it.

They entered the mist. It had grown even thicker since the initial sighting and was higher now, around waist height. Although it was vapour, it felt like wading through something much more substantial, as if they were being dragged. She never saw the limbs or talons again, but the reek was horrific, even filtered through their masks.

Another opening loomed ahead, this time on the right. It

looked like a larger portal and for a few moments she dared to hope for a way out, away from the stench and the mist. As they reached it, Kesh and the others were afforded a much deeper view into the maze, a long passageway perpendicular to the one they were in and stretching off for several hundred feet. She was about to order the troops into it when she stopped. Something was moving in the distance, and as she saw it she heard a high-pitched scraping sound that set her teeth on edge.

Scrape... pause... *scrape*. Over and over, like a cripple dragging an injured limb.

It was large, the figure, its silhouette nearly filling the corridor. Moving slowly and heavily, the *scrape...* pause... *scrape* punctuating every step.

'Holy Throne...' gasped Kesh, as she saw the figure properly for the first time.

Rostov and his party reached the deck plate and the deep plunge down to the level below. He eyed it warily, conscious of his own physical limitations.

'My lord?' asked Nirdrangar, noticing his hesitation.

'I've come this far,' said Rostov, after a short pause. Like the storm troopers, he was wearing a grav-chute, a compact propulsion device commonly used in drop assaults but utilised here in quick controlled bursts to effect a safe descent. In short order Nirdrangar was leading the line into the beckoning darkness, his men jumping over the edge.

Syreniel had no need for such a device. She leapt into the great nothing with acrobatic confidence, landing on each step with feline poise before springing off to the next. As Rostov followed, his own trajectory less certain and much more functional, he marvelled at the Silent Sister's brutal elegance.

Gratefully he made it to the ground, though the pain had intensified, and found the Silent Sister waiting for him. She had evidently gone ahead to scout the way. Another shot of morphia barely touched his pain, but it kept him upright, at least. Several openings presented themselves, leading off into a veritable labyrinth of corridors, and Rostov looked to Syreniel, who nodded to one of the openings. In they went, moving fast and surefooted in spite of the terrain.

She is here, signed Syreniel after a few moments, hanging back to stay with Rostov, who was struggling with the pace.

'Your former comrade? With the Militarum?'

Syreniel nodded. *We must reach her. Something is near.*

'The Hand?'

A monster in the labyrinth.

Chapter Forty

THE GODS BEAR WITNESS

A SACRIFICE

PROPHECIES

A monster lurked in the well below. Its silent agonies trembled the blackstone around her, a dying leviathan willing for its end.

Yheng had been staring into the depths, into churning black and tentacular horror. It felt simultaneously huge, a being of ancient and dread majesty, and yet also pitiable and small to have been brought so low. She had suffered in her life; she had been subservient to cruel and uncaring masters; she had felt her potential stymied, her faith abused. Perhaps this was why the fortress had chosen her.

'How can I...?' Yheng began. She had her staff, her knife and her knowledge of sorcery, but this was small magic, crude against the task before her.

'The gods bear witness, Yheng,' said Augury, the strange amorphous creature standing behind her with their face hidden by a deep hood.

At these words, Yheng looked up into the vaulted ceiling and she remembered the ritual and the supplicant, what felt like aeons ago, his genhanced body hex-marked by each of the Eight, the shards pushed into his flesh. His burden. One that could only be borne by a warrior of the Traitor Astartes. And she remembered the gods and their eager regard. It was upon her again now, only this time she did not quail before it – she welcomed it.

At a murmured incantation, she fed power into the head of her staff. It crackled in a dark nimbus, a tempest confined to the thrice-cursed wood.

'A sacrifice demands a blade, Tharador Yheng,' uttered Augury, and with a slow nod of understanding Yheng drew her knife as well. She regarded the morass below, the dying core of the Blackstone Fortress.

'It has no heart to pierce, no neck to slash,' she said.

'*Intent*, Yheng, there can be no true sacrifice without intent. You must offer this kill to the gods... and please them.'

A mote of fear fluttered in her chest but Yheng quashed it.

'Enter the darkness, Yheng, and make your kill. It is ordained, you are ready.'

Yheng looked back at Augury, but they merely nodded, urging her to proceed.

'What will happen?' she asked.

'The fortress will die, its anima extinguished. It has served its purpose as a place to hide us, and our purpose with the shards. The others depart already, though some remain to hold our enemy's attention. That is why we are still here, Yheng, to pull the Imperium's eye towards us so that my agent can finish his journey. It has drawn our enemies in, the fortress, a black candle flame in the outer darkness. They are here, Yheng, within these halls. Far away for now, but the servants of the Corpse-Emperor are coming. Do this, devote your soul to the gods, and be rewarded. Receive apotheosis.'

Yheng murmured a few words of power and a macabre wind

blew up around her. Slowly she rose off the ground, buoyed by the souls of the damned, their stretched faces fashioned by the wind and screaming in muted torment. Her staff held aloft like a flaming brand, she drifted over the gaping mouth of the well and descended into blackness.

Abject and all-consuming. A silent tempest. An obsidian desert. An ocean of ink. The azure flame at the head of her staff guttered and died. She gagged as the darkness swept over her, suffocating, sending her mind reeling – and then her nerves steadied and she felt the overburdening presence.

It *saw* her.

Something brushed against her ankle, her shoulder, the back of her neck, like the touch of fish swimming through a river. Yheng fought the urge to recoil, and merely stood and closed her eyes. The staff's flame rekindled, the lightning across the haft crackled back to life. She wove it around her, expanding the energies into a terrifying storm. Lightning arcs stabbed outwards and the formless darkness spasmed, as if stung. It shrank, and Yheng felt its weakness.

Something coalesced amidst roiling shadow. A mass, withered and diseased, emitting a soft beat.

You will bare your neck to me...

She raised the knife, and plunged it down into the black mass.

There was no scream, no obvious reaction of any kind. As she opened her eyes again, the writhing darkness in its many forms had simply gone, and the well was empty. The fortress was still. Inert.

Yheng drifted upwards and back out of the well. Her skin tingled, and like a night-rose opening up inside her, she felt it. *Power.*

'Gods...' she breathed, and saw cinder crackle on the air.

Augury watched her quietly. Yheng smiled, her eyes wide and eager.

'I feel it,' she said, her voice deeper now, and oddly resonant. 'I feel the favour of the gods.'

Augury bowed, all of a sudden the supplicant. 'It is yours, Mistress Yheng. You are to be their priestess, their sorceress.'

'Tell me what they would will of me.'

'All in good time. First, we have an errand. Our departure from this place is long overdue.'

Augury threw open their cloak and Yheng beheld the warp in all its wondrous horror. It wrapped around her, enfolded her in a sea of unreality. Her mind was suddenly awash with prophetic visions: of a throne in flames, of the corpse-lord her gods so despised.

Chapter Forty-One

THE BUTCHER KING

AS ONE

SOMETHING HAS CHANGED

Not all of the hanging bodies were corpses. One of them detached itself from the chains above and fell upon Areios with a manic cry. It stabbed with a heavy knife, two-handed, but Areios threw it off and into one of the columns. The bone shattered audibly.

More crazed cultists were dropping from the chains, like chiropterans diving for prey. They landed on the backs of the Astartes, hacking with axes and swords and chainblades.

'Eyes up!' shouted Areios, raking the hanging bodies with a burst of bolter fire. Torsos exploded over the Ultramarines in a grisly rain.

Cicero cut down another flock, blasting them apart in midair. Limbs pinwheeled, ripped from their bodies. Drussus caught one as it descended and slammed it into the ground. Bones cracked. He hauled it up again straight away, leaving a red smear in the ice, and proceeded to fling the wretch across the room to collide with three others. The cultists went sprawling, lost to the frozen mist.

Some of the Militarum soldiers were screaming, less durable than the Astartes, attacked in a frenzy of hatchets and knives. Their blood ran in rivers across the frozen abattoir floor.

Amused, the Butcher King raised his cleaver and gestured to Areios and his brothers.

'Skulls for the Skull Throne,' he growled.

They charged.

Violence erupted across the abattoir. The grim torrent of falling bodies was like a flesh shield for the charging Traitor Astartes, though Areios shot one in the shoulder guard and saw the warrior spin on his heel. Bolter fire thinned out the cultists quickly, turning them into chunks of exploded meat, but it gave the Traitor Space Marines a short reprieve and time enough to gain ground. Spurring himself into a run, batting aside anything that fell into his path, Areios took the lead. He felt a body carom off his battle plate but kept moving. A cultist sprang onto his shoulder guard, clinging on with an embedded axe, but Areios tore them off, blade and all. The heady thunder of war drummed in his ears, beating out a belligerent tattoo in his hearts. He trampled a cultist underfoot, running and gunning now, determined to reach the true foe.

In the Traitor Astartes, he saw a dark mirror-image of himself and his brothers. Their armour, though of an ancient pattern, was just as formidable. Their enhancements were not so dissimilar. But the Butcher King and his ilk had sworn pacts to the Dark Gods. They reeked of corruption. It gave them strength, resilience. He and his brothers had something the traitors did not: the absolute belief that they would prevail, and the honour to see it done.

A traitor bulled his way through the thronging cultists, his chainaxe leaving red ruin wherever it fell. The wretches were nothing to him, *less* than nothing. Areios shot him through the throat, and the traitor's headless corpse collapsed bloodily a few seconds later.

He moved on, into the fray, his squad by his side.

'For honour, brothers!' he bellowed.

Next to Areios, Drussus cut the legs from under an armoured brute, then fired almost point-blank into the warrior's face. Its roared invective soon fell silent. Cicero was more sparing, lining up headshots with a marksman's skill. He took out three in rapid succession, hanging back as his brothers pushed up, fighting as a unit.

A Traitor Space Marine came at Areios from the flank, half seen in his peripheral vision. He turned to engage, a fraction late, and saw the warrior felled with a precise shot through the left eye.

Gratitude, Cicero.

But the grind was relentless, and even Areios felt his strength being taxed. 'For courage!' he roared, blasting apart the breastplate of an enemy, its innards spilling through the ravaged mesh beneath. He finished it with a bolt-shell to the face. As gore spattered his helm, he quickly took stock.

Uxio fell to a traitor's savage blow, the axe blade buried in his chest. Tiberon staggered back with blood fountaining from his neck; two of his brothers brought his killer down with a coordinated attack. It was brutal, a melee of staggering violence. Astartes-on-Astartes warfare, conducted at dizzying pace and without restraint. The Astra Militarum could not hope to match it. They fought off the cultist horde, while Areios and his men kept the Traitor Astartes focused on them and them alone.

As the ranks of the enemy thinned and the fighting grew stretched, Areios felt rather than saw the champion of the Dark Gods coming for him. A heady blood-stench preceded him, fouling Areios' olfactory sensors. A brute of a warrior stepped forwards, bellowing in incoherent fury. Ortho and Demidies engaged him, seeking to intercede on their brother-lieutenant's behalf, but the Butcher King tore them down as though they were children, rather than warriors Areios had fought and bled beside. In two swings of the fell champion's axe, Ortho slumped to his knees, decapitated, and Demidies was carved down the middle, his bifurcated halves parting with monstrous slowness.

'Your skull will adorn Khorne's throne,' the Butcher King promised, levelling his gore-slicked blade at Areios.

Guilliman grant me strength, Areios willed, preparing to face the monster when Sergeant Trajus rushed in from the flank, his chainsword wet with traitor blood.

The blow was so swift that it almost didn't register. Trajus appeared to stall, then staggered to a halt. When he tried to turn, the upper portion of his torso parted diagonally from the lower in a gruesome slide.

Areios cried out, 'Avenging Son!' and charged the Butcher King.

A hasty burst of mass-reactives exploded against the traitor's armour but did nothing to slow him, and all too quickly Areios found himself face to face with a monster. He stared up at his foe, finding only rage and hatred in the Butcher King's bloodshot eyes.

About to fire again, Areios recoiled as his bolt rifle came apart in his hand, destroyed by the monstrous warrior's axe. The explosion blasted Areios onto his back but he rose to his feet immediately, letting go of the useless bolt rifle and drawing the thunder hammer. It crackled with power, a lightning arc rippling across the head. His dead captain had named it Honour, but all Areios could feel was wrath, and a desire for vengeance against the one who had slain his brothers.

Vengeance is the undoing of honour, Epathus had once said.

For now, vengeance will have to be enough, thought Areios as Drussus and Cicero came to his side.

'As one,' said Drussus.

'As one,' echoed Areios.

They charged the Butcher King together. A savage swing kept them back, the cleaver carving a shallow furrow in Cicero's armour, a near miss. He fired at close range, a snapshot, but it pranged off the dark crown the monster wore and barely made a scratch. The Butcher King blinked back sparks, snarling and frothing. Drussus leapt at the opening, and managed to stab his gladius into the meat of the monster's thigh. A backhand blow sent him reeling and crashing into Cicero, his blade still embedded, and the Butcher King not even limping as he bore down on Areios.

A hasty parry with the hammer's haft prevented him from being cut in half, but it was taking all of Areios' strength to hold on. The fight against Pridor Vrakon came back to him, the last time he had fought a foe of such potency and experience. Areios had almost died that day. He had lost an arm instead. He vowed he would not be found wanting this time.

A kick to his midriff propelled him backwards. He hit one of the columns, felt his shoulder jar as the stone cracked with the impact. Still dazed, Areios swerved instinctively to avoid a beheading.

His foe reeked of blood, his body wreathed in a hot red mist that melted the ice around him. Areios found himself on the defensive, unable to land a blow, the heavy thunder hammer an anchor in his unfamiliar grip.

Another swipe of the cleaver cut through a chain attached to the wall mounting, and the body it had been holding crashed down. Areios leapt aside, scrambling. A glancing blow scraped his arm and pain lanced through the bone. He retreated up a set of low steps, mounting a dais overlooking the abattoir, the Butcher King pursuing in a relentless frenzy. The traitor was raw aggression and unfettered wrath. Wild.

Since facing Pridor Vrakon, Areios had learned never to underestimate an enemy. He had also learned patience, though it railed against the eager fire within him, and to choose his moment carefully.

The Butcher King made a reckless swipe and Areios lunged, the hammer head punching into the traitor's chest. It staggered him, and for a moment his guard opened up. Areios swung a blow into his flank, crushing armour plate, cracking and denting it inwards. He followed up with a smash to the traitor's shoulder, though this had less impact and the Butcher King was able to lash out with a heavy punch that caught Areios on the chin. His vision crazed through his retinal lenses and he tasted blood.

Another savage attack followed and Areios parried. His return swing caught his foe against the knee, destroying the knee plate and much of the bone. The Butcher King collapsed as his leg gave way beneath him. He lashed out, roaring his defiance, but Areios stayed back to let him rage.

A blow to the shoulder took out the cleaver. Bleeding, foaming at the mouth, the Butcher King bellowed to his god to grant him strength.

'They're not listening,' Areios said, and smashed his skull with Honour, ending it.

Deranged and unhinged, the rest of the Traitor Astartes were straightforward to pick apart after that. The Ultramarines fought them in packs, taking each one down like a rabid beast, and when that was done they put the last of the cultists to the sword.

Areios was amidst the aftermath when a pale, bloody-faced Militarum colonel approached him.

'We are victorious, my lord,' he said, breathless. His considerably thinned ranks gathered behind him. Proud and courageous, they nonetheless looked disturbed by what they had done and witnessed.

Favouring the colonel with a nod of acknowledgement, he turned to Valentius, who had been ministering to the dying and the dead. Considering the carnage around the abattoir, the Apothecary's work was not yet over.

'Eight of our brothers have fallen, lieutenant,' he reported grimly. 'A high price, though I will take the Chapter's due.'

'Remain here to perform the rites,' Areios said, and gestured to the exhausted-looking Mordians. 'And keep them with you. They have honoured the Emperor, and I would ask no more of them.'

Valentius saluted and went to his task.

'It feels...' Cicero tried to catch the right word. '*Still*?' He and Drussus had survived the slaughter and had converged on their leader, as always.

'Quieter, yes,' Drussus agreed. He regarded the crushed skull of the dead Butcher King, lying not so far away. 'Is this it? Is this the great enemy we are meant to find and kill?'

Areios had been wondering the same thing, but shook his head. 'This isn't over yet. I think they were put here to slow us down.'

'Something *has* changed though,' said Cicero. He crouched down to place his hand against the ground. 'No tremors or vibrations. It's as if it suddenly stopped. I think the machine is dead.'

'Dead or alive, we need to reach its heart and make sure,' Areios replied.

'And kill whatever else is lurking there,' added Drussus.

Areios gave a nod. 'And kill whatever else.'

Chapter Forty-Two

DEAD MEN

ON ALL SIDES

SAINTED

His pockmarked armour plate straining at his bulk, the hulking plague lord ambled for the kill.

A bucket helm covered a diminutive head, a tripartite eye staring through its same-shaped slit. He dragged an immense bell on a long and rusted anchor chain, the metal tarnished, cracked and riddled with black patches of contagion like its bearer. A huge double-bladed broadsword was scabbarded on his lumpen back. He had a kinship to the Heretic Astartes Kesh had killed at the Last Stronghold, only he was larger. Much larger.

And he was not alone. Lesser versions of the plague lord gathered behind him. They wore the same sickly-coloured armour, clusters of suppurating boils and fleshy goitres pushing through the gaps between plates. Filth-encrusted knives were held low in their pudgy fists. They carried dirty boltguns with corroded bayonets. But it was their belts to which Kesh found her eye inexorably drawn. Helmets, cobalt blue, corroded and blood-stained, hung from strings of gut.

The missing Astartes. Dead to a man.

As he appeared to register the horror on Kesh's face, the plague lord stopped to pull on the chain until it grew slack and the bell hung pendulously from his gauntleted fist.

Kesh stared, unable to move, to act, the same paralysing fear gripping her troopers, who were looking through the gap in the conduit wall.

'Doom...' the plague lord thundered, a voice of gurgling virulence, and he hoisted up the bell and brought it crashing down, chain and all.

A dolorous *gong!* rippled down the conduit, growing in amplitude the farther it travelled in a great clangour. As it reached them the Mordians were already cowering, hands pressed to the sides of their helms. Visors cracked under sudden pressure. The strange mist leaked in. Some of the troopers collapsed.

Kesh and a few others raised their lasguns and started firing, the bright bolts splashing against the monstrous bell-ringer and his cohorts but seemingly leaving them unharmed. Mavin shouted – at least Kesh thought it was the vox-operator; her ears were still ringing painfully. His warning made her and several others turn. Through the mist that had been ahead of them more figures were emerging. They staggered on uncertain limbs, moving awkwardly in shuffling steps.

It was Lieutenant Rultich. For a second, Kesh praised the Emperor that he was alive – until she saw the boils, the carbuncles and the unnaturally decomposed flesh. The entire incursion group had been afflicted by a contagion, as if they had died and returned as shambling revenants. They clutched their weapons in curled, claw-like fingers but wielded them like clubs and spears.

'Doom...' the plague lord pronounced again, the horrible din rattling bone and popping armour seals.

Something hot brushed against Kesh, the same warm-skin

feeling that comes from a fever. Sweat dappled her neck and back. She heard someone choke and fall towards the rear of her group, the third or fourth platoon down. At the same time, the *scrape...* pause... *scrape* started up again as the bell-ringer advanced. His retinue crept forward in his wake, patient for their moment. So too the ghastly revenants of Lieutenant Rultich and his men. She was hemmed in from every direction.

The sounds of a scuffle came from the back. Someone screamed, a trooper she couldn't place. And then came the las-fire. From *within* her rear ranks. More shouting. Closer. Kesh turned about, away from the bell-ringer and his warriors, past Lieutenant Rultich and back to the rear ranks. There were dead men there too, turned by the mist. It was killing them and bringing them back. Kesh felt the walls pressing in, arching over her with coffin-like finality, closing off the light...

...burying me with the dead, under their bones.

She felt a hand shake her vigorously, but she was slipping under, her fear as heavy as lead, pulling her down; sweat in her eyes, skin prickling with sickly heat. At the edge of her perception, she heard Munser give the order to fire, a sustained fusillade at the plague lord.

Somewhere at the back of their group, a flamer-burst lit the shadows, so bright and sudden that it shocked her. The harrowed faces of the dead ones were thrown into stark relief, fighting against their own, biting and clawing...

Then the flamer exploded and fire was running rampant, funnelled by the corridor. Men burned, both the living and the dead. Her world narrowed inward to a cacophony of las-fire and screaming, so commingled that she couldn't tell them apart.

She had sunk to her knees, weapon discarded and on the ground, her arms wrapped around her body. Preparing to meet the end.

Suddenly Kesh felt the coin against her palm. She wasn't

aware of having fished it from her pocket but it had found its way into her hand. It felt cool to the touch and that balm spread through her, first lifting the heat and then moving outwards... *as light*. Pearlescent, purifying, where the light touched the Mordians they straightened and found their courage. The light was only small; it protected but a few.

But the plague lord hesitated before it.

Emboldened, a handful of Mordians moved to intercept him but the plague lord swung the great bell like a morning star, sweeping away the troopers almost lethargically. He waded into the rest and sent bodies tumbling before him, crushed to death. His retinue followed him, and the slaughter began.

'Retreat!' bellowed Munser, and Kesh felt herself pulled backwards through the throng. The Mordians fell back even as the monstrous bell-ringer and his warriors came for them.

A sudden burst of momentum brought the plague lord within a few feet of Kesh, and with slow deliberation he pulled the broadsword off his back. Las-fire pattered off his body like rain. Even a plasma-bolt barely scorched his armour. They fared no better against his retinue, who were dismembering any surviving Mordians with almost casual ease.

Backing away, firing as they went, the Mordians had nothing that could stop their pursuers. A long thrust of the fell broadsword impaled three troopers, their bodies liquifying in moments at the blade's touch. Two more were crushed by the overhand swing of the great bell, the resulting clang as it hit the floor putting more troopers on their knees.

'Hold him back!' shouted Munser, dragging Kesh, who was struggling to get to her feet. A flailing trooper hit him across the torso and he was snatched away, out of her sight.

Fallen to her knees again, she looked up into the tripartite eye of the plague lord. His armour was blackened by the purifying light, some of it having partly dissolved in places, but it wasn't bright enough to repel him. The blood lathering the broadsword's blade sizzled and burned away. He raised it up, an ugly sneer visible where part of his helm had disintegrated to reveal his pallid face.

The blade never fell. A silver-armoured warrior impeded it, her own greatsword braced against the blow.

Syreniel.

She held him back with a two-handed grip on her sword, but the strain was evident. The plague lord struggled, as if the presence of the Silent Sister hurt him.

'Magda Kesh,' a voice shouted to her against the fading echoes of the bell strike. She looked up to see a gaunt-faced man, pale as death. He had a stylised 'I' emblazoned on his armour. 'Embrace it,' he was saying. 'Embrace His will, and the blessing of the Emperor's chosen.'

Kesh wavered, but Syreniel was slipping as the plague lord exerted his strength. Her mind reeled at the unexpected reunion, at the confluence of events that had brought her to this moment. It could not be coincidence. Her many escapes from certain death had been for a reason. Her miracles.

The Silent Sister buckled and was swept aside by a monstrous arm.

Rostov fired his pistol into the plague lord's face, aiming for the eye. It caused no more than irritation, an insect sting to the monster as it wrenched up a giant bell attached to a chain and swung it in an arc. The rusted chain struck Rostov and several others across the body. He felt ribs crack as something else broke inside him. His feet left the ground, and then he was flying backwards into Nirdrangar and his men, who were faring no better than the Mordians.

Agony knifed through his limbs, and it took an effort of will for Rostov to lurch onto his elbows.

He saw Kesh get to her feet, her fear seemingly overcome as she stood before the plague lord.

Brave, he thought. *Brave but foolish.* She was about to die and there was nothing he or anyone could do to stop it.

Instead, Kesh blazed into a coruscation of light. It rose up like white fire within, burning through her, and through the dead men, the ones he and Syreniel had fought through to reach her. It swept outwards, purging the damned, their rotting bodies crackling into purified white, destroying them utterly but leaving the living untouched.

Where it struck the plague lord, he withered and blackened. The great bell split and shuddered to dust, the rusted broadsword flaking away like smoke on the air. He staggered, unsure how to fight, until Kesh reached out and touched him. A fiery nova cored the plague lord hollow, resonating from the point of contact. It spread like a dawning sun until eventually there was nothing left – no trace but for a blackened scar on the ground and Kesh refulgent, powerful, standing where the monster had once been. Black wings rippled in the smoke from her back, stark against the blinding white of her transformation.

Syreniel picked herself up and then sank to one knee, bowing her head before a living saint of the Emperor. All of the Mordians bowed, too. Some of them were openly weeping, clutching holy talismans to their chests.

Rostov made the sign of the aquila as the light washed over him, the white fire that did not burn, and he felt a purity stir within. A cleansing. His pain ebbed, his broken ribs healed. Old strength he had not known for months returned.

He stood and proclaimed, 'All hail Saint Magda Kesh, blessed by the Emperor!'

'Ave Sanctus Kesh!' every man and woman rejoined.

Kesh remained impassive as she regarded the worshippers, imbued with His will, His grace. Rostov watched as she drew her sword and raised it up. A simple officer's blade, it could have been the flaming sword of the Emperor for the cheer it evoked.

The bell-ringer's retinue had begun to retreat, firing as they went, hands raised to ward off the light. Now they fell: to the las-fire, to the plasma-bolts, to the purging Mordian flame. To the counter-attack led by Saint Kesh, who sprang amongst the putrified host, buoyed on black wings, and set about them with her sword. Diseased armour and flesh parted before her blade, purified, annihilated. She left chunks of smoking metal and bone behind her.

On Kesh drove, into the hordes, into cultists and cybernetic horrors, into the Traitor Space Marines who had forsaken their oaths. She smote them all, her voice a glorious clarion calling the faithful to arms.

At her side, the loyal Guardsmen of her regiment, an inquisitor she did not know, and the Silent Sister she had befriended in a war that seemed so long ago. She felt changed, strong, the strength that came from certainty of purpose.

She felt *Him,* the Emperor's sword in her hand, His courage filling her heart. The protection of His glorious and holy aegis.

It guided her and peeled back the shadows of the fortress.

Until the light of her apotheosis faded as they reached the throne room of the Hand.

Chapter Forty-Three

EIGHT THRONES

SHARDS

FAR FROM OVER

It was a light – a perfect white light, so bright and striking against the darkness of the abattoir. Areios followed it, leaving the corpses of the Butcher King and his minions behind.

'What is this?' murmured Drussus, wary of another trap.

'I aim to find out,' said Areios, though the light felt like a beacon.

It guided them through the tangled innards of the fortress until they found its source.

Across a large dais stained with blood, he saw a Militarum captain enter from the opposite side of the room. Except she was no mere mortal Guardsman. Her hair was stark white, like snowfall, her eyes aflame and bright as young stars. Every inch of her radiated with light, and he realised this was what had drawn him here, to this place. Black corvid wings framed her otherwise angelic aspect, the great feathers shimmering as if they were made of smoke. She carried a simple sword, white fire bleeding from its edge.

As the light faded like a lantern slowly shuttered, Areios' eye was drawn to the room itself. Eight thrones. There were eight thrones set around a black chamber. Empty and forgotten, much like the chamber itself.

Then he saw that the Militarum captain led an army. More intriguing still was the fact he recognised the inquisitor and Silent Sister amongst their ranks.

'I do not remember her in the original war party,' said Cicero dryly, referring to the saintly figure.

'Nor I,' answered Areios, as his salute of fealty to her was echoed by his brothers. 'Nor I.'

Rostov assessed their surroundings immediately. The ritual dais had been used, though not recently. He noticed dried blood in its recesses. A fresher trail led off from the dais itself and he ordered Nirdrangar and a small cohort of his men to chase it to its terminus, whilst he investigated the room further.

The Mordians in their company took up defensive positions, even as the Astartes maintained their own perimeter, but there was an odd sense of tension – of a victory apparent, but not quite won. Neither side really knew what to do in this moment. They had expected another fight. They had expected the Hand. Not this... anticlimax.

Syreniel remained aloof. She kept her eye on Rostov, but her gaze moved from the inquisitor to the living saint who had miraculously manifested in their midst. Rostov would attend to that question later. For now, he craved other answers.

A statue overlooked the dais, partly cloistered in an alcove. It was a vile thing, a carving in stone of some Neverborn abomination. It had eight limbs, its claws and hands extended as if they had each once held something. The absences were concerning, and aroused an unpleasant suspicion in the inquisitor.

Were we too late?

Rostov felt the presence of one of the Astartes, and it arrested his thoughts. The scent of gun oil, blood and a protein stench gave the warrior away even without considering the low growl of their armour. He turned to meet the steady gaze of Lieutenant Ferren Areios. The Space Marine had removed his helm but looked all the fiercer for it. Rostov noticed a few more scars, and a resolve to the Ultramarine's countenance that hadn't been there when they had last met.

'I would be careful of that,' Areios warned him, and his eyes flicked to the statue. 'Our most recent dealings with something not so dissimilar ended in tragedy.'

'Noted, and my condolences, but I believe it is merely stone,' Rostov replied, though he used his psychic gifts to apply the merest mental brush against the statue. As he had expected, its malevolence was limited to its aesthetics alone. 'I am more concerned with what it once held in its hands.'

Areios maintained his stare, which Rostov took as an invitation to explain further.

'The Anathame was split into eight shards.'

'"A weapon of ancient malice".'

'The very same,' Rostov concluded.

'It is gone, then.'

'I suspect it was never even here, at least not when it would have mattered. We were lured, and took the bait.' He tried not to sound too bitter.

'And the Hand?'

Here, Rostov turned his attention to the thrones. Each had a sigil carved in its headrest. A few he even recognised, symbols – or variations of them – that he had seen during his career as an inquisitor. They were sigils of Ruin.

'I think we fought some of them.'

'Them?' said Areios, before his eyes widened a fraction in realisation. 'There were eight. I believe I killed one.'

'And...' Rostov struggled for the right word with which to

refer to Kesh. In the end, he settled for the prosaic: '*She* took another.'

It had been her light, the Emperor's light, that had healed him, *was* still healing him. The corruption had been purged from his flesh: a miracle. But his mind soon turned to darker thoughts.

'It never sat well with me that Tenebrus was the Hand.' Rostov exhaled ruefully. 'And now I know why.'

'I recognise that name.' Something shadowy passed over Areios' expression as he said, 'From Srinagar.'

'Yes. He claimed the title as his own. It seems it was not an outright lie.'

Rostov was about to go on when Areios raised a hand for silence. He listened to the vox-bead in his ear for a moment.

'Your rogue trader and the Kin are inbound,' Areios told him, glancing at one of his men. Rostov didn't know the warrior's name but recognised him as having been with Areios at the briefing. 'The Blackstone Fortress is dead, its defences deactivated. Whatever foul anima inhabited it is gone.'

'And yet,' uttered Rostov, eyeing the empty statue and the blood trail, and seeing Nirdrangar return with a subtle shake of the head, 'this is far from over.'

Chapter Forty-Four

ONLY FIRE REMAINS

REFORGED

THE LACKEY

His strength ebbing, Herek mounted the steps to the anvil.

Only fire remains, the warsmith had said, watching the renegade now as he hauled his weary body to the summit. The slaying of Rathek had harrowed him, his last tether to the old ways severed. He briefly thought of Kurgos, wondered if he was still alive. It might not matter, depending on what happened next.

As he reached the uppermost dais, Herek's will collapsed at last, and he with it. On his knees, he glowered at the warsmith with bloodshot eyes, his skin as pale and thin as paper.

'Fire, then...' he rasped, and grimaced as he felt the susurration bite, as the shards wormed inside him with an animus of their own. 'Let's get it over with.'

The Anathame.

He had borne its pieces just as Augury had told him to. His part of the pact: willing sufferance for the prospect of something greater. It tasted bitter, as bitter as a brother's blood on his tongue.

The gods demand much...

From the shadows came the hooded attendants he had seen as he and Rathek had entered the forge. Up close they were huge, hulking things. Having abandoned their shovels and picks, they carried saws and drills and other tools. They went to work, cutting away Herek's armour. He flinched at first, but the grip of the attendants was strong and he did not resist. The pieces of plate came away in scraps at first, then swathes; then off came the mesh beneath, like a serpent sloughs away its dead skin. Naked, exposed, Herek saw the hexes marked onto his skin for the first time since the Eight had bestowed them. They throbbed, burning with a painful eagerness. He the vessel for the power they had allowed him to bear.

One of the attendants brought forth a savage-looking pair of tongs. Its pincers were sharp, like a set of fangs. The warsmith took the tool and lumbered around to the front of the anvil, where Herek awaited him down on his knees.

'Thus is the anointing done,' said the warsmith, 'and there are eight and so shall the supplicant carry the eight, a vessel for the power of the sacred Octed and the Eightfold Path. The blade of Horus' rebirth. The bringer of illumination. The shards of Erebus. Anathame.'

The tongs grew white-hot in an instant, and he plunged them searingly into Herek's flesh.

Despite himself, Herek screamed. Every bone in his body felt like it was burning, his skin, his nerves, his eyes, his organs – even his soul, alight and blazing. A heavy clang resounded as a dark splinter was pulled out of his body and laid to rest upon the face of the anvil.

'Of the eight, this is the first,' the warsmith intoned.

Seven more to go.

He went in again.

Herek just kept on screaming. He was near unconsciousness by the time the final shard of the Anathame had been removed, and he had to be supported by the attendants, one at each shoulder. The creatures took care to face away from the warsmith's labours even whilst hooded, and Herek felt their trembling.

The warsmith exhaled a shuddered breath when he was done.

'And lo, there were eight, and from the eight shall come the one,' he said.

As the last piece was removed, Herek felt the burden he had been carrying lift. His senses sharpened again, and some of his fatigue fell away. Thick, bloody scars covered his body from where the shards had been pulled out. They lay, all eight of them, on the anvil now, and the warsmith was already lumbering back around to resume his former position. From a glowing pit of fire, he wrenched forth a hammer. It dripped with molten promise, with the heartblood of this terrible place. He raised it, and turned his eye on Herek.

'As the bearer, you may choose.'

The shards resembled crude daggers in their own right but arrayed just so, Herek discerned the greater whole they had once been. But that was the past. An axe had been his first thought – the executioner his preferred soubriquet. But then his mind turned to his brother's sacrifice. He would honour that.

His voice was a reedy croak but found its purpose after he had cleared his throat.

'A sword...'

'Dark metals shall be amalgamated with the shards to form the blade. It shall have a hilt of cursed iron. A black sapphire shall make the pommel, unbreakable and cut with the essence of Neverborn ichor. It is the Anathame reforged,' the warsmith pronounced. 'It is...'

'Culler,' said Herek, dragging himself to his feet to stand before the warsmith. 'Call it Culler.'

The warsmith gave a solemn nod. 'So it is spoken, so it shall be.'

He hammered the shards, and with each blow the screams of the damned resounded and dark, unholy visions filled Herek's mind.

A woman with a saint's fiery halo, wings arising from her back...

A horned priestess, with chains of fate threaded through her flesh, carrying a staff of azure flame...

A figure seated upon a throne, encircled by fire, its sword aloft and then its cup, until the flames consumed it.

He blinked, breathless, as the warsmith struck a final tempering blow.

'The third is fire,' he intoned and quenched the blade in a vat of blood. Then he pulled it forth, the sword steaming with malevolence both old and renewed. It had tasted the flesh of demigods, Herek knew, and now it was his.

He held out his hand.

It was heavier than he had imagined. Herek clasped Culler and felt the power running through it. *A weapon to slay a god.* He knew of one whose craven followers revered him as a god, and who recently bestrode the galaxy again.

The attendants came forward, heads bowed, one with a belted scabbard and another with a simple brown cloak, which Herek wrapped around his naked body. Then he donned the belt, sheathed the blade, and departed the forge.

Herek kept his gaze away from Rathek, who remained where he had fallen, and tried not to think about the sacrifices he had made to get here. As the gates parted with a loud clamour, he stepped out into the red desert and made for the river mouth. Once there, he could retrace their steps and find Kurgos, if the chirurgeon was still alive. He hoped he was.

Behind him, the pyroclastic cloud closed up and the forge was lost to his sight. A storm threatened on the horizon and Herek pulled the cloak tighter around his neck. The reek of sulphur and warm copper on the breeze stirred his survival instincts, and he drew the blade, though he saw no foe ahead of him.

'Declare yourself,' he demanded of the desert wind, which was rising and dirtying the air.

Then he lurched forward, arching in agony as hot fire pierced his back and punched out through his chest in a welter of blood.

A rapid paralysis overtook his limbs and Culler fell from nerveless fingers to land softly on the desert sand. Herek fell less gracefully, collapsed onto his side, a long knife still jutting from his chest, the hilt still lodged in his back. As he stared at it, disbelieving, he saw it had a shiny black blade.

'The Lackey,' uttered a voice he knew – several voices, all overlaid atop one another.

Augury. He stared open-mouthed at his patron before his eyes came to rest on the figure with them.

A sorceress. She held a staff, its head flickering with azure fire. She had silver piercings in her skin, and the gemstones embedded in her flesh caught the light of the sun as she reached down for Culler. Her hands were stained red with his blood.

'That belongs to me,' she said, her voice resonant with power, 'though I thank you for carrying it.' The smile was venomous.

Herek could not move, though his mind raged and his fingers tried to clench into claws, into fists. The sorcerer took the sword and disappeared from view.

Augury remained, looking down on him, their face largely concealed.

'You were a good servant, Graeyl Herek,' they said, 'but you have done your part. It was only ever ordained that you would deliver the weapon, not bear it. That part is over now, though, and the children of the gods must have you.'

'I was...' Herek rasped, as his lifeblood leaked eagerly from his body, '*chosen*.'

'Yes, you were,' Augury replied, not unkindly, 'for the gods choose all their servants, willing and otherwise. Not all may ascend, as Yheng of Gathalamor does before you. Farewell, Herek.'

They departed then, leaving a trace of blood and brimstone with their passing, and the lightest tang of electrified rain.

Chapter Forty-Five

A DEBT IS OWED

A FLICKER OF LIGHT

DUTY

Rostov met the kâhl in his quarters aboard the *Wyrmslayer Queen*, this visit much more cordial than the first time she had set foot on the ship. She had come alone, not that Rostov believed for a moment she needed protection.

'You look well, Imperial,' she began, a smile on her face that the inquisitor had never quite decoded. 'Better than when last we met.'

'The benefits of a well-earned rest,' he lied.

It had been several hours since they had breached the throne room only to find it empty and the shards absent. After an initial search, Rostov and the other troopers had returned to the ship. The Kin had been left to their salvage and wasted no time in starting the process of stripping the Blackstone Fortress bare. They went in armed and in force, clearance teams ridding the place of any lingering inhabitants, every scrap of resource being slowly conveyed back to Vutred's fleet in short order. It would take days, even weeks, but Rostov's time in the Stygius Gilt was coming to an end.

Vutred sat down heavily in a wooden chair that creaked against her armoured weight. She paid it no mind, nor appeared to notice she had not been invited to sit.

'I think you are someone unaccustomed to rest, Imperial.' She gave him a querying look. 'Was it something on the fortress? Did you find some restorative? Is it valuable?' Now she jabbed a thick finger his way, one eye shut as the other appraised and chastised equally. 'Do not think to hold out on me, Imperial. I will know, true as wrought, and I swear by the ancestors that if you try to skim off our agreement... Well.' She leaned back and the chair creaked further, threatening collapse. 'You would find us far less amenable.'

'The Blackstone Fortress is yours, kâhl, lock stock and whatever else you can fill your gunwales with. I have no interest in it now. But I thank you for your part in this. You have earned my gratitude, and that of the Imperium.'

Vutred nodded at this, pleased with his show of respect, as he had known she would be.

'Fair is fair, and a deal is a deal. You have held up your end, and I mine.' She rose to her feet, letting out a small grunt of effort. 'This concludes our accord, though if you ever have need of the Kin again, I would not be averse to pulling your hide out of the fire one more time.'

Rostov didn't take the bait, and considered the possibility that she might actually like him to a degree.

'I appreciate you coming to say that in person,' he said.

'I prefer to finish my business face to face.' Another smile, just as inscrutable as the first, before her expression became more readable, more serious. 'Grudgement has been settled. I am able to reclaim my honour, Rostov. This is no small matter for my Kindred. A debt owed that will not be forgotten.'

She lingered, her gaze appraising as ever, and then finally she left.

Rostov watched her leave, his satisfaction at making a new ally souring at the prospect of what he had to do next. He sealed the room and activated a hololithic recorder. Encased by the cone of light, he began his report to Lord Inquisitor Greyfax.

The Hand had been dealt a serious blow, but some yet lived. And the shards had been taken, their whereabouts now unknown. A threat had ended only for another worse one to take its place. The irony of it left a bitter taste as he concluded his verbal missive for now.

And yet he felt hopeful. The one who travelled with him now, the one known to Syreniel: she was surely an indication of the Emperor's presence and protection. To what that portended, Rostov was at a loss, but he had felt something as the taint was purged from his flesh, his vitality restored and purified. A miracle, a chink of light to lift the darkness.

If only a flicker.

She hit the target right in the middle. A perfect shot. Well, not perfect, not exactly. That word had taken on a different meaning now.

She fired again, three more shots, three more bullseyes, all marksman's skill and no miracles needed.

At least I still have this, Kesh thought, and tried not to dwell on what had happened to her on the fortress. Only a few hours ago she had blazed with light, spat fire from her sword. It had felt... unreal, as if it had been someone else experiencing those things.

She saw her face reflected in the plastek shielding of the range alcove. Apart from the stark white hair, she looked as she always had, though there was a certain lustre in her eyes that had not been there before. The miracle, the light and the fire – that had faded. She considered it a mercy, and as time wore on she found she remembered less and less of her deeds.

Not for the first time since coming aboard ship, Kesh sank

her face into her hands and just focused on breathing. And also not for the first time, she was grateful for the ship's captain graciously acceding to her request for a place where she could be alone.

She was no longer aboard the *Venerated Sword* but a rogue trader vessel called the *Wyrmslayer Queen.* She had not been allowed to speak with her comrades, the inquisitor having sequestered her almost immediately in the aftermath of the miracle. He had said little to her, beyond the fact that she was to accompany him; that she would be presented to his master and a high-ranking priest of the Ecclesiarchy.

She had not the heart nor the audacity to tell him that this had been tried before, to no great fanfare. Though she supposed it was different now. Everything was different now – and yet she was still Magda Kesh, still a daughter of Mordian, still grieving for a father figure she hadn't realised she had until she'd lost him, and wondering if she might speak again with the silent ally she had made on Kamidar.

As Kesh lifted her face from her hands, she saw that same ally standing behind her, the reflection of the Silent Sister far less distinct than her own. She turned to face Syreniel.

'Am I meant to feel empowered?' Kesh asked her. 'Because all I feel right now is fear.'

It is human to fear what is unknown.

Kesh gave her a wry look. 'I had hoped for a more encouraging reply.'

You are chosen, Magda Kesh. I see in you His will made manifest.

'I only ever wanted to serve, as a soldier, one amongst many. I could fulfil my duty and die with honour. I *should* have died. More than once.'

And what will you do, then, with the life that has been given?

'I wish I knew the answer to that question.' Remembering something, Kesh suddenly fiddled around in her pocket, until she produced the coin she had been gifted. Syreniel's impassive expression softened as she laid eyes on it.

'This is what saved me. I honestly think I would be dead without it.'

Then I am glad you have it.

'How did you even come to be here? I thought once everything was done with Kamidar that I would never see you again.'

As did I, Magda, but who am I to understand–

'If you are about to say the will of the Emperor, I will shoot you with this lasgun. And as you can see, I am a damn good shot.'

Syreniel's eyes smiled in a rare flash of warmth amidst the ice. *Then I will not. Say it, I mean.*

Kesh leaned against the alcove, exhausted. 'I never asked for any of this.'

Syreniel's face hardened. *The true faithful rarely do, but we must observe our duty all the same.*

Kesh caught on to the sudden change in mood and straightened up.

'You're not really here to reminisce, are you, Syreniel?'

No.

'Then why are you here?'

Because it is my duty.

'You want to know if I can be trusted,' Kesh realised. 'And you will kill me if I cannot.'

Syreniel nodded.

'And what do you think?'

It does not matter what I think. I am merely to watch and be vigilant.

Kesh's gaze lingered on the Silent Sister for a moment, then she turned back to the firing range. She reloaded her lasgun, taking aim at the furthest target. She regretted the bitterness in what she said next, but could not take it back.

'Then you had better do your duty well.'

Another hit, dead in the middle.

Epilogue

THE WILL TO LIVE

THE SWORD IS MINE

THREE REMAIN

It took every iota of his will, but Tenebrus had managed to crawl from the black chamber before the Imperials arrived. He knew the paths of the fortress, even inert as it now was, and had taken a secret way into its depths. He was bleeding – *dying*, he realised – but only needed to find a place to rest. With sorcery, he would reknit his wounds. He would regain his strength, and he would have his vengeance against the acolyte who had betrayed him.

Gods of the abyss, she will suffer.

He heard them now, the servants of the False Emperor, the blind fools who followed a corpse-lord on an empty throne. They were far above him, and even in his weakened state Tenebrus was confident that they would not find him before he had restored himself and found a way off the fortress.

Anger was a powerful motivator, and he drank deep of it now as he dragged his broken body across obsidian. At one point during his flight, he had heard soldiers closing in, but using a little of his power Tenebrus had masked his presence and the soldiers had given up their pursuit.

Idiots.

He had found the perfect place for his recovery, a deep chamber, hard to reach and even harder to find. He felt confident he would be undisturbed for several hours at least. All the time he needed, during which he would nurture thoughts of revenge.

Slumping against a pillar, Tenebrus peeled open his robes to reveal the damage she had done to his body. The wounds were deep, and bleeding. He wondered how much of himself he had left smeared on the floor. A fair amount, judging by his failing strength. He just needed to gather his wits, focus his mind. Fingers moving like a puppeteer's pulling on invisible strings, Tenebrus began to work at his injuries. Skin pulled together, began to heal.

He was deep into this process when he heard the faintest cry. It was high-pitched, an animalistic call. He had heard it before. Heart beating loudly, he summoned a crackle of dark lightning to his fingertips. The spell took a toll; it was harder to manifest than comparatively simple biomancy.

It didn't have eyes, the thing that regarded him from the shadows. Rather, it smelled him, turning its nasal pits to the air and taking in a sucking breath. It was gangly, its limbs pallid and taut with rangy muscle. It shuffled towards him, hunched over and with an apelike gait. Tenebrus recognised the ur-ghul, one of the denizens of the fortress. A wretched creature, killing it would be a mercy.

The lightning spark swelled as he prepared to unleash it, but as it grew it lit the room around it, and Tenebrus saw then that the ur-ghul was not alone. It had brought its kin, the ones from the amphitheatre, the ones who had come to witness Yheng's ascension.

Hundreds of them, gathering in the dark. One cry became

many, a sharp and hungry drone that filled the chamber even as they advanced on him.

'Oh, gods...' breathed Tenebrus as the light faded and the creatures lunged, tearing him limb from limb.

The light came and went, warm and red at first then cold like ice. Herek felt his body dragged, a hand fastened around his ankle. Through sand, through water that smelled like metal and then upwards, a rope, a chain around his waist.

And then blackness, as all meaning of time faded, and him with it.

Until...

He awoke on a slab of metal, the air thick with mist and edged with chill. He was naked but for a cloth to hide his modesty, his many wounds exposed. Some of them had been stitched and cauterised.

A face resolved before him, malformed, riddled with lesions and ugly masses.

'Kurgos...' he croaked, recognising his chirurgeon. He took a breath, and it felt like shattered glass raking his lungs. 'Rathek... he's dead. I killed him, brother.'

'I know.'

'The blade... I lost it. Taken...' As he remembered, his anger began to harden to a sharp point.

'I know.'

He tried to rise, but Kurgos held him down with a strong hand.

'You are still weak, brother. Rest. Heal.' He wheezed then, betraying his own hurts. 'We all must heal. Clortho is alive – take that for a blessing or a curse as you see fit. I am in the process of replacing your missing hand. This bionic is less refined than the one you lost, but it will serve.'

'Where is my armour?'

'Gone, I am afraid, without hope of recovery. Another suit is being prepared. There was plenty of spare war plate for the task,' Kurgos added grimly.

'How did you survive, chirurgeon?'

'I refused to die. I am hard to kill, brother. Like you.' Kurgos busied himself at his instrument table. 'You were murmuring in your sleep. Babbling, really. Saints and priestesses, a throne in flames.'

Herek remembered, and his flesh-and-blood hand flexed its fingers at the absence of the sword. 'I want it back. Rathek gave his life for that sword. It is mine.'

'And if the ones who have it refuse to return it?' asked Kurgos, as he paused in his ministrations.

'Then we take it,' vowed Herek, 'and kill anyone who gets in our way.'

Only three remained, where once there had been eight.

They gathered on a desolate promontory under a slate-grey sky. Creatures hunted in that bleak expanse and on the ash plains below, but none dared approach the three. It had been inhabited once, this world, but that was long ago and only tortured ghosts existed here now. The degraded shells of cities persisted too, but these were down in the valley, far from the heath and the hill.

The Host of Masks bowed to the Wretched Prince, a mocking gesture, his face wearing an overlong grin. An assassin preferred to fight from the shadows; it had no interest in open warfare. The Prince said nothing, merely wrapped his ragged cloak closer to his withered frame, his coven of witchlings lurking nearby, and sought out the third of their order.

This one came through the ether, subsisting on the tortured souls of the dead city. Its feasts had been frugal and the Sin of Six Knives looked all the weaker for it. It regarded the others hungrily but would dare not act against them.

Another survivor, unlooked for, climbed onto the hill, and the three became four. Half of the original covenant. Her robes were singed and black. She gained the craggy summit with difficulty, pain evident on her burned face. She appraised them all with cool disdain, breathless from her climb.

'I am now First amongst us,' she declared.

'What of Tenebrus?' the Wretched Prince enquired in a reedy, despicable voice.

'Tenebrus is dead. I am First. Do any of you wish to gainsay?'

None did. Even the Host of Masks was content to bow, and did so with courtly poise.

'Then I have two edicts,' said the Iron Magus with a determination that bordered on anger. 'Replenish our ranks, and slaughter the ones who betrayed us.'

Appendix: Notes on the Crusade

THE BLACKSTONE FORTRESSES

Humanity is not the first species to claim dominance over the heavens. Scattered throughout the galaxy are artefacts created by creatures long fallen into obscurity or extinction. Many of these objects are little more than curios of interest only to the technoarchaeologists of Mars and the historitors of Terra. Alas, war has ever stained the light of the stars with blood. The debris of past conflicts is found everywhere, and hidden within it are many powerful weapons. Among the most deadly of these relics are the battle stations known as the Blackstone Fortresses.

ANCIENT ARMAMENTS

A Blackstone Fortress is an immense, warp-capable vessel bigger than most Imperial battle stations and armed with warp-based weaponry potent enough to destroy a world. When the fortresses were first encountered, the strange obsidian-like material they were built from was initially unknown, and defied efforts to analyse it. One of the least problems this novel stone presented was dating the fortresses. Imperial scholars put their ages at anywhere between tens of thousands and tens of millions of years old, though current thinking tends to the more extreme end of these estimations. The aeldari call them the Talismans of Vaul, and their legends say they are relics of the long-ago War in Heaven. The mythic cycle of the aeldari tells that this galaxy-shattering war was fought between their gods and the evil C'tan, gods born from the stars, who were the masters of the necrontyr.

THE GOTHIC WAR

Mankind first encountered the Blackstone Fortresses in the Gothic Sector, where six were discovered adrift and powerless in the stars. The fortresses at that time were completely inert, their true capabilities unguessed at. The Imperium nevertheless saw their potential as deep-space Naval bases. The Adeptus Mechanicus gleaned enough knowledge to access the fortresses' semi-dormant energy systems, tapping into them to provide power for retrofitted Imperial facilities. Human-built defence turrets, command centres and star docks soon encrusted the fortresses' ancient hulls, and for a time they served the Imperium well.

This did not last. Another galactic power had an eye on these machines. Abaddon the Despoiler launched his Twelfth Black Crusade into the Gothic Sector in early M41 with the express aim of securing as many of the Blackstone Fortresses as possible. War raged throughout space. Abaddon secured three of the six. Somehow, the son of Horus had learned how to unlock the fortresses' full potential. Once awoken, the fortresses sloughed off their Imperial additions, their engines came online, and their awful weaponry was activated. Abaddon soon demonstrated that just one of these gargantuan battle stations was capable of destroying a world. Yet that was not the limit of their power, for their weaponry's warp-beams could be combined, and Abaddon used this ability of his new prizes to destroy the star of the Taranis System.

Harried by a vast armada of aeldari and Imperial ships, Abaddon retreated back to the Eye of Terror. One of the three Blackstone Fortresses seized by Chaos was boarded by Imperial forces and retaken. However, the moment the ship fell back into Imperial hands, it and the other three remaining under Imperial control disintegrated utterly, leaving the last two in the hands of the Archenemy.

THE FALL OF CADIA

Hundreds of years later, Abaddon's Blackstone Fortresses were once more seen in Imperial space. One, Abaddon gave to Huron Blackheart to secure the aid of the Red Corsairs, who have since adopted it as a major base in the Maelstrom. The other, dubbed the *Will of Eternity*, was heavily damaged by the Imperial Fists fortress-battleship *Phalanx* over Cadia. Abaddon had the crippled fortress crashed into the surface of the bastion world, shattering it utterly, breaking the necron pylon network, and finally opening the Cadian Gate to the forces of Chaos.

BLACKSTONE FORTRESSES TODAY

The six fortresses of the Gothic Sector were the only known examples for a long time. Yet in recent years others have come to light. Of course, verification of these reports in the Era Indomitus is nigh on impossible, but there are possibly four or more Blackstone Fortresses in the galaxy currently known to the Imperium.

One has been positively identified far to the west of the Segmentum Pacificus. Surrounded by a ship graveyard a million miles across, this seventh fortress seems to be active and awake. It is possessed by an ancient machine intelligence that is able to reconfigure the vessel's internal layout at will, and is defended by a number of automata. Even so, there are many who brave these dangers, and the creatures and renegades who have made the fortress their home, for the fortress' passageways are scattered with archeotech of the highest value from myriad spacefaring species. From the void-city of Precipice, humans and xenos alike plumb its sinister depths for treasure.

From the experiences of Imperial boarding crew in the Gothic War, the adventurers of Precipice and the testimony of Roboute Guilliman himself, who was held prisoner for a time aboard the fortress of the Red Corsairs, a clearer picture of the true nature of the fortresses has begun to emerge. Firstly, it is now widely agreed that the vessels are made from the material noctilith, colloquially referred to in Low Gothic as 'blackstone'. Indeed, these ships were the first place that noctilith was encountered. Because of a commonality in substance, it is suspected that the fortresses share some kinship with the equally ancient necron pylons. It is also probable that when operating correctly, each Blackstone Fortress possesses its own alien abominable intelligence, which, according to some unsubstantiated reports, can be usurped by a sufficiently powerful daemon. The sainted primarch tells that the core of the fortress he escaped from had multiple portals into the webway, including gates big enough to take voidships. Whether this is because the fortresses were made by the aeldari as some historians assert, or by the race of their long-disappeared masters, is hotly debated. All that is truly known is that the Blackstone Fortresses are ancient, powerful and terrible weapons, and that the galaxy would be a safer place if they did not exist at all.

ABOUT THE AUTHOR

Nick Kyme is the author of many Horus Heresy novels, novellas and audio dramas, including *Old Earth, Promethean Sun* and *Nightfane.* His novella *Feat of Iron* was a *New York Times* bestseller in the Horus Heresy collection *The Primarchs.* For Warhammer 40,000, Nick has written *Volpone Glory* and the Dawn of Fire novel *The Iron Kingdom.* He is also well known for his popular Salamanders series and the Cato Sicarius novels *Damnos* and *Knights of Macragge.* His work for Age of Sigmar includes the short story 'Borne by the Storm', included in the novel *War Storm,* and the audio drama *The Imprecations of Daemons.* He has also written the Warhammer Horror novel *Sepulturum.* He lives and works in Nottingham.

An extract from
The Lion: Son of the Forest
by Mike Brooks

The river sings silver notes: a perpetual, chaotic babble in which a fantastically complex melody seems to hang, tantalising, just out of reach of the listener. He could spend eternity here trying to find the heart of it, without ever succeeding, yet still not consider the time wasted. The sound of water over stone, the interplay of energy and matter, creates a quiet symphony that is both unremarkable and unique. He does not know how long he has been here, just listening.

Nor, he realises, does he know where *here* is.

The listener becomes aware of himself in stages, like a sleeper passing from the deepest, darkest depths of slumber, through the shallows of semi-consciousness where thought swirls in confusing eddies, and then into the light. First comes the realisation that he is not the song of the river; that he is in fact separate from it, and listening to it. Then sensation dawns, and he realises he is sitting on the river's bank. If there is a sun, or suns, then he cannot see them through the branches of the trees overhead and the mist that hangs heavily in the air, but there is still light enough for him to make out his surroundings.

The trees are massive, and mighty, with great trunks that could not be fully encircled by one, two, perhaps even half a dozen people's outstretched arms. Their rough, cracked bark pockmarks them with shadows, as though the trees themselves are camouflaged. The ground beneath their branches is fought over by tough shrubs: sturdy, twisted, thorny things strangling each other in the contest for space and light, like children unheeded at the feet of adults. The earth in which they grow is dark and rich, and when the listener digs his fingers into it, it smells of life, and death, and other things besides. It is a familiar smell, although he cannot say from where, or why.

His fingers, he realises as they penetrate the ground, are armoured. His whole body is armoured, in fact, encased in a great suit of black plates with the faintest hint of dark green. This is a familiar sensation, too. The armour feels like a part of him – an extension, as natural as the shell of any crustacean that might lurk in the nooks and crannies of the river in front of him. He leans forward and peers down into the still water next to the bank, sheltered from the main flow by an outcropping just upstream. It becomes an almost perfect mirror surface, as smooth as a dream.

The listener does not recognise the face that looks back at him. It is deeply lined, as though a world of cares and worries has washed over it like the river water, scoring the marks of their passage into the skin. His hair is pale, streaked with blond here and there, but otherwise fading into grey and white. The lower part of his face is obscured by a thick, full beard and moustache, leaving only the lips bare; it is a distrustful mouth, one more likely to turn downwards in disapproval than quirk upwards in a smile.

He raises one hand, the fingers still smeared with dirt, before his face. The reflection does the same. This is surely his face, but the sight sparks no memory. He does not know who he is, and he does not know where he is, for all that it feels familiar.

That being the case, there seems little point in remaining here.

The listener gets to his feet, then hesitates. He cannot explain to himself why he should move, given the song of the river is so beautiful. However, the realisation of his lack of knowledge has opened something inside him, a hunger which was not there before. He will not be satisfied until he has answers.

Still, the river's song calls to him. He decides to walk along the bank, following the flow of the water and listening to it as he goes, and since he does not know where he is, one direction is as good as the other. There is a helmet on the bank, next to where he was sitting. It is the same colour as his armour, with vertical slits across the mouth, like firing slits in a wall. He picks it up, and clamps it to his waist with a movement that feels instinctual.

He does not know for how long he walks. Time is surely passing, in that one moment slips into another, and he can remember ones that came before and consider the concept of ones yet to come, but there is nothing to mark it. The light neither increases nor decreases, instead remaining an almost spectral presence which illuminates without revealing its source. Shadows lurk, but there is no indication as to what casts them. The walker is unperturbed. His eyes can pierce those shadows, just as he can smell foliage, and he can hear the river. There is no soughing of wind in the branches, for the air is still, but the moist air carries the faint hooting, hollering calls of animals of some kind, somewhere in the distance.

The river's course begins to flatten and widen. The walker follows it around a bend, then comes to a halt in shock.

On the far bank stands a building.

It is built of cut and dressed stone, a dark blue-grey rock in which brighter specks glitter. It is not immense – the surrounding trees tower over it – but it is solid. It is a castle of some kind, a fortress, intended to keep the unwanted out and whatever people and treasures lie within safe from harm. It is neither new and pristine, nor ancient and weathered. It looks as though it has always stood here, and always shall. And on the wide, calm water in front of it sits a boat.

It is small, wooden, and unpainted. It is large enough for one person, and indeed one person is sitting in it. The walker's eyes can make him out, even at distance. He is old, and not old in the same way as the walker's face is. Time has not lined his features, it has ravaged them. His cheeks are sunken, his limbs are wasted; skin that was once clearly a rich chestnut now has an ashen patina, and his long hair is lifeless, dull grey, and matted. However, that grey head supports a crown: little more than a circlet of gold, but a crown nonetheless.

In his hands, swollen of knuckle and weak of grip, he holds a rod. The line is already cast into the water. Now he sits, hunched over as though in pain, a small, ancient figure in a small, simple boat.

The walker does not stop to wonder why a king would be fishing in such a manner. He is aware of the context of such things, but he does not know from where, and they do not matter to him. Here is someone who might have some answers for him.

'Greetings!' he calls. His voice is strong, rich and deep, although rough around the edges from age or disuse, or both. It carries across the water. The old king in the boat blinks, and when his eyes open again, they are looking at the walker.

'What is this place?' the walker demands.

The old king blinks again. When his eyes open this time, they are focused on the water once more. It is as though the walker is not there at all, a dismissal of minimal effort.

The walker discovers that he is not used to being ignored, and nor does he appreciate it. He steps into the water, intending to wade across the river so the king cannot so easily dismiss him. He is unconcerned about the current: he is strong of limb, and knows without knowing that his armour is waterproof, and that should he don his helmet he will be able to breathe even if he is submerged.

He has only gone a few steps, in up to his knees, when he realises there are shadows in the water: large shadows that circle the small boat, around and around. They do not bite on the line, and nor do they capsize the craft in which the fisher sits, but either could be disastrous.

Moreover, the walker realises, the king is wounded. The walker cannot see the wound, but he can smell the blood. A rich, copperish tang tickles his nose. It is not a smell that delights him, but neither does he find it repulsive. It is simply a scent, one that he is able to parse and understand. The king is bleeding into the water, drip by drip. Perhaps that is what has drawn the shadows to this place. Perhaps they would have been here anyway.

Some of the shadows start to peel away, and head towards the walker.

The walker is not a being to whom fear comes naturally, but nor is he unfamiliar with the concept of danger. The shadows in the water are unknown to him, and move like predators.

+Come back to the bank.+

The walker whirls. A small figure stands on the land, swathed in robes of dark green, so that it nearly blends into the background against which it stands. It is the size of a child, perhaps, but the walker knows it to be something else.

It is a Watcher in the Dark.

+Come back to the bank,+ the Watcher repeats. Although its communication can hardly be called a voice – there is no sound, merely a sensation inside the walker's head that imparts meaning – it feels increasingly urgent nonetheless. The walker realises that he is not normally one to turn away from a challenge, but nor is he willing to ignore a Watcher in the Dark. It feels like a link, a connection to what came before, to what he should be able to remember.

He wades back, and steps up onto the bank. The approaching shadows hesitate for a moment, then circle away towards the king in his boat.

+They would destroy you,+ the Watcher says. The walker understands that it is talking about the shadows. There are layers to the feelings in his head now, feelings that are the mental aftertaste of the Watcher's communication. Disgust lurks there, but also fear.

'Where is this place?' the walker asks.

+Home.+

The walker waits, but nothing else is forthcoming. Moreover, he understands that there will not be. So far as the Watcher is concerned, that is not simply all the information that is required, but all that is available to give.

He looks out over the water, towards the king. The old man still sits hunched over, rod in his hands, blood leaking from his wounds one drip at a time.

'Why does he ignore me?'

+You did not ask the correct question.+

The walker looks around. The shadows in the water are still there, so it seems foolish to try to cross. However, he has seen no bridge over the river, nor another boat. He has no tools with which to build such a craft from the trees around him, and the knowledge of how to do so does not come easily to his mind. He is not like some of his brothers, for whom creation is natural...

His brothers. Who are his brothers?

Shapes flit through his mind, as ephemeral as smoke in a storm. He cannot get a grip, cannot wrestle them into anything that makes sense, or anything onto which his reaching mind can latch. The peace brought about by the song of the river is gone, and in its place is uncertainty and frustration. Nonetheless, the walker would not return to his former state. To knowingly welcome ignorance is not his way.

He catches a glimpse of something pale, a long way off through the trees, but on his side of the river. He begins to walk towards it, leaving the river behind him – he can always find it again, he knows its song – and making his way through the undergrowth. The plants are thick and verdant, but he is strong and sure. He ducks under spines, slaps aside strangling tendrils reaching out for anything that passes, and avoids breaking the twigs, which would leak sap so corrosive it might damage even his armour.

He does not wonder how he knows these things. The Watcher said that this was home.

The Watcher itself has been left behind, but it keeps reappearing, stepping out of the edge of shadows. It says nothing; not until the walker passes through a thicket of thorns and finally gets a clearer view of what he had seen.

It is a building, or at least the roof of one; that is all he can see from here. It is a dome of beautiful pale stone, supported by pillars. Whereas before he had been finding his own route through the forest, now there is a clear path ahead, a route of short grass hemmed in on either side by bushes and tree trunks. It curves away, rather than arrowing straight towards the pale building, but the walker knows that is where it leads.

+Do not take that path,+ the Watcher cautions him. +You are not yet strong enough.+

The walker looks down at this tiny creature, barely knee-high to him, then breathes deeply and rolls his shoulders within his armour. He presumes he had a youth, given he now looks old. Perhaps he was stronger then. Nonetheless, his body does not feel feeble.

+That is not the strength you will need.+

The walker narrows his eyes. 'You caution me against anything that might help me make sense of my situation. What would you have me do instead?'

+Follow your nature.+

The walker breathes in again, ready to snap an answer, for he finds he is just as ill-disposed towards being denied as he is to being ignored. However, he pauses, then sniffs.

He sniffs again.

Something is amiss.

He is surrounded by the deep, rich scent of the forest, which smells of both life and death. However, now his nose detects something else: a rancid undercurrent, something that is not merely rot or decay – for these are natural odours – but far worsc, far more jarring.

Corruption.

This is something wrong, something twisted. It is something that should not be here: something that should not, in fact, exist at all.

The walker knows what he must do. He must follow his nature.

The hunter steps forward, and starts to run in pursuit of his quarry.